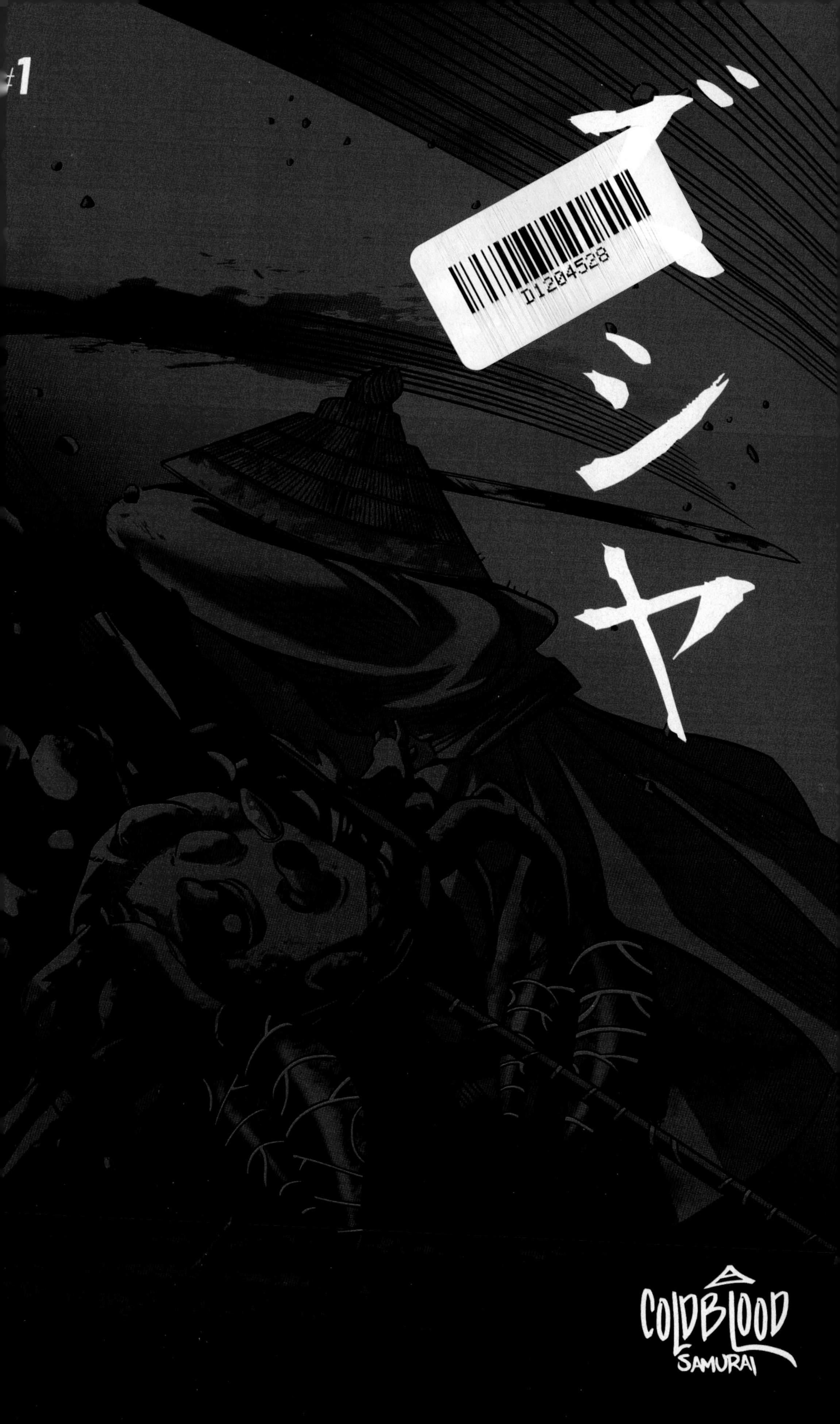
#1
ズシャ
COLDBLOOD
SAMURAI

COLDBLOOD SAMURAI

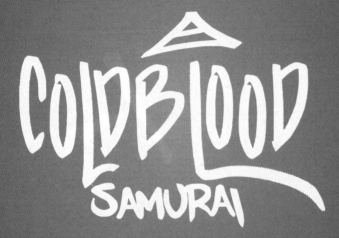

CREDITS

Story
MASSIMO ROSI

Pencils
LUDOVICA CEREGATTI

Colors
RENATO STEVANATO

Lettering
MATTIA GENTILI

Bryan Seaton: Publisher/ CEO
Shawn Gabborin: Editor In Chief
Jason Martin: Publisher-Danger Zone
Nicole D'Andria: Marketing Director/Editor
Jessica Lowrie: Social Media Czar
Danielle Davison: Executive Administrator
Chad Cicconi: King Lizard
Shawn Pryor: President of Creator Relations

Printed in USA. First Printing.

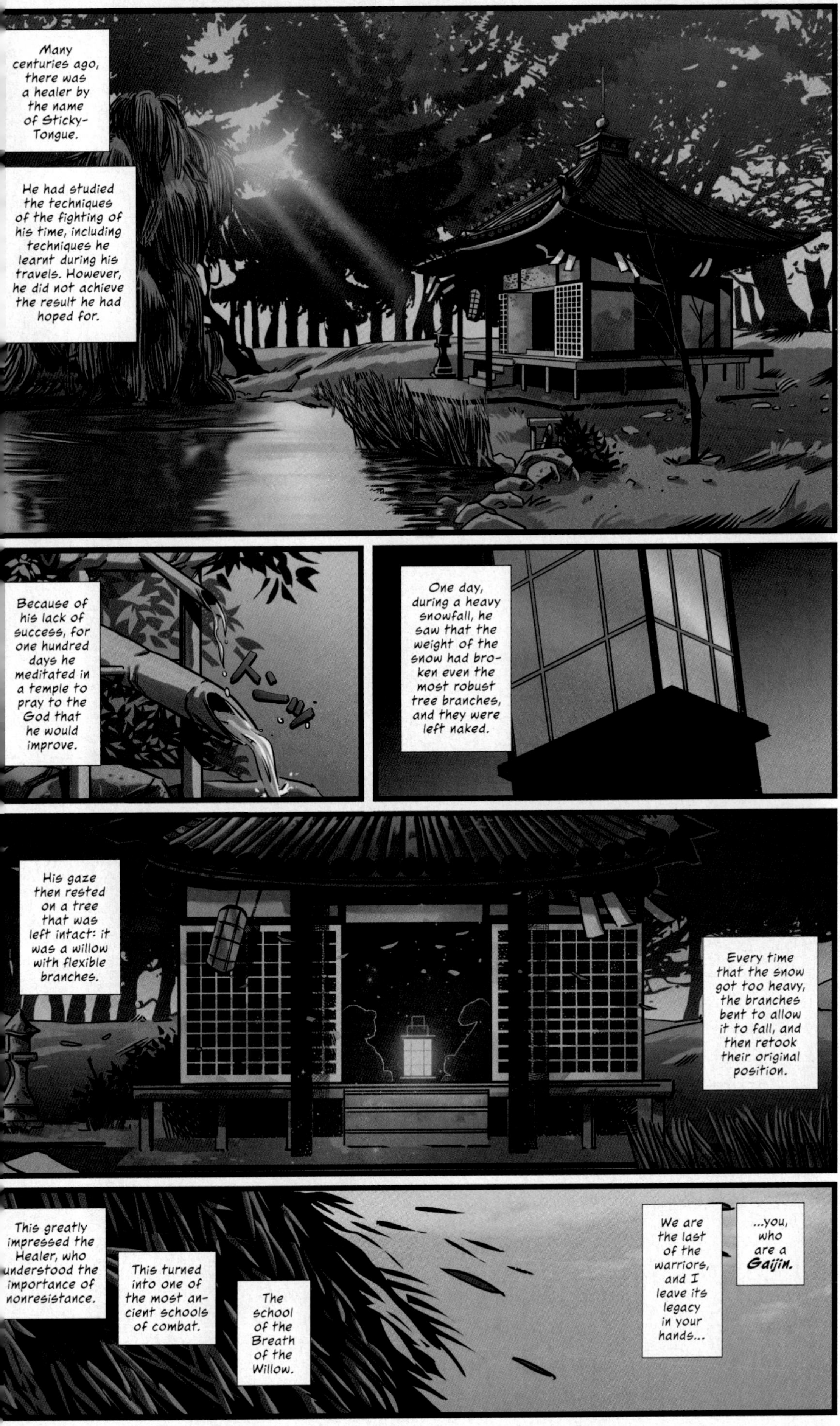

Many centuries ago, there was a healer by the name of Sticky-Tongue.
He had studied the techniques of the fighting of his time, including techniques he learnt during his travels. However, he did not achieve the result he had hoped for.
Because of his lack of success, for one hundred days he meditated in a temple to pray to the God that he would improve.
One day, during a heavy snowfall, he saw that the weight of the snow had broken even the most robust tree branches, and they were left naked.
His gaze then rested on a tree that was left intact: it was a willow with flexible branches.
Every time that the snow got too heavy, the branches bent to allow it to fall, and then retook their original position.
This greatly impressed the Healer, who understood the importance of nonresistance.
This turned into one of the most ancient schools of combat.
The school of the Breath of the Willow.
We are the last of the warriors, and I leave its legacy in your hands...
...you, who are a **Gaijin.**

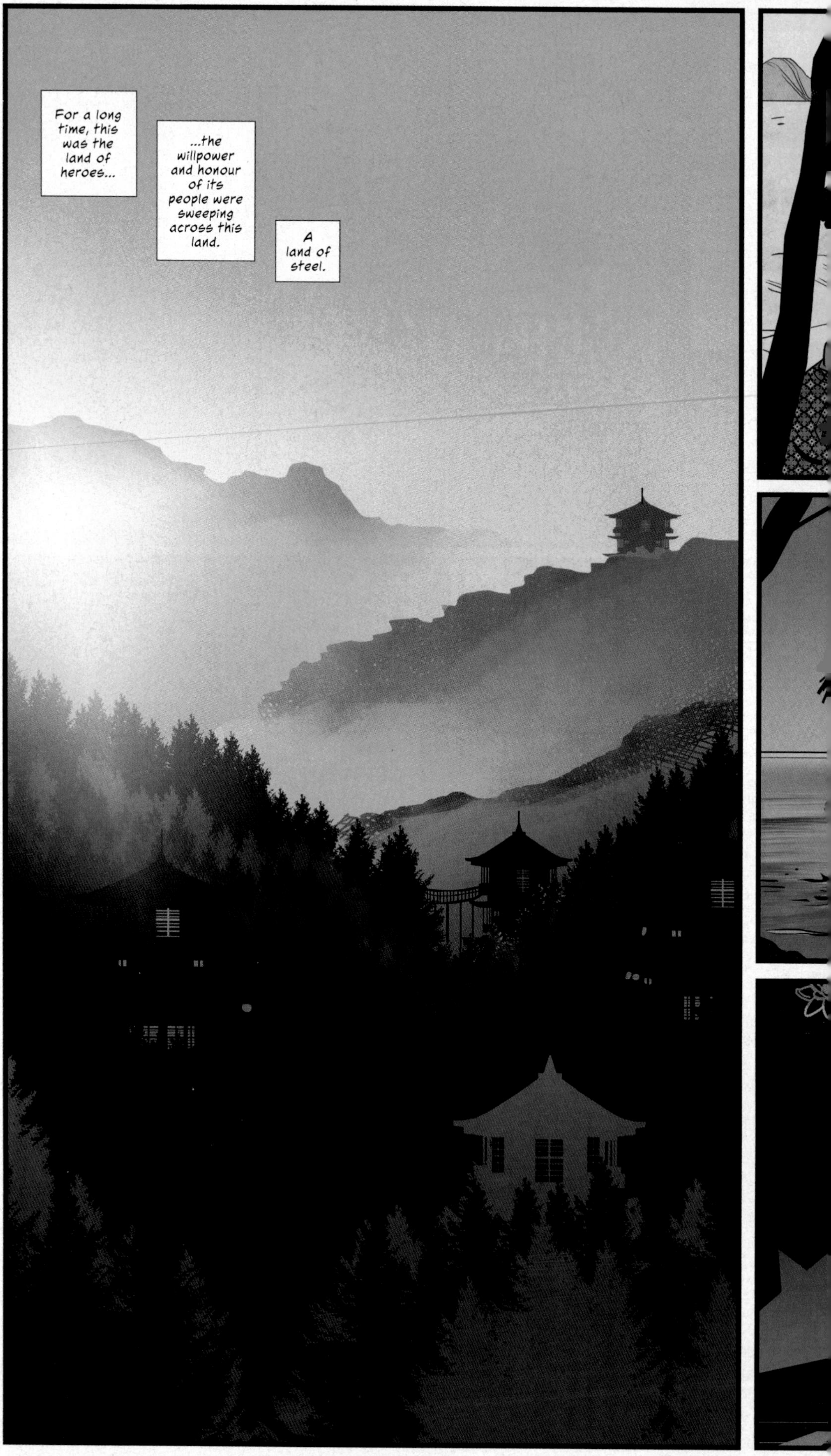
For a long time, this was the land of heroes...
...the willpower and honour of its people were sweeping across this land.
A land of steel.

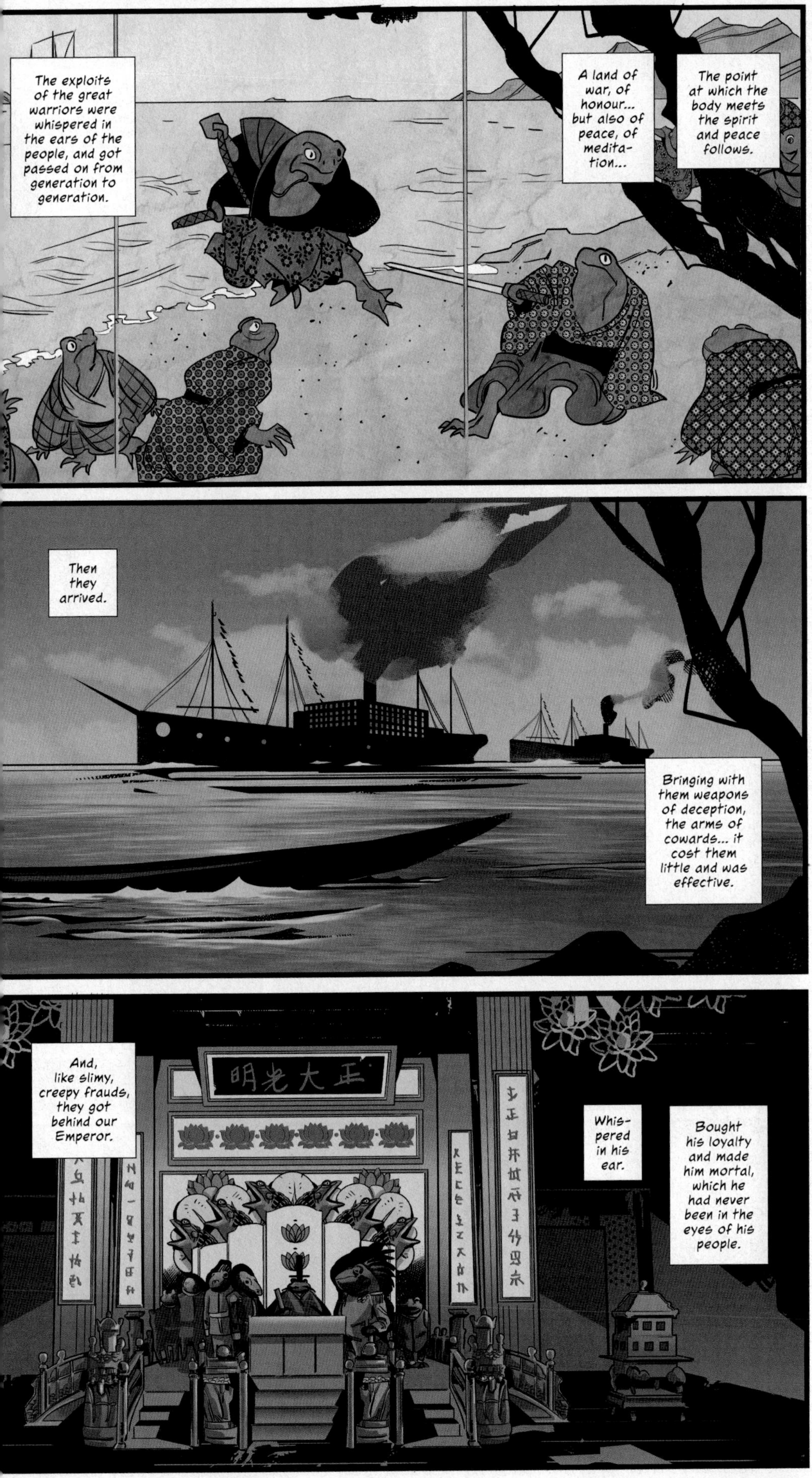
The exploits of the great warriors were whispered in the ears of the people, and got passed on from generation to generation.
A land of war, of honour... but also of peace, of medita-tion...
The point at which the body meets the spirit and peace follows.
Then they arrived.
Bringing with them weapons of deception, the arms of cowards... it cost them little and was effective.
And, like slimy, creepy frauds, they got behind our Emperor.
正大光明
Whis-pered in his ear.
Bought his loyalty and made him mortal, which he had never been in the eyes of his people.

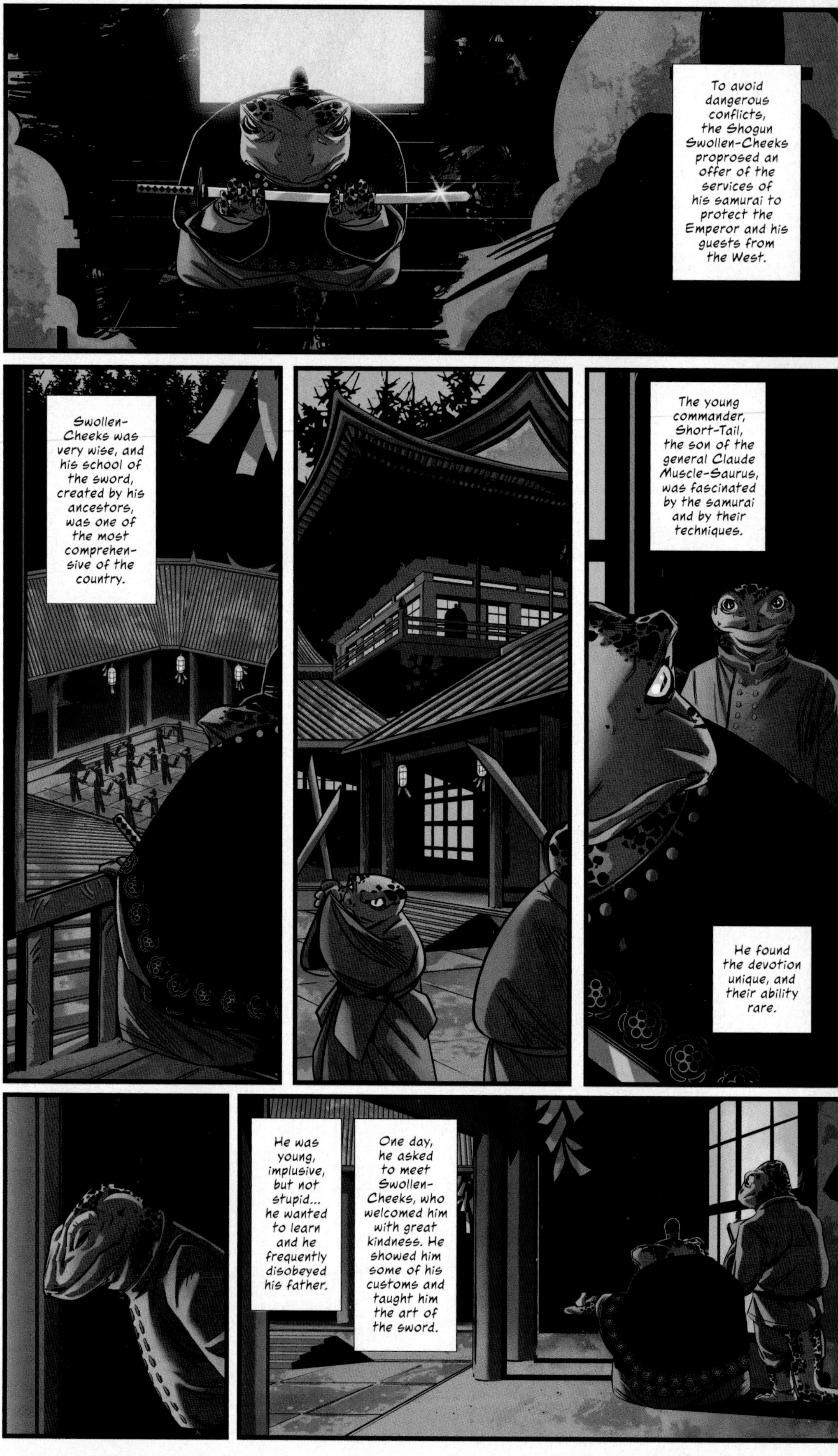
To avoid dangerous conflicts, the Shogun Swollen-Cheeks proprosed an offer of the services of his samurai to protect the Emperor and his guests from the West.
Swollen-Cheeks was very wise, and his school of the sword, created by his ancestors, was one of the most comprehen-sive of the country.
The young commander, Short-Tail, the son of the general Claude Muscle-Saurus, was fascinated by the samurai and by their techniques.
He found the devotion unique, and their ability rare.
He was young, implusive, but not stupid... he wanted to learn and he frequently disobeyed his father.
One day, he asked to meet Swollen-Cheeks, who welcomed him with great kindness. He showed him some of his customs and taught him the art of the sword.

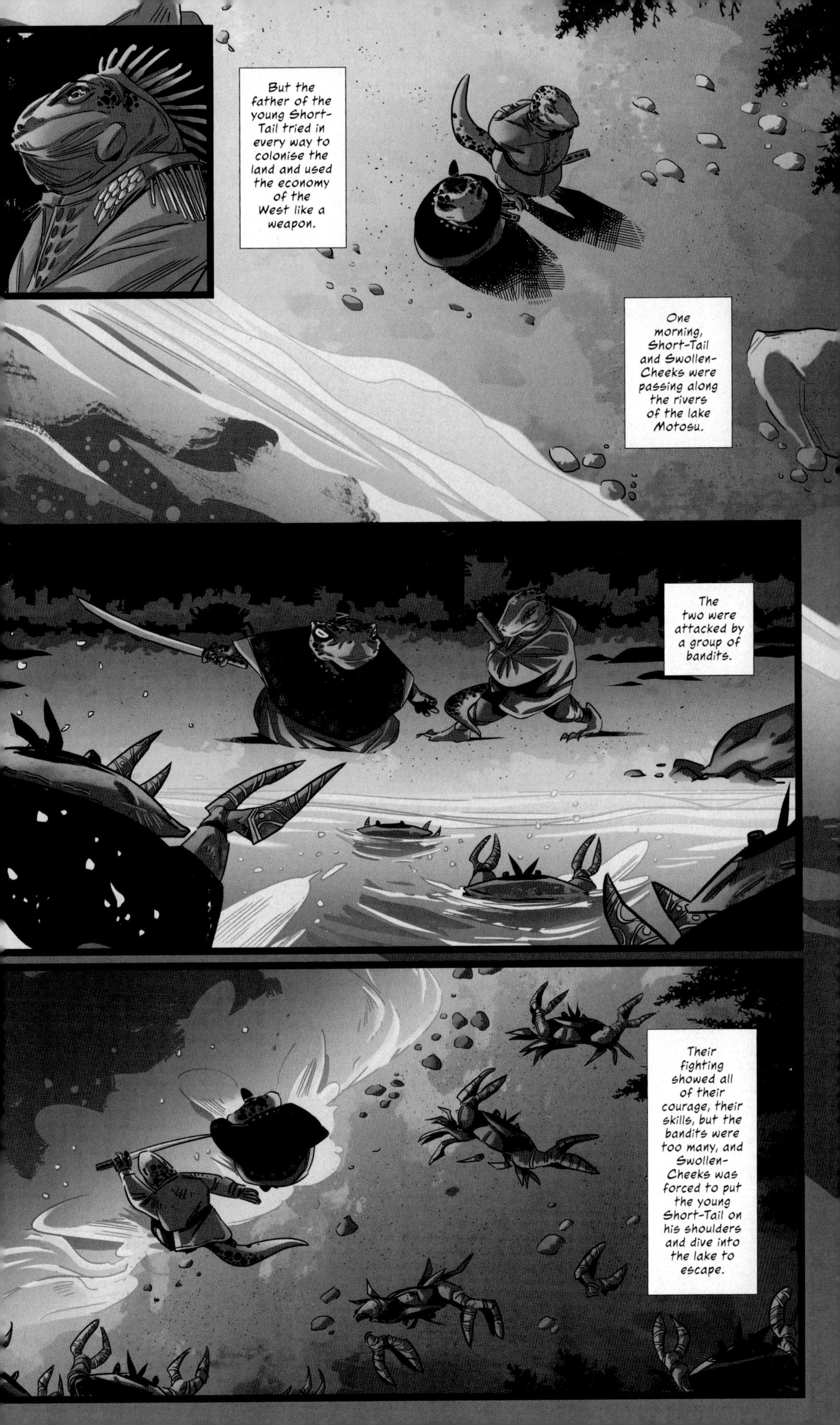
But the father of the young Short-Tail tried in every way to colonise the land and used the economy of the West like a weapon.
One morning, Short-Tail and Swollen-Cheeks were passing along the rivers of the lake Motosu.
The two were attacked by a group of bandits.
Their fighting showed all of their courage, their skills, but the bandits were too many, and Swollen-Cheeks was forced to put the young Short-Tail on his shoulders and dive into the lake to escape.

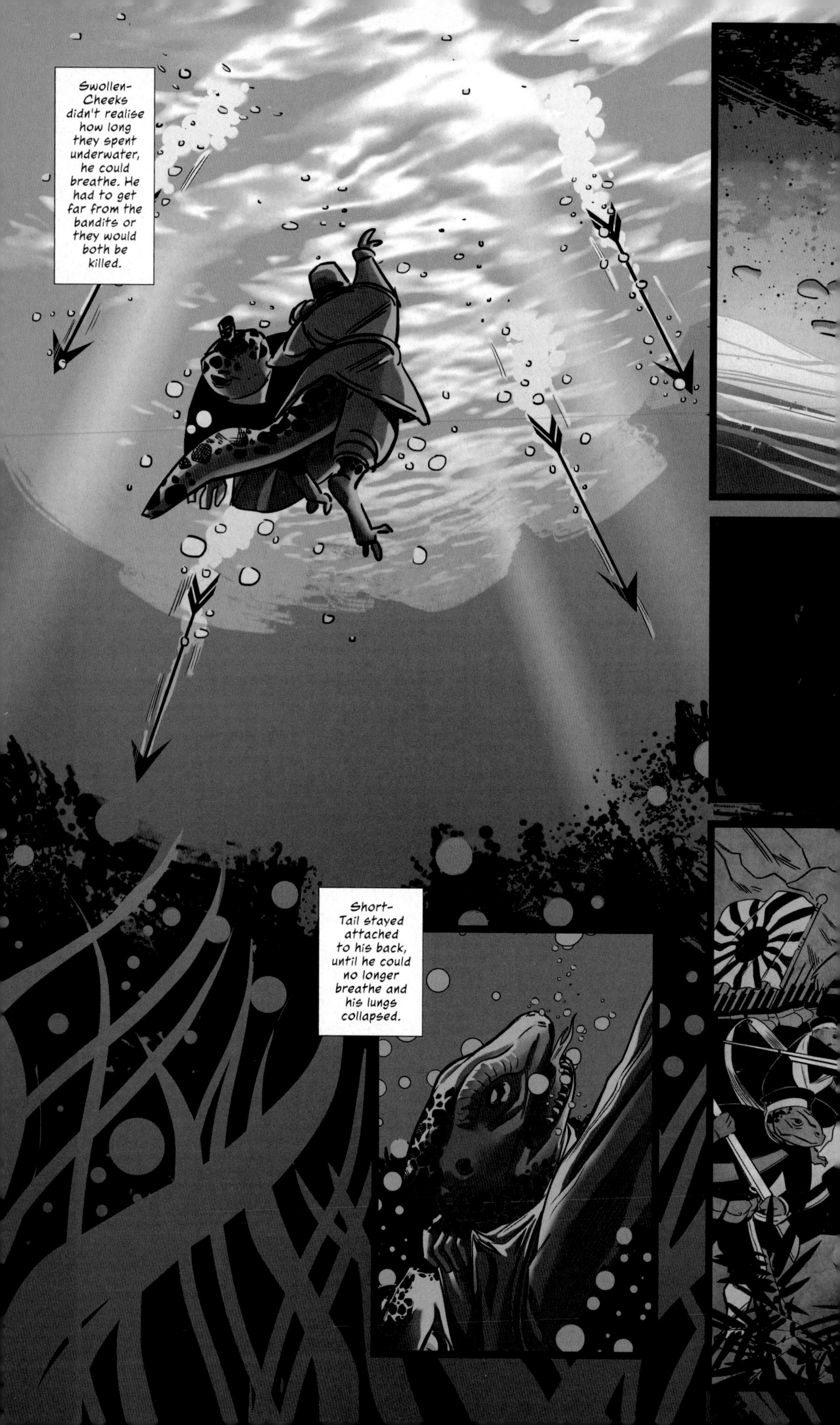
Swollen-Cheeks didn't realise how long they spent underwater, he could breathe. He had to get far from the bandits or they would both be killed.
Short-Tail stayed attached to his back, until he could no longer breathe and his lungs collapsed.

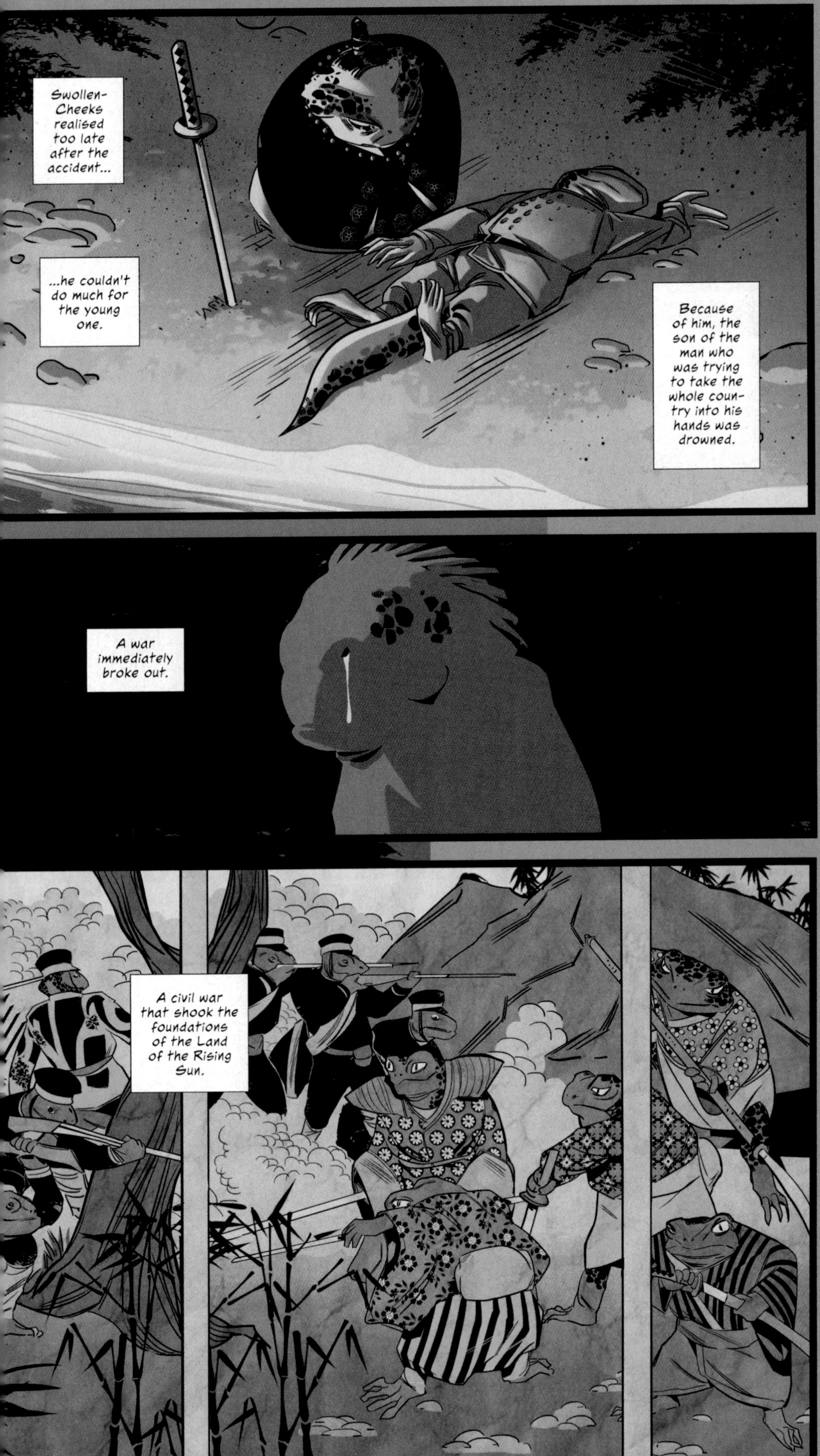
Swollen-Cheeks realised too late after the accident...
...he couldn't do much for the young one.
Because of him, the son of the man who was trying to take the whole country into his hands was drowned.
A war immediately broke out.
A civil war that shook the foundations of the Land of the Rising Sun.

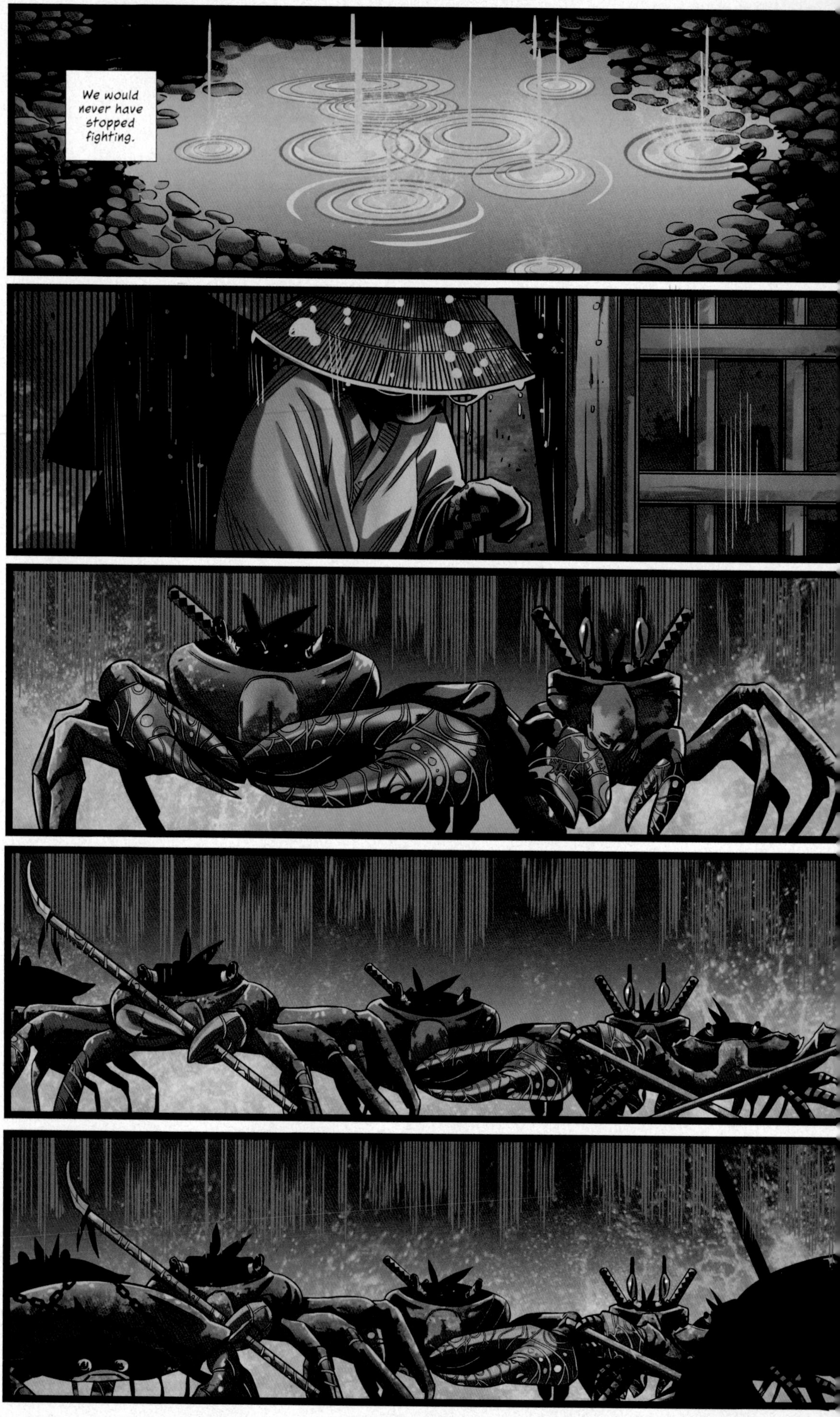
We would never have stopped fighting.

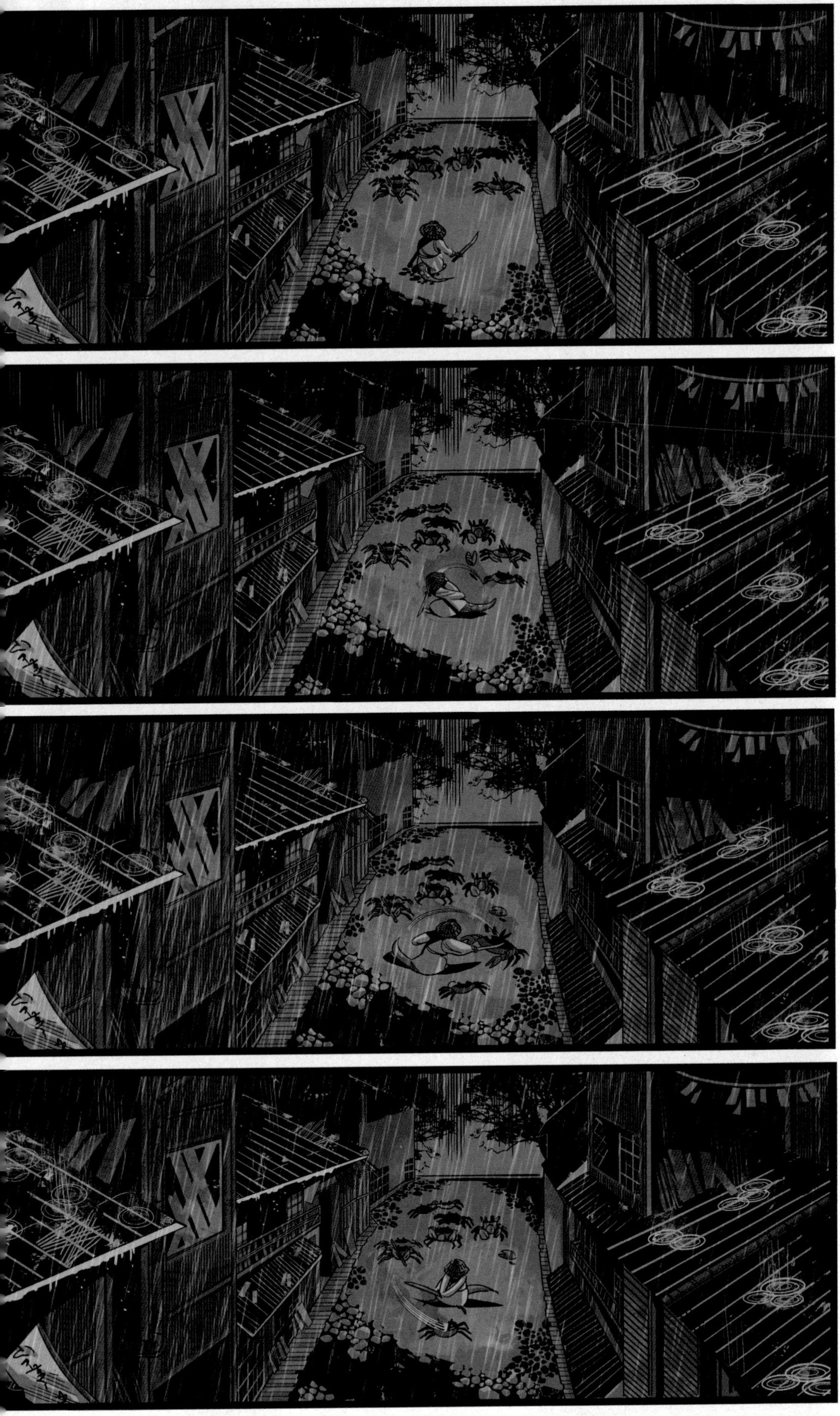

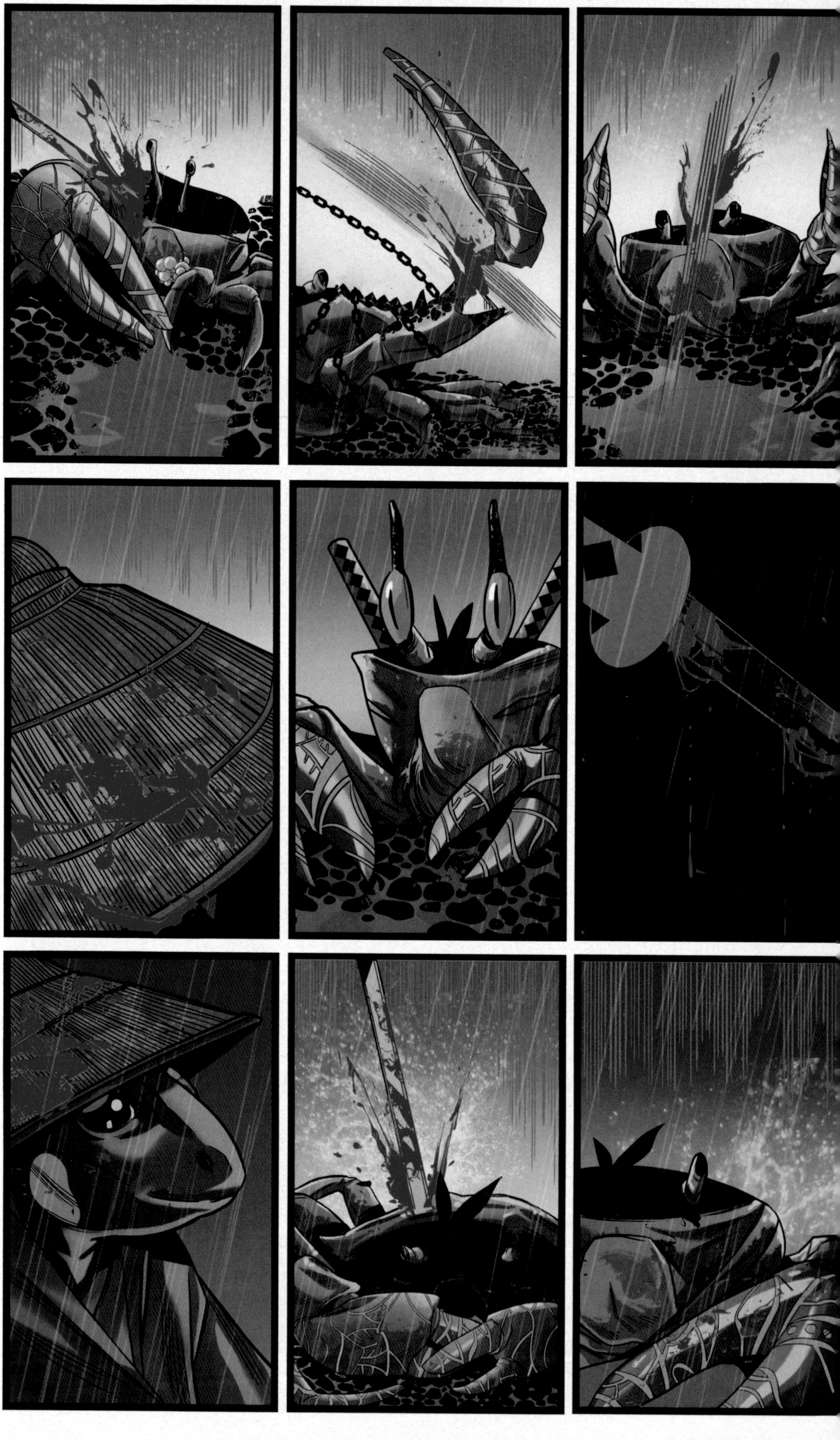

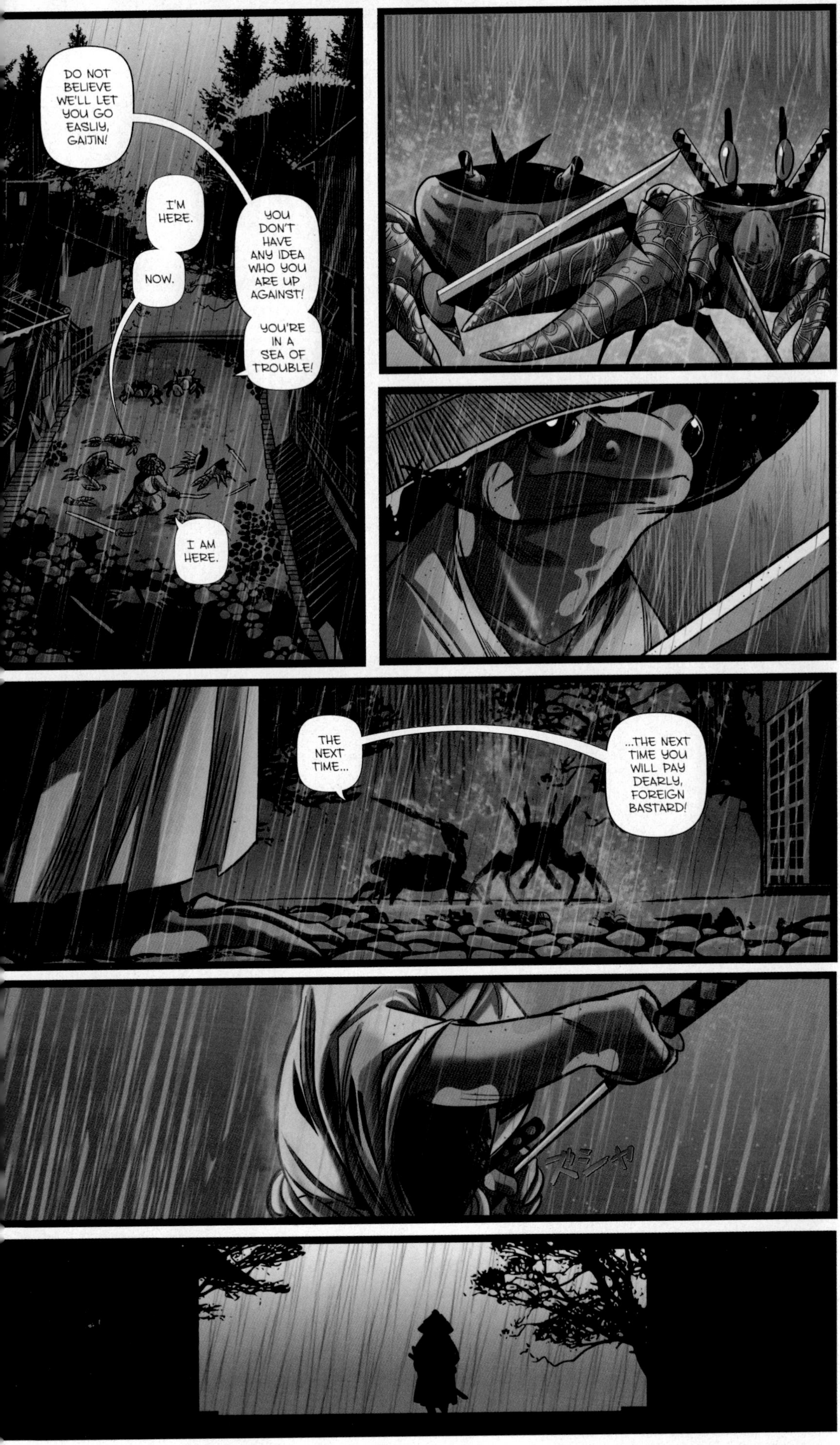
DO NOT BELIEVE WE'LL LET YOU GO EASLIY, GAIJIN!
YOU DON'T HAVE ANY IDEA WHO YOU ARE UP AGAINST!
YOU'RE IN A SEA OF TROUBLE!
I'M HERE.
NOW.
I AM HERE.
THE NEXT TIME...
...THE NEXT TIME YOU WILL PAY DEARLY, FOREIGN BASTARD!

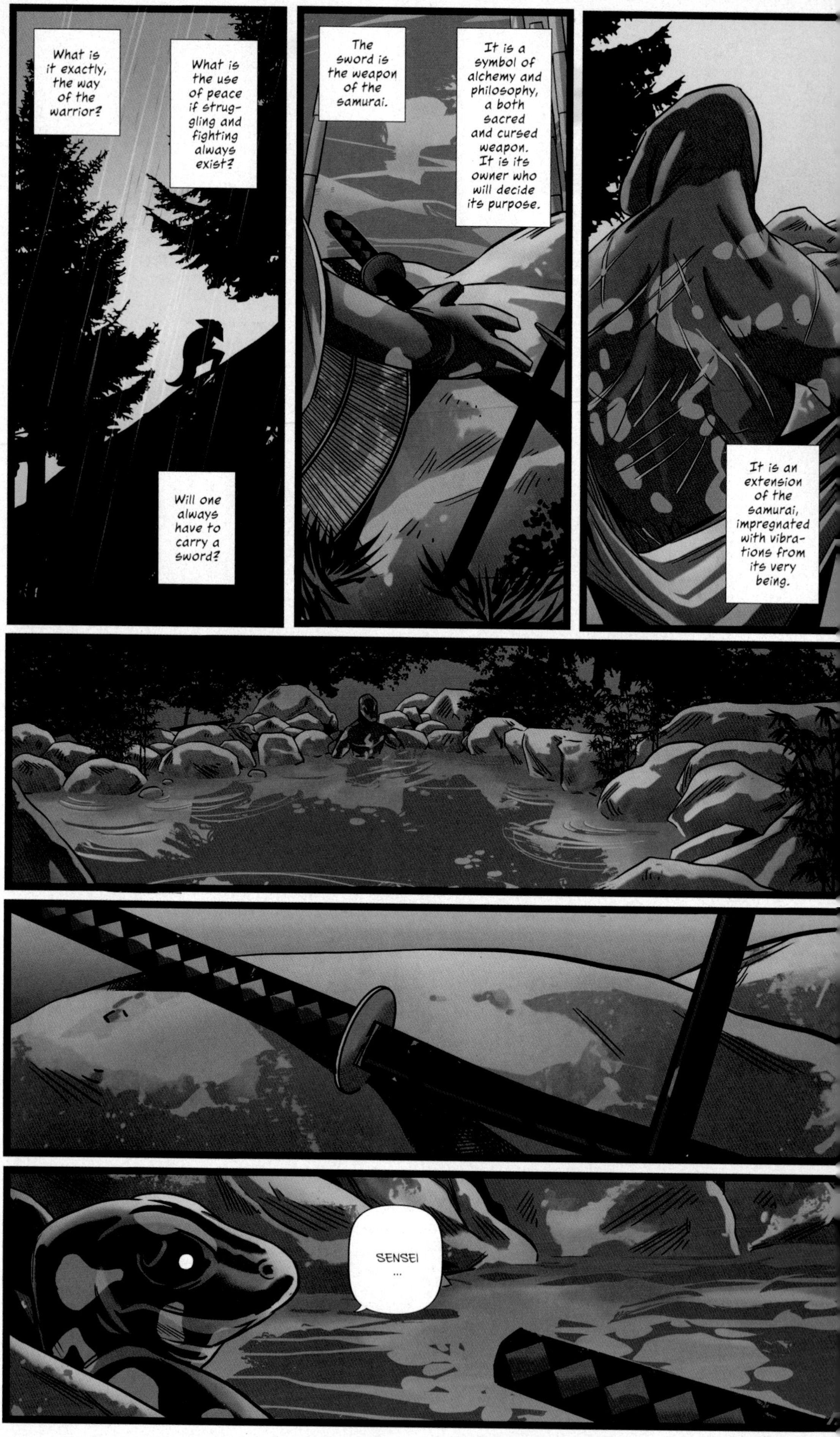
What is it exactly, the way of the warrior?
What is the use of peace if struggling and fighting always exist?
Will one always have to carry a sword?
The sword is the weapon of the samurai.
It is a symbol of alchemy and philosophy, a both sacred and cursed weapon. It is its owner who will decide its purpose.
It is an extension of the samurai, impregnated with vibrations from its very being.
SENSEI ...

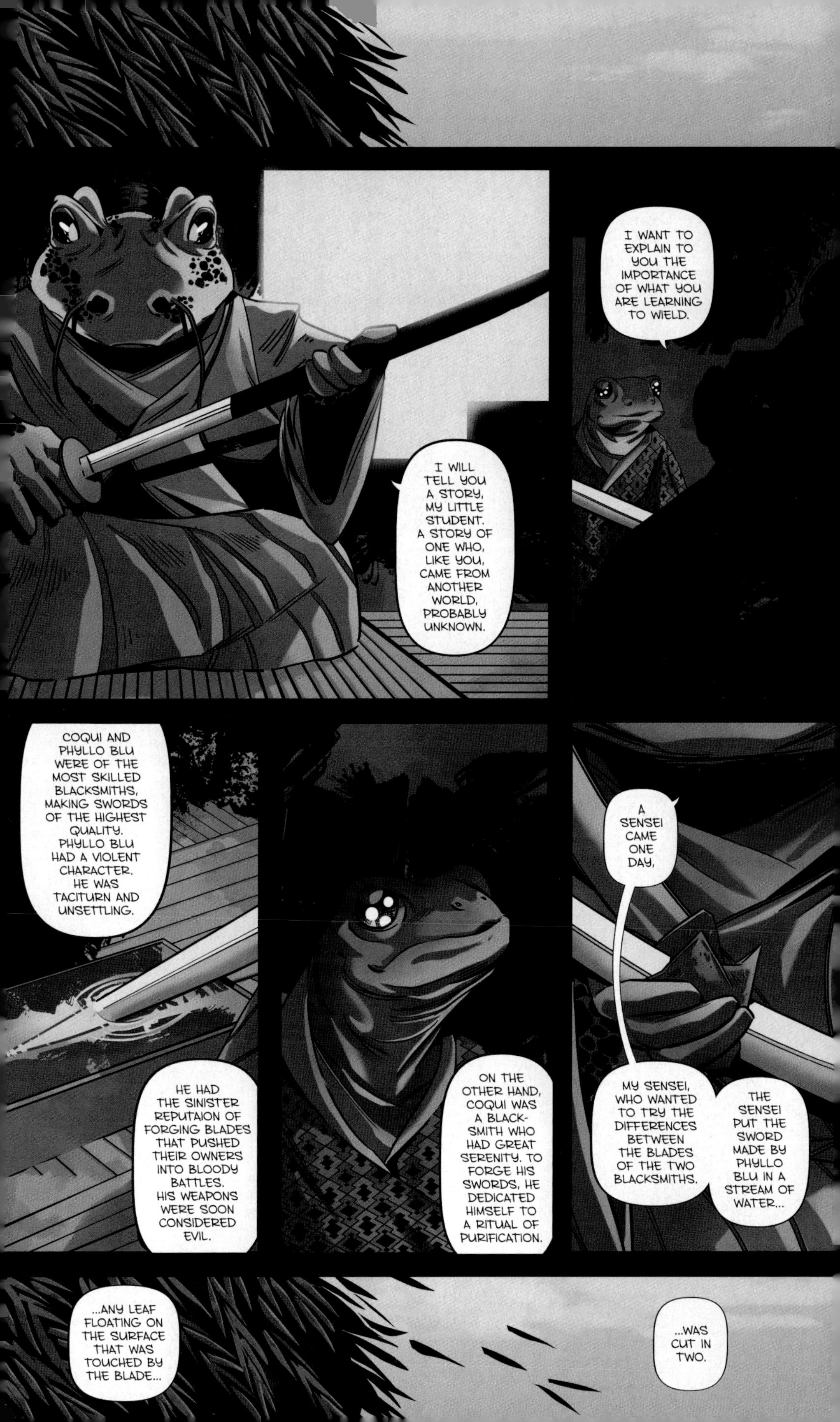
I WANT TO EXPLAIN TO YOU THE IMPORTANCE OF WHAT YOU ARE LEARNING TO WIELD.
I WILL TELL YOU A STORY, MY LITTLE STUDENT. A STORY OF ONE WHO, LIKE YOU, CAME FROM ANOTHER WORLD, PROBABLY UNKNOWN.
COQUI AND PHYLLO BLU WERE OF THE MOST SKILLED BLACKSMITHS, MAKING SWORDS OF THE HIGHEST QUALITY. PHYLLO BLU HAD A VIOLENT CHARACTER. HE WAS TACITURN AND UNSETTLING.
HE HAD THE SINISTER REPUTAION OF FORGING BLADES THAT PUSHED THEIR OWNERS INTO BLOODY BATTLES. HIS WEAPONS WERE SOON CONSIDERED EVIL.
ON THE OTHER HAND, COQUI WAS A BLACK-SMITH WHO HAD GREAT SERENITY. TO FORGE HIS SWORDS, HE DEDICATED HIMSELF TO A RITUAL OF PURIFICATION.
A SENSEI CAME ONE DAY,
MY SENSEI, WHO WANTED TO TRY THE DIFFERENCES BETWEEN THE BLADES OF THE TWO BLACKSMITHS.
THE SENSEI PUT THE SWORD MADE BY PHYLLO BLU IN A STREAM OF WATER...
...ANY LEAF FLOATING ON THE SURFACE THAT WAS TOUCHED BY THE BLADE...
...WAS CUT IN TWO.

NONE OF THEM WERE CUT, THEY ALL SLIPPED, INTACT, ALONG THE BLADE, AS THOUGH THE BLADE WANTED TO SAVE THEM.

THE SENSEI THEN GAVE THEM HIS VERDICT...

THEN, HE PUT THE SWORD MADE BY COQUI IN THE STREAM...

...THE LEAVES SEEMED TO AVOID THE BLADE.

"THE SWORD OF PHYLLO BLU-SAMA IS TERRIBLE, BUT THAT OF COQUI-SAMA IS BATRA-CHIAN."*

*THIS IS
STORY
JAPANESE
IN THE O
TEXT, IT IS
THAT THE
IS "HUMAN
THAT I
SETTING A
OF HUMA
TERM "BA
INDICA
CREATUR
THE FROG
THEREFO
SWORD IN
IS NOT HU
BATRAC

ガシャン

ガ

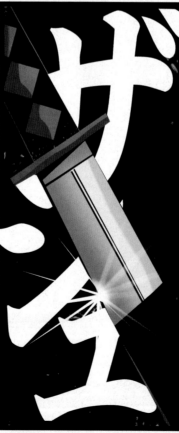

ザ
ン

NO SIR, PLEASE... WE ARE NOT BANDITS!

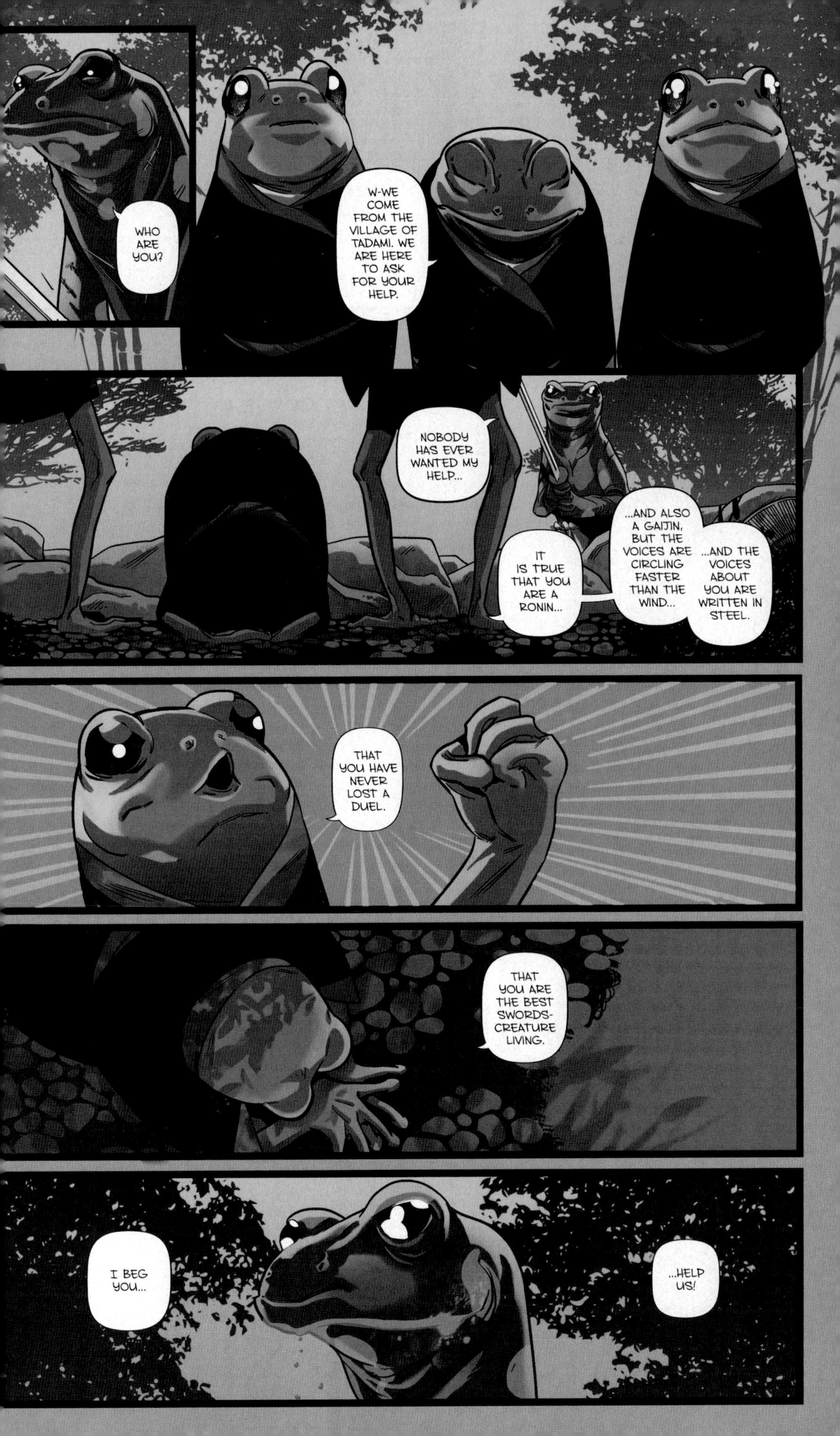
WHO ARE YOU?
W-WE COME FROM THE VILLAGE OF TADAMI. WE ARE HERE TO ASK FOR YOUR HELP.
NOBODY HAS EVER WANTED MY HELP...
IT IS TRUE THAT YOU ARE A RONIN...
...AND ALSO A GAIJIN, BUT THE VOICES ARE CIRCLING FASTER THAN THE WIND...
...AND THE VOICES ABOUT YOU ARE WRITTEN IN STEEL.
THAT YOU HAVE NEVER LOST A DUEL.
THAT YOU ARE THE BEST SWORDS-CREATURE LIVING.
I BEG YOU...
...HELP US!

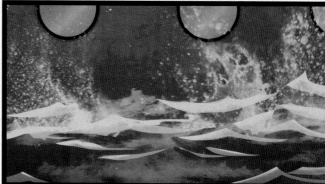

HIS ROLE HAS ALWAYS OSCILLATED BETWEEN THAT OF A HIGH-GRADE RELIGIOUS FIGURE...

...AND THAT OF IMPERIAL KING. WE ARE TALKING OF A VENERABLE FIGURE.

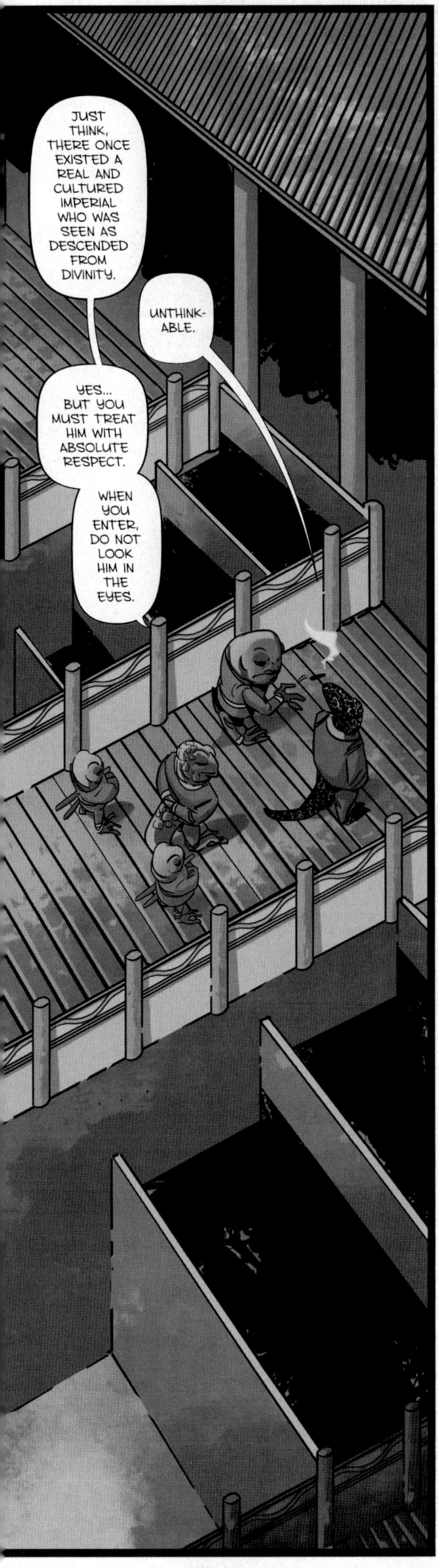
JUST THINK, THERE ONCE EXISTED A REAL AND CULTURED IMPERIAL WHO WAS SEEN AS DESCENDED FROM DIVINITY.
UNTHINK-ABLE.
YES... BUT YOU MUST TREAT HIM WITH ABSOLUTE RESPECT.
WHEN YOU ENTER, DO NOT LOOK HIM IN THE EYES.

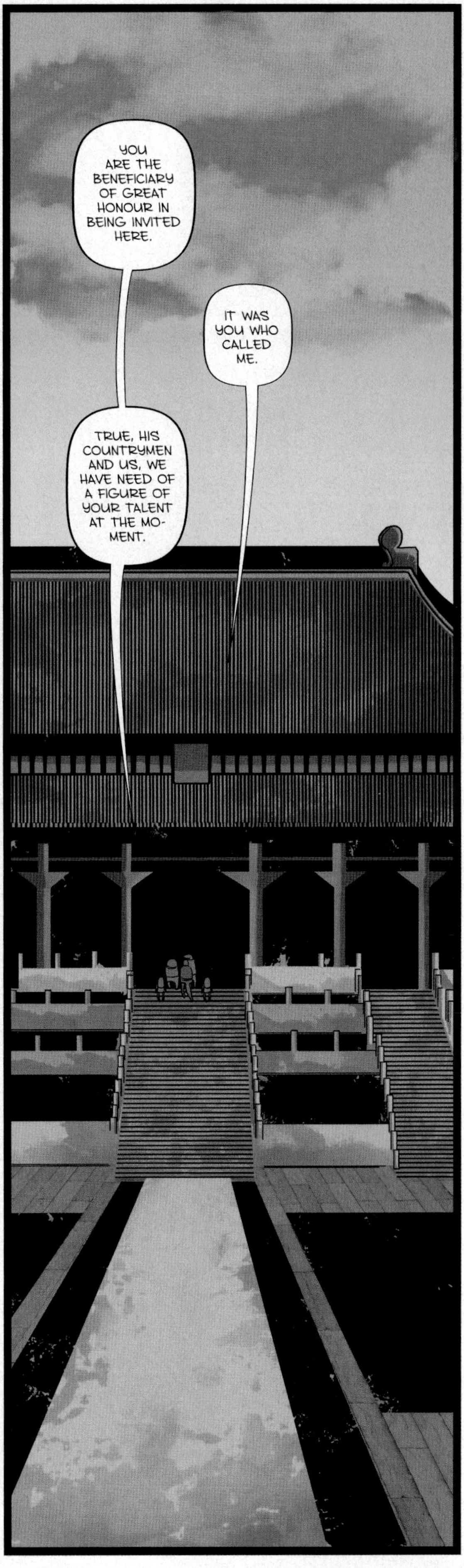
YOU ARE THE BENEFICIARY OF GREAT HONOUR IN BEING INVITED HERE.
IT WAS YOU WHO CALLED ME.
TRUE, HIS COUNTRYMEN AND US, WE HAVE NEED OF A FIGURE OF YOUR TALENT AT THE MO-MENT.

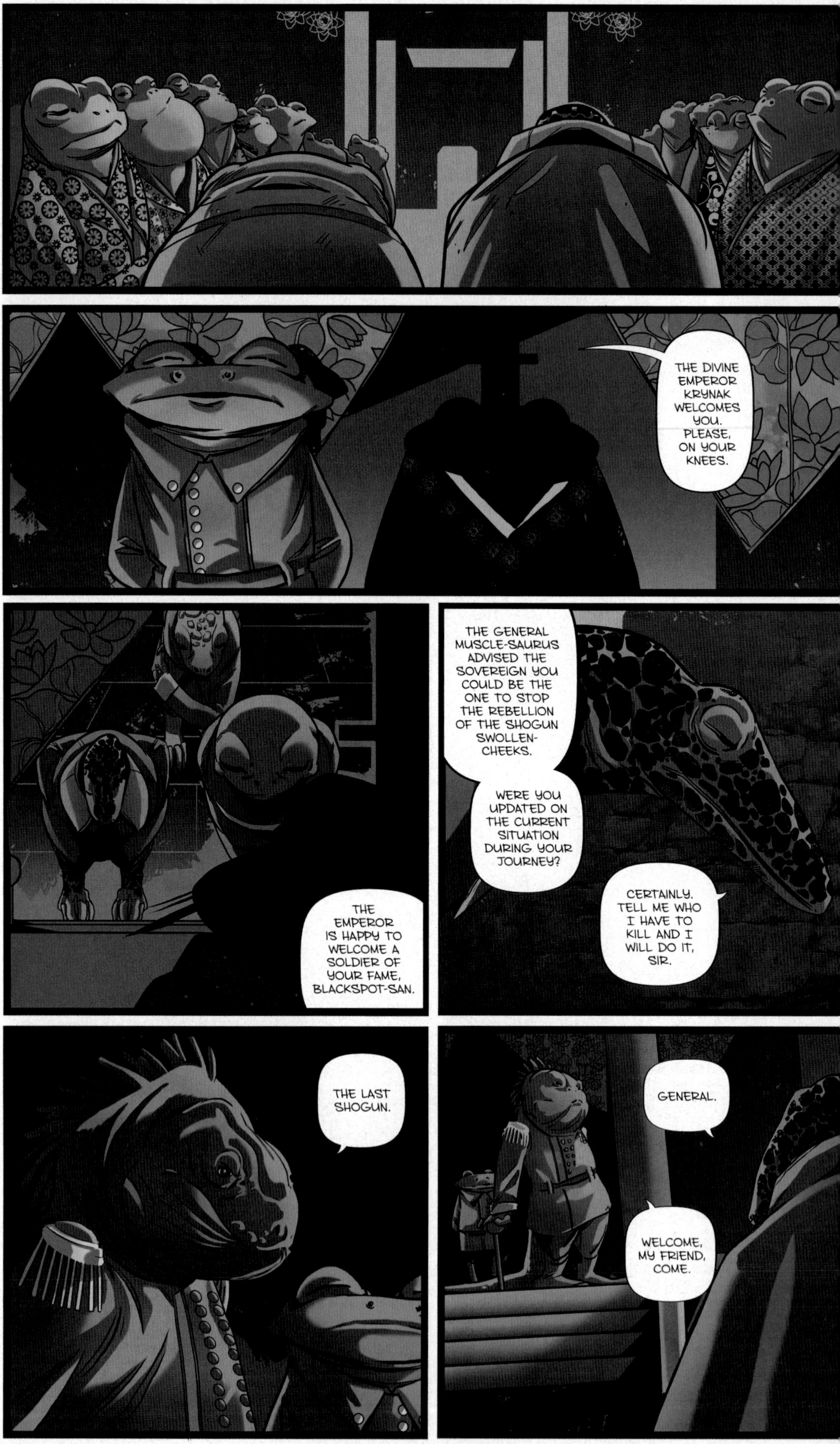
THE DIVINE EMPEROR KRYNAK WELCOMES YOU. PLEASE, ON YOUR KNEES.
THE EMPEROR IS HAPPY TO WELCOME A SOLDIER OF YOUR FAME, BLACKSPOT-SAN.
THE GENERAL MUSCLE-SAURUS ADVISED THE SOVEREIGN YOU COULD BE THE ONE TO STOP THE REBELLION OF THE SHOGUN SWOLLEN-CHEEKS.
WERE YOU UPDATED ON THE CURRENT SITUATION DURING YOUR JOURNEY?
CERTAINLY. TELL ME WHO I HAVE TO KILL AND I WILL DO IT, SIR.
THE LAST SHOGUN.
GENERAL.
WELCOME, MY FRIEND, COME.

THE SITUATION HERE IS CRITICAL... THE SHOGUN HAS BETRAYED AND KILLED MY SON AND A GROUP OF LOCAL DELINQUENTS HAVE TAKEN THE BLAME.

BUT I THINK THAT THEY KNOW DEEP DOWN THAT WE WANTED TO START A TREATY TO GOVERN THE COUNTRY, AND THEREFORE THEY ATTACKED ME PERSONALLY.

NOW THEY ARE IN A FORTRESS IN THE SOUTH, HIDING LIKE RATS WITH THEIR SAMURAI.

THE PROBLEM IS THAT THE FROGS STILL, IN SOME WAYS, LOVE THIS BARBARIAN WARRIOR.

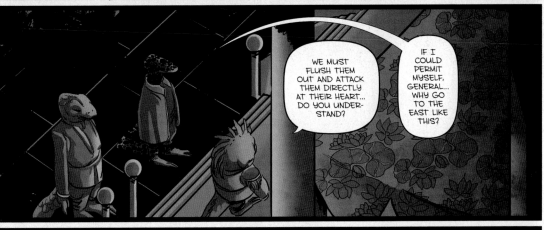

WE MUST FLUSH THEM OUT AND ATTACK THEM DIRECTLY AT THEIR HEART... DO YOU UNDERSTAND?

IF I COULD PERMIT MYSELF, GENERAL... WHY GO TO THE EAST LIKE THIS?

WE ARE GUARANTEEING THE IMPORT OF FIREARMS, EXCLUSIVELY, TO THE WHOLE COUNTRY.

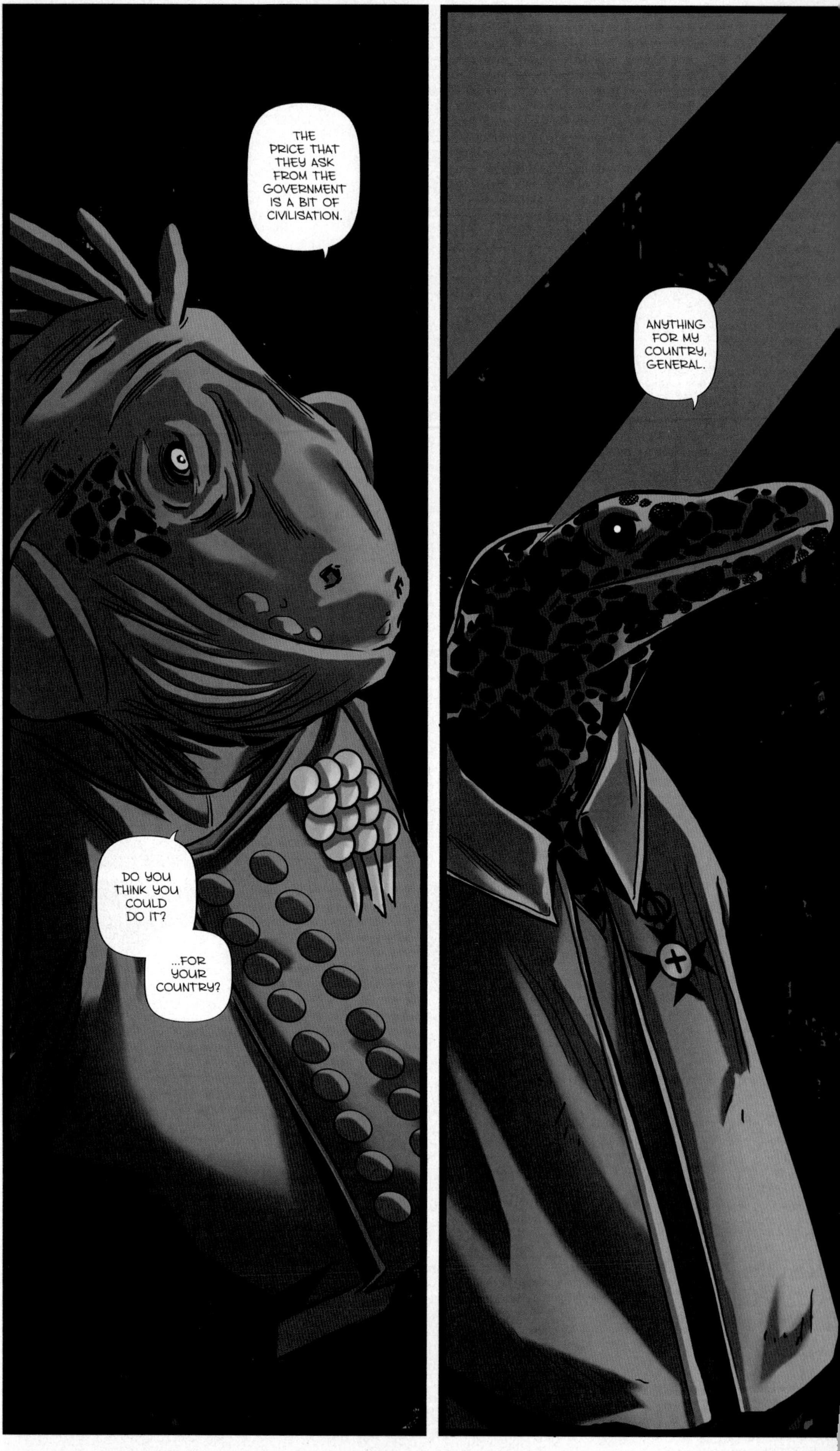
THE PRICE THAT THEY ASK FROM THE GOVERNMENT IS A BIT OF CIVILISATION.
DO YOU THINK YOU COULD DO IT?
...FOR YOUR COUNTRY?
ANYTHING FOR MY COUNTRY, GENERAL.

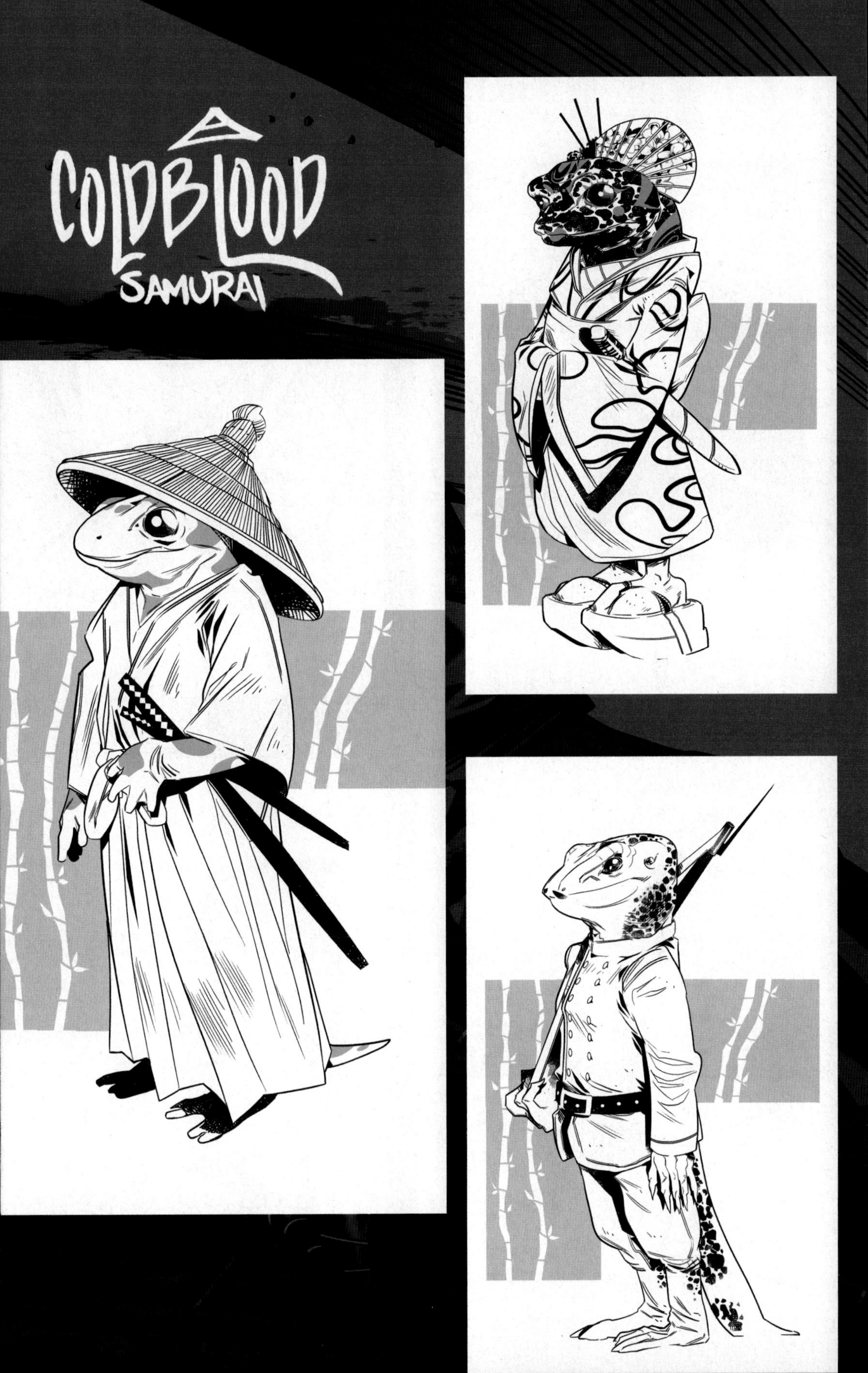
COLDBLOOD
SAMURAI

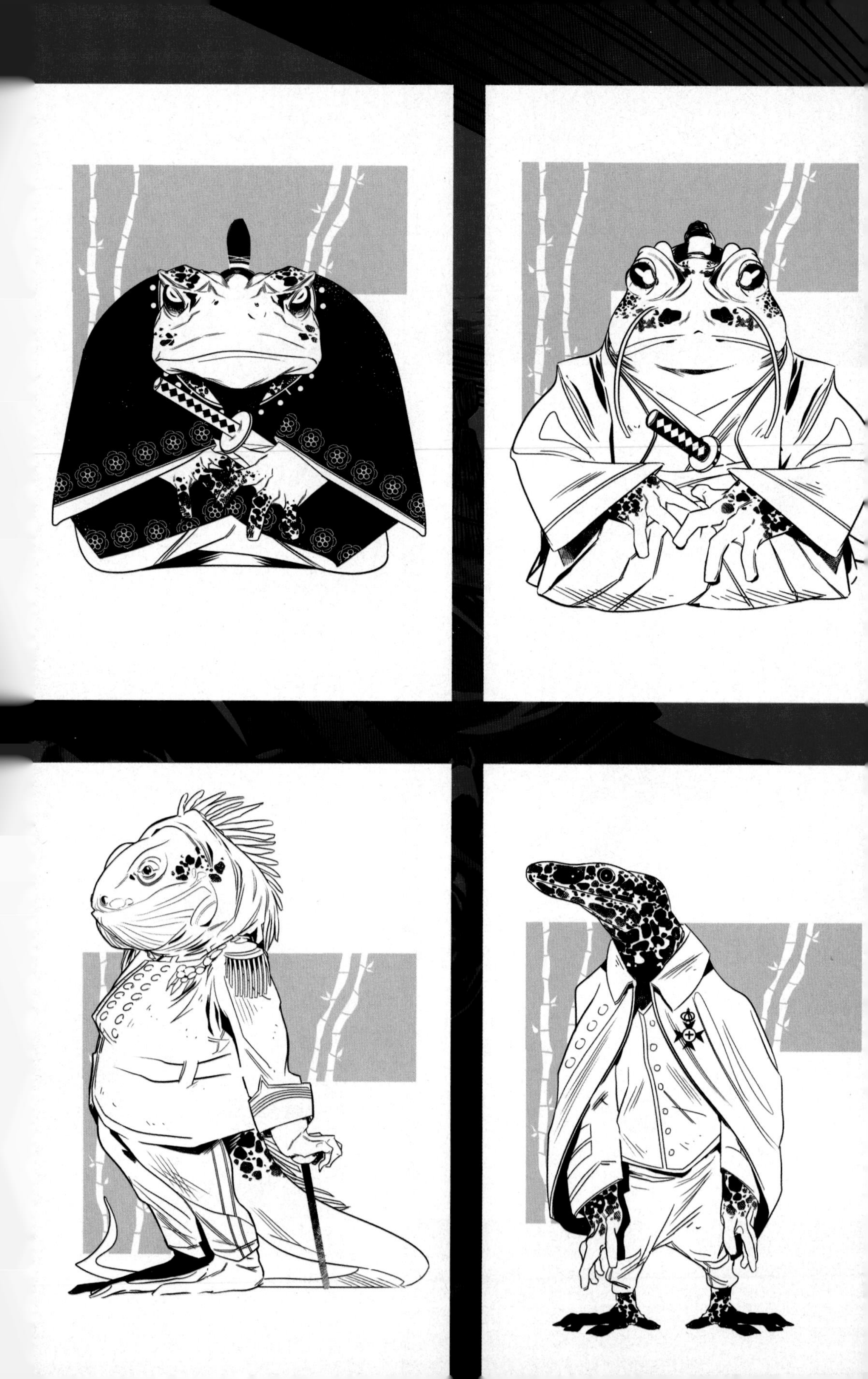

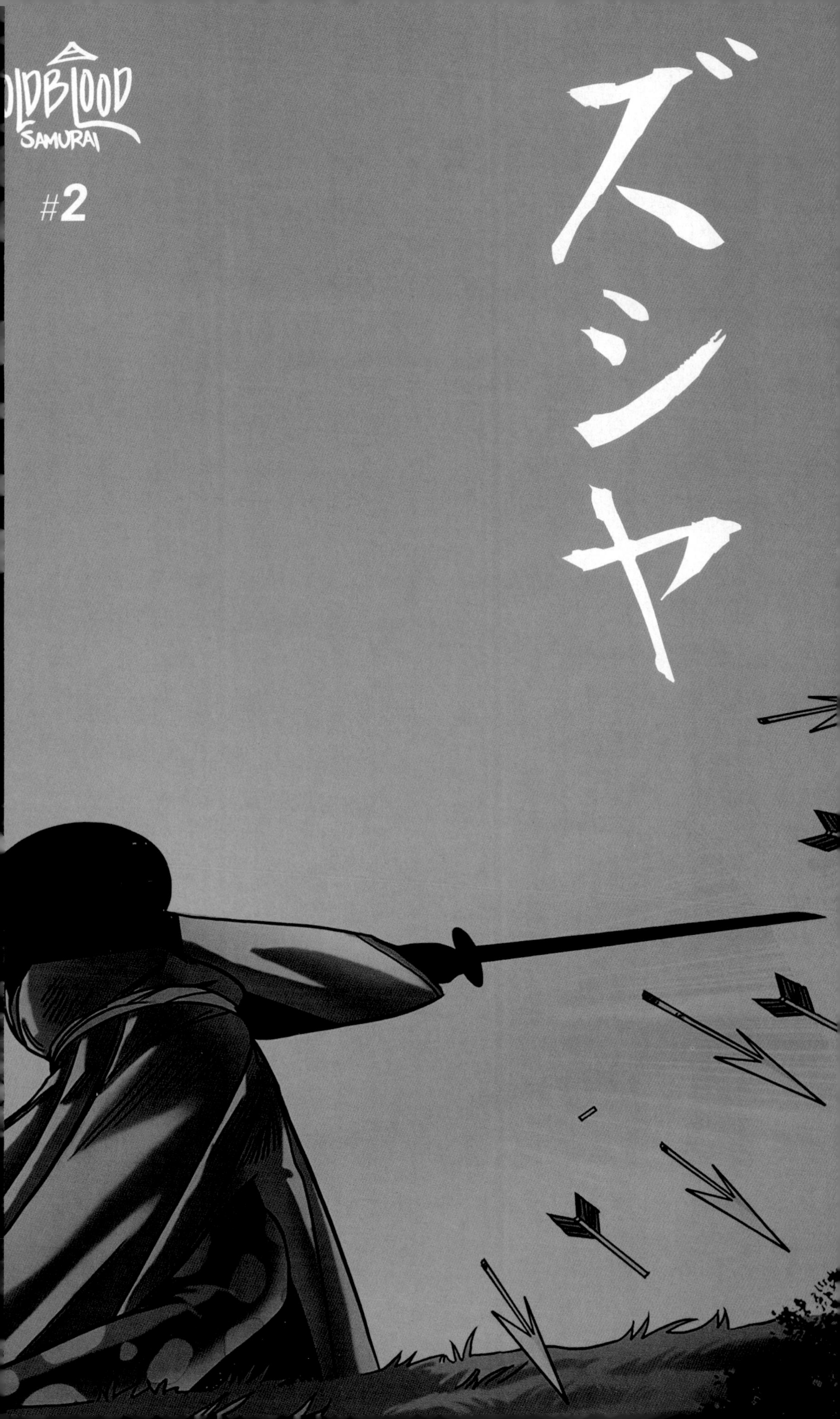

ズシャ

COLD BLOOD SAMURAI

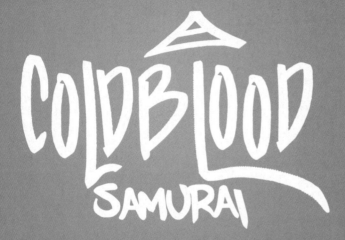

CREDITS

Story
MASSIMO ROSI

Pencils
LUDOVICA CEREGATTI

Colors
RENATO STEVANATO

Lettering
MATTIA GENTILI

Bryan Seaton: Publisher/ CEO
Shawn Gabborin: Editor In Chief
Jason Martin: Publisher-Danger Zone
Nicole D'Andria: Marketing Director/Editor
Jessica Lowrie: Social Media Czar
Danielle Davison: Executive Administrator
Chad Cicconi: King Lizard
Shawn Pryor: President of Creator Relations

Printed in USA. First Printing.

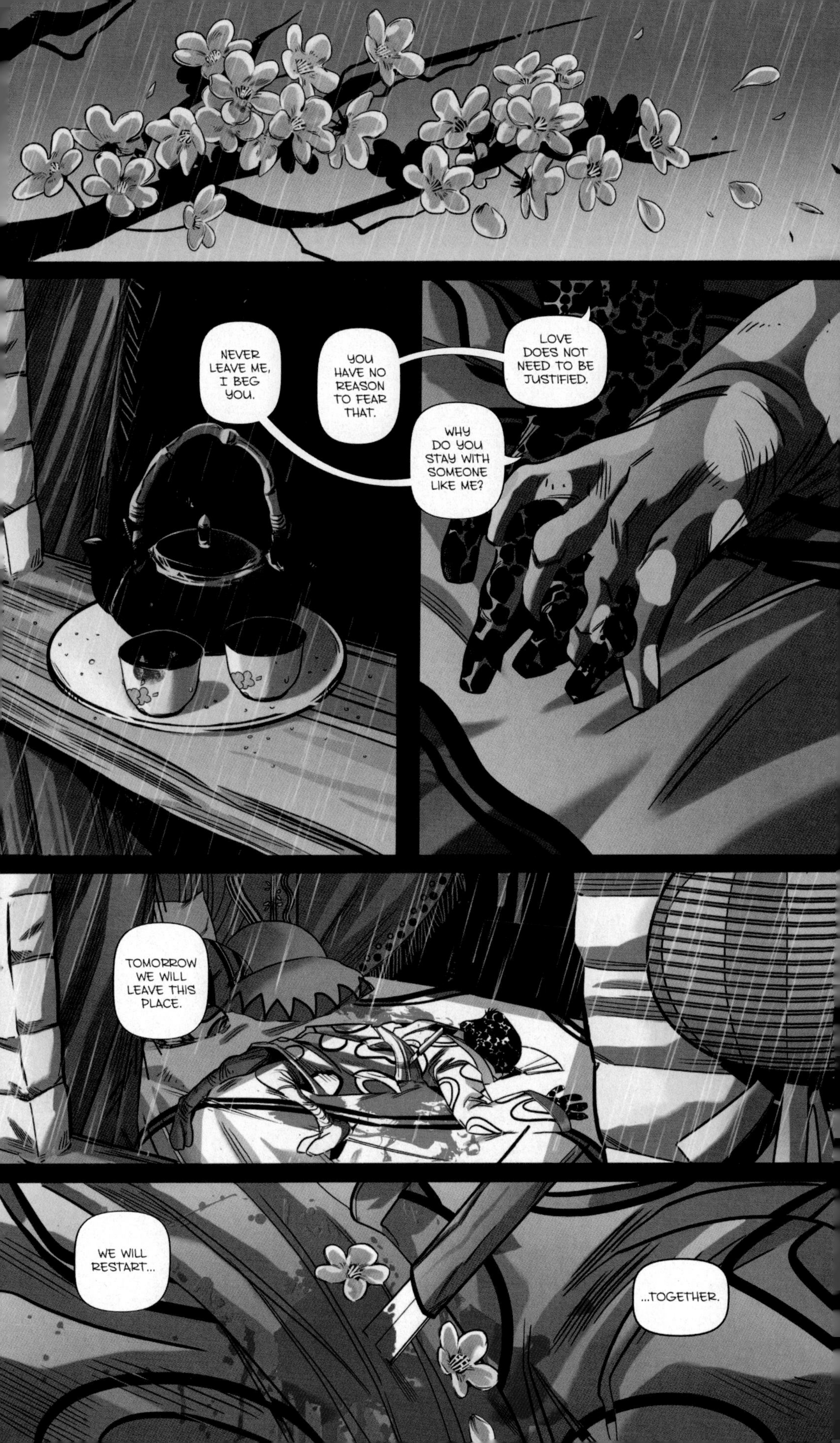
NEVER LEAVE ME, I BEG YOU.
YOU HAVE NO REASON TO FEAR THAT.
LOVE DOES NOT NEED TO BE JUSTIFIED.
WHY DO YOU STAY WITH SOMEONE LIKE ME?
TOMORROW WE WILL LEAVE THIS PLACE.
WE WILL RESTART...
...TOGETHER.

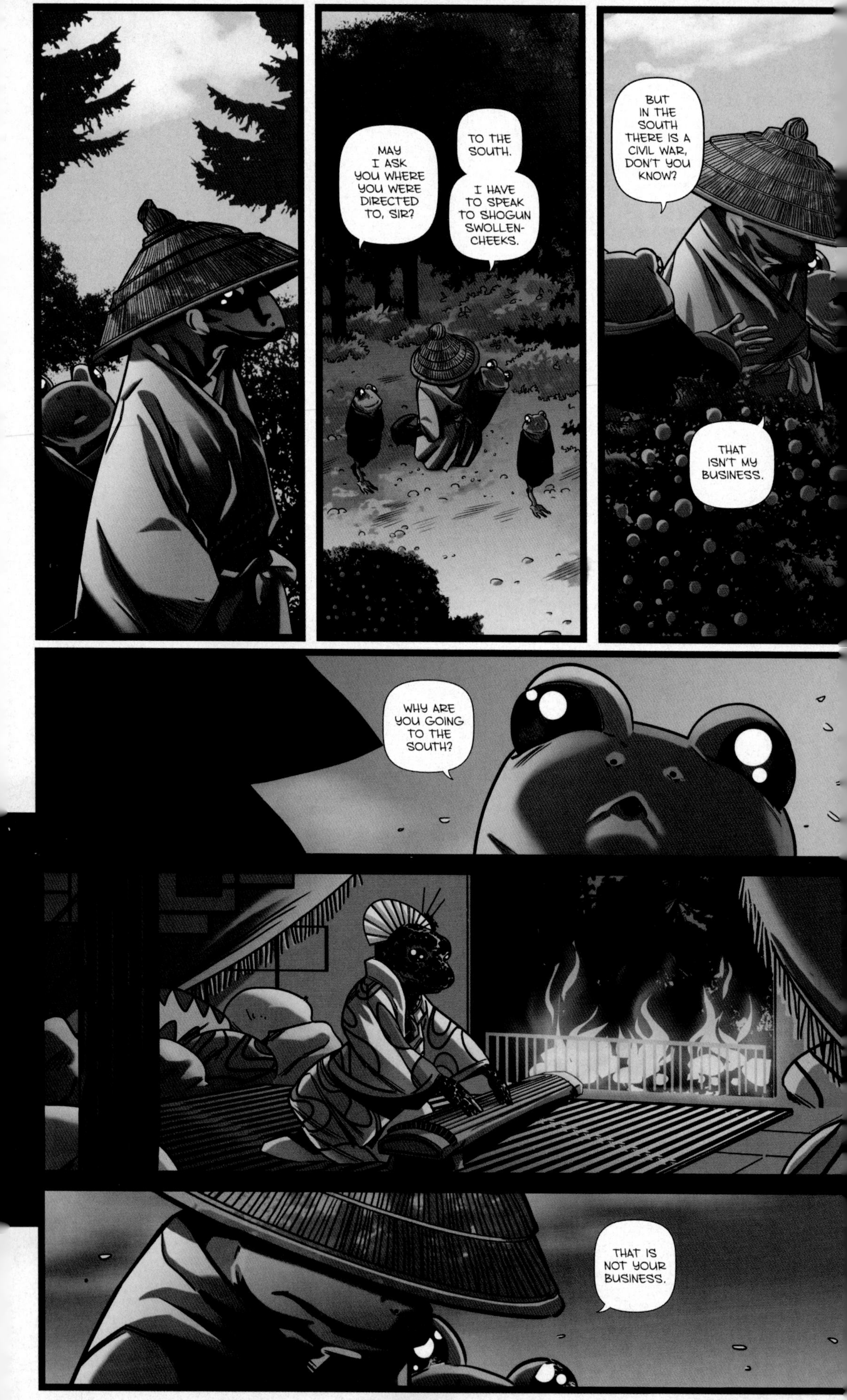
MAY I ASK YOU WHERE YOU WERE DIRECTED TO, SIR?
TO THE SOUTH.
I HAVE TO SPEAK TO SHOGUN SWOLLEN-CHEEKS.
BUT IN THE SOUTH THERE IS A CIVIL WAR, DON'T YOU KNOW?
THAT ISN'T MY BUSINESS.
WHY ARE YOU GOING TO THE SOUTH?
THAT IS NOT YOUR BUSINESS.

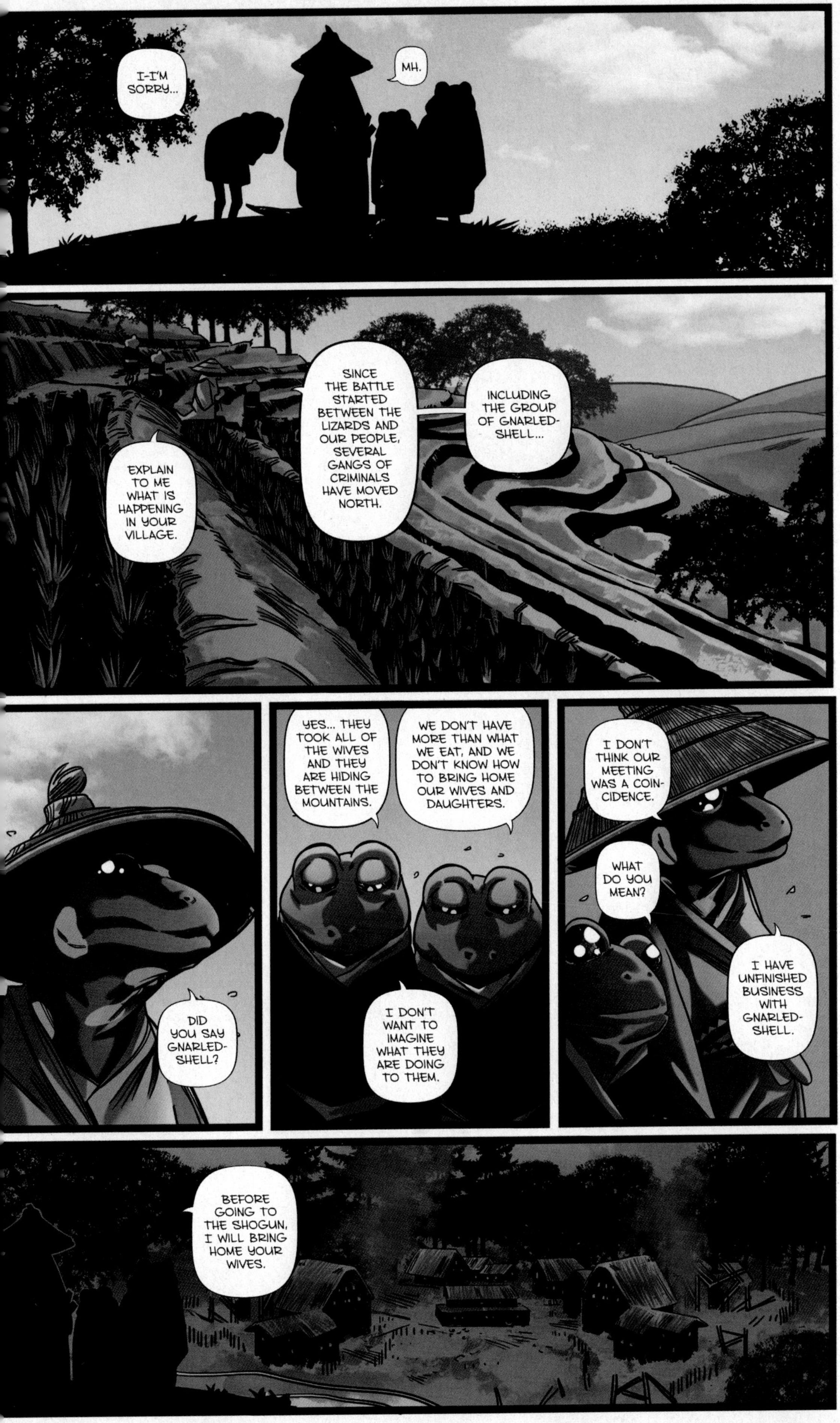
I-I'M SORRY...
MH.
EXPLAIN TO ME WHAT IS HAPPENING IN YOUR VILLAGE.
SINCE THE BATTLE STARTED BETWEEN THE LIZARDS AND OUR PEOPLE, SEVERAL GANGS OF CRIMINALS HAVE MOVED NORTH.
INCLUDING THE GROUP OF GNARLED-SHELL...
DID YOU SAY GNARLED-SHELL?
YES... THEY TOOK ALL OF THE WIVES AND THEY ARE HIDING BETWEEN THE MOUNTAINS.
WE DON'T HAVE MORE THAN WHAT WE EAT, AND WE DON'T KNOW HOW TO BRING HOME OUR WIVES AND DAUGHTERS.
I DON'T WANT TO IMAGINE WHAT THEY ARE DOING TO THEM.
I DON'T THINK OUR MEETING WAS A COIN-CIDENCE.
WHAT DO YOU MEAN?
I HAVE UNFINISHED BUSINESS WITH GNARLED-SHELL.
BEFORE GOING TO THE SHOGUN, I WILL BRING HOME YOUR WIVES.

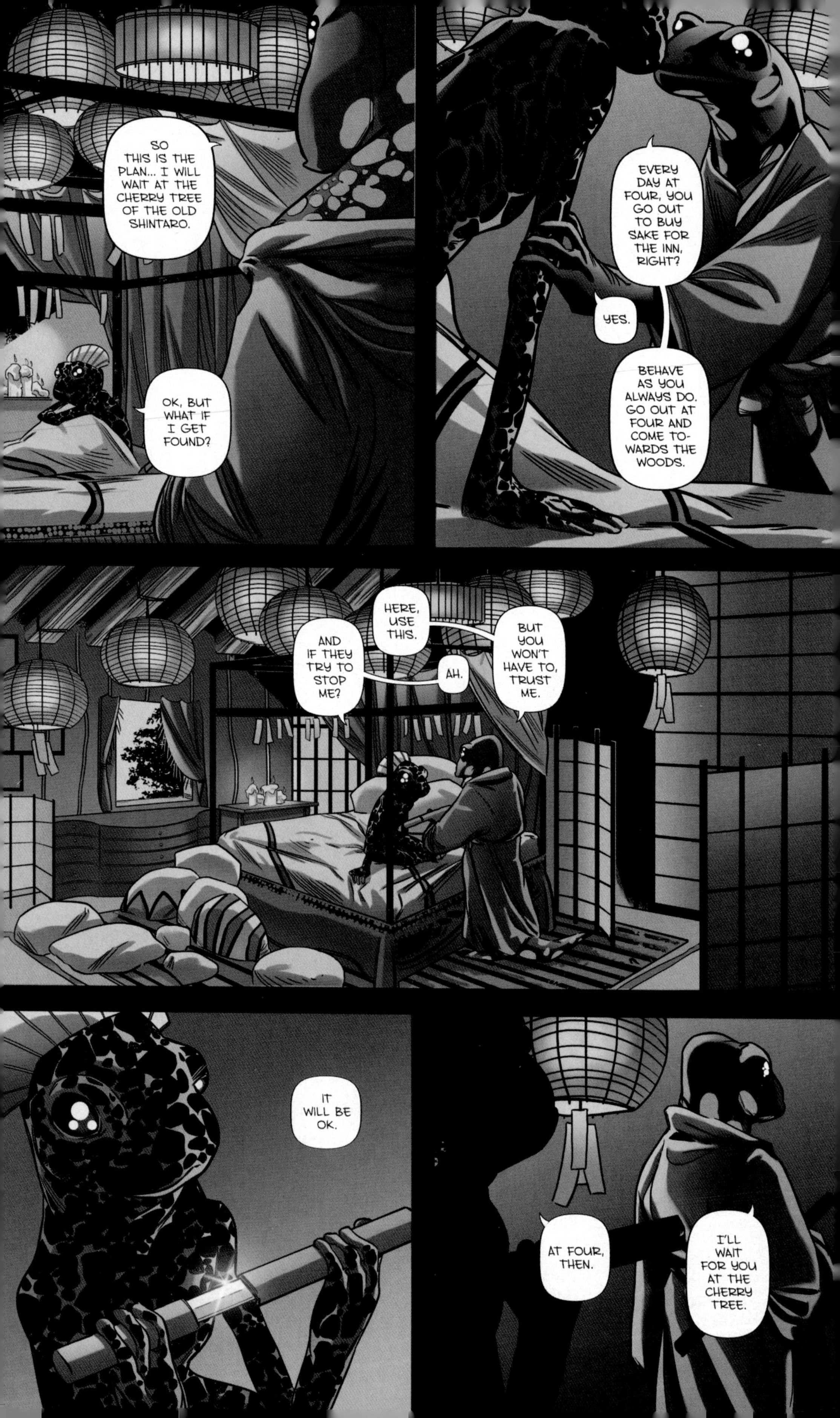
SO THIS IS THE PLAN... I WILL WAIT AT THE CHERRY TREE OF THE OLD SHINTARO.
OK, BUT WHAT IF I GET FOUND?
EVERY DAY AT FOUR, YOU GO OUT TO BUY SAKE FOR THE INN, RIGHT?
YES.
BEHAVE AS YOU ALWAYS DO. GO OUT AT FOUR AND COME TO-WARDS THE WOODS.
AND IF THEY TRY TO STOP ME?
HERE, USE THIS.
AH.
BUT YOU WON'T HAVE TO, TRUST ME.
IT WILL BE OK.
AT FOUR, THEN.
I'LL WAIT FOR YOU AT THE CHERRY TREE.

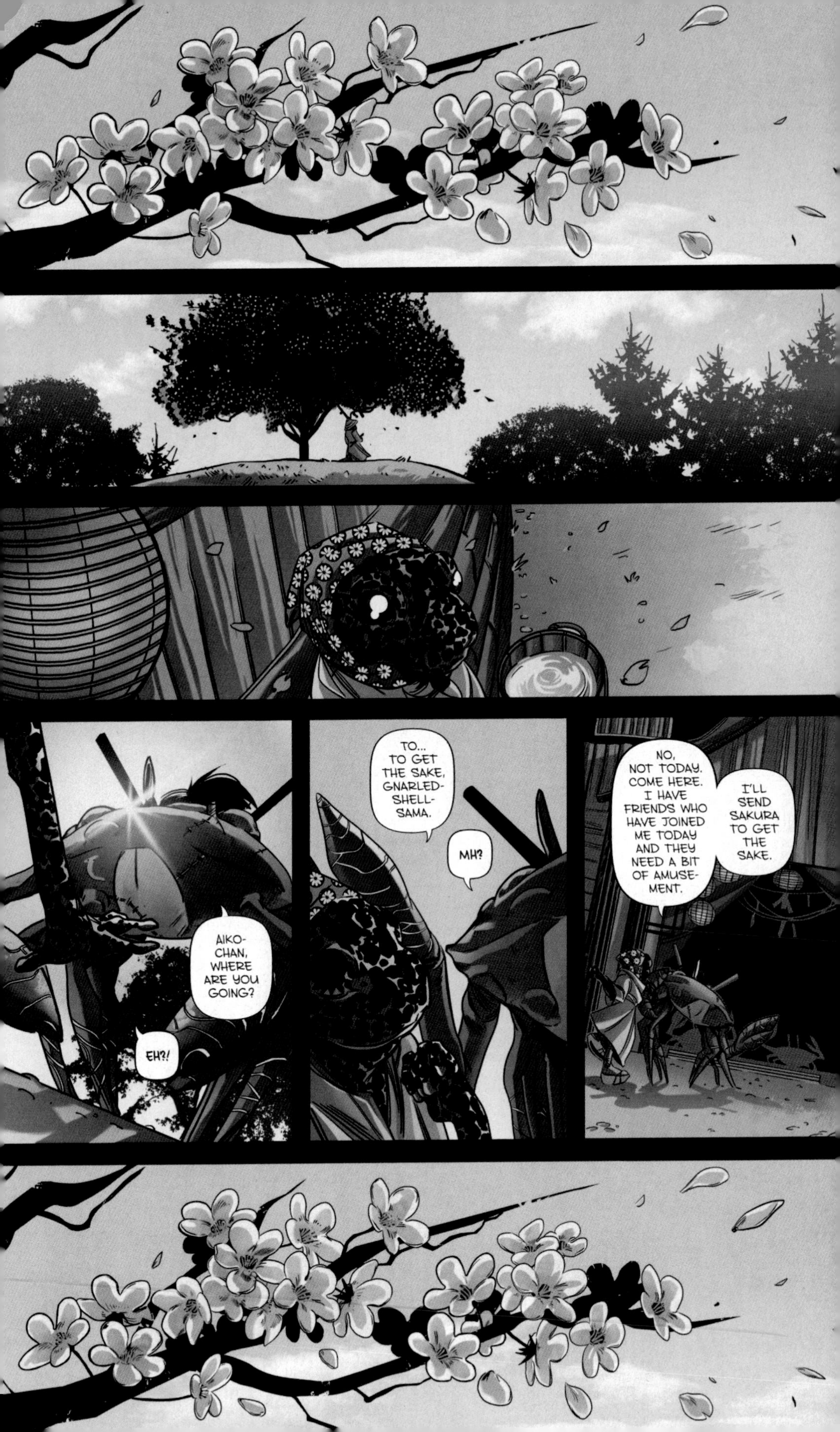
AIKO-CHAN, WHERE ARE YOU GOING?
EH?!
TO... TO GET THE SAKE, GNARLED-SHELL-SAMA.
MH?
NO, NOT TODAY. COME HERE. I HAVE FRIENDS WHO HAVE JOINED ME TODAY AND THEY NEED A BIT OF AMUSE-MENT.
I'LL SEND SAKURA TO GET THE SAKE.

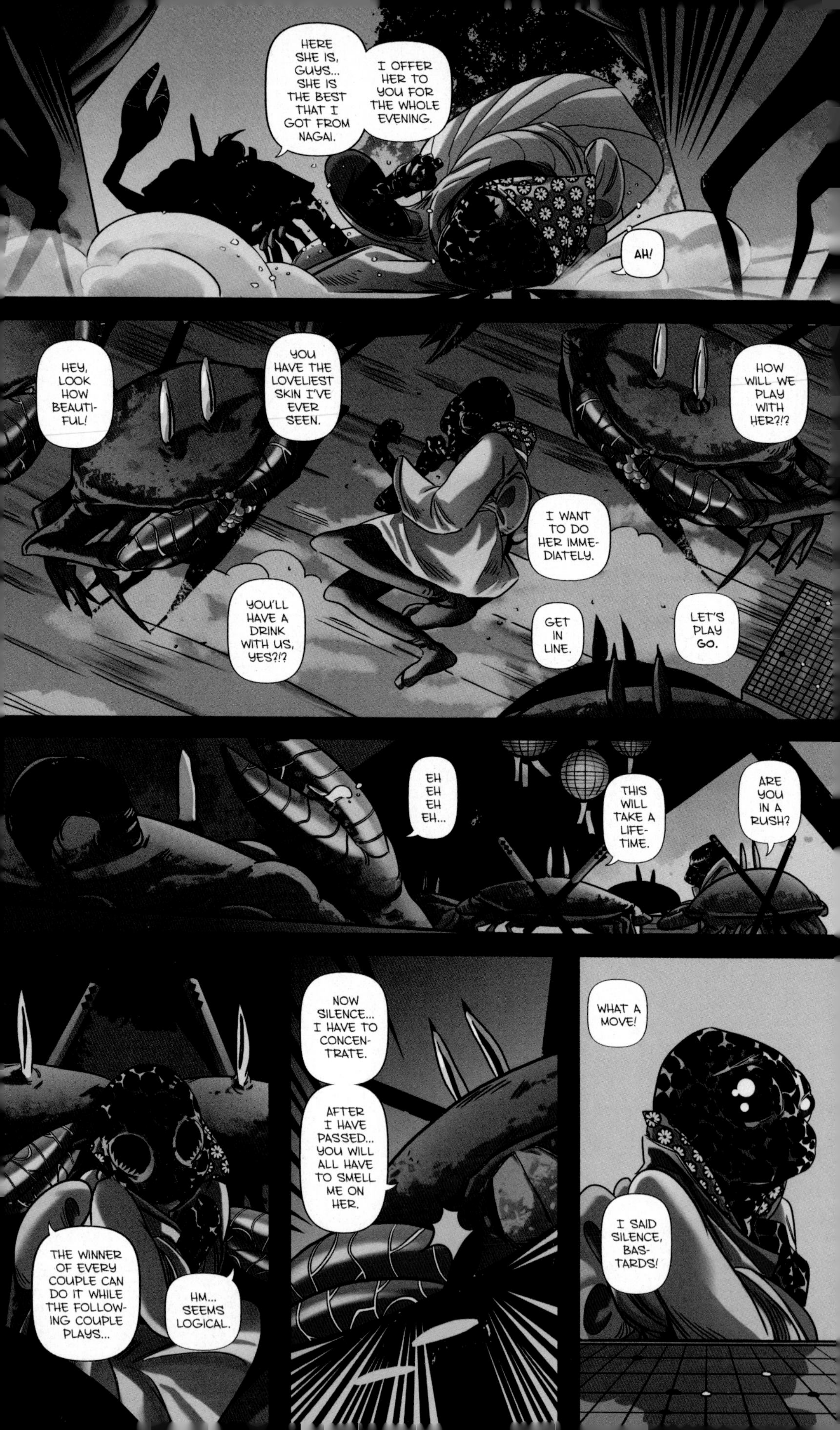
HERE SHE IS, GUYS... SHE IS THE BEST THAT I GOT FROM NAGAI.
I OFFER HER TO YOU FOR THE WHOLE EVENING.
AH!
HEY, LOOK HOW BEAUTI-FUL!
YOU HAVE THE LOVELIEST SKIN I'VE EVER SEEN.
HOW WILL WE PLAY WITH HER?!?
I WANT TO DO HER IMME-DIATELY.
YOU'LL HAVE A DRINK WITH US, YES?!?
GET IN LINE.
LET'S PLAY GO.
EH EH EH EH...
THIS WILL TAKE A LIFE-TIME.
ARE YOU IN A RUSH?
THE WINNER OF EVERY COUPLE CAN DO IT WHILE THE FOLLOW-ING COUPLE PLAYS...
HM... SEEMS LOGICAL.
NOW SILENCE... I HAVE TO CONCEN-TRATE.
AFTER I HAVE PASSED... YOU WILL ALL HAVE TO SMELL ME ON HER.
WHAT A MOVE!
I SAID SILENCE, BAS-TARDS!

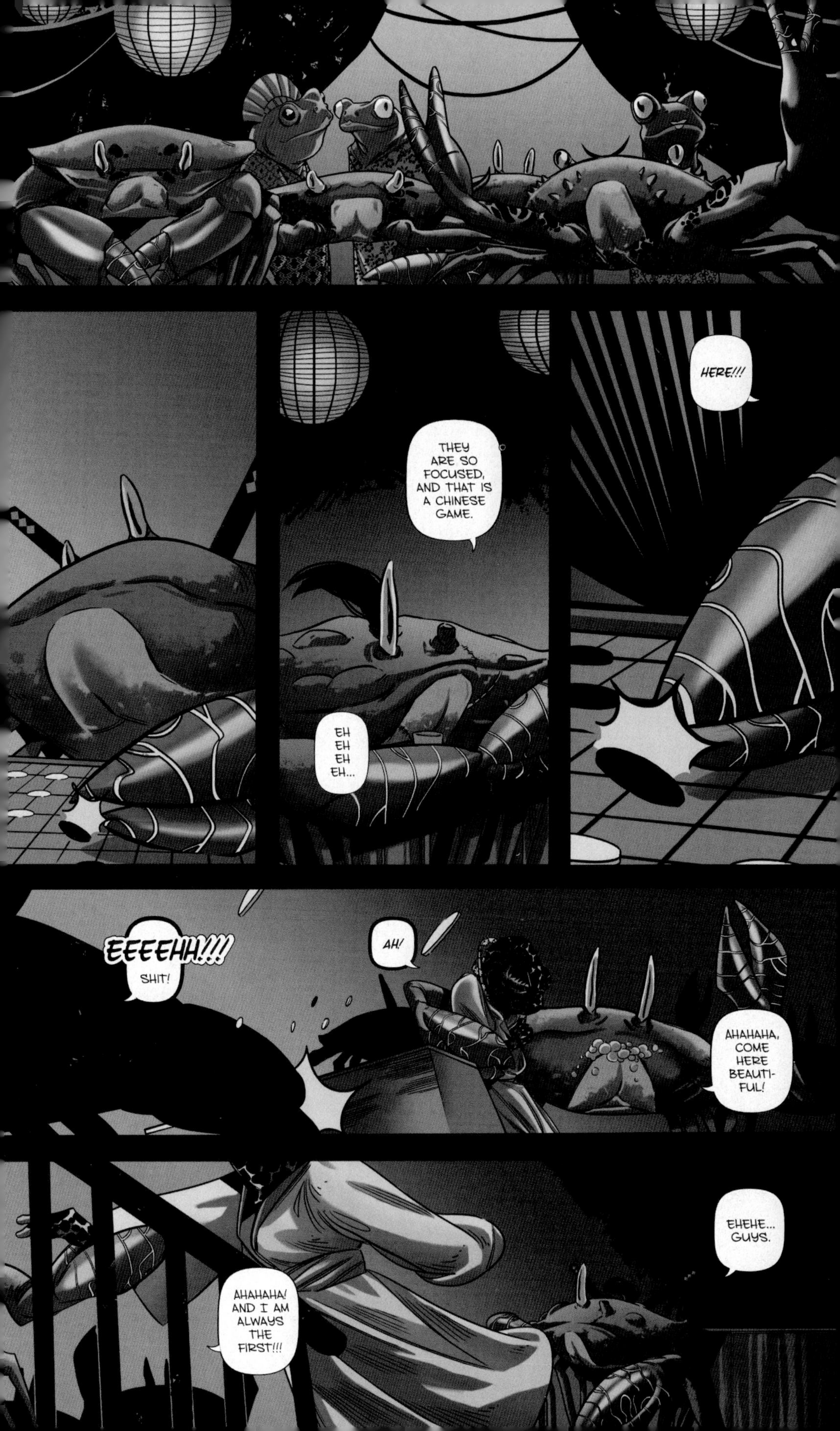
HERE!!!
THEY ARE SO FOCUSED, AND THAT IS A CHINESE GAME.
EH EH EH EH...
EEEEEHH!!!
SHIT!
AH!
AHAHAHA, COME HERE BEAUTI-FUL!
EHEHE... GUYS.
AHAHAHA! AND I AM ALWAYS THE FIRST!!!

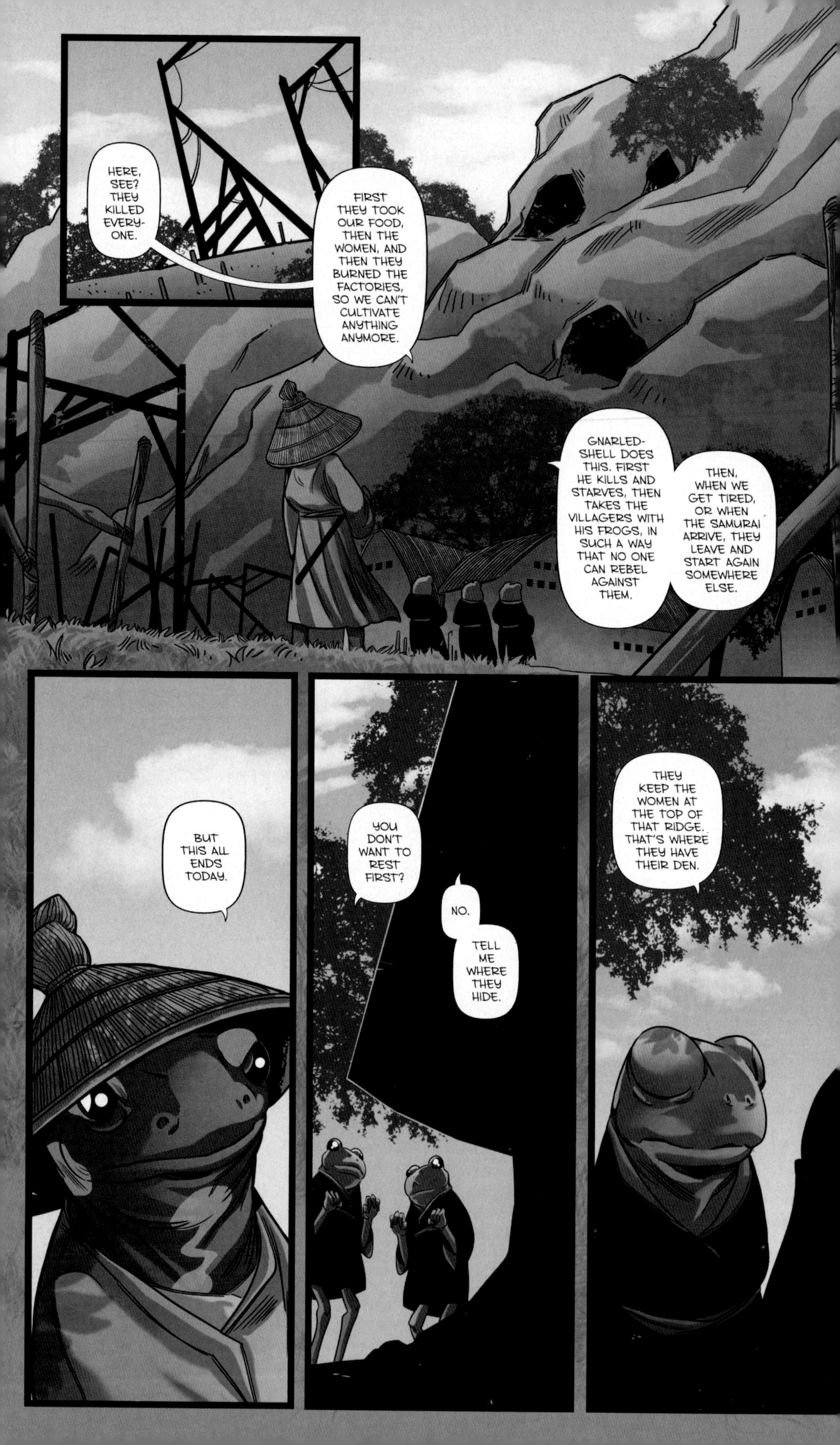
HERE, SEE? THEY KILLED EVERY-ONE.
FIRST THEY TOOK OUR FOOD, THEN THE WOMEN, AND THEN THEY BURNED THE FACTORIES, SO WE CAN'T CULTIVATE ANYTHING ANYMORE.
GNARLED-SHELL DOES THIS. FIRST HE KILLS AND STARVES, THEN TAKES THE VILLAGERS WITH HIS FROGS, IN SUCH A WAY THAT NO ONE CAN REBEL AGAINST THEM.
THEN, WHEN WE GET TIRED, OR WHEN THE SAMURAI ARRIVE, THEY LEAVE AND START AGAIN SOMEWHERE ELSE.
BUT THIS ALL ENDS TODAY.
YOU DON'T WANT TO REST FIRST?
NO.
TELL ME WHERE THEY HIDE.
THEY KEEP THE WOMEN AT THE TOP OF THAT RIDGE. THAT'S WHERE THEY HAVE THEIR DEN.

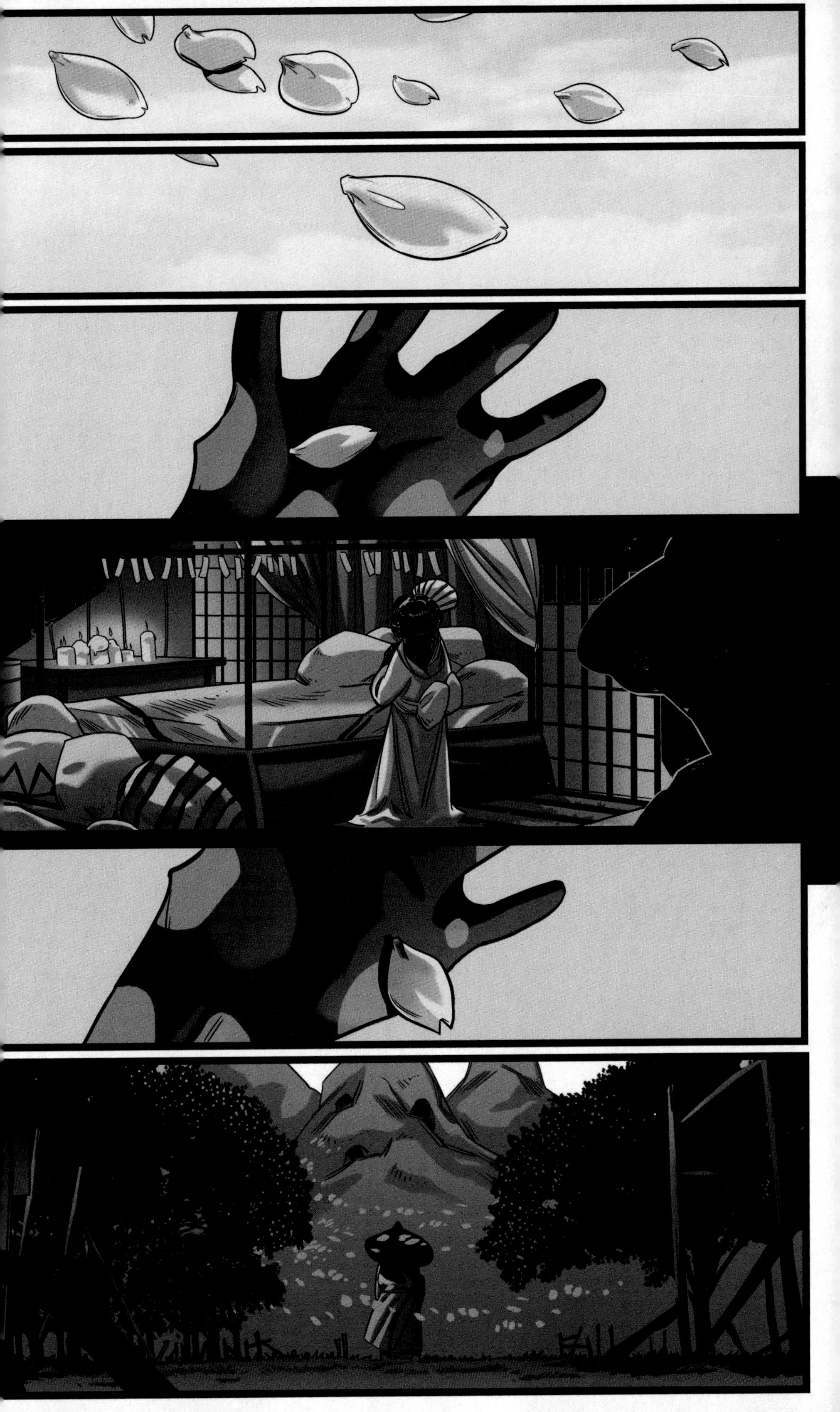

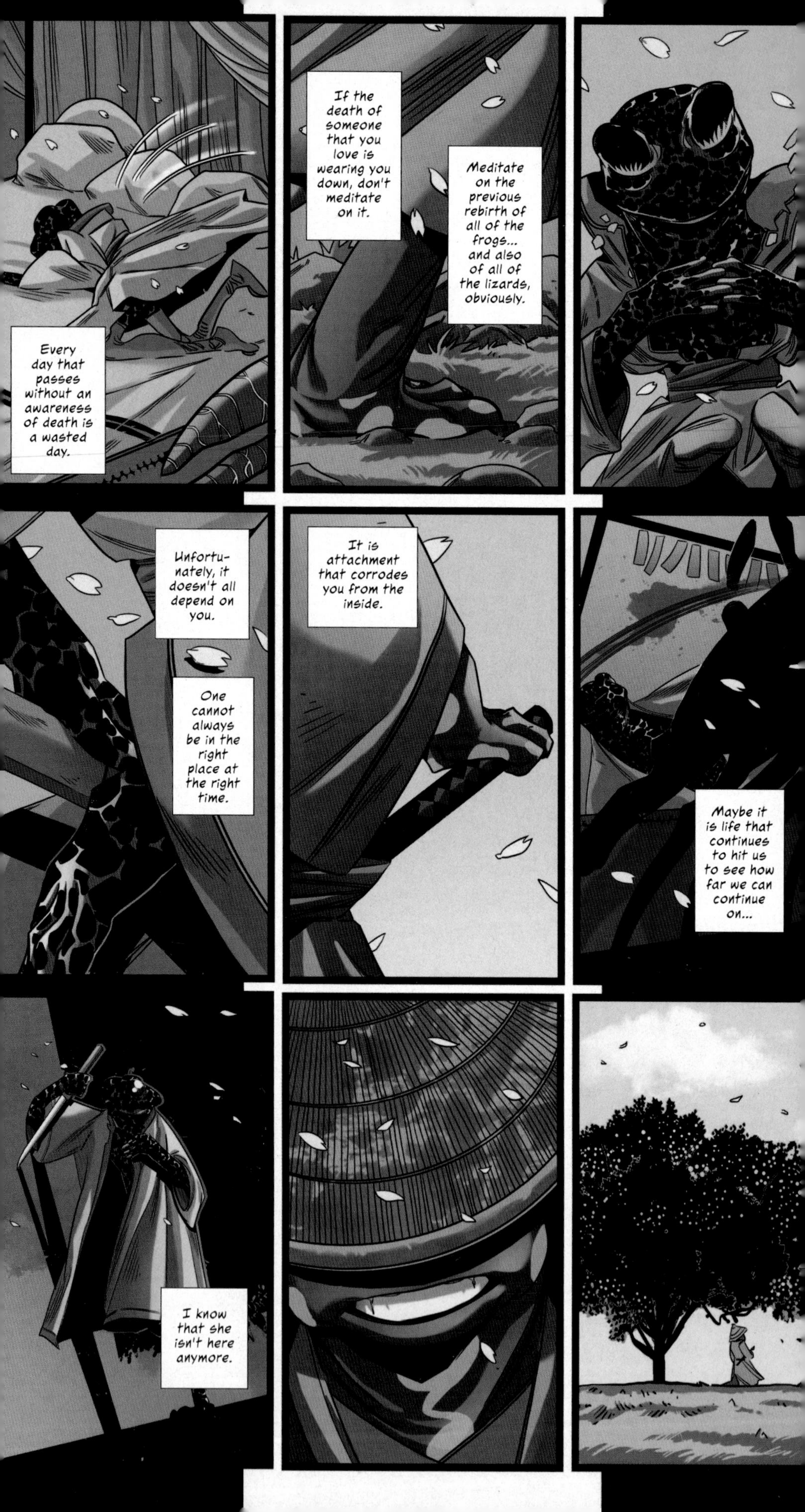
Every day that passes without an awareness of death is a wasted day.
If the death of someone that you love is wearing you down, don't meditate on it.
Meditate on the previous rebirth of all of the frogs... and also of all of the lizards, obviously.
Unfortu-nately, it doesn't all depend on you.
One cannot always be in the right place at the right time.
It is attachment that corrodes you from the inside.
Maybe it is life that continues to hit us to see how far we can continue on...
I know that she isn't here anymore.

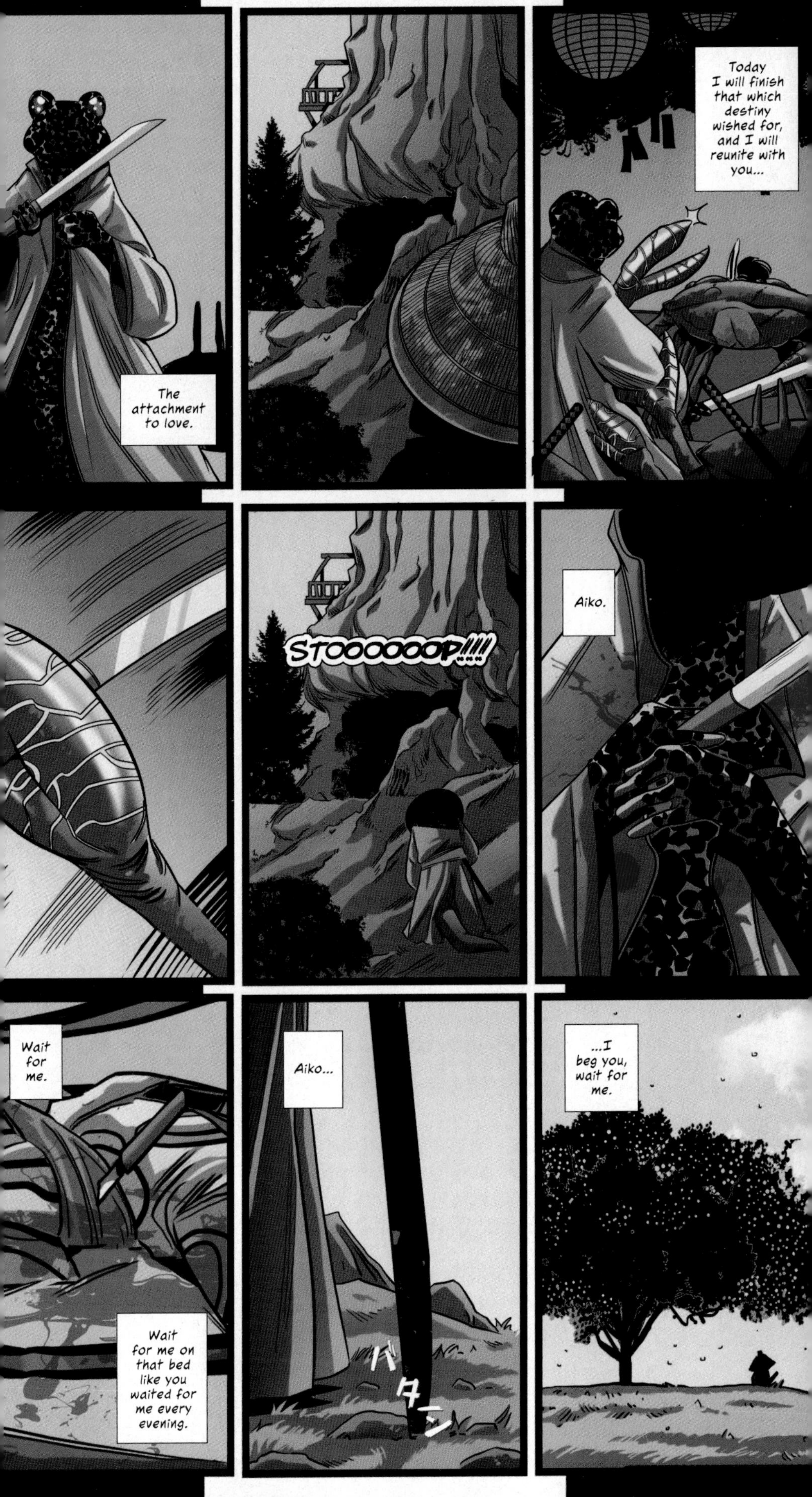
The attachment to love.
Today I will finish that which destiny wished for, and I will reunite with you...
STOOOOOOP!!!!
Aiko.
Wait for me.
Wait for me on that bed like you waited for me every evening.
Aiko...
バタン
...I beg you, wait for me.

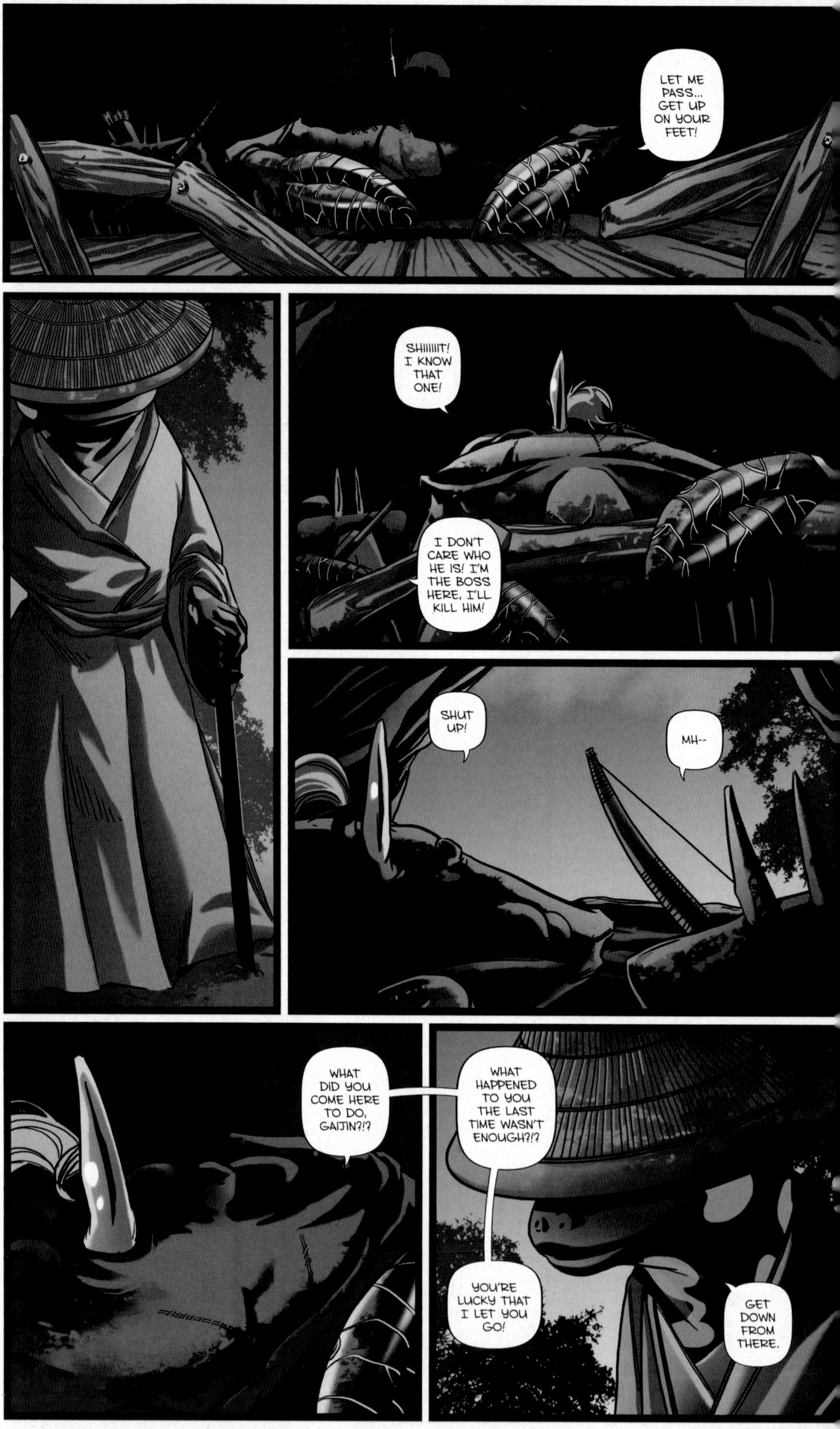
LET ME PASS... GET UP ON YOUR FEET!
SHIIIIIIT! I KNOW THAT ONE!
I DON'T CARE WHO HE IS! I'M THE BOSS HERE, I'LL KILL HIM!
SHUT UP!
MH--
WHAT DID YOU COME HERE TO DO, GAIJIN?!?
WHAT HAPPENED TO YOU THE LAST TIME WASN'T ENOUGH?!?
YOU'RE LUCKY THAT I LET YOU GO!
GET DOWN FROM THERE.

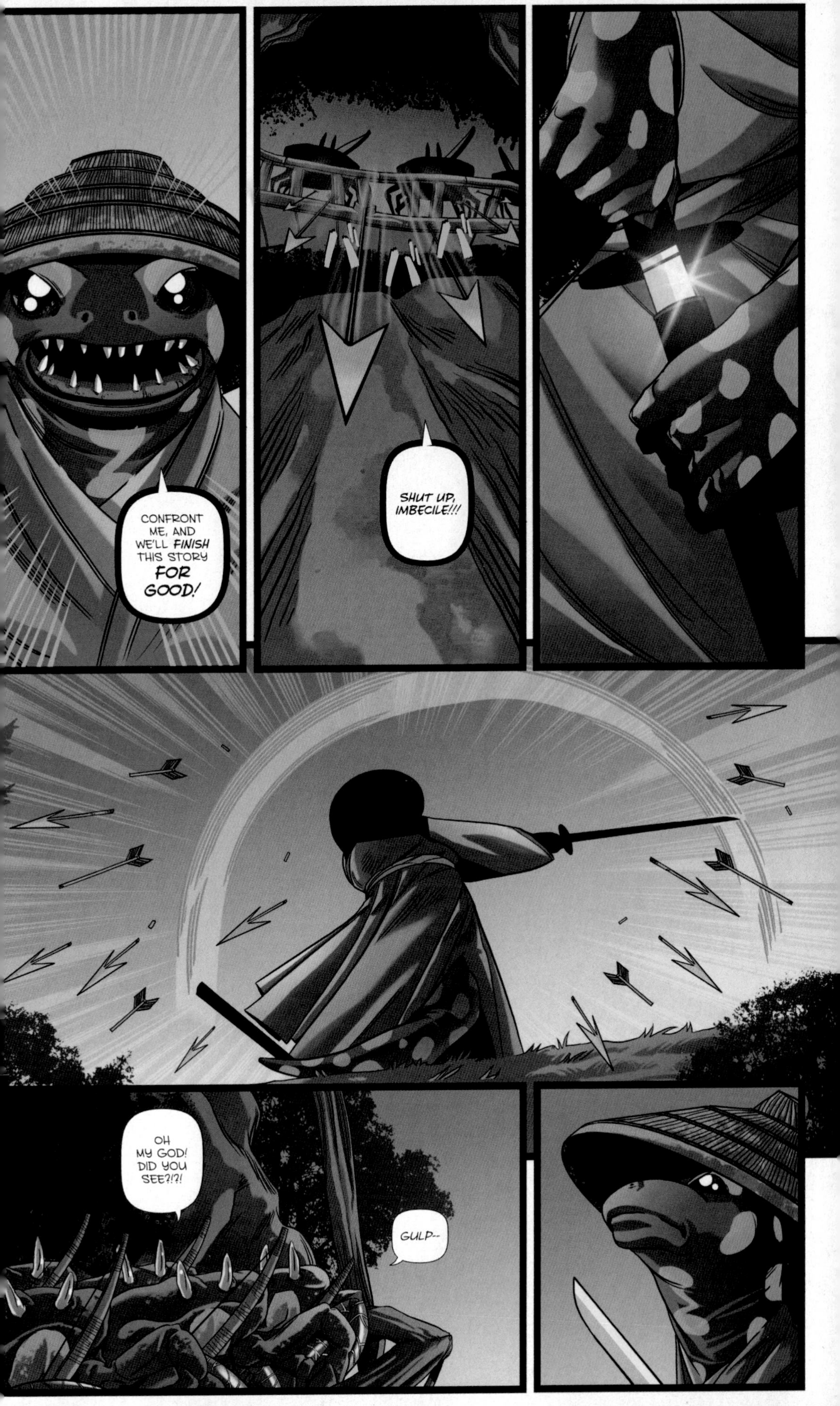
CONFRONT ME, AND WE'LL FINISH THIS STORY FOR GOOD!
SHUT UP, IMBECILE!!!
OH MY GOD! DID YOU SEE?!?!
GULP--

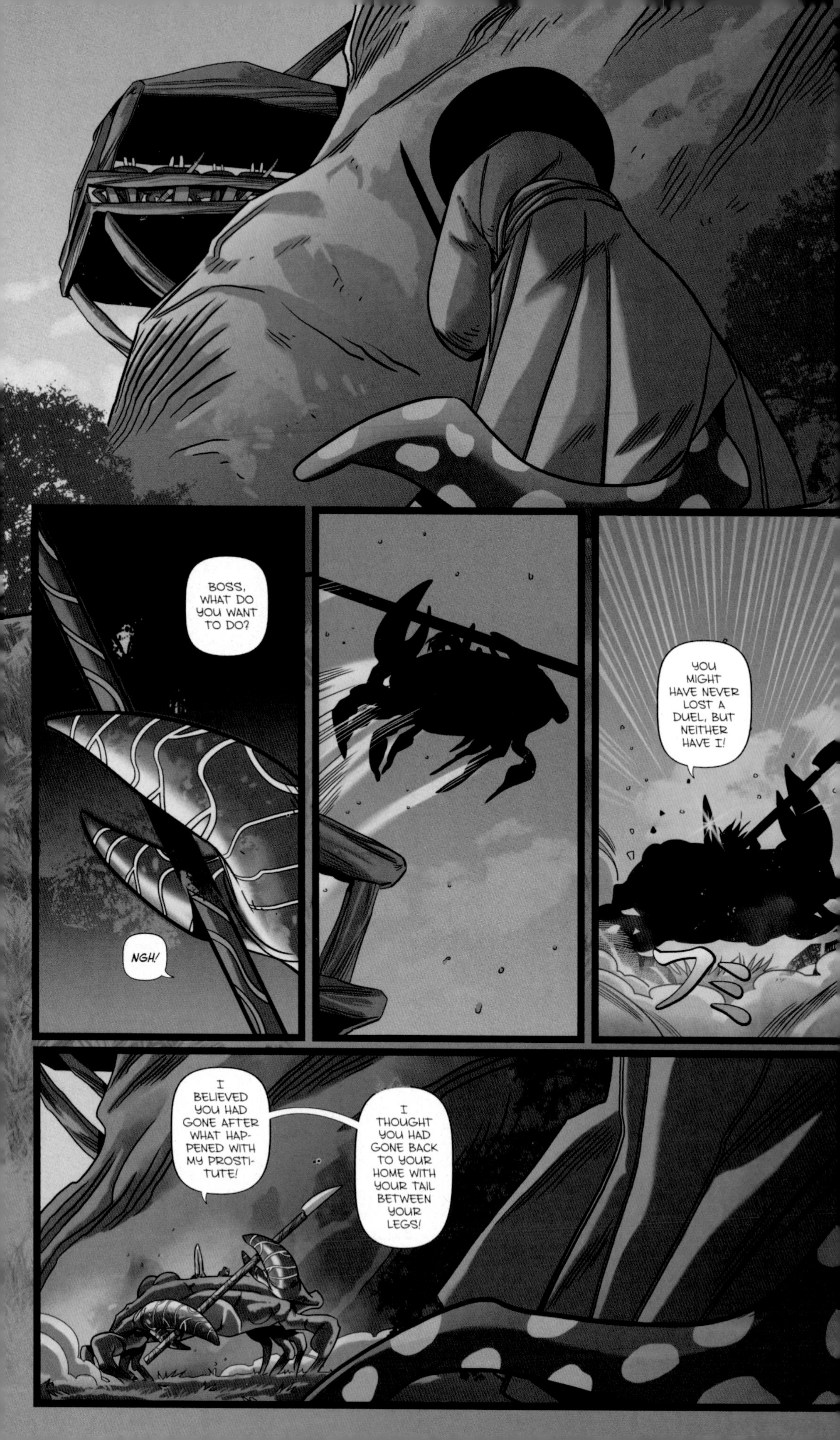
BOSS, WHAT DO YOU WANT TO DO?
NGH!
YOU MIGHT HAVE NEVER LOST A DUEL, BUT NEITHER HAVE I!
I BELIEVED YOU HAD GONE AFTER WHAT HAP-PENED WITH MY PROSTI-TUTE!
I THOUGHT YOU HAD GONE BACK TO YOUR HOME WITH YOUR TAIL BETWEEN YOUR LEGS!

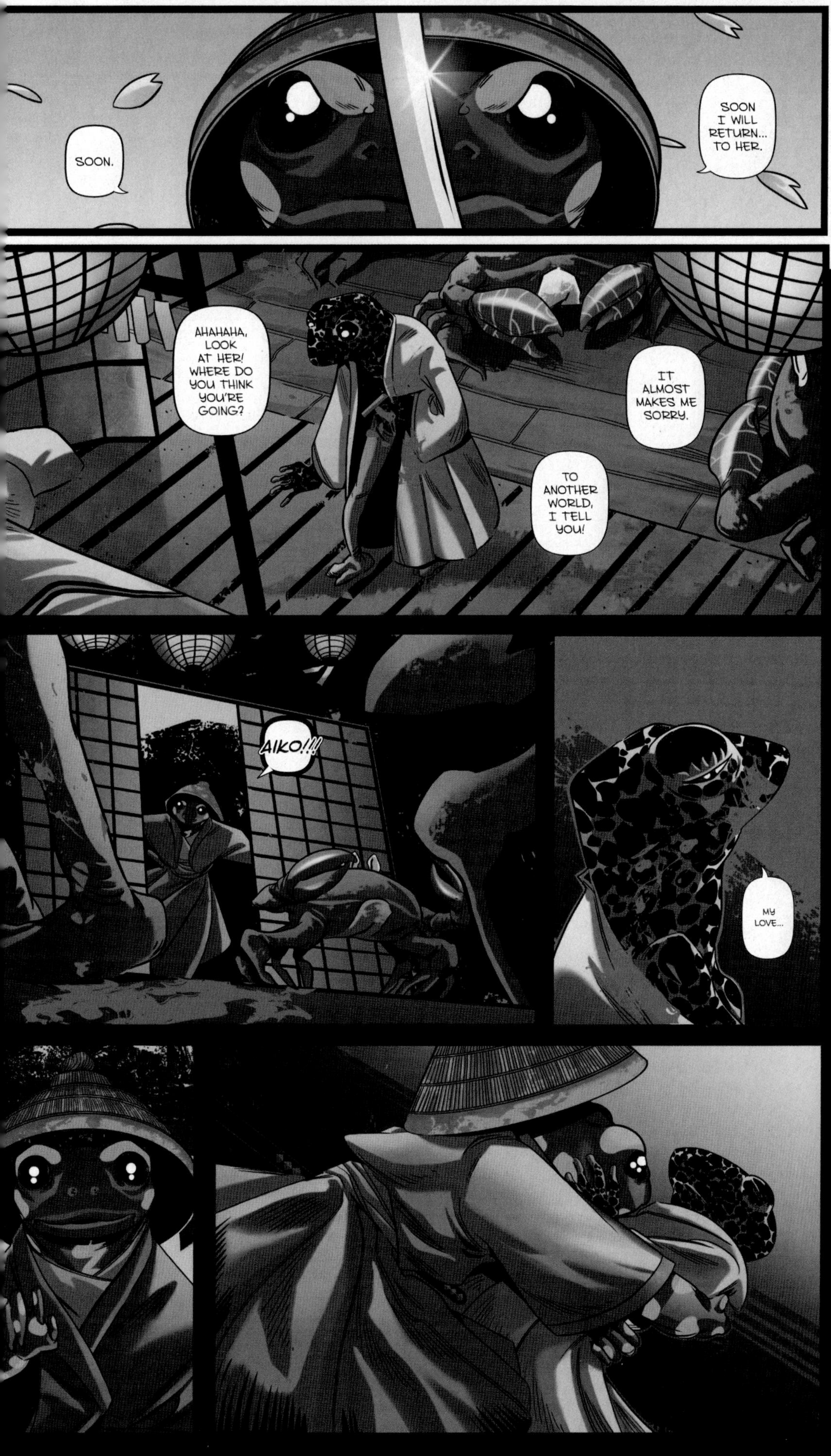
SOON.
SOON I WILL RETURN... TO HER.
AHAHAHA, LOOK AT HER! WHERE DO YOU THINK YOU'RE GOING?
IT ALMOST MAKES ME SORRY.
TO ANOTHER WORLD, I TELL YOU!
AIKO!!!
MY LOVE...

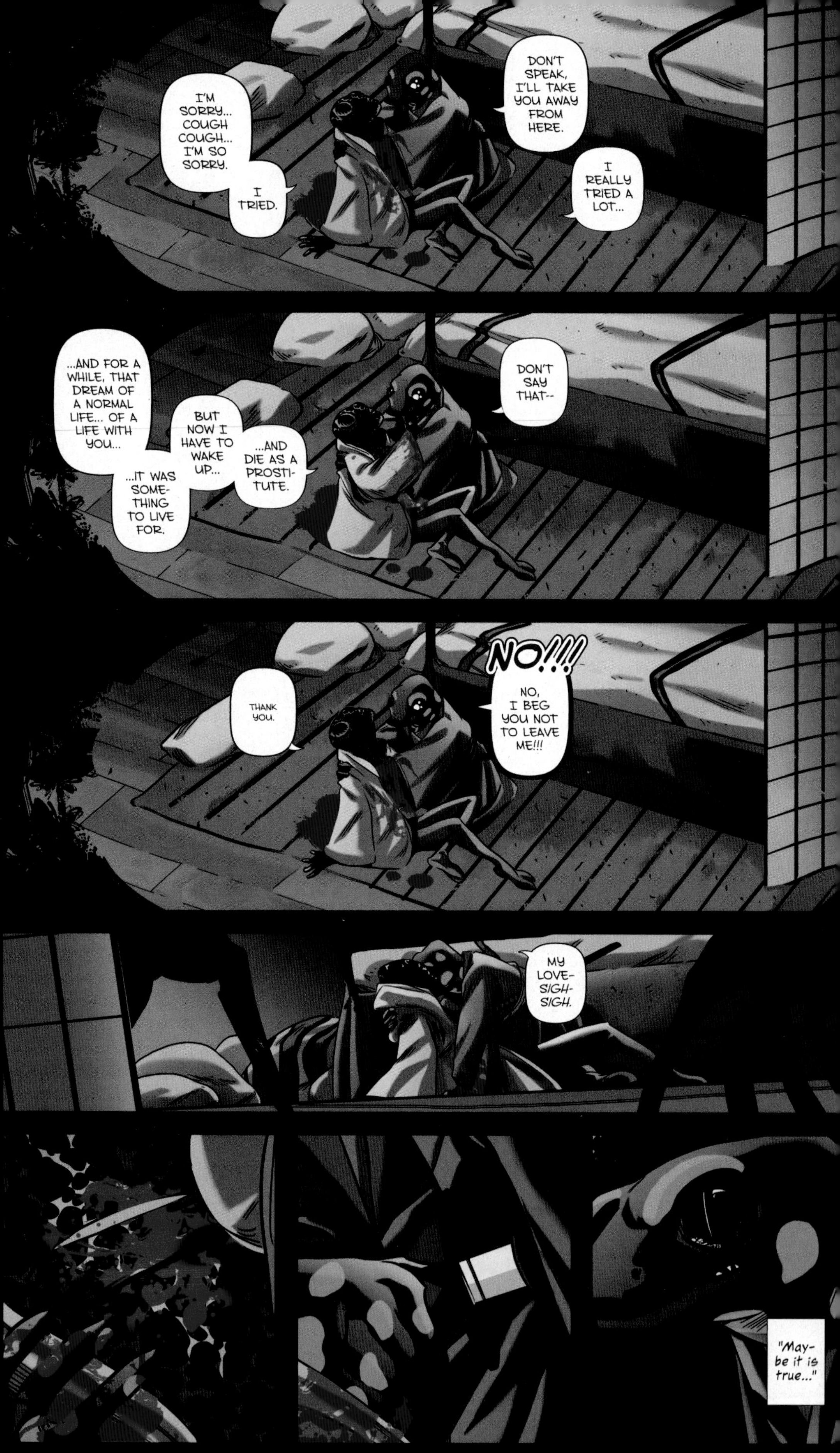
I'M SORRY... COUGH COUGH... I'M SO SORRY.
I TRIED.
DON'T SPEAK, I'LL TAKE YOU AWAY FROM HERE.
I REALLY TRIED A LOT...
...AND FOR A WHILE, THAT DREAM OF A NORMAL LIFE... OF A LIFE WITH YOU...
...IT WAS SOME-THING TO LIVE FOR.
BUT NOW I HAVE TO WAKE UP...
...AND DIE AS A PROSTI-TUTE.
DON'T SAY THAT--
THANK YOU.
NO!!!!
NO, I BEG YOU NOT TO LEAVE ME!!!
MY LOVE-SIGH-SIGH.
"May-be it is true..."

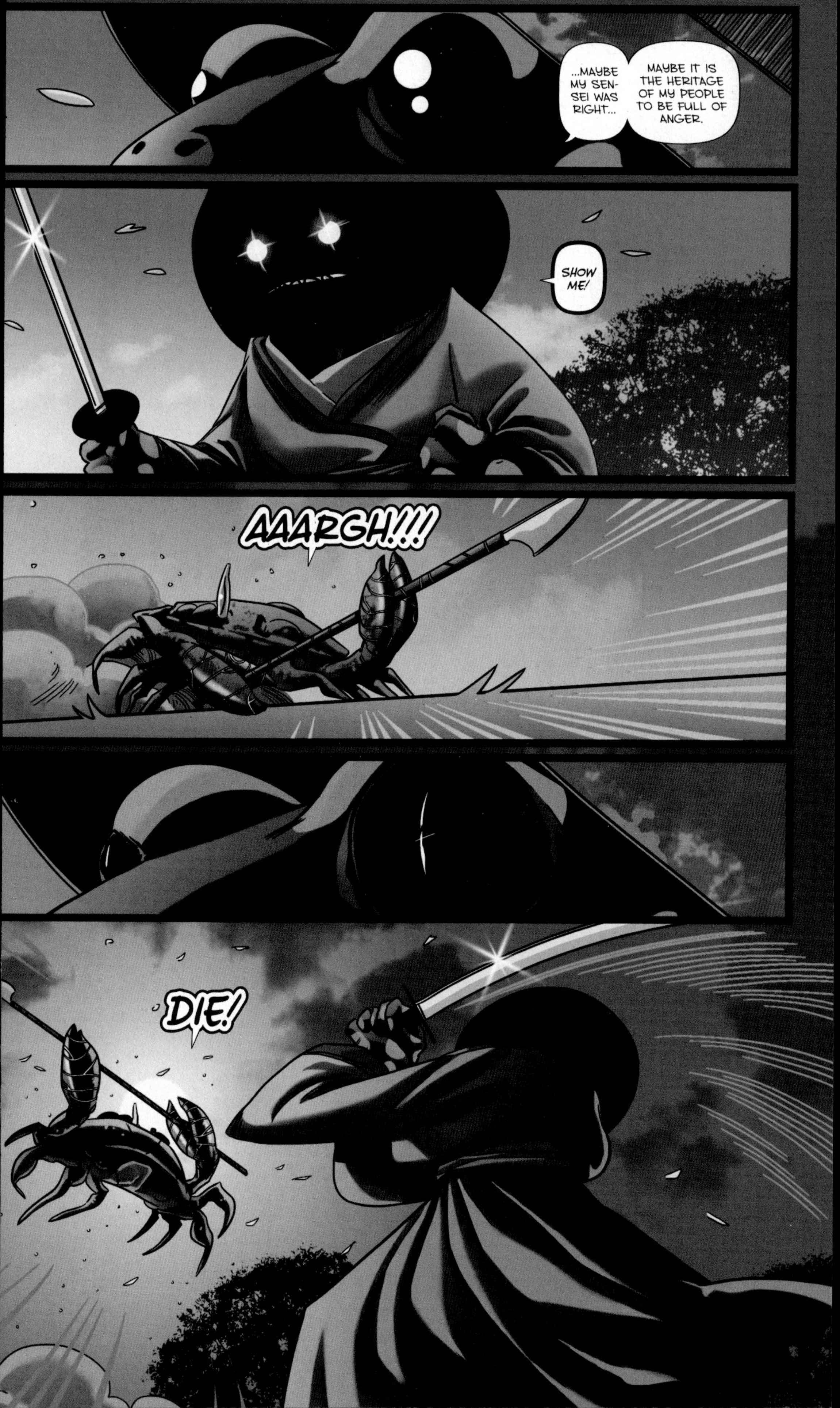
...MAYBE MY SEN-SEI WAS RIGHT...
MAYBE IT IS THE HERITAGE OF MY PEOPLE TO BE FULL OF ANGER.
SHOW ME!
AAARGH!!!
DIE!

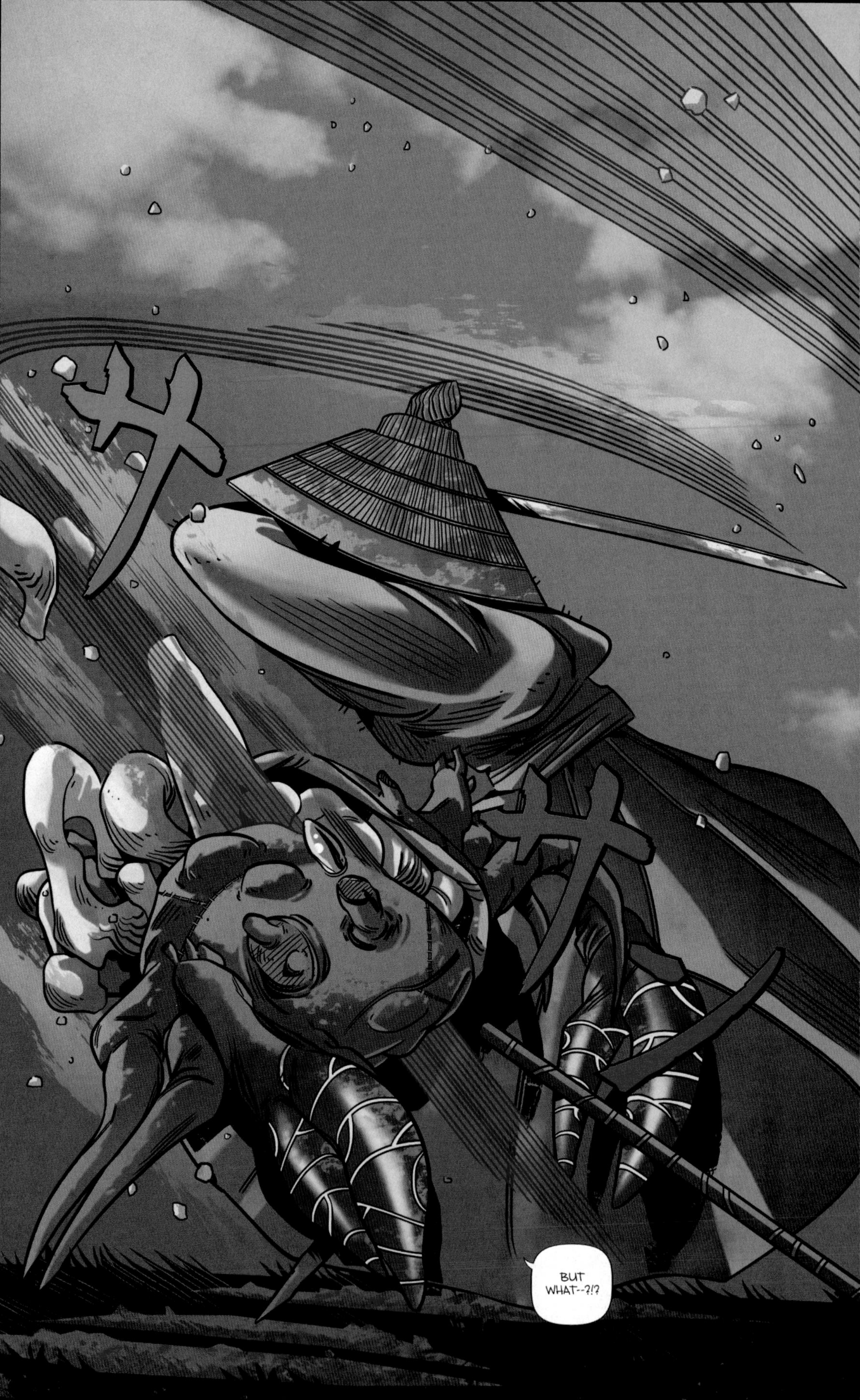
BUT WHAT--?!?

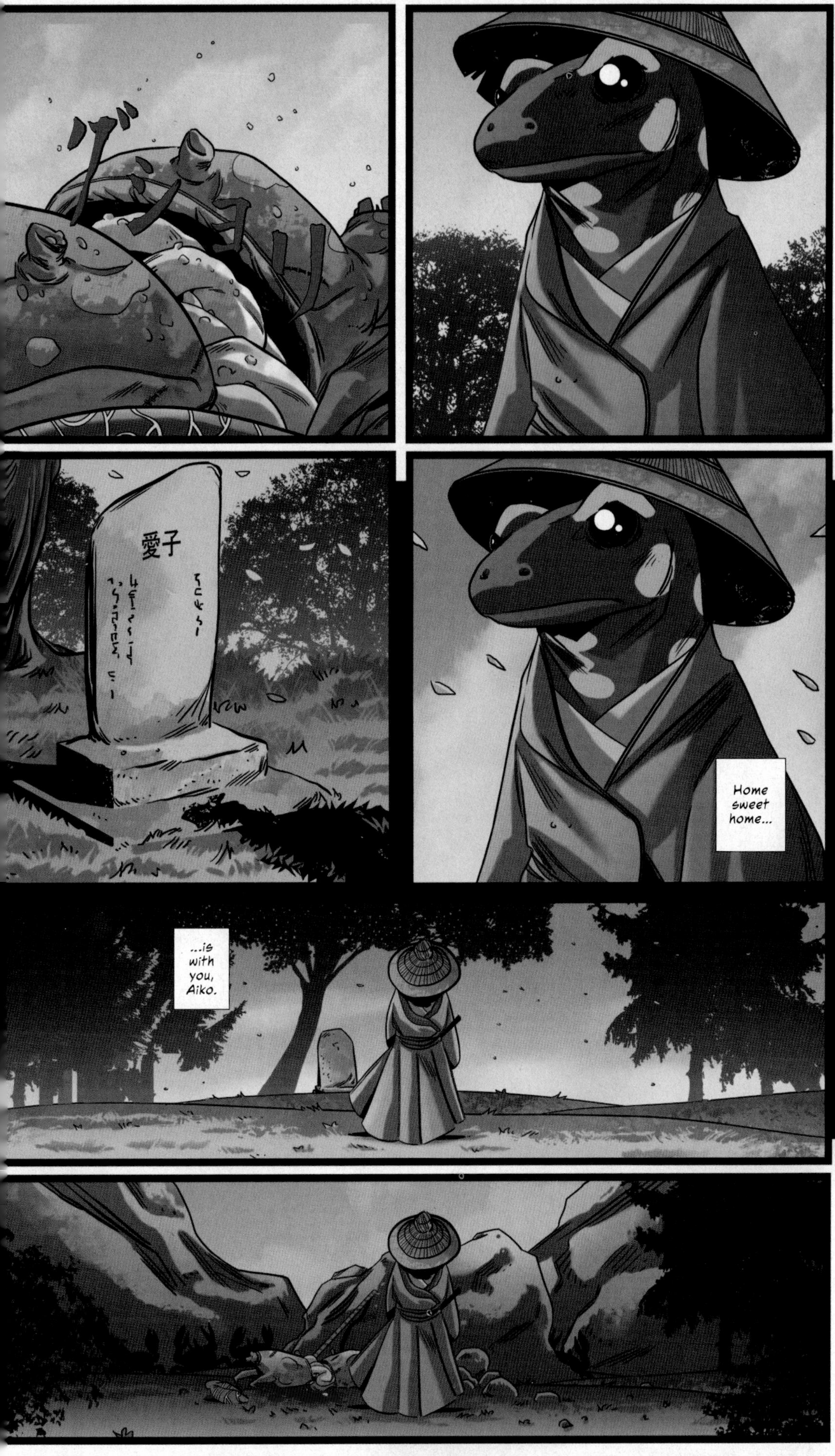
愛子
Home sweet home...
...is with you, Aiko.

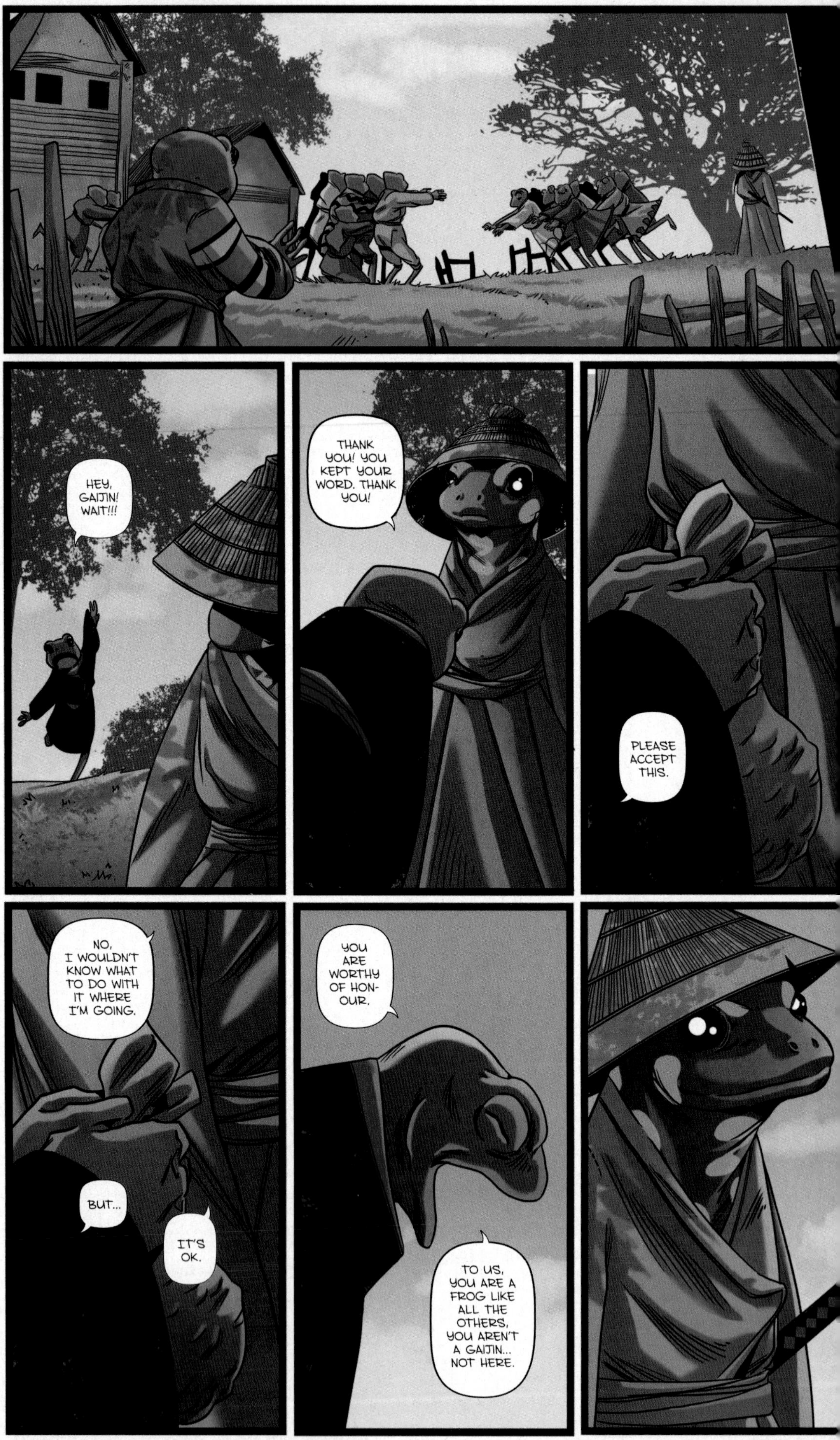
HEY, GAIJIN! WAIT!!!
THANK YOU! YOU KEPT YOUR WORD. THANK YOU!
PLEASE ACCEPT THIS.
NO, I WOULDN'T KNOW WHAT TO DO WITH IT WHERE I'M GOING.
BUT...
IT'S OK.
YOU ARE WORTHY OF HON-OUR.
TO US, YOU ARE A FROG LIKE ALL THE OTHERS, YOU AREN'T A GAIJIN... NOT HERE.

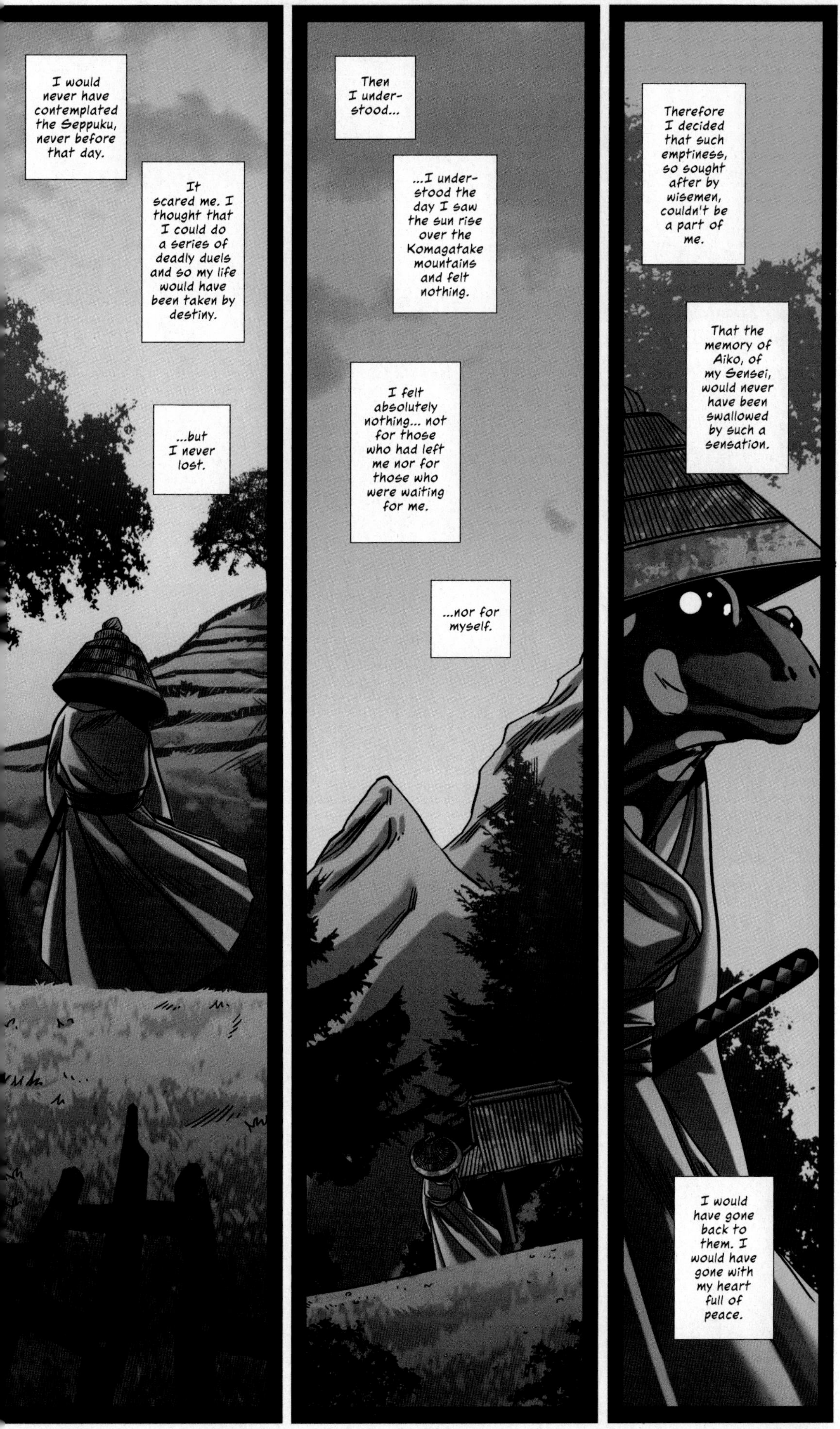
I would never have contemplated the Seppuku, never before that day.
It scared me. I thought that I could do a series of deadly duels and so my life would have been taken by destiny.
...but I never lost.
Then I under-stood...
...I under-stood the day I saw the sun rise over the Komagatake mountains and felt nothing.
I felt absolutely nothing... not for those who had left me nor for those who were waiting for me.
...nor for myself.
Therefore I decided that such emptiness, so sought after by wisemen, couldn't be a part of me.
That the memory of Aiko, of my Sensei, would never have been swallowed by such a sensation.
I would have gone back to them. I would have gone with my heart full of peace.

HERE, SIR. HE WENT OFF LIKE NOTHING HAD HAPPENED.

HIS SWORD?

HE DIDN'T WANT TO GIVE IT UP, FOR THIS...

ALRIGHT THEN.

HERE IT IS, SIR.

MH... HOLD HIM STILL.

NNNGH!!! AARGH!!!

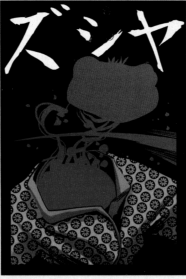

ズシヤ

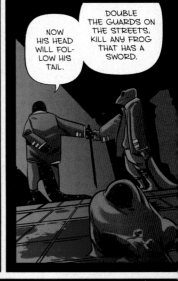

NOW HIS HEAD WILL FOLLOW HIS TAIL.

DOUBLE THE GUARDS ON THE STREETS, KILL ANY FROG THAT HAS A SWORD.

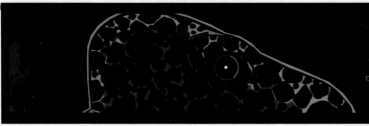

SOON, THIS COUNTRY WILL BE OURS.

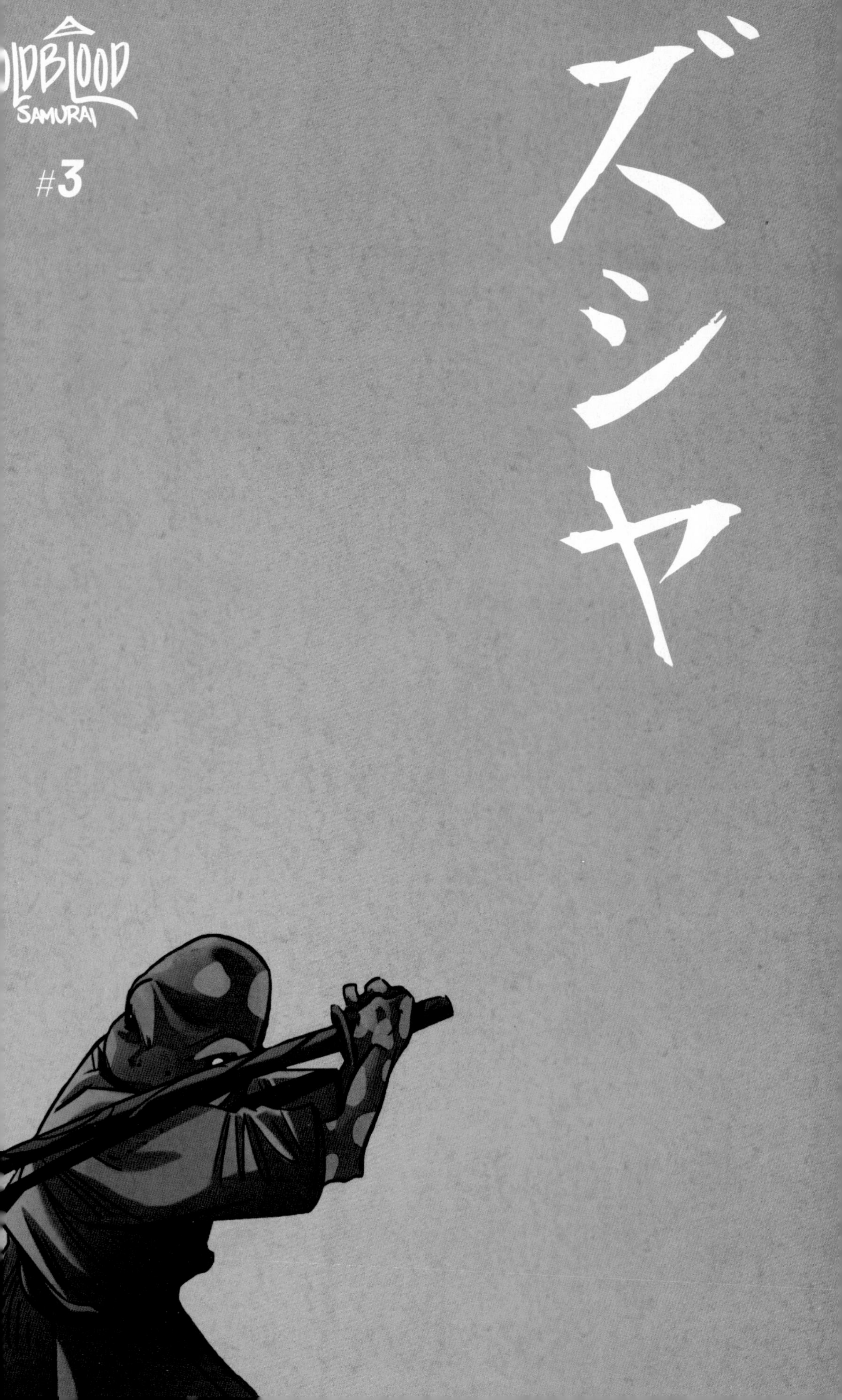

LDBLOOD
SAMURAI
#3
ズシャ

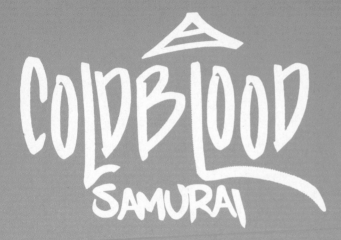

COLDBLOOD SAMURAI

CREDITS

Story
MASSIMO ROSI

Pencils
LUDOVICA CEREGATTI

Colors
RENATO STEVANATO

Lettering
MATTIA GENTILI

Bryan Seaton: Publisher/ CEO
Shawn Gabborin: Editor In Chief
Jason Martin: Publisher-Danger Zone
Nicole D'Andria: Marketing Director/Editor
Jessica Lowrie: Social Media Czar
Danielle Davison: Executive Administrator
Chad Cicconi: King Lizard
Shawn Pryor: President of Creator Relations

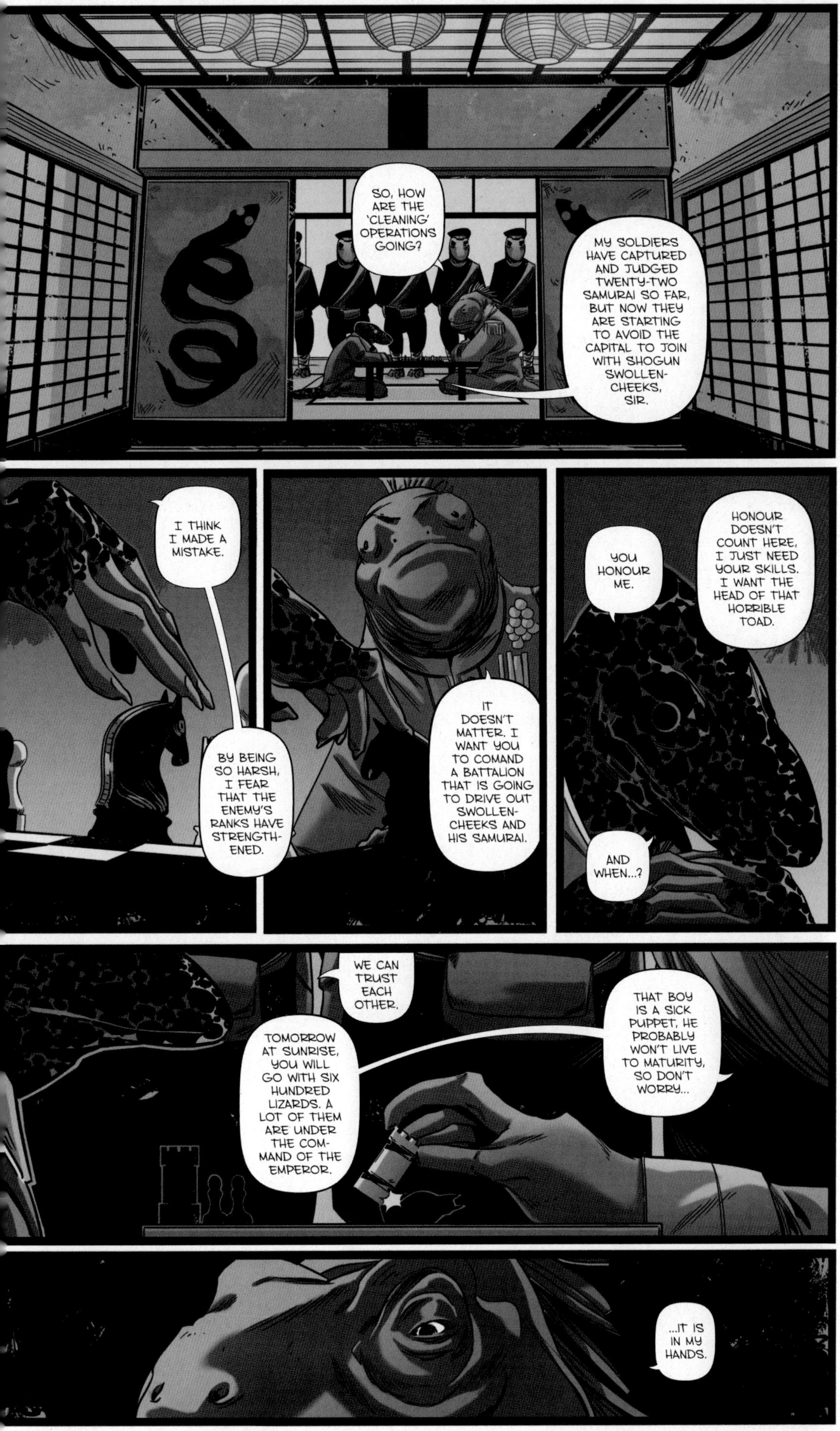
SO, HOW ARE THE 'CLEANING' OPERATIONS GOING?
MY SOLDIERS HAVE CAPTURED AND JUDGED TWENTY-TWO SAMURAI SO FAR, BUT NOW THEY ARE STARTING TO AVOID THE CAPITAL TO JOIN WITH SHOGUN SWOLLEN-CHEEKS, SIR.
I THINK I MADE A MISTAKE.
BY BEING SO HARSH, I FEAR THAT THE ENEMY'S RANKS HAVE STRENGTH-ENED.
IT DOESN'T MATTER. I WANT YOU TO COMAND A BATTALION THAT IS GOING TO DRIVE OUT SWOLLEN-CHEEKS AND HIS SAMURAI.
YOU HONOUR ME.
HONOUR DOESN'T COUNT HERE, I JUST NEED YOUR SKILLS. I WANT THE HEAD OF THAT HORRIBLE TOAD.
AND WHEN...?
TOMORROW AT SUNRISE, YOU WILL GO WITH SIX HUNDRED LIZARDS. A LOT OF THEM ARE UNDER THE COM-MAND OF THE EMPEROR.
WE CAN TRUST EACH OTHER.
THAT BOY IS A SICK PUPPET, HE PROBABLY WON'T LIVE TO MATURITY, SO DON'T WORRY...
...IT IS IN MY HANDS.

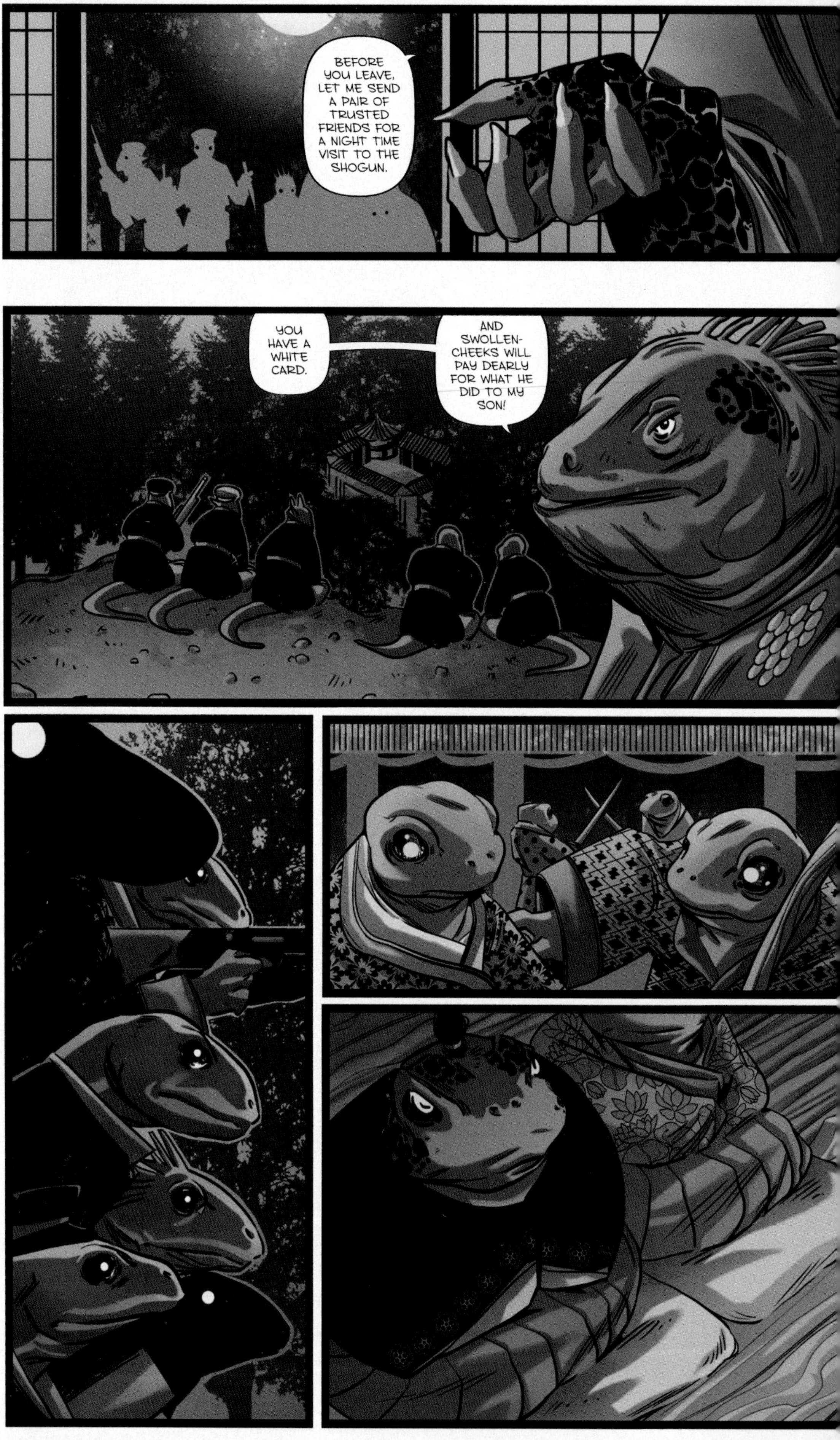
BEFORE YOU LEAVE, LET ME SEND A PAIR OF TRUSTED FRIENDS FOR A NIGHT TIME VISIT TO THE SHOGUN.
YOU HAVE A WHITE CARD.
AND SWOLLEN-CHEEKS WILL PAY DEARLY FOR WHAT HE DID TO MY SON!

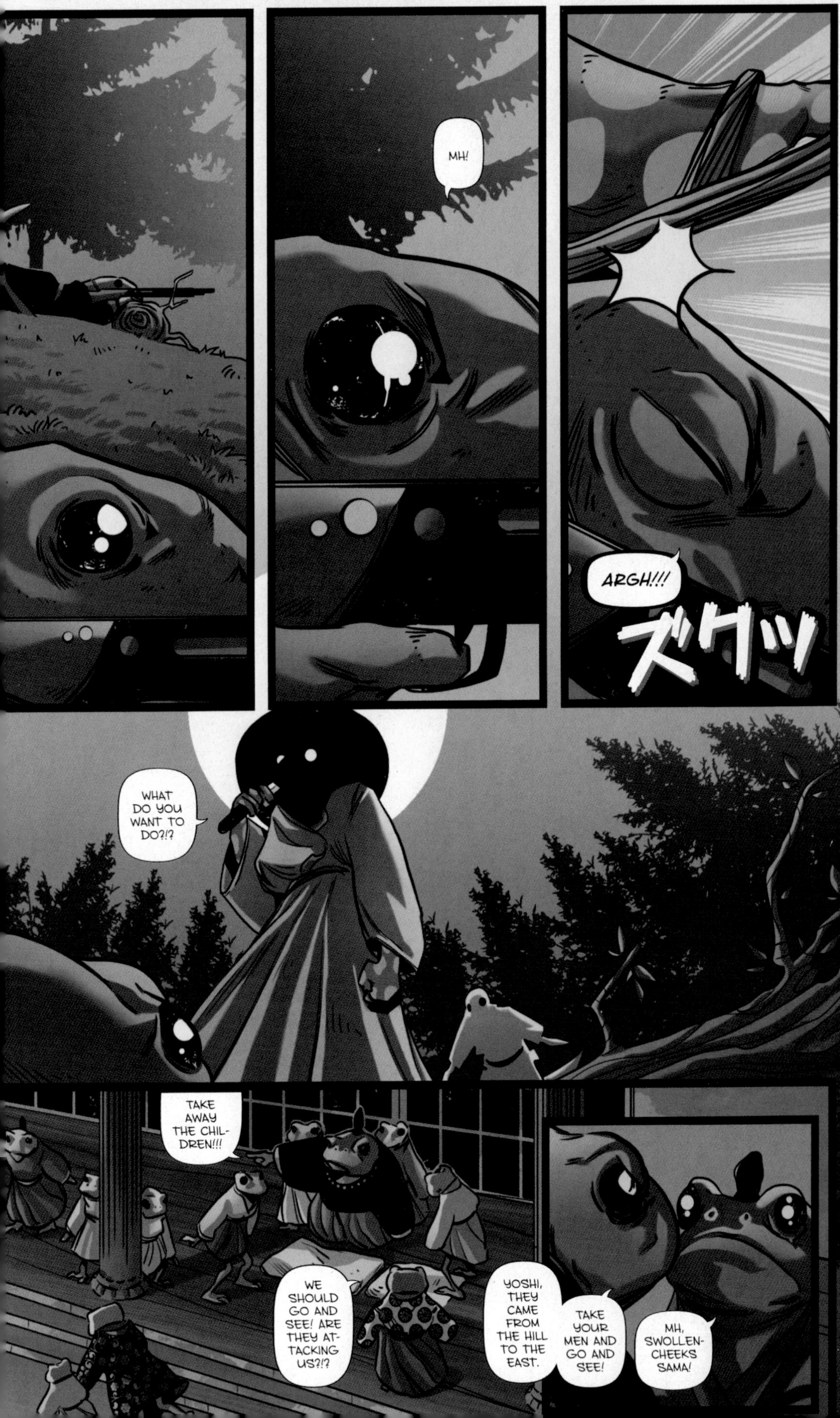
MH!
ARGH!!!
ズゲッ
WHAT DO YOU WANT TO DO?!?
TAKE AWAY THE CHIL-DREN!!!
WE SHOULD GO AND SEE! ARE THEY AT-TACKING US?!?
YOSHI, THEY CAME FROM THE HILL TO THE EAST.
TAKE YOUR MEN AND GO AND SEE!
MH, SWOLLEN-CHEEKS SAMA!

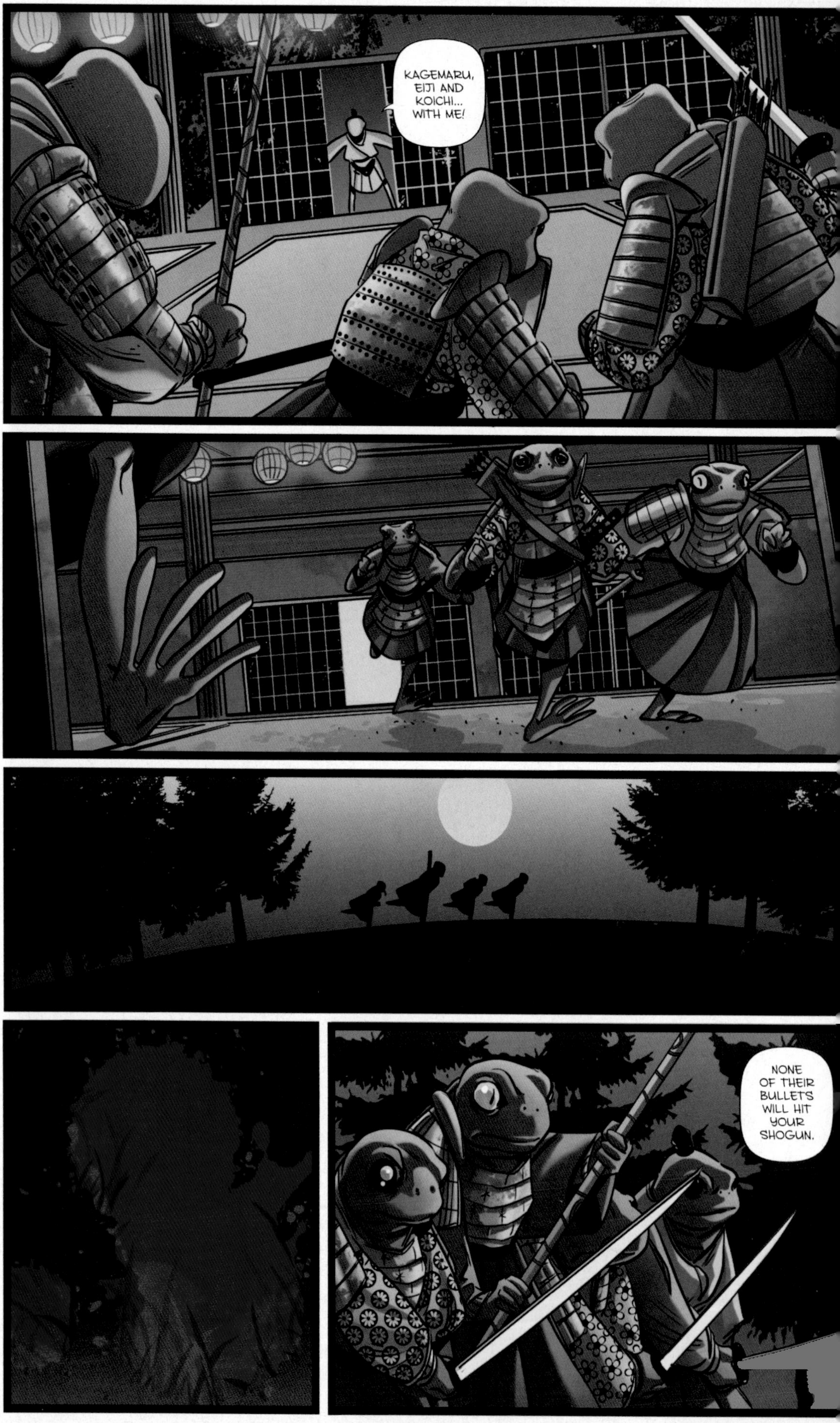
KAGEMARU, EIJI AND KOICHI... WITH ME!
NONE OF THEIR BULLETS WILL HIT YOUR SHOGUN.

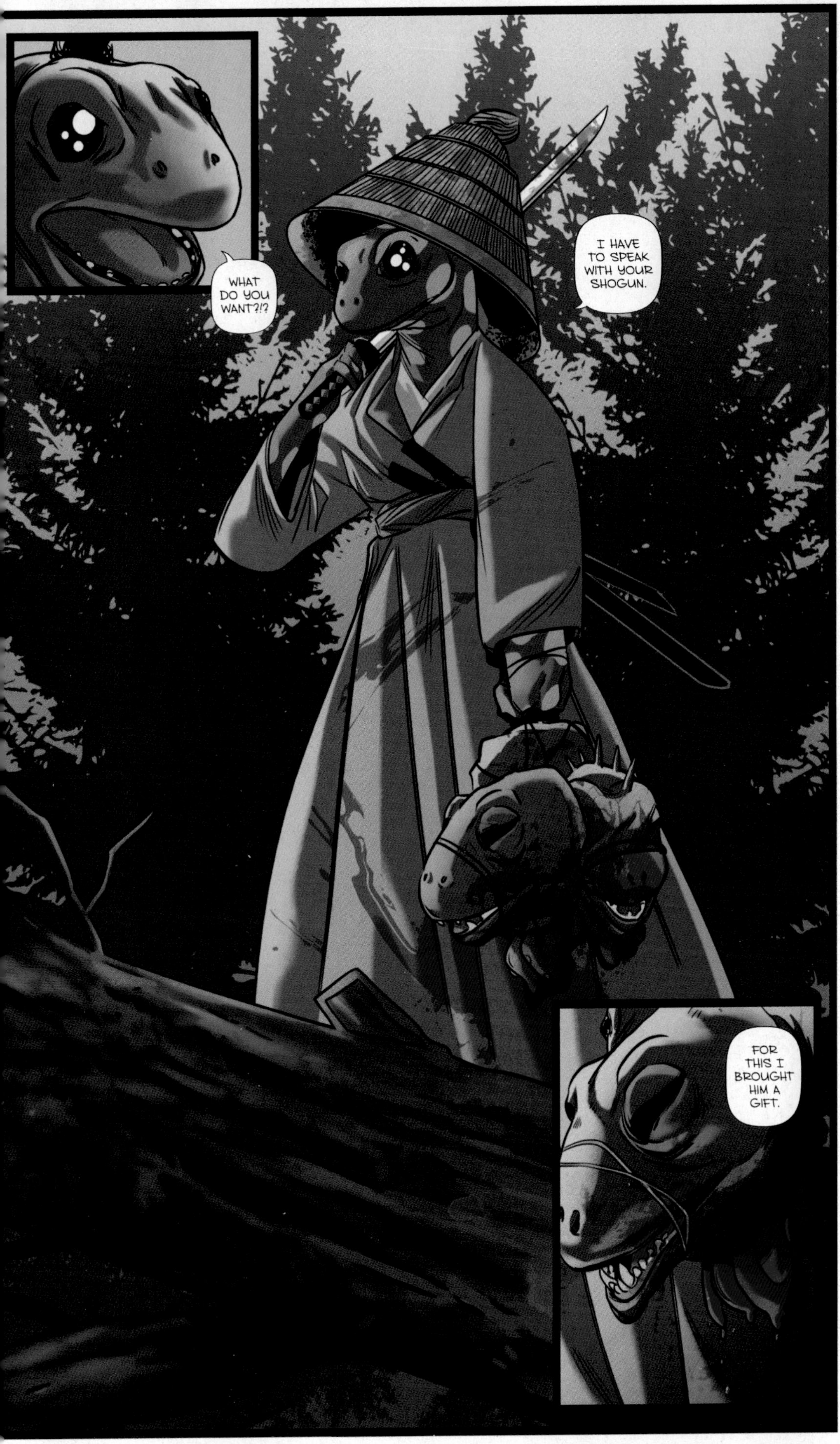
WHAT DO YOU WANT?!?
I HAVE TO SPEAK WITH YOUR SHOGUN.
FOR THIS I BROUGHT HIM A GIFT.

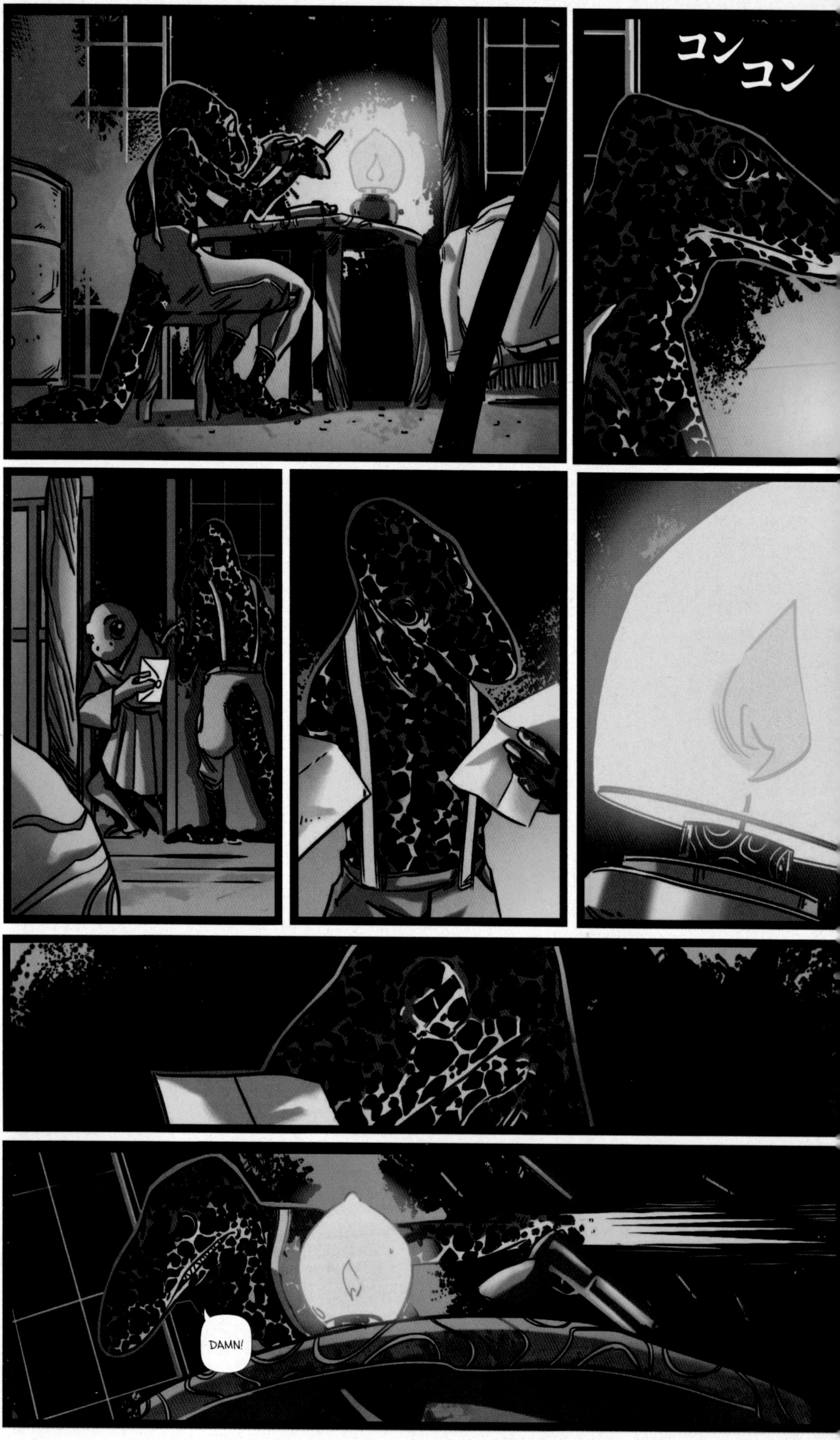
コンコン
DAMN!

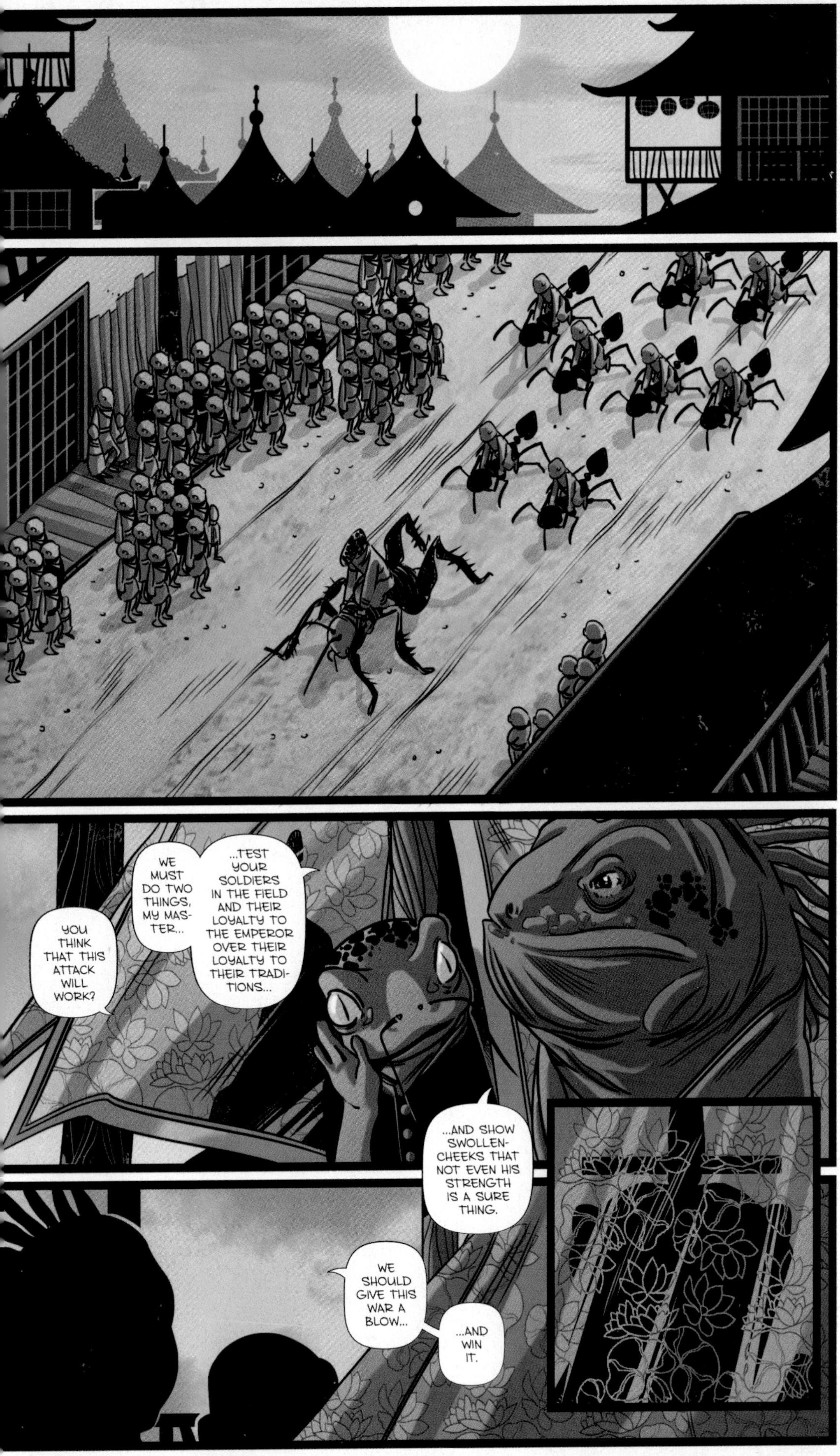
YOU THINK THAT THIS ATTACK WILL WORK?
WE MUST DO TWO THINGS, MY MASTER...
...TEST YOUR SOLDIERS IN THE FIELD AND THEIR LOYALTY TO THE EMPEROR OVER THEIR LOYALTY TO THEIR TRADITIONS...
...AND SHOW SWOLLEN-CHEEKS THAT NOT EVEN HIS STRENGTH IS A SURE THING.
WE SHOULD GIVE THIS WAR A BLOW...
...AND WIN IT.

I WISH TO HAVE A WORD WITH YOU, GENERAL.

CERTAINLY.

FOLLOW ME.

EM-PER-OR.

GEN-ERAL. GO.

EM-PER-OR.

AS YOU HAVE NOTICED, THE EMPEROR IS NO LONGER THE SAME. THE SICKNESS IS TAKING HIM FAR, EVEN FROM HIS KNOWLEDGE OF US.

I NO-TICED.

ONCE, HE WAS A DIFFERENT TYPE OF FROG, BUT TODAY... WITH THINGS LIKE THIS... WE HAVE TO THINK OF OUR FUTURE.

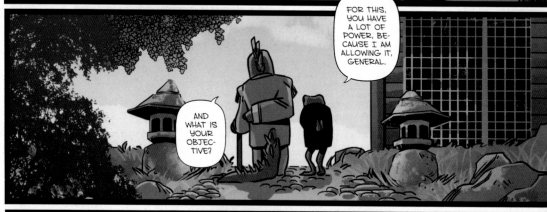

FOR THIS, YOU HAVE A LOT OF POWER, BE-CAUSE I AM ALLOWING IT, GENERAL.

AND WHAT IS YOUR OBJEC-TIVE?

A CIVILIZED COUNTRY.

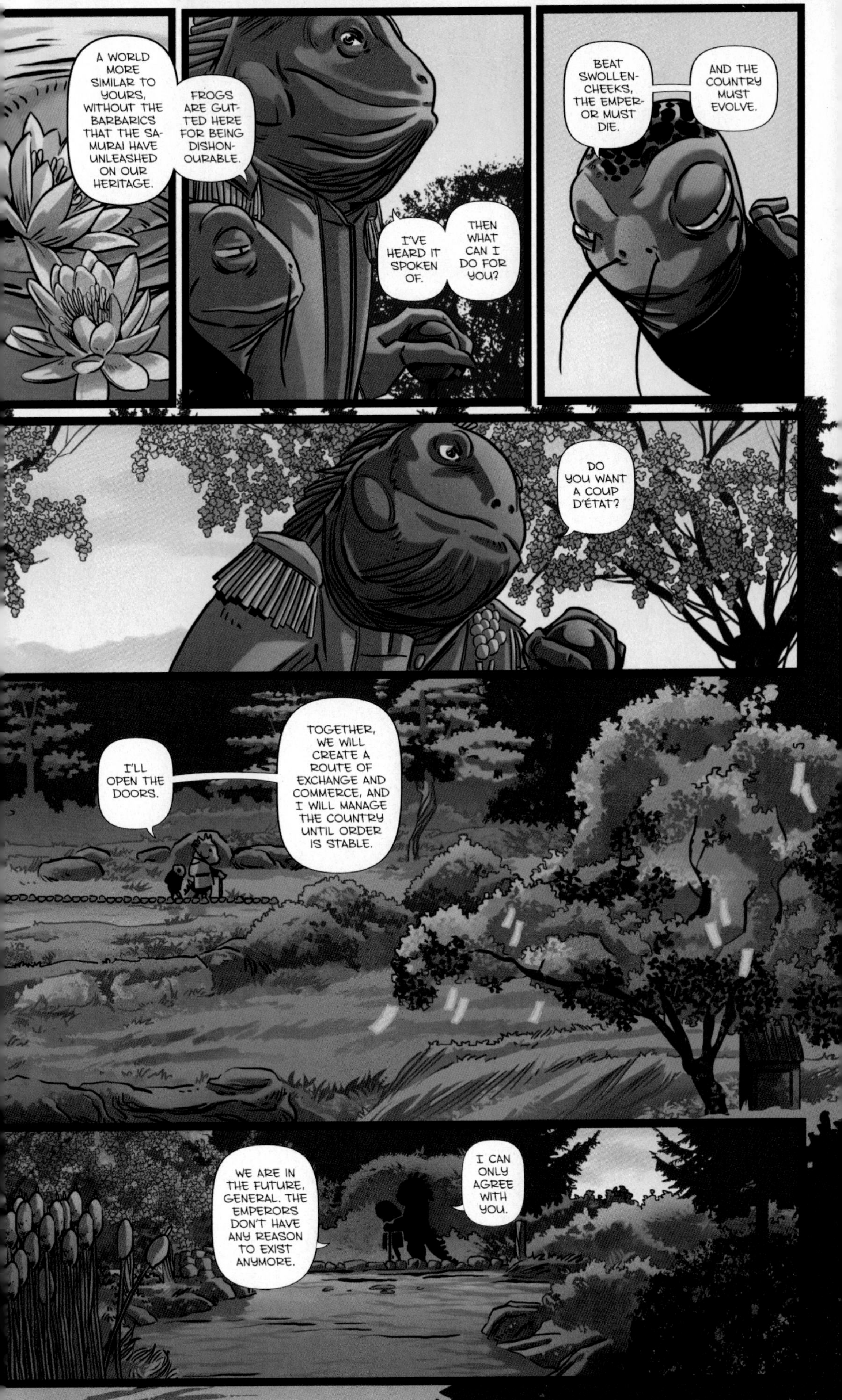
A WORLD MORE SIMILAR TO YOURS, WITHOUT THE BARBARICS THAT THE SAMURAI HAVE UNLEASHED ON OUR HERITAGE.
FROGS ARE GUTTED HERE FOR BEING DISHONOURABLE.
I'VE HEARD IT SPOKEN OF.
THEN WHAT CAN I DO FOR YOU?
BEAT SWOLLEN-CHEEKS, THE EMPEROR MUST DIE.
AND THE COUNTRY MUST EVOLVE.
DO YOU WANT A COUP D'ÉTAT?
I'LL OPEN THE DOORS.
TOGETHER, WE WILL CREATE A ROUTE OF EXCHANGE AND COMMERCE, AND I WILL MANAGE THE COUNTRY UNTIL ORDER IS STABLE.
WE ARE IN THE FUTURE, GENERAL. THE EMPERORS DON'T HAVE ANY REASON TO EXIST ANYMORE.
I CAN ONLY AGREE WITH YOU.

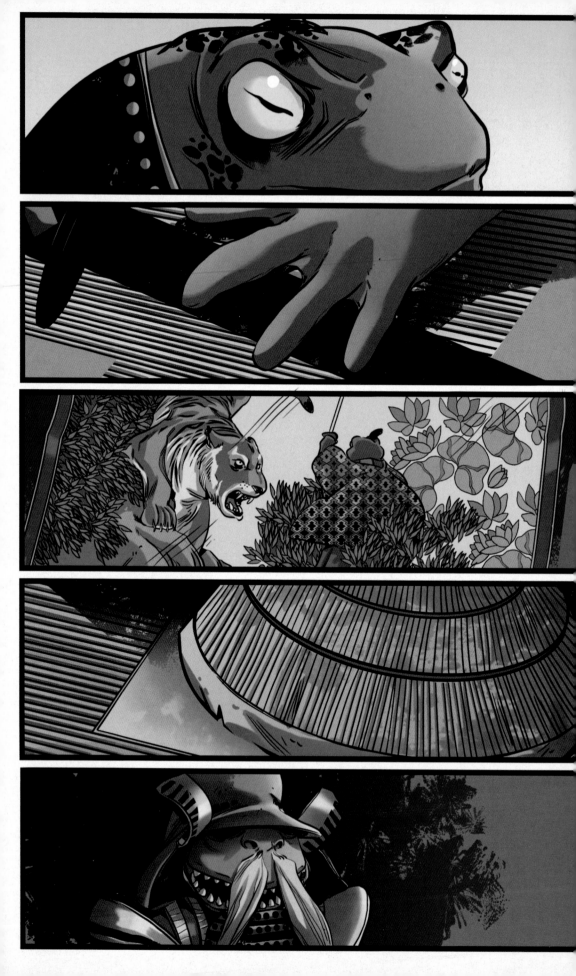

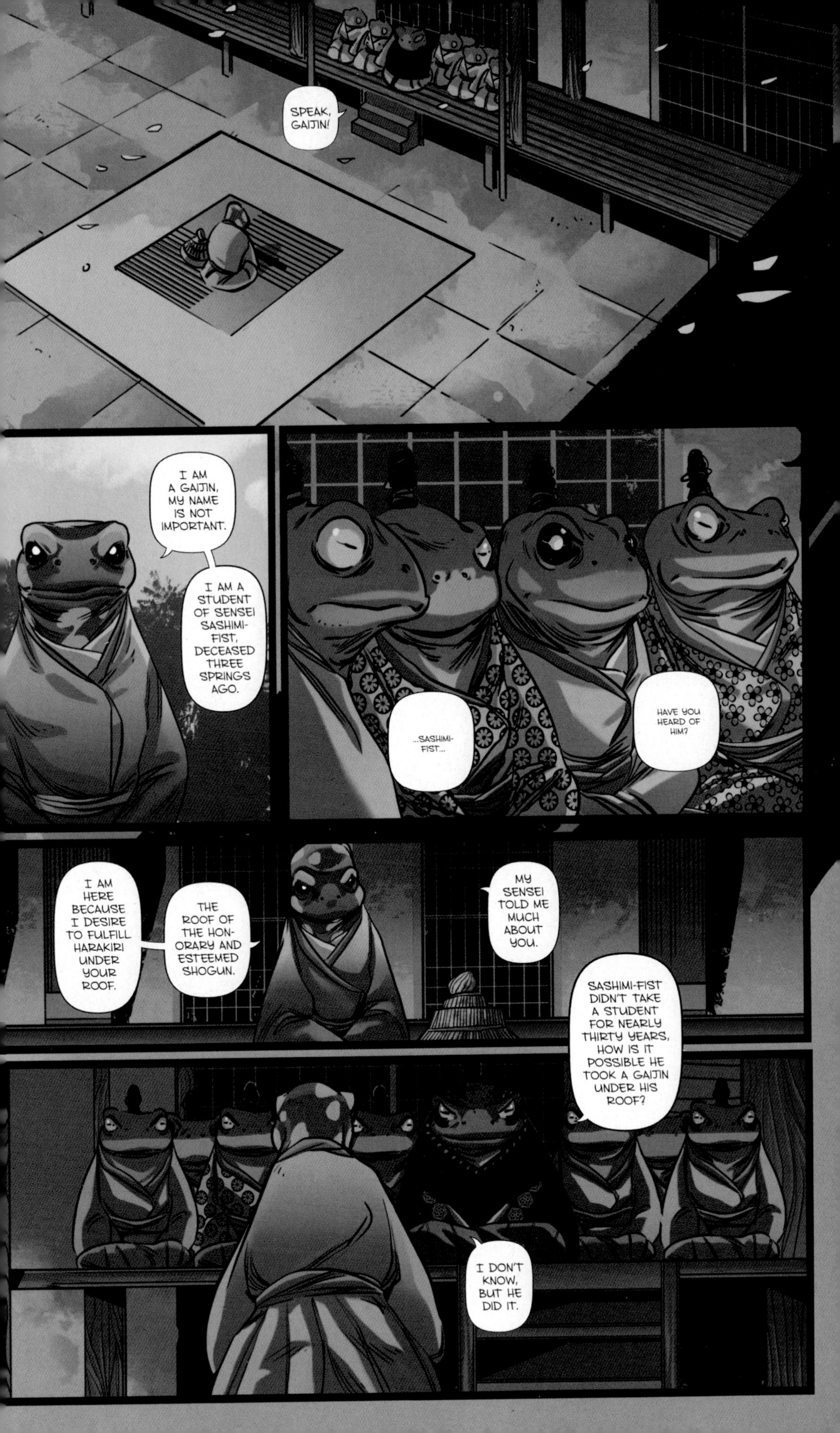
SPEAK, GAIJIN!
I AM A GAIJIN, MY NAME IS NOT IMPORTANT.
I AM A STUDENT OF SENSEI SASHIMI-FIST, DECEASED THREE SPRINGS AGO.
...SASHIMI-FIST...
HAVE YOU HEARD OF HIM?
I AM HERE BECAUSE I DESIRE TO FULFILL HARAKIRI UNDER YOUR ROOF.
THE ROOF OF THE HON-ORARY AND ESTEEMED SHOGUN.
MY SENSEI TOLD ME MUCH ABOUT YOU.
SASHIMI-FIST DIDN'T TAKE A STUDENT FOR NEARLY THIRTY YEARS, HOW IS IT POSSIBLE HE TOOK A GAIJIN UNDER HIS ROOF?
I DON'T KNOW, BUT HE DID IT.

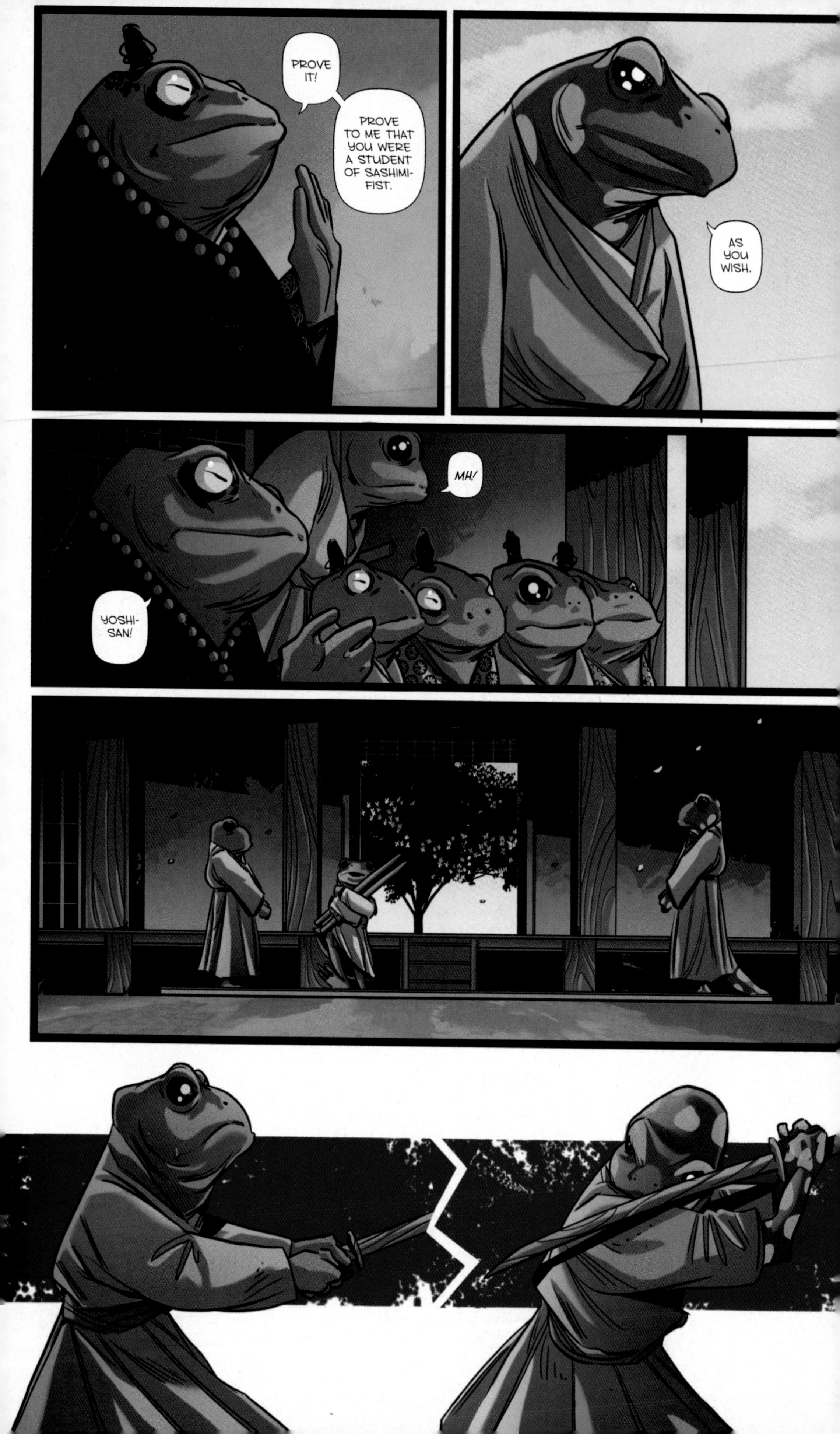
PROVE IT!
PROVE TO ME THAT YOU WERE A STUDENT OF SASHIMI-FIST.
AS YOU WISH.
MH!
YOSHI-SAN!

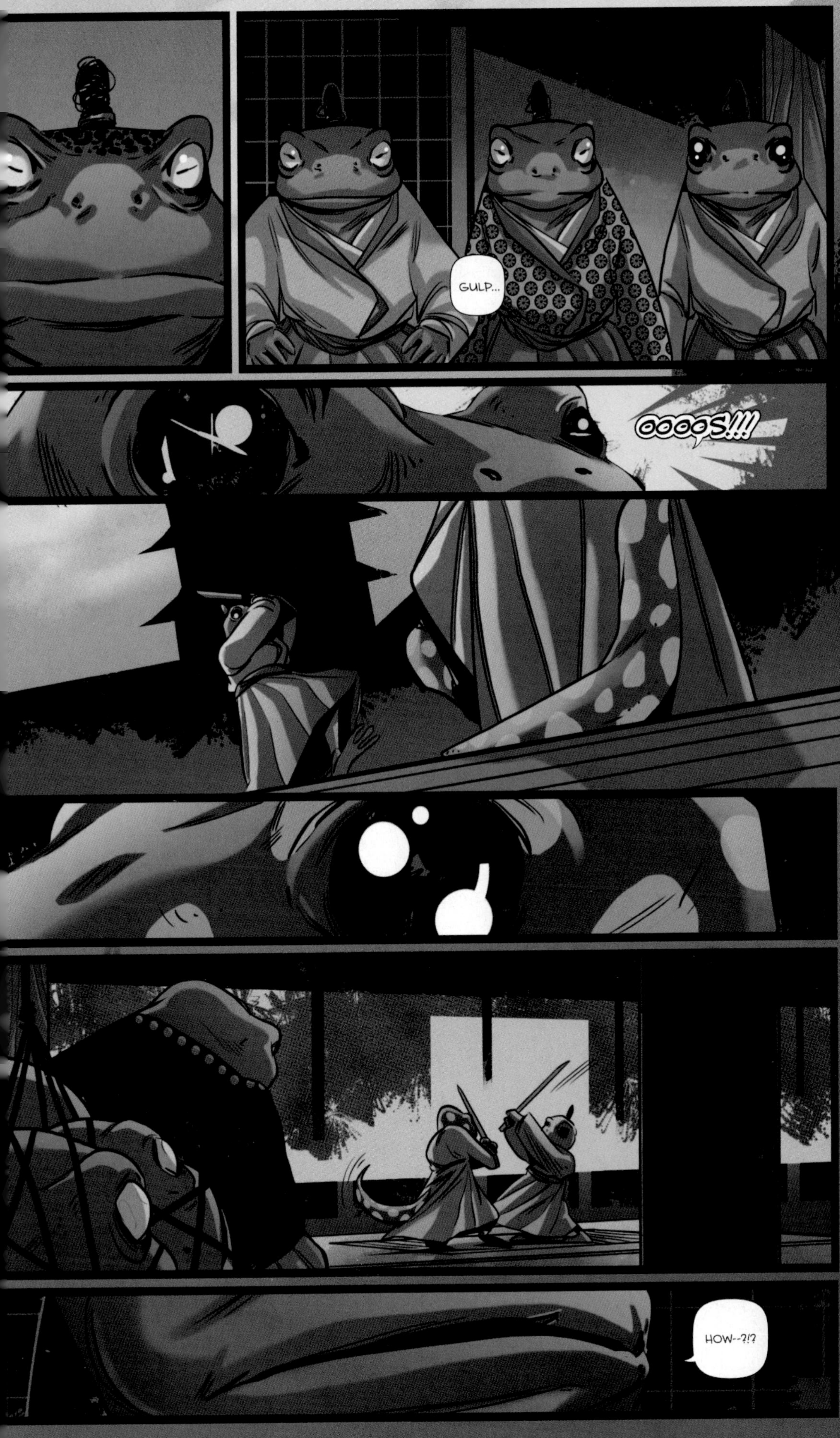
GULP...
OOOOS!!!
HOW--?!?

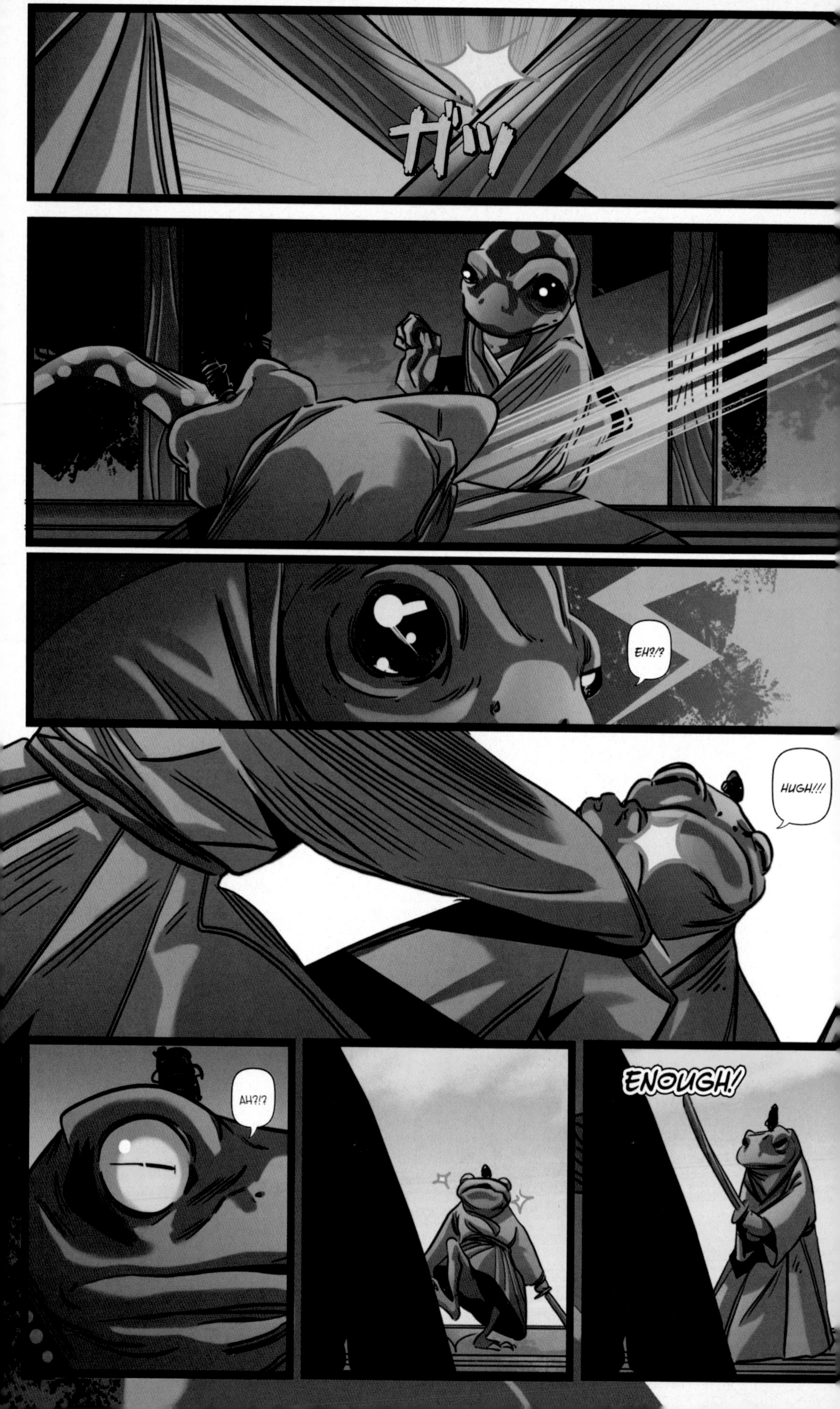

ガッ
EH?!?
HUGH!!!
AH?!?
ENOUGH!

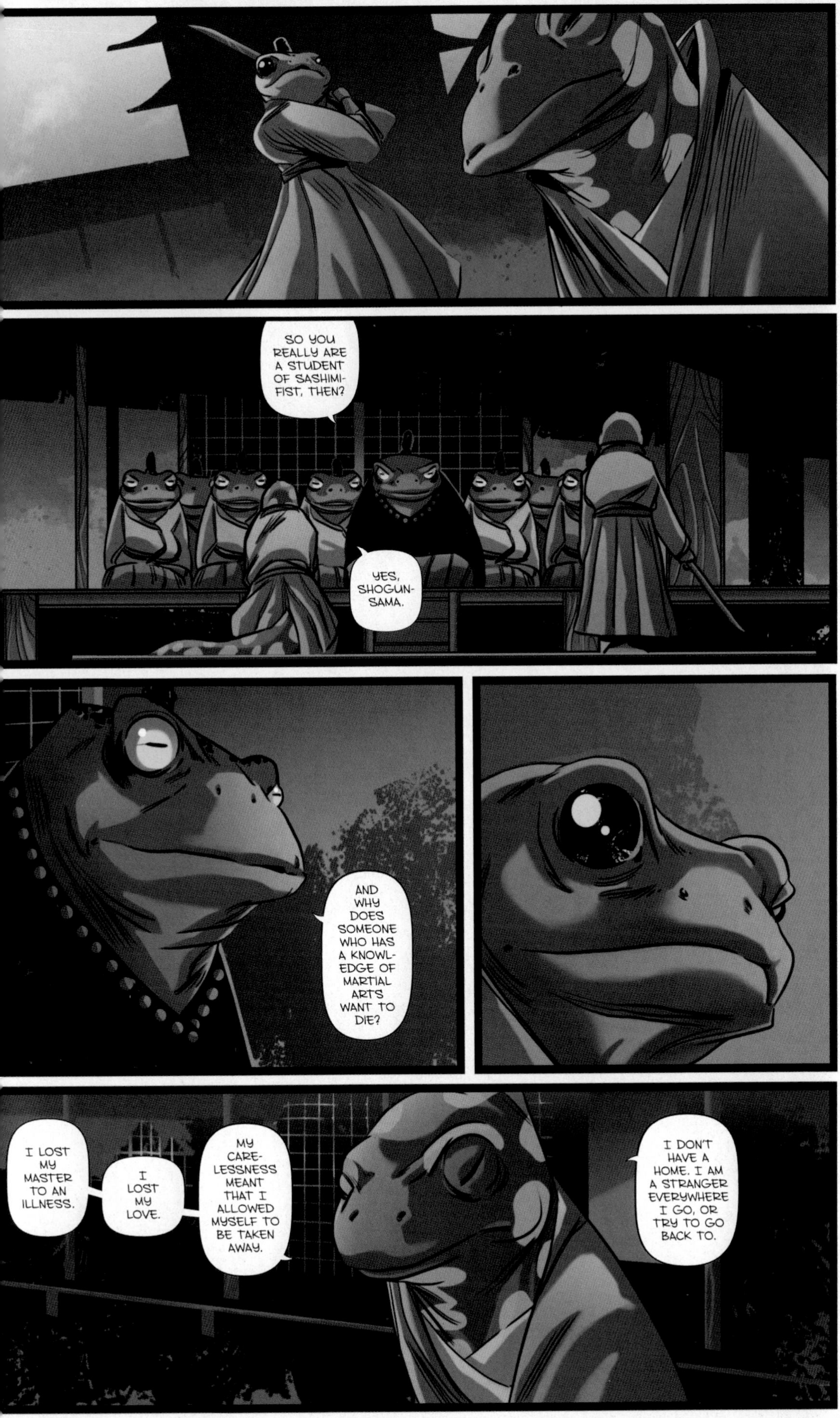
SO YOU REALLY ARE A STUDENT OF SASHIMI-FIST, THEN?
YES, SHOGUN-SAMA.
AND WHY DOES SOMEONE WHO HAS A KNOWL-EDGE OF MARTIAL ARTS WANT TO DIE?
I LOST MY MASTER TO AN ILLNESS.
I LOST MY LOVE.
MY CARE-LESSNESS MEANT THAT I ALLOWED MYSELF TO BE TAKEN AWAY.
I DON'T HAVE A HOME. I AM A STRANGER EVERYWHERE I GO, OR TRY TO GO BACK TO.

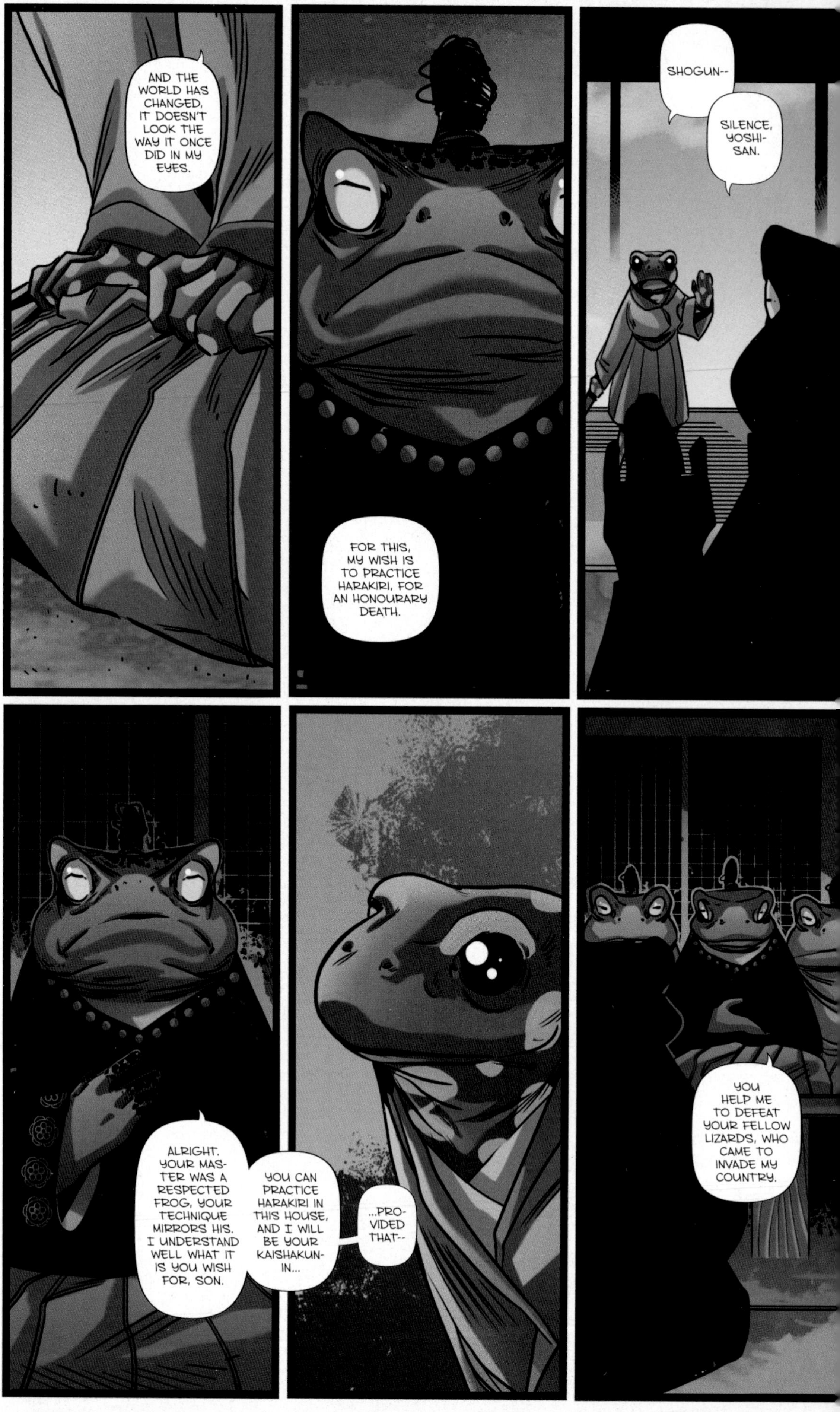
AND THE WORLD HAS CHANGED, IT DOESN'T LOOK THE WAY IT ONCE DID IN MY EYES.
FOR THIS, MY WISH IS TO PRACTICE HARAKIRI, FOR AN HONOURARY DEATH.
SHOGUN--
SILENCE, YOSHI-SAN.
ALRIGHT. YOUR MASTER WAS A RESPECTED FROG, YOUR TECHNIQUE MIRRORS HIS. I UNDERSTAND WELL WHAT IT IS YOU WISH FOR, SON.
YOU CAN PRACTICE HARAKIRI IN THIS HOUSE, AND I WILL BE YOUR KAISHAKUNIN...
...PROVIDED THAT--
YOU HELP ME TO DEFEAT YOUR FELLOW LIZARDS, WHO CAME TO INVADE MY COUNTRY.

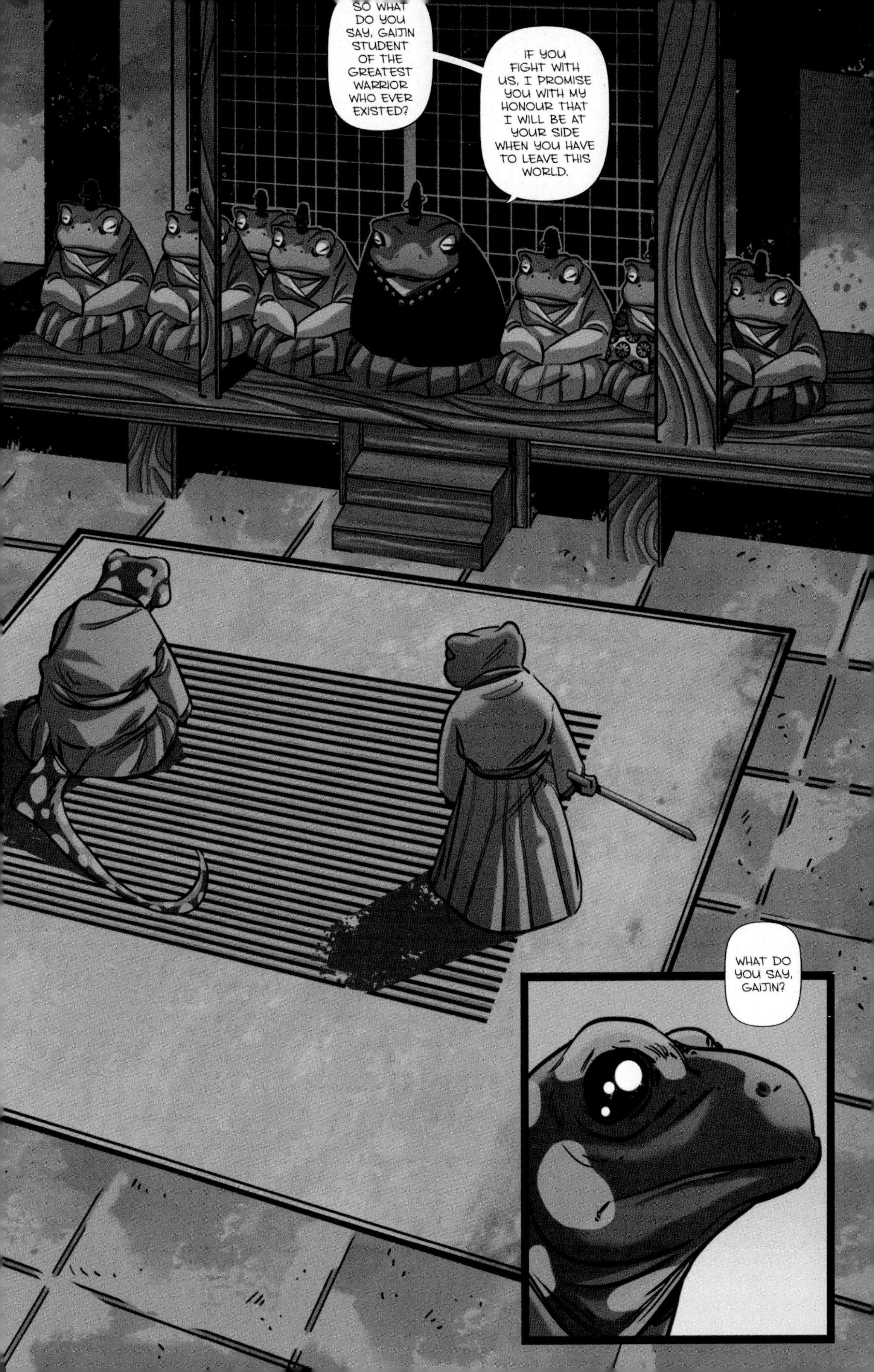
SO WHAT DO YOU SAY, GAIJIN STUDENT OF THE GREATEST WARRIOR WHO EVER EXISTED?
IF YOU FIGHT WITH US, I PROMISE YOU WITH MY HONOUR THAT I WILL BE AT YOUR SIDE WHEN YOU HAVE TO LEAVE THIS WORLD.
WHAT DO YOU SAY, GAIJIN?

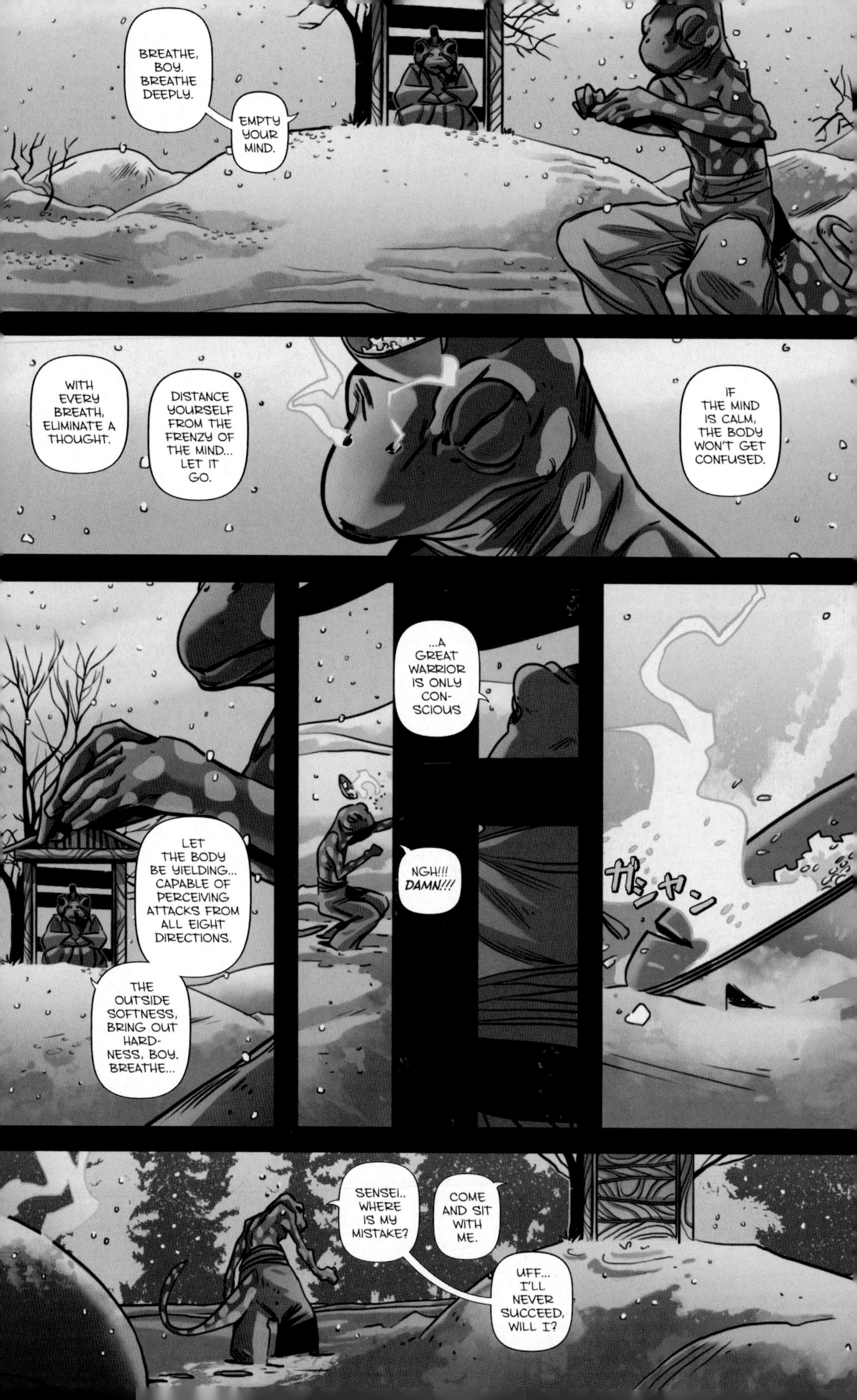
BREATHE, BOY. BREATHE DEEPLY.
EMPTY YOUR MIND.
WITH EVERY BREATH, ELIMINATE A THOUGHT.
DISTANCE YOURSELF FROM THE FRENZY OF THE MIND... LET IT GO.
IF THE MIND IS CALM, THE BODY WON'T GET CONFUSED.
LET THE BODY BE YIELDING... CAPABLE OF PERCEIVING ATTACKS FROM ALL EIGHT DIRECTIONS.
THE OUTSIDE SOFTNESS, BRING OUT HARD-NESS, BOY. BREATHE...
...A GREAT WARRIOR IS ONLY CON-SCIOUS
NGH!!! *DAMN!!!*
ガシャン
SENSEI.. WHERE IS MY MISTAKE?
COME AND SIT WITH ME.
UFF... I'LL NEVER SUCCEED, WILL I?

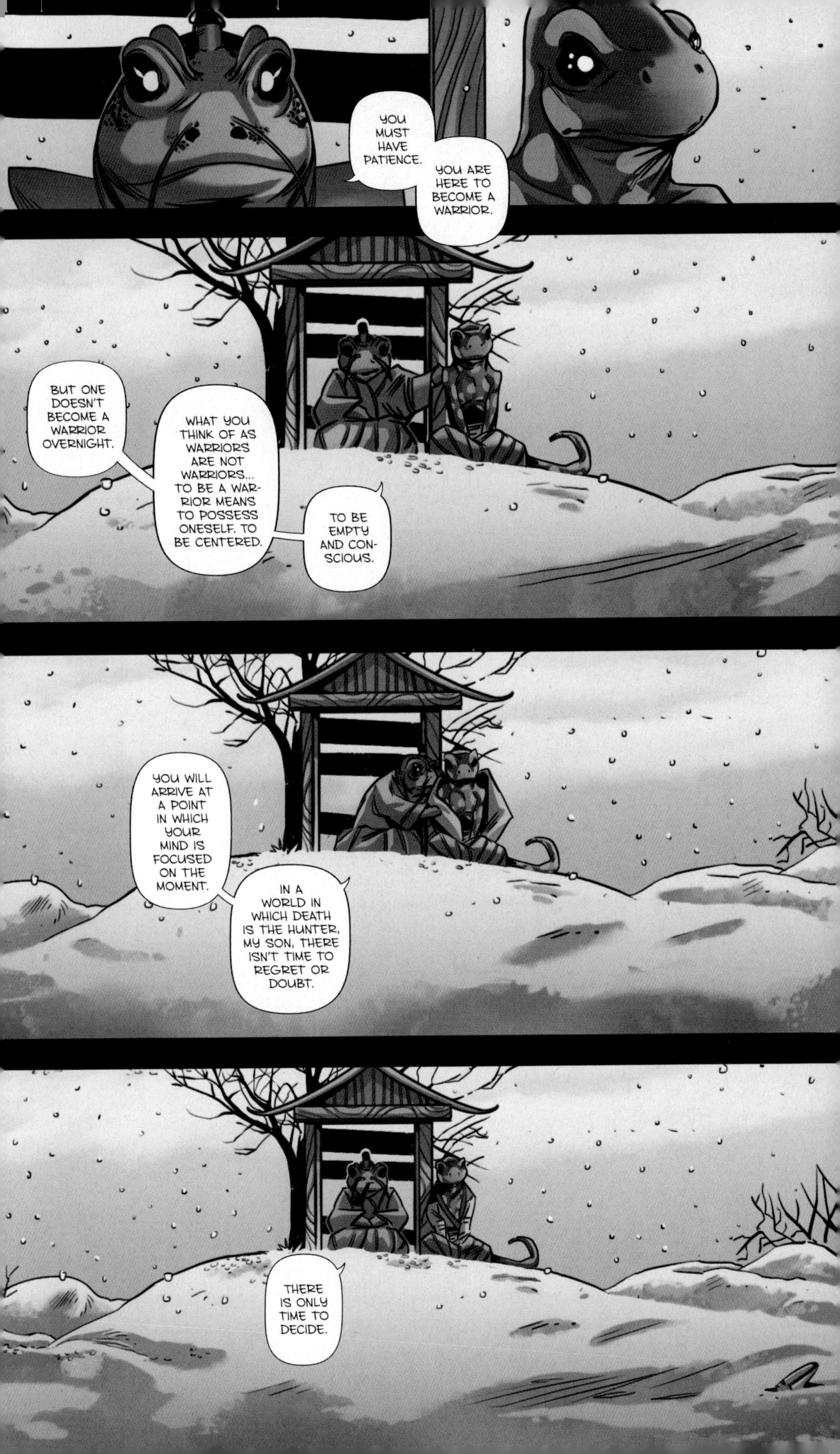

YOU MUST HAVE PATIENCE.
YOU ARE HERE TO BECOME A WARRIOR.
BUT ONE DOESN'T BECOME A WARRIOR OVERNIGHT.
WHAT YOU THINK OF AS WARRIORS ARE NOT WARRIORS... TO BE A WAR-RIOR MEANS TO POSSESS ONESELF. TO BE CENTERED.
TO BE EMPTY AND CON-SCIOUS.
YOU WILL ARRIVE AT A POINT IN WHICH YOUR MIND IS FOCUSED ON THE MOMENT.
IN A WORLD IN WHICH DEATH IS THE HUNTER, MY SON, THERE ISN'T TIME TO REGRET OR DOUBT.
THERE IS ONLY TIME TO DECIDE.

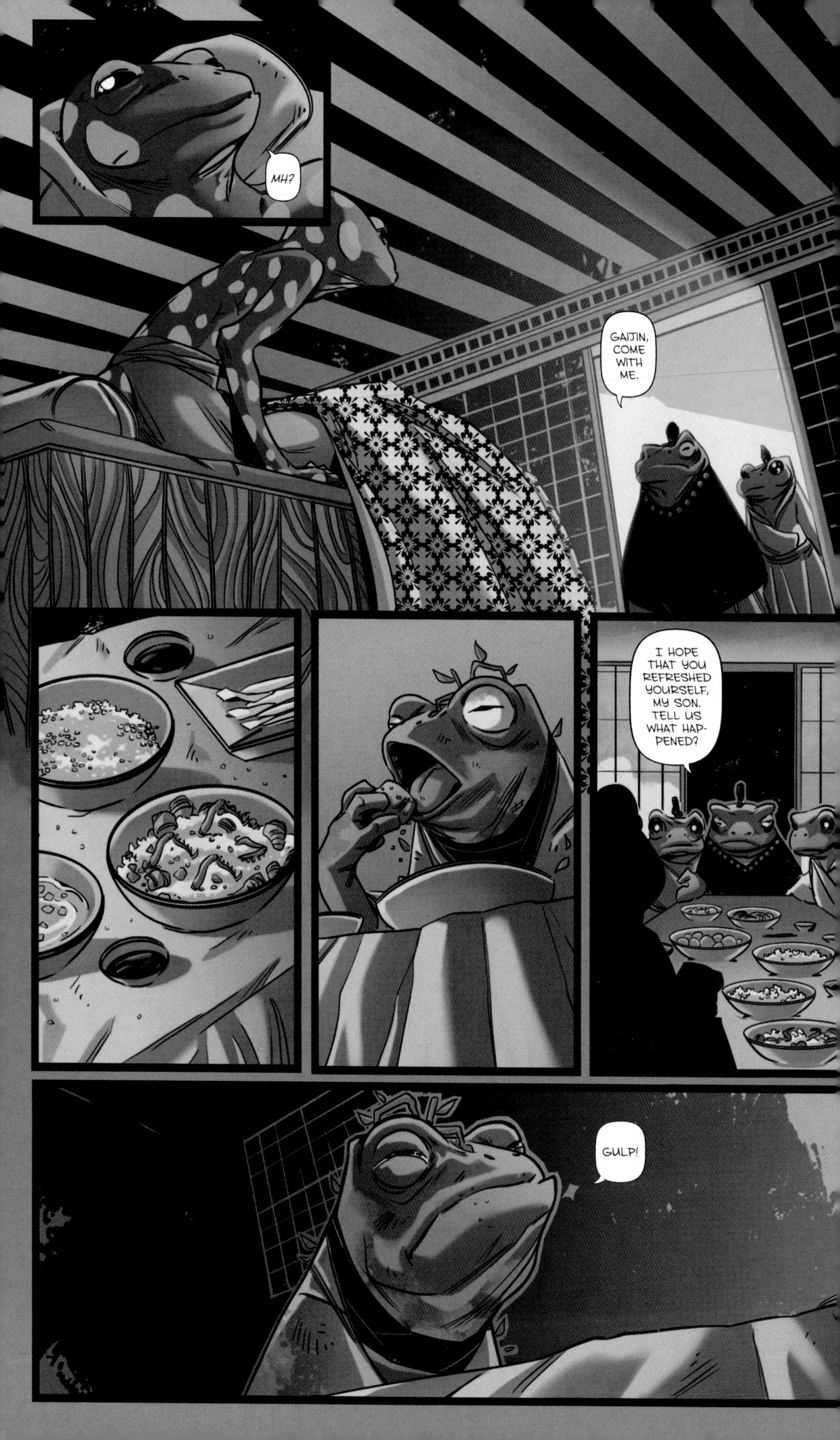
MH?
GAIJIN, COME WITH ME.
I HOPE THAT YOU REFRESHED YOURSELF, MY SON. TELL US WHAT HAP-PENED?
GULP!

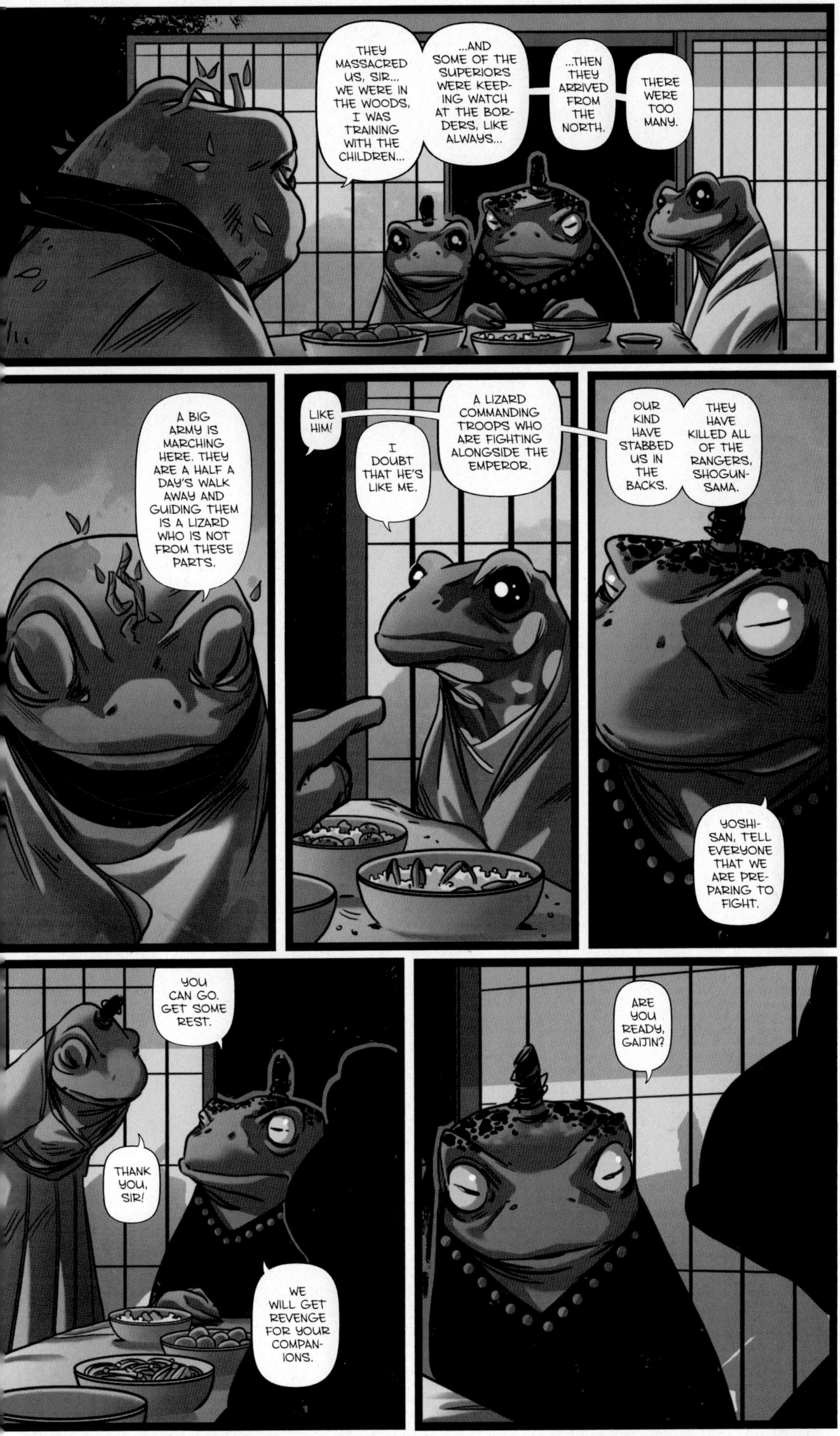
THEY MASSACRED US, SIR... WE WERE IN THE WOODS, I WAS TRAINING WITH THE CHILDREN...
...AND SOME OF THE SUPERIORS WERE KEEPING WATCH AT THE BORDERS, LIKE ALWAYS...
...THEN THEY ARRIVED FROM THE NORTH.
THERE WERE TOO MANY.
A BIG ARMY IS MARCHING HERE. THEY ARE A HALF A DAY'S WALK AWAY AND GUIDING THEM IS A LIZARD WHO IS NOT FROM THESE PARTS.
LIKE HIM!
A LIZARD COMMANDING TROOPS WHO ARE FIGHTING ALONGSIDE THE EMPEROR.
I DOUBT THAT HE'S LIKE ME.
OUR KIND HAVE STABBED US IN THE BACKS.
THEY HAVE KILLED ALL OF THE RANGERS, SHOGUN-SAMA.
YOSHI-SAN, TELL EVERYONE THAT WE ARE PREPARING TO FIGHT.
YOU CAN GO. GET SOME REST.
THANK YOU, SIR!
WE WILL GET REVENGE FOR YOUR COMPANIONS.
ARE YOU READY, GAIJIN?

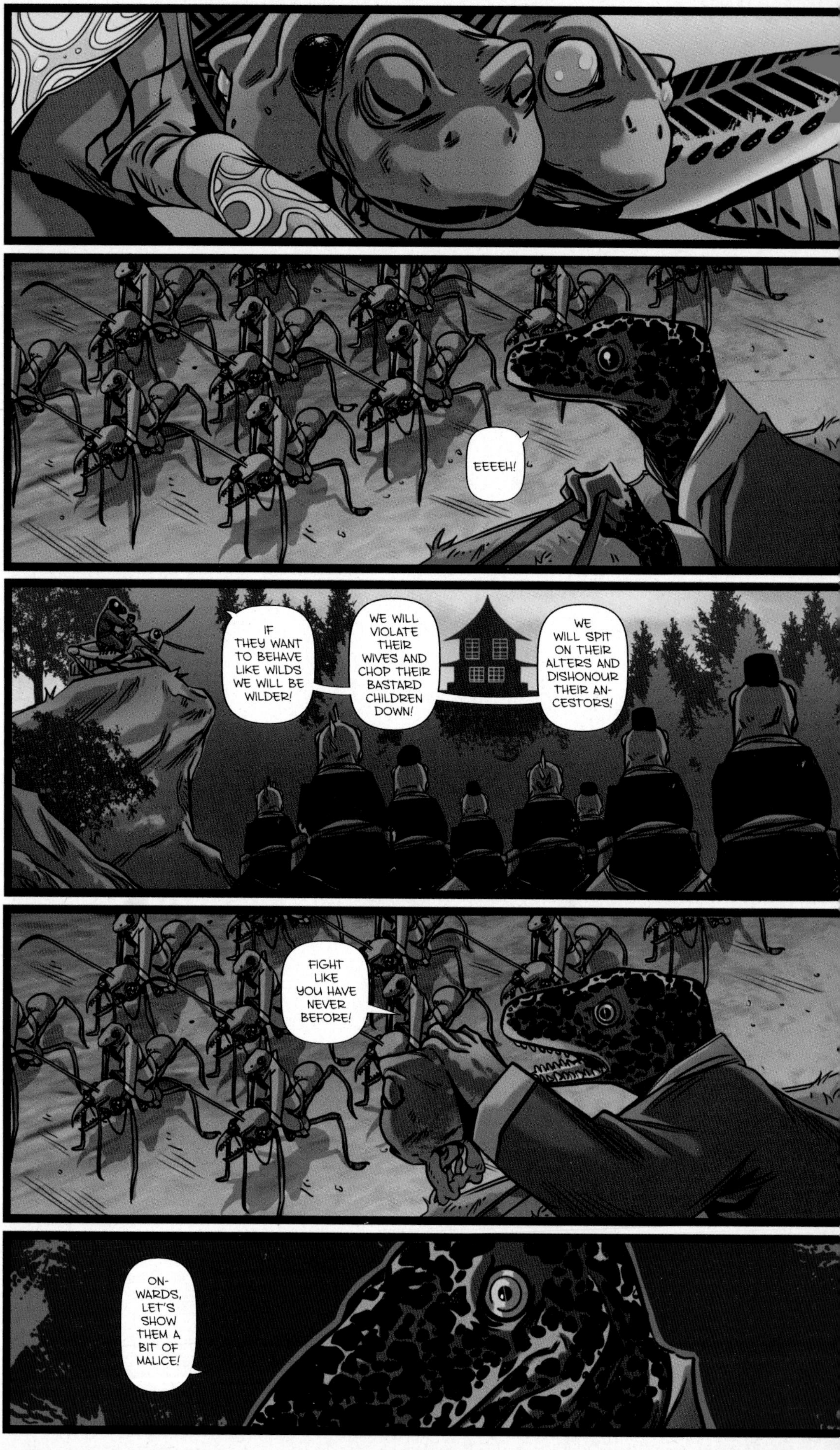
EEEEH!
IF THEY WANT TO BEHAVE LIKE WILDS WE WILL BE WILDER!
WE WILL VIOLATE THEIR WIVES AND CHOP THEIR BASTARD CHILDREN DOWN!
WE WILL SPIT ON THEIR ALTERS AND DISHONOUR THEIR ANCESTORS!
FIGHT LIKE YOU HAVE NEVER BEFORE!
ONWARDS, LET'S SHOW THEM A BIT OF MALICE!

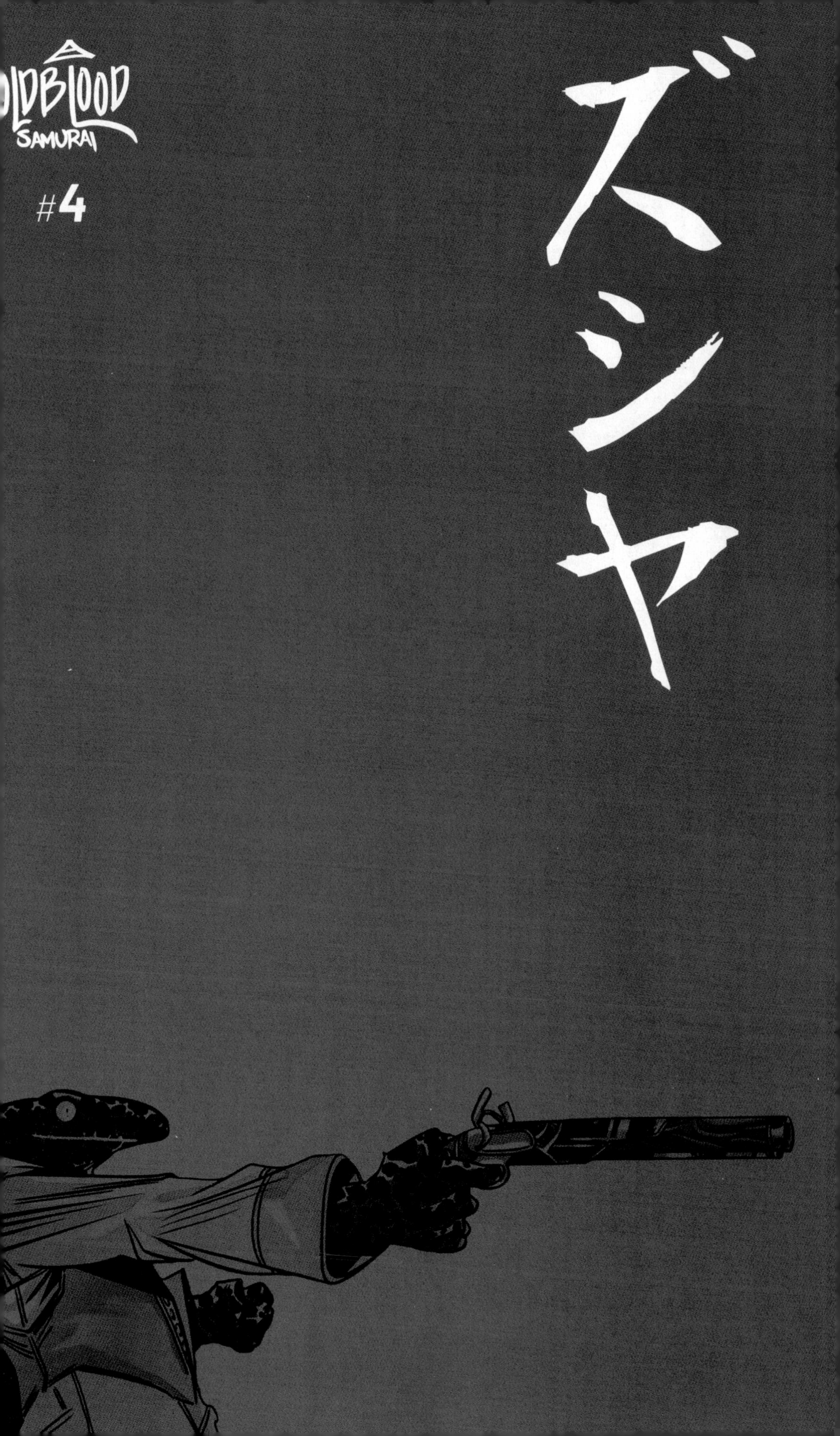
SAMURAI
#4
ズシャ

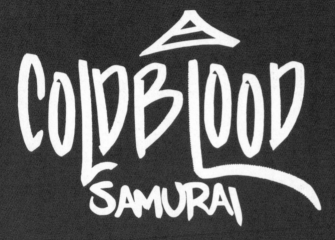

CREDITS

Story
MASSIMO ROSI

Pencils
LUDOVICA CEREGATTI

Colors
RENATO STEVANATO

Lettering
MATTIA GENTILI

Bryan Seaton: Publisher/ CEO
Shawn Gabborin: Editor In Chief
Jason Martin: Publisher-Danger Zone
Nicole D'Andria: Marketing Director/Editor
Jessica Lowrie: Social Media Czar
Danielle Davison: Executive Administrator
Chad Cicconi: King Lizard
Shawn Pryor: President of Creator Relations

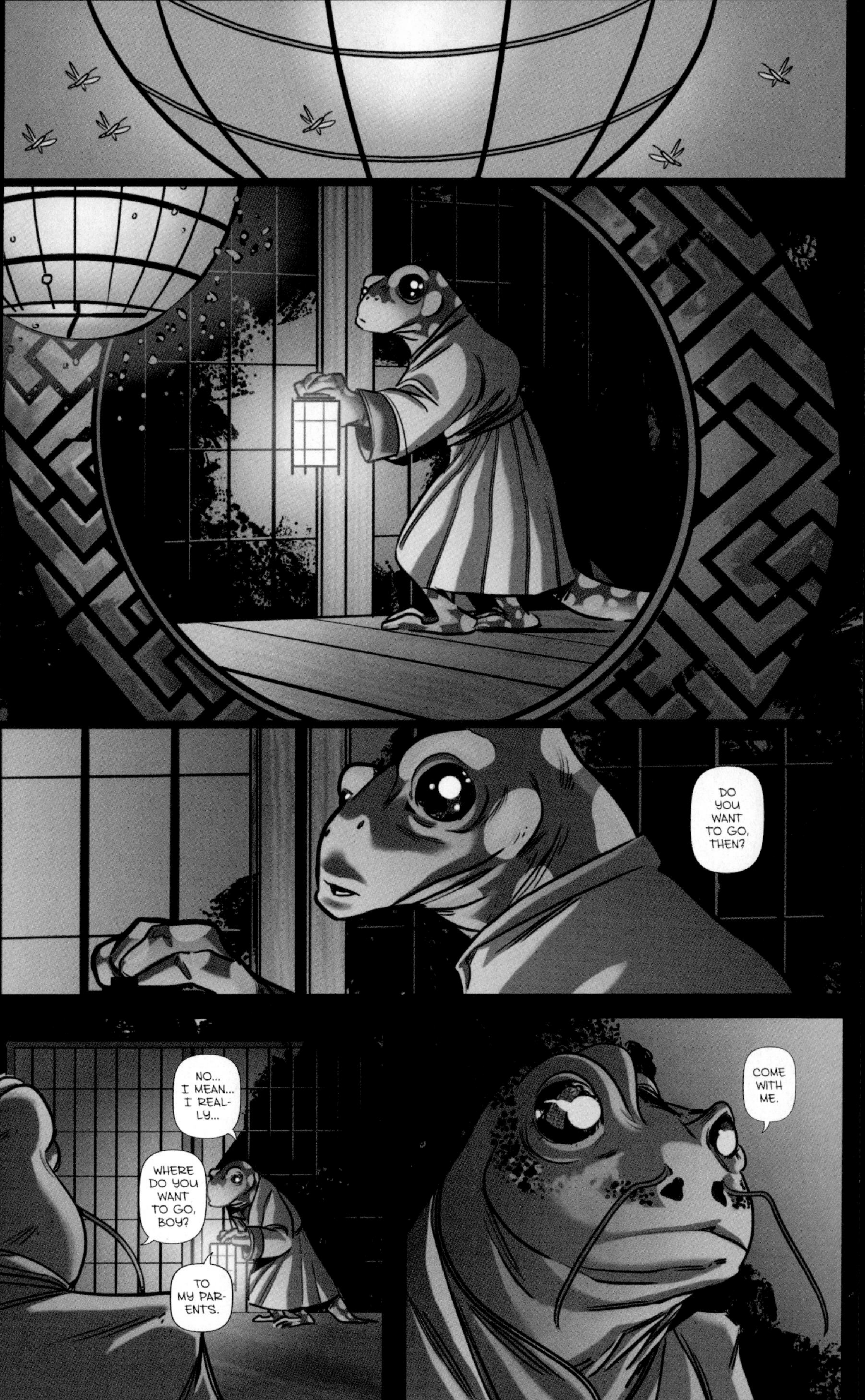
DO YOU WANT TO GO, THEN?
NO... I MEAN... I REALLY...
WHERE DO YOU WANT TO GO, BOY?
TO MY PARENTS.
COME WITH ME.

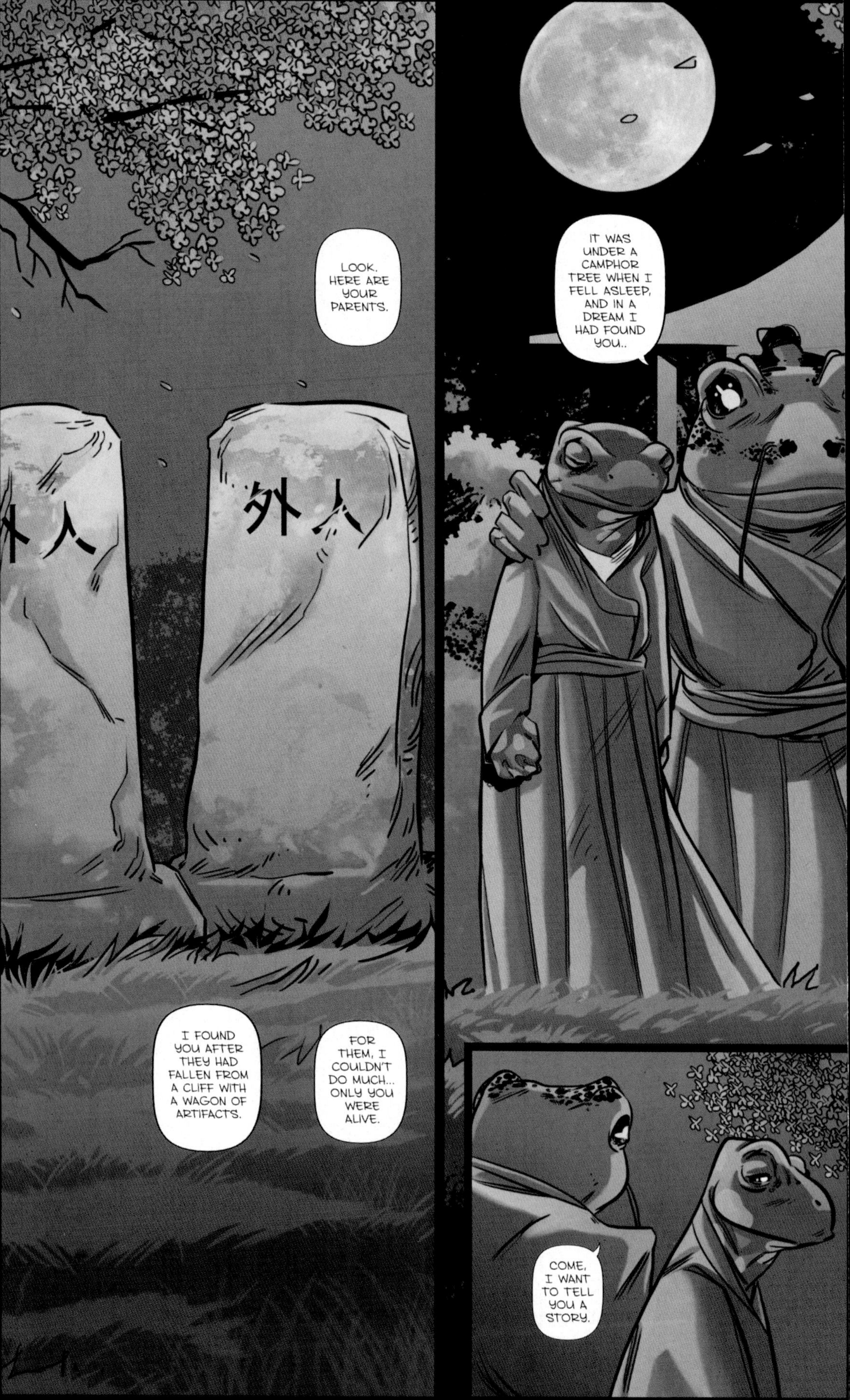
LOOK. HERE ARE YOUR PARENTS.
外人
外人
I FOUND YOU AFTER THEY HAD FALLEN FROM A CLIFF WITH A WAGON OF ARTIFACTS.
FOR THEM, I COULDN'T DO MUCH... ONLY YOU WERE ALIVE.
IT WAS UNDER A CAMPHOR TREE WHEN I FELL ASLEEP, AND IN A DREAM I HAD FOUND YOU..
COME, I WANT TO TELL YOU A STORY.

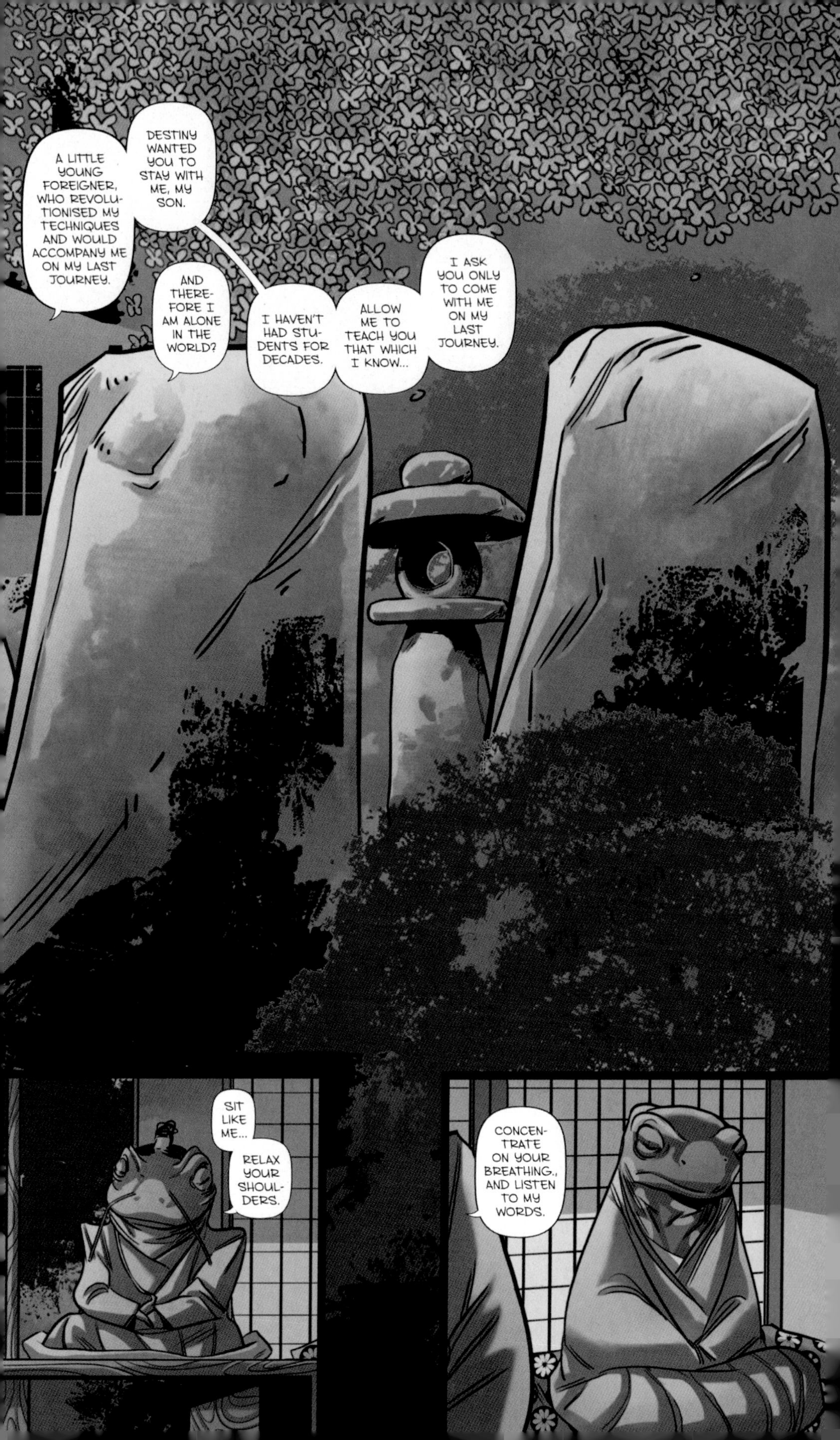
A LITTLE YOUNG FOREIGNER, WHO REVOLUTIONISED MY TECHNIQUES AND WOULD ACCOMPANY ME ON MY LAST JOURNEY.
DESTINY WANTED YOU TO STAY WITH ME, MY SON.
AND THEREFORE I AM ALONE IN THE WORLD?
I HAVEN'T HAD STUDENTS FOR DECADES.
ALLOW ME TO TEACH YOU THAT WHICH I KNOW...
I ASK YOU ONLY TO COME WITH ME ON MY LAST JOURNEY.
SIT LIKE ME...
RELAX YOUR SHOULDERS.
CONCENTRATE ON YOUR BREATHING., AND LISTEN TO MY WORDS.

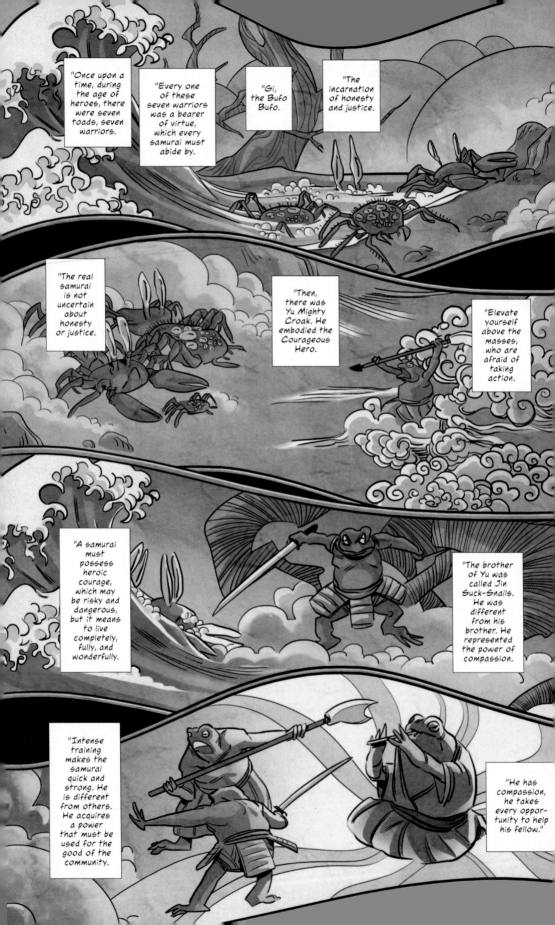

"Once upon a time, during the age of heroes, there were seven toads, seven warriors.

"Every one of these seven warriors was a bearer of virtue, which every samurai must abide by.

"Gi, the Bufo Bufo.

"The incarnation of honesty and justice.

"The real samurai is not uncertain about honesty or justice.

"Then, there was Yu Mighty Croak. He embodied the Courageous Hero.

"Elevate yourself above the masses, who are afraid of taking action.

"A samurai must possess heroic courage, which may be risky and dangerous, but it means to live completely, fully, and wonderfully.

"The brother of Yu was called Jin Suck-Snails. He was different from his brother. He represented the power of compassion.

"Intense training makes the samurai quick and strong. He is different from others. He acquires a power that must be used for the good of the community.

"He has compassion, he takes every opportunity to help his fellow."

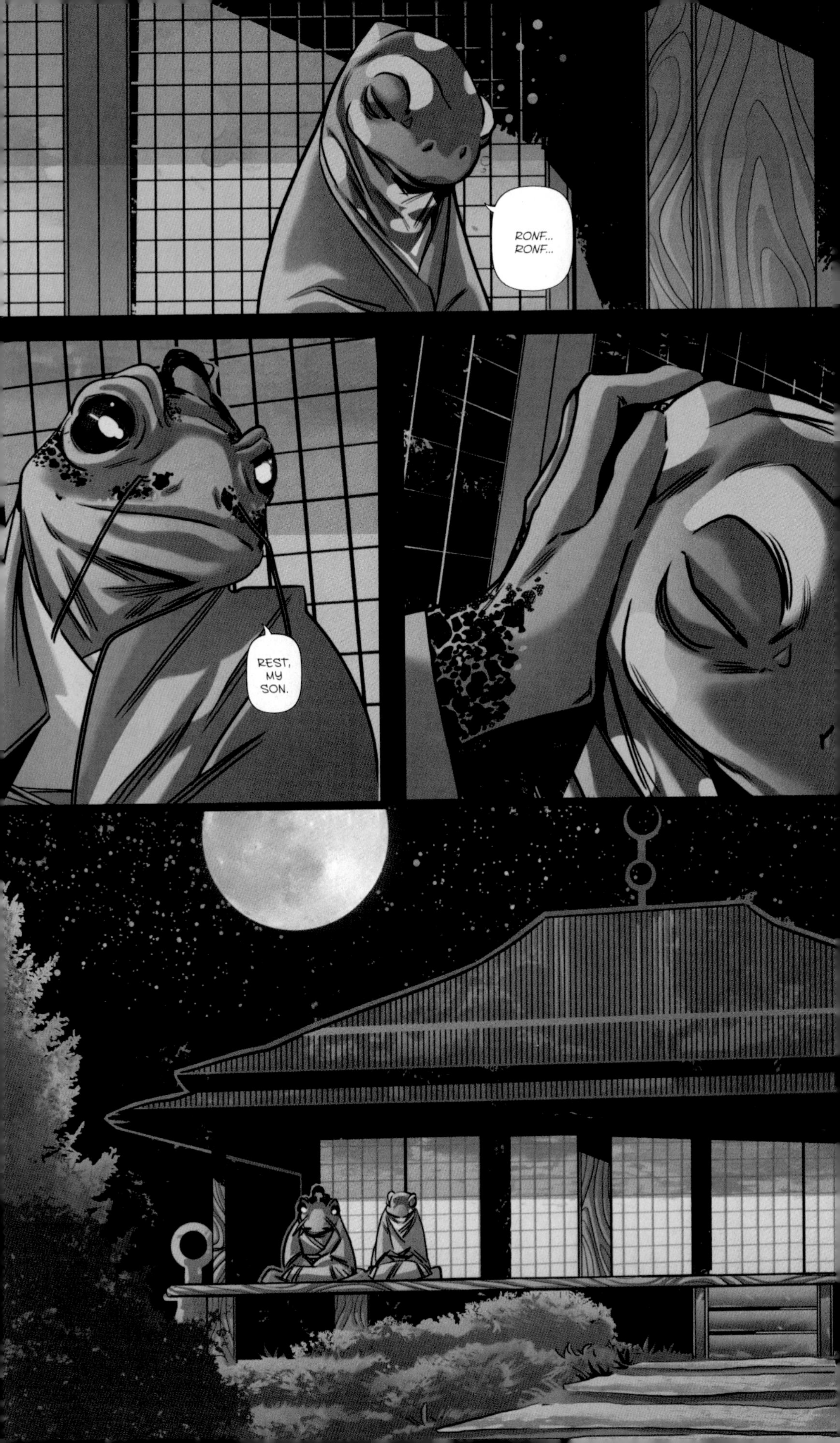
RONF... RONF...
REST, MY SON.

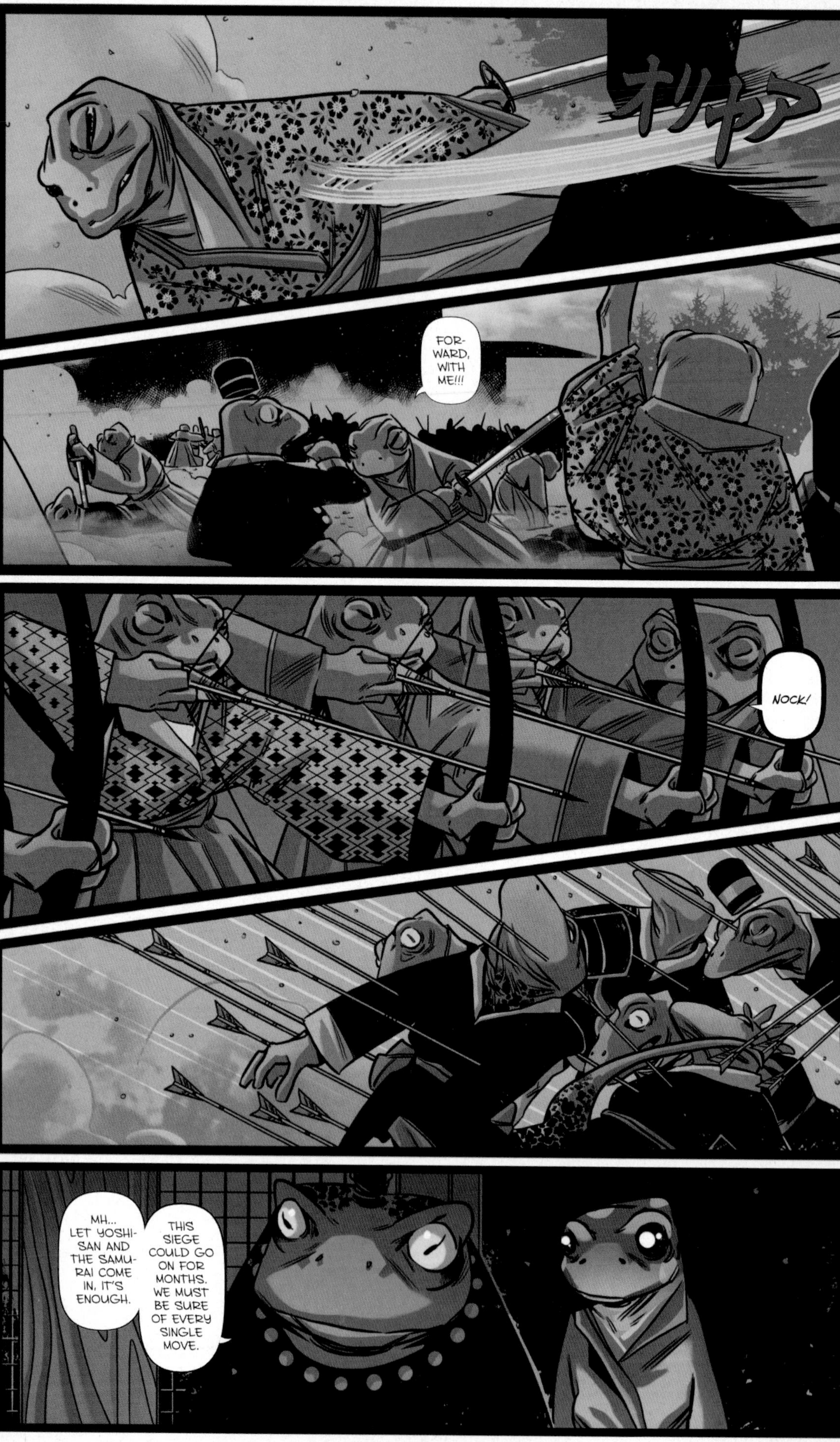
オリャア
FOR-WARD, WITH ME!!!
NOCK!
MH... LET YOSHI-SAN AND THE SAMU-RAI COME IN, IT'S ENOUGH.
THIS SIEGE COULD GO ON FOR MONTHS. WE MUST BE SURE OF EVERY SINGLE MOVE.

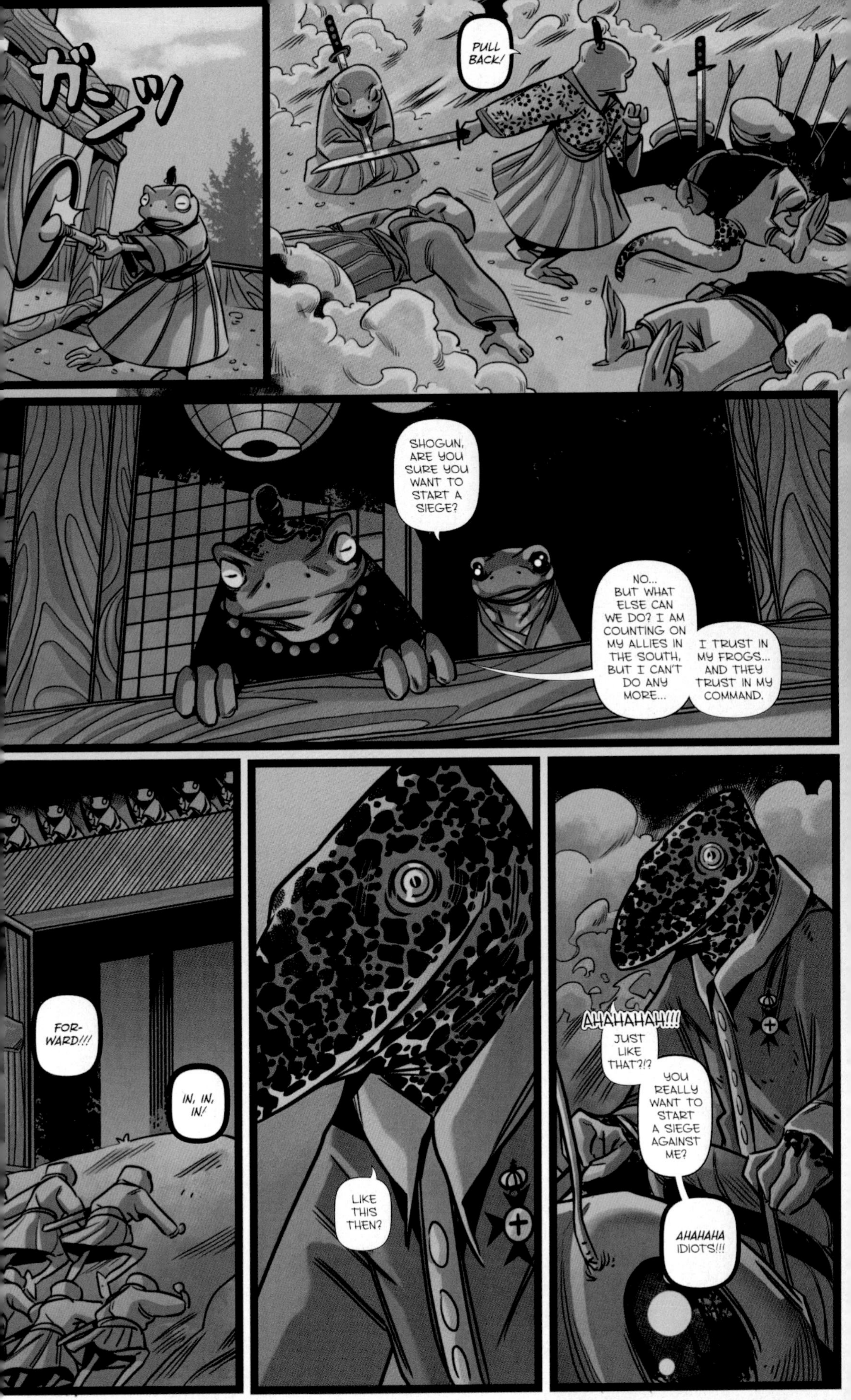
ガーンッ
PULL BACK!
SHOGUN, ARE YOU SURE YOU WANT TO START A SIEGE?
NO... BUT WHAT ELSE CAN WE DO? I AM COUNTING ON MY ALLIES IN THE SOUTH, BUT I CAN'T DO ANY MORE...
I TRUST IN MY FROGS... AND THEY TRUST IN MY COMMAND.
FOR-WARD!!!
IN, IN, IN!
LIKE THIS THEN?
AHAHAHAH!!!
JUST LIKE THAT?!?
YOU REALLY WANT TO START A SIEGE AGAINST ME?
AHAHAHA IDIOTS!!!

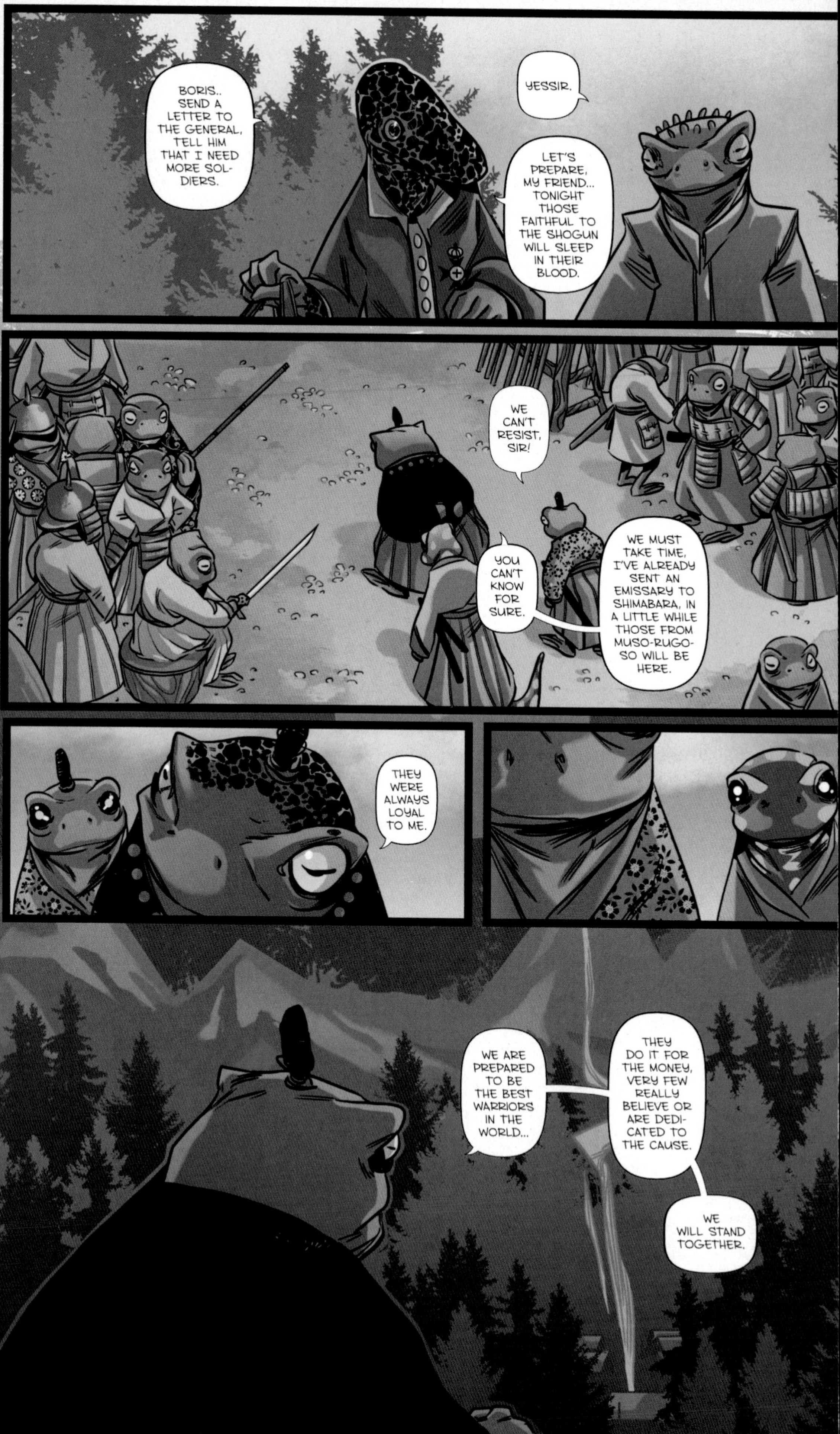
BORIS.. SEND A LETTER TO THE GENERAL, TELL HIM THAT I NEED MORE SOL-DIERS.
YESSIR.
LET'S PREPARE, MY FRIEND... TONIGHT THOSE FAITHFUL TO THE SHOGUN WILL SLEEP IN THEIR BLOOD.
WE CAN'T RESIST, SIR!
WE MUST TAKE TIME, I'VE ALREADY SENT AN EMISSARY TO SHIMABARA, IN A LITTLE WHILE THOSE FROM MUSO-RUGO-SO WILL BE HERE.
YOU CAN'T KNOW FOR SURE.
THEY WERE ALWAYS LOYAL TO ME.
WE ARE PREPARED TO BE THE BEST WARRIORS IN THE WORLD...
THEY DO IT FOR THE MONEY, VERY FEW REALLY BELIEVE OR ARE DEDI-CATED TO THE CAUSE.
WE WILL STAND TOGETHER.

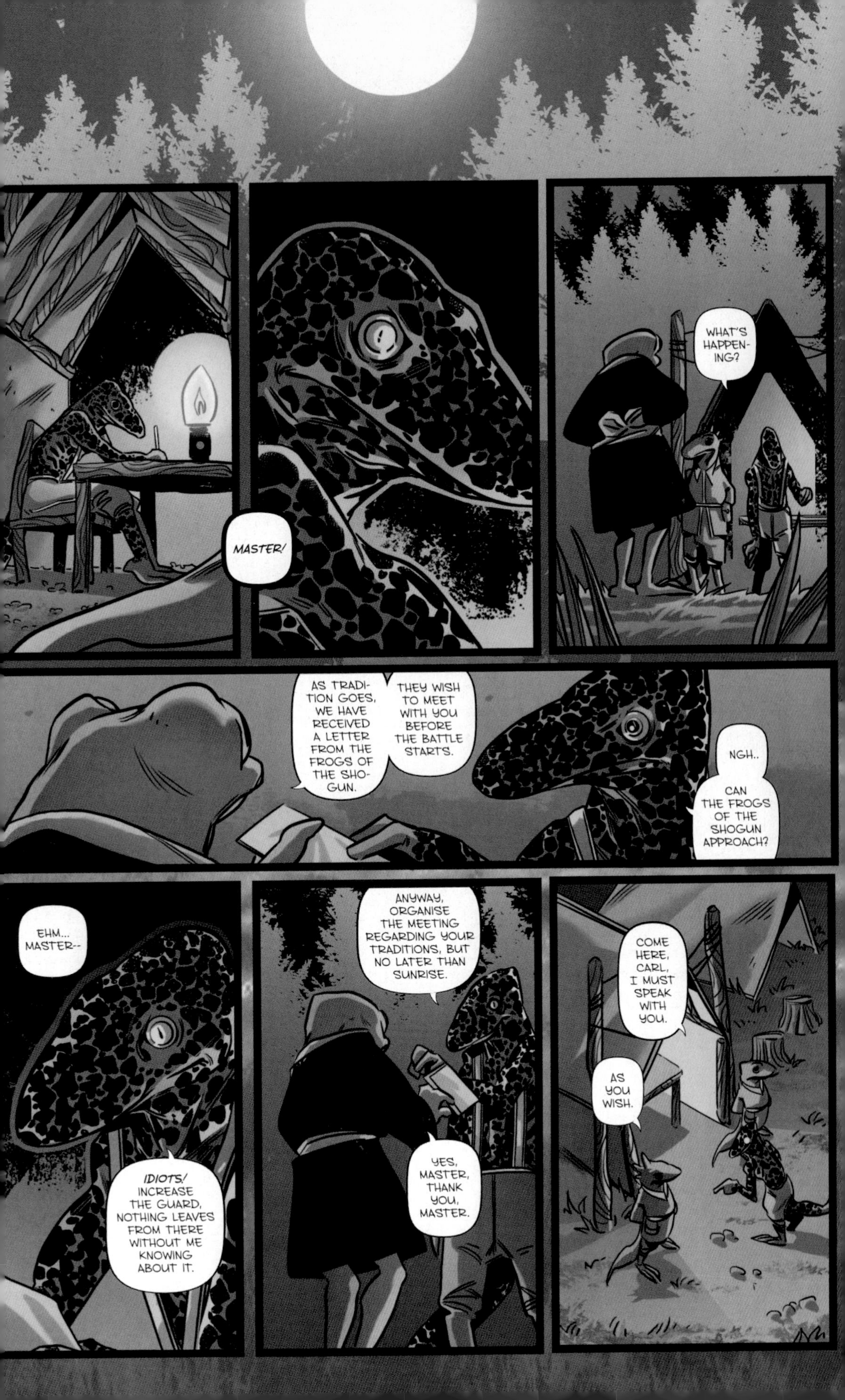
MASTER!
WHAT'S HAPPENING?
AS TRADITION GOES, WE HAVE RECEIVED A LETTER FROM THE FROGS OF THE SHOGUN.
THEY WISH TO MEET WITH YOU BEFORE THE BATTLE STARTS.
NGH..
CAN THE FROGS OF THE SHOGUN APPROACH?
EHM... MASTER--
IDIOTS! INCREASE THE GUARD, NOTHING LEAVES FROM THERE WITHOUT ME KNOWING ABOUT IT.
ANYWAY, ORGANISE THE MEETING REGARDING YOUR TRADITIONS, BUT NO LATER THAN SUNRISE.
YES, MASTER, THANK YOU, MASTER.
COME HERE, CARL, I MUST SPEAK WITH YOU.
AS YOU WISH.

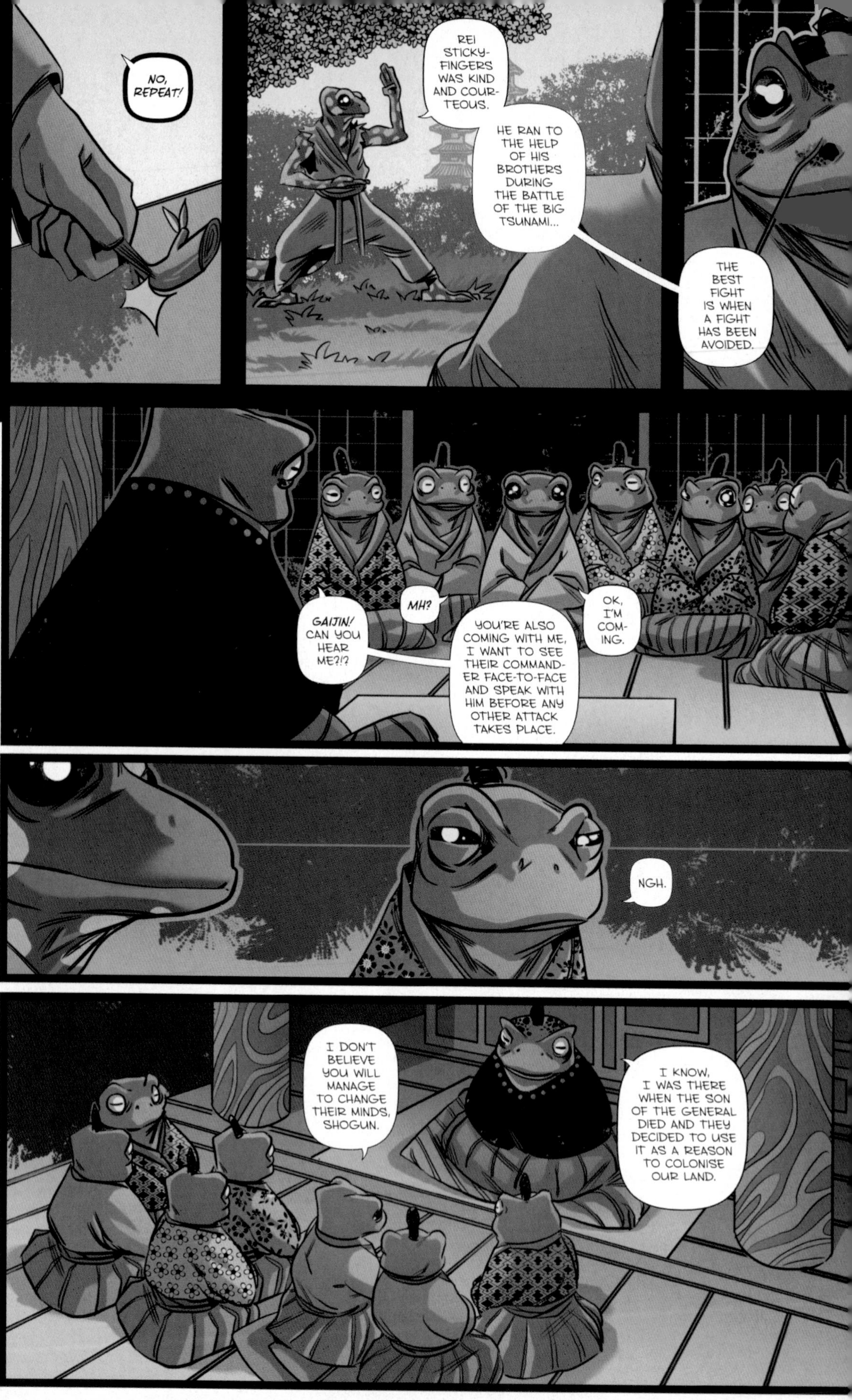
NO, REPEAT!
REI STICKY-FINGERS WAS KIND AND COURTEOUS.
HE RAN TO THE HELP OF HIS BROTHERS DURING THE BATTLE OF THE BIG TSUNAMI...
THE BEST FIGHT IS WHEN A FIGHT HAS BEEN AVOIDED.
GAIJIN! CAN YOU HEAR ME?!?
MH?
YOU'RE ALSO COMING WITH ME, I WANT TO SEE THEIR COMMANDER FACE-TO-FACE AND SPEAK WITH HIM BEFORE ANY OTHER ATTACK TAKES PLACE.
OK, I'M COMING.
NGH.
I DON'T BELIEVE YOU WILL MANAGE TO CHANGE THEIR MINDS, SHOGUN.
I KNOW, I WAS THERE WHEN THE SON OF THE GENERAL DIED AND THEY DECIDED TO USE IT AS A REASON TO COLONISE OUR LAND.

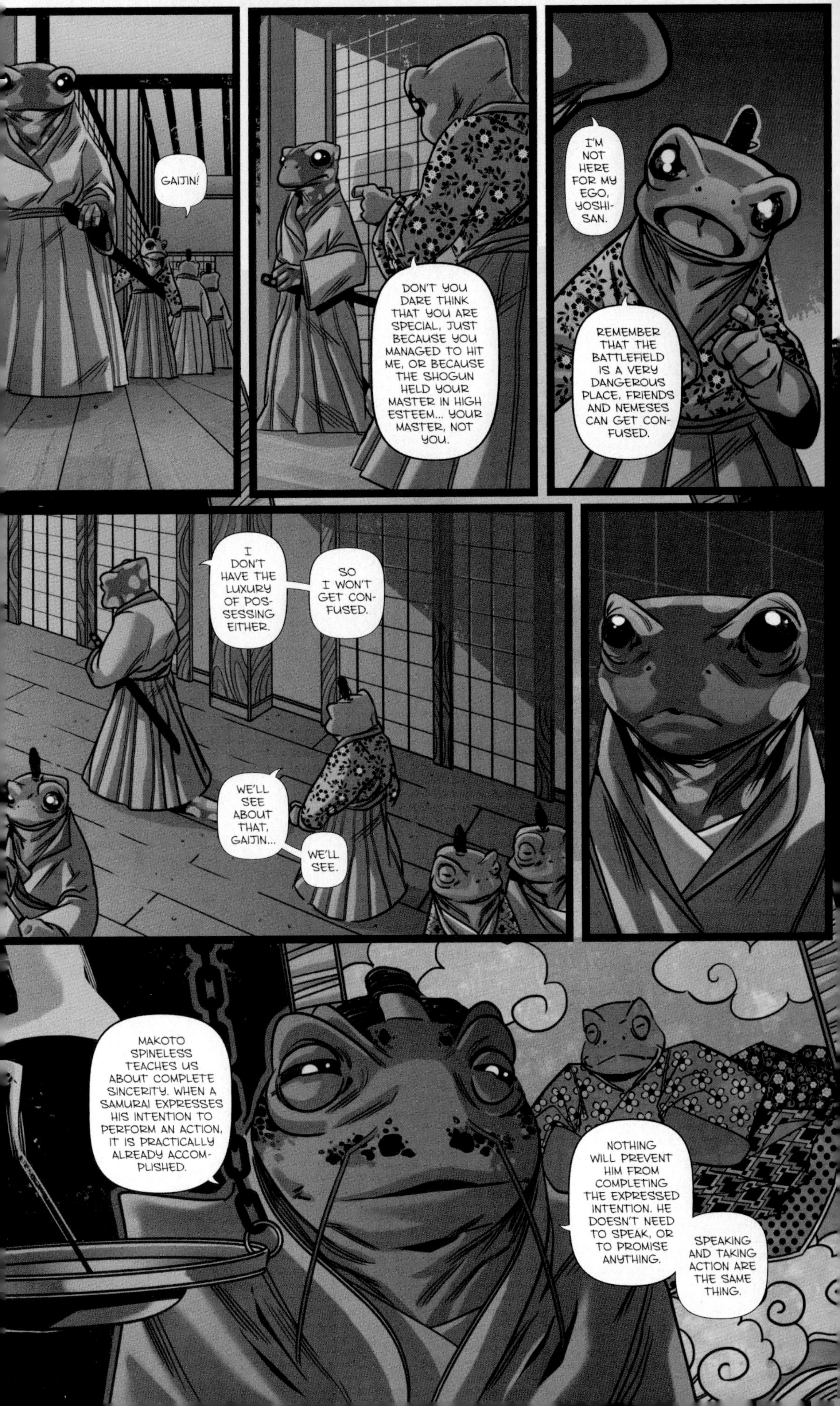
GAIJIN!
DON'T YOU DARE THINK THAT YOU ARE SPECIAL, JUST BECAUSE YOU MANAGED TO HIT ME, OR BECAUSE THE SHOGUN HELD YOUR MASTER IN HIGH ESTEEM... YOUR MASTER, NOT YOU.
I'M NOT HERE FOR MY EGO, YOSHI-SAN.
REMEMBER THAT THE BATTLEFIELD IS A VERY DANGEROUS PLACE, FRIENDS AND NEMESES CAN GET CON-FUSED.
I DON'T HAVE THE LUXURY OF POS-SESSING EITHER.
SO I WON'T GET CON-FUSED.
WE'LL SEE ABOUT THAT, GAIJIN...
WE'LL SEE.
MAKOTO SPINELESS TEACHES US ABOUT COMPLETE SINCERITY. WHEN A SAMURAI EXPRESSES HIS INTENTION TO PERFORM AN ACTION, IT IS PRACTICALLY ALREADY ACCOM-PLISHED.
NOTHING WILL PREVENT HIM FROM COMPLETING THE EXPRESSED INTENTION. HE DOESN'T NEED TO SPEAK, OR TO PROMISE ANYTHING.
SPEAKING AND TAKING ACTION ARE THE SAME THING.

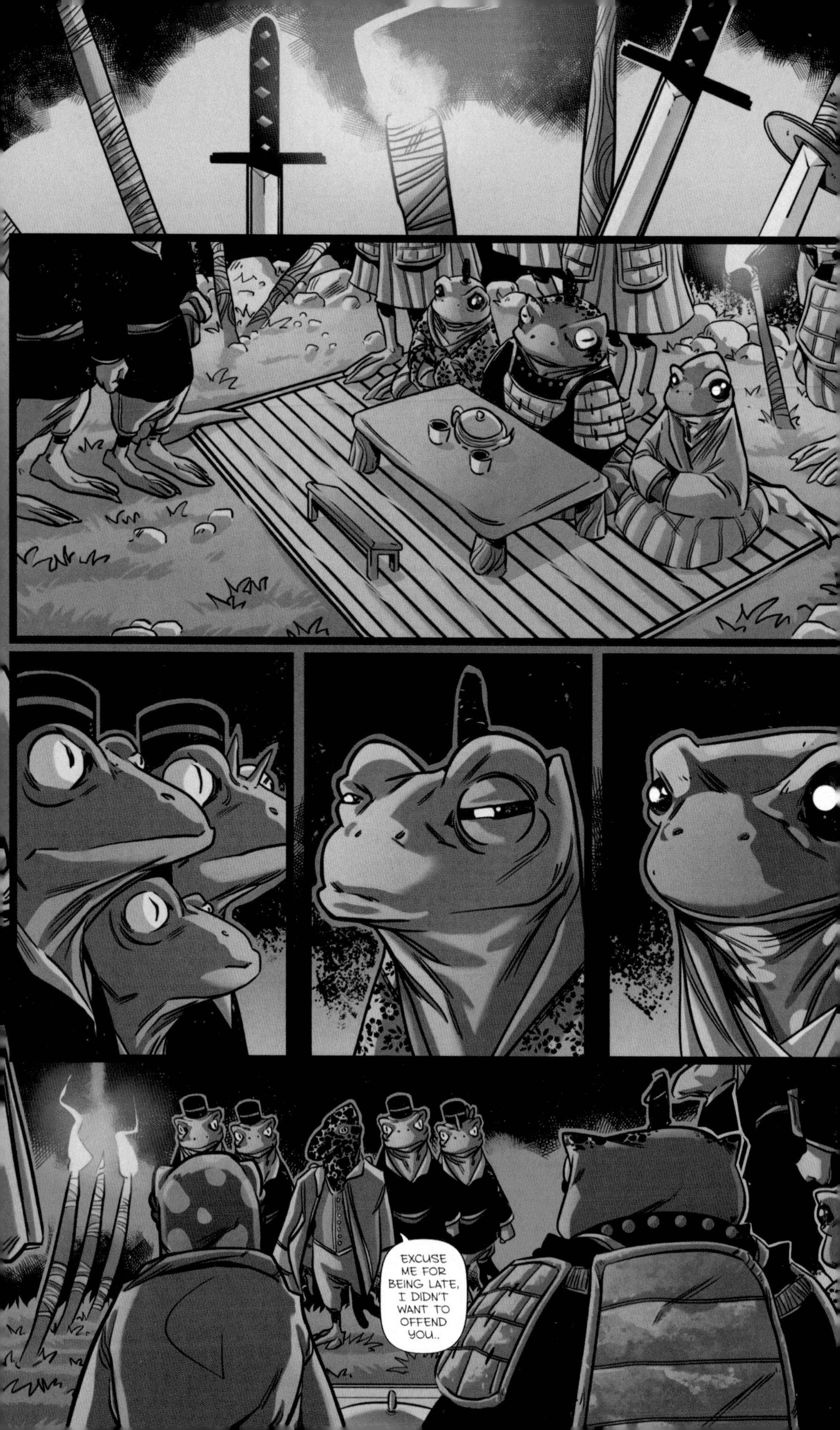
EXCUSE ME FOR BEING LATE, I DIDN'T WANT TO OFFEND YOU..

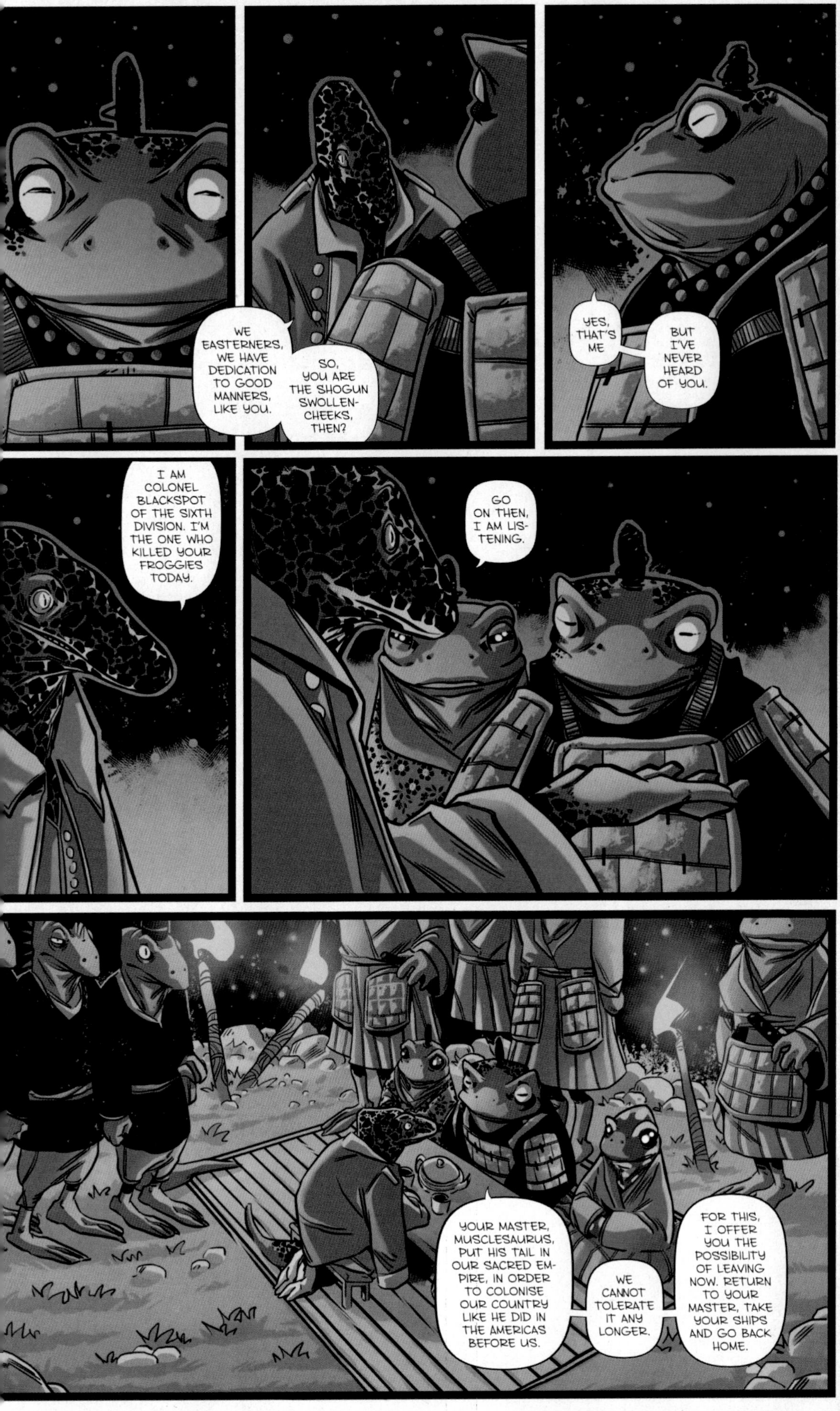

WE EASTERNERS, WE HAVE DEDICATION TO GOOD MANNERS, LIKE YOU.
SO, YOU ARE THE SHOGUN SWOLLEN-CHEEKS, THEN?
YES, THAT'S ME
BUT I'VE NEVER HEARD OF YOU.
I AM COLONEL BLACKSPOT OF THE SIXTH DIVISION. I'M THE ONE WHO KILLED YOUR FROGGIES TODAY.
GO ON THEN, I AM LISTENING.
YOUR MASTER, MUSCLESAURUS, PUT HIS TAIL IN OUR SACRED EMPIRE, IN ORDER TO COLONISE OUR COUNTRY LIKE HE DID IN THE AMERICAS BEFORE US.
WE CANNOT TOLERATE IT ANY LONGER.
FOR THIS, I OFFER YOU THE POSSIBILITY OF LEAVING NOW. RETURN TO YOUR MASTER, TAKE YOUR SHIPS AND GO BACK HOME.

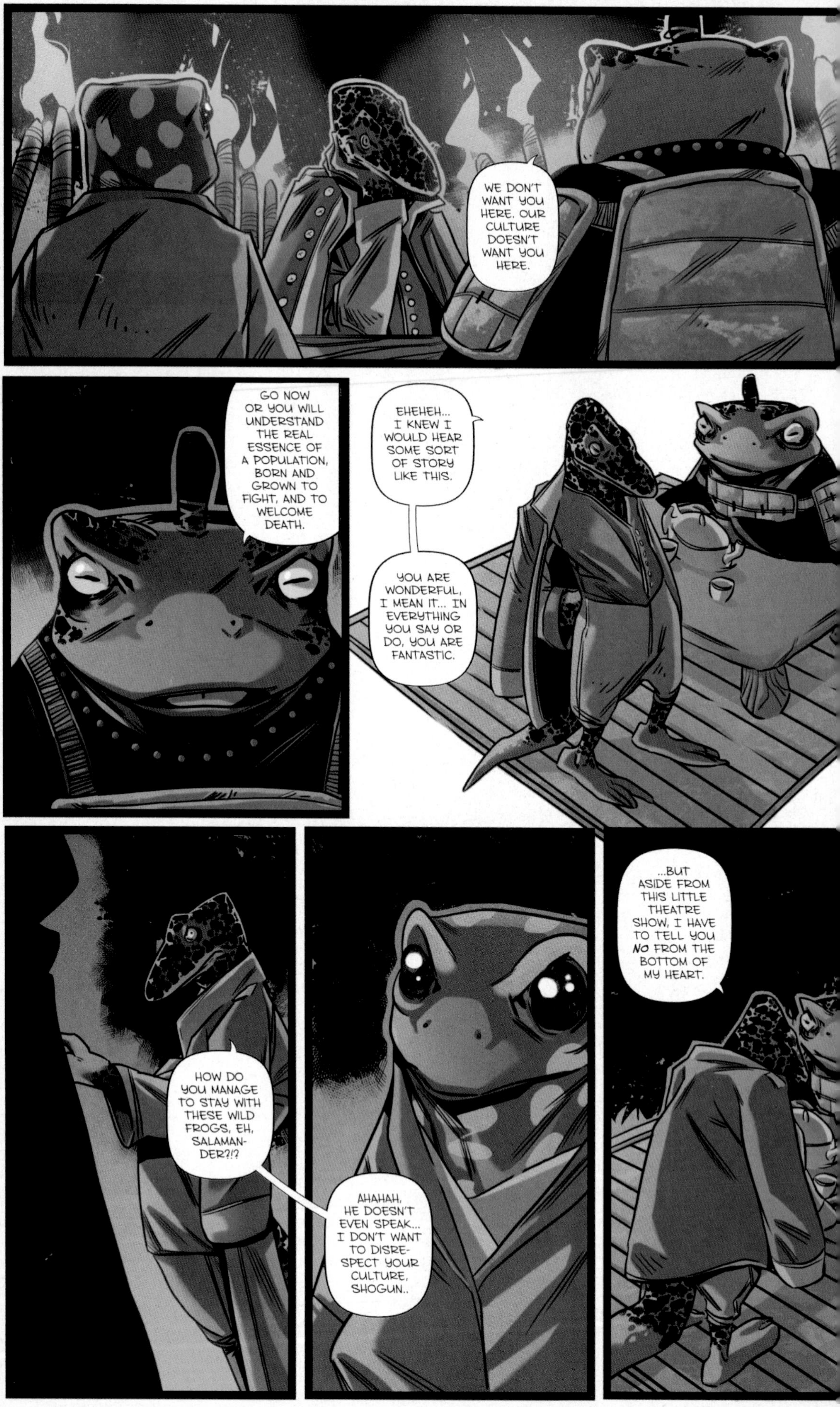
WE DON'T WANT YOU HERE. OUR CULTURE DOESN'T WANT YOU HERE.
GO NOW OR YOU WILL UNDERSTAND THE REAL ESSENCE OF A POPULATION, BORN AND GROWN TO FIGHT, AND TO WELCOME DEATH.
EHEHEH... I KNEW I WOULD HEAR SOME SORT OF STORY LIKE THIS.
YOU ARE WONDERFUL, I MEAN IT... IN EVERYTHING YOU SAY OR DO, YOU ARE FANTASTIC.
HOW DO YOU MANAGE TO STAY WITH THESE WILD FROGS, EH, SALAMANDER?!?
AHAHAH, HE DOESN'T EVEN SPEAK... I DON'T WANT TO DISRESPECT YOUR CULTURE, SHOGUN..
...BUT ASIDE FROM THIS LITTLE THEATRE SHOW, I HAVE TO TELL YOU NO FROM THE BOTTOM OF MY HEART.

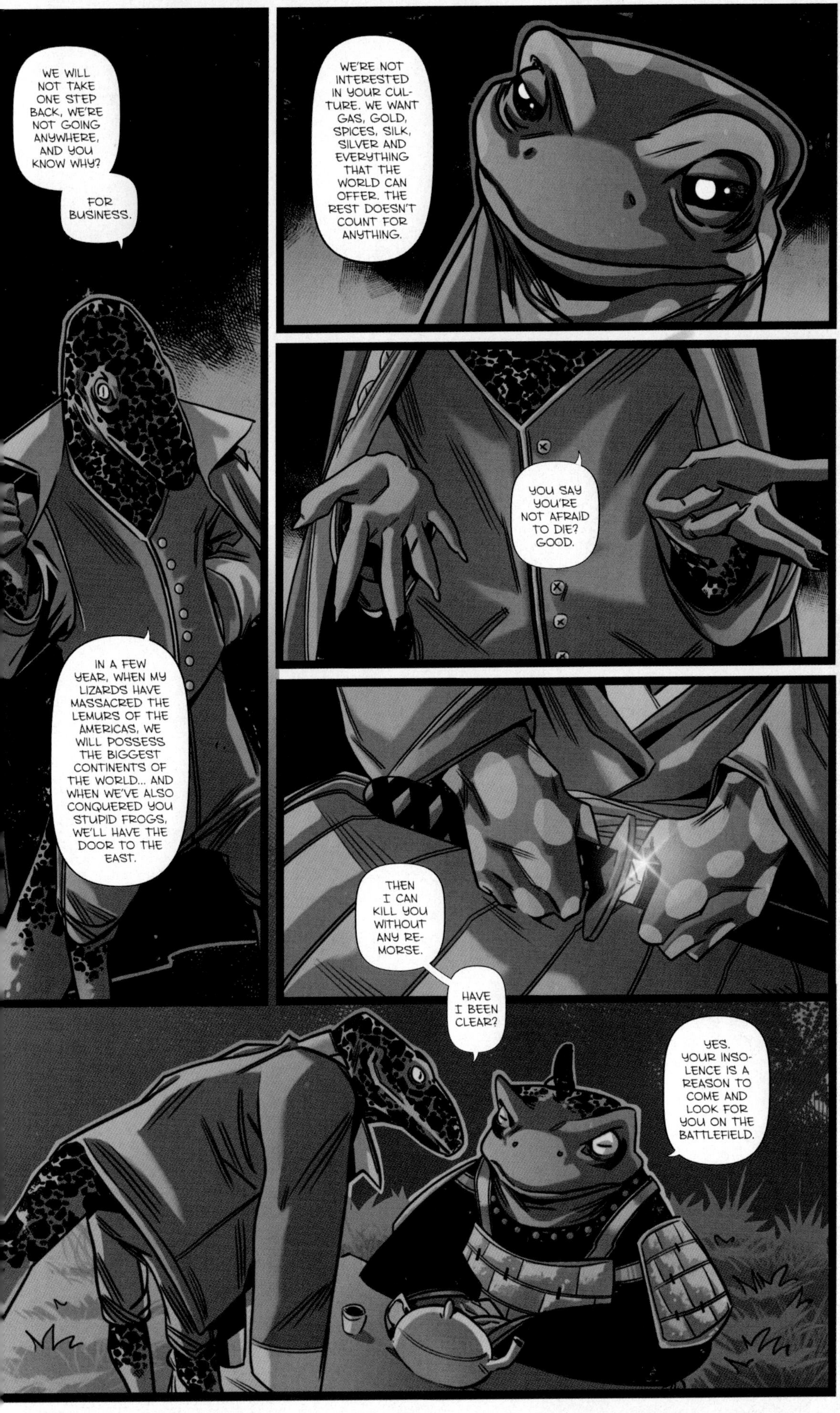

WE WILL NOT TAKE ONE STEP BACK, WE'RE NOT GOING ANYWHERE, AND YOU KNOW WHY?
FOR BUSINESS.
WE'RE NOT INTERESTED IN YOUR CUL-TURE. WE WANT GAS, GOLD, SPICES, SILK, SILVER AND EVERYTHING THAT THE WORLD CAN OFFER. THE REST DOESN'T COUNT FOR ANYTHING.
IN A FEW YEAR, WHEN MY LIZARDS HAVE MASSACRED THE LEMURS OF THE AMERICAS, WE WILL POSSESS THE BIGGEST CONTINENTS OF THE WORLD... AND WHEN WE'VE ALSO CONQUERED YOU STUPID FROGS, WE'LL HAVE THE DOOR TO THE EAST.
YOU SAY YOU'RE NOT AFRAID TO DIE? GOOD.
THEN I CAN KILL YOU WITHOUT ANY RE-MORSE.
HAVE I BEEN CLEAR?
YES. YOUR INSO-LENCE IS A REASON TO COME AND LOOK FOR YOU ON THE BATTLEFIELD.

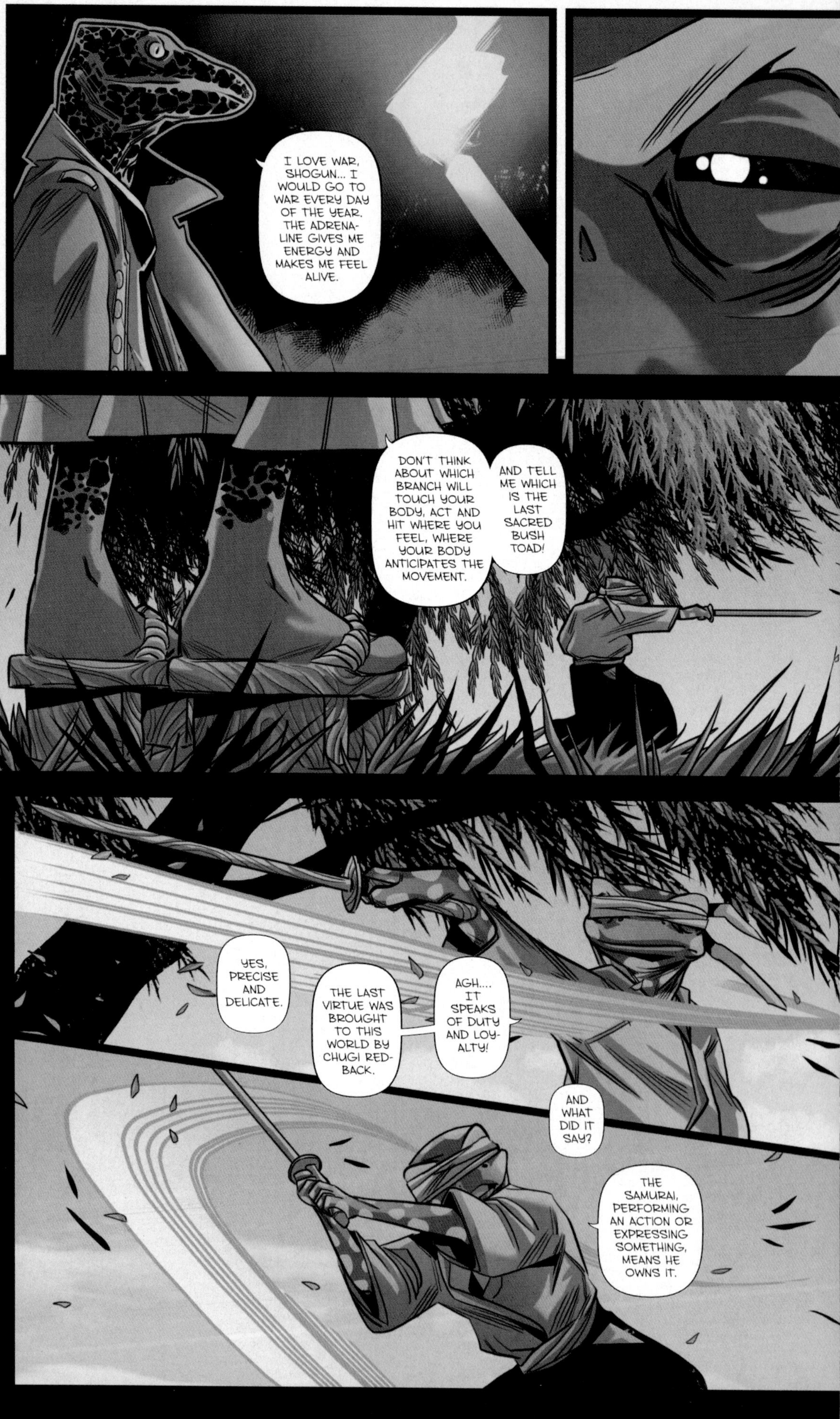
I LOVE WAR, SHOGUN... I WOULD GO TO WAR EVERY DAY OF THE YEAR. THE ADRENALINE GIVES ME ENERGY AND MAKES ME FEEL ALIVE.
DON'T THINK ABOUT WHICH BRANCH WILL TOUCH YOUR BODY, ACT AND HIT WHERE YOU FEEL, WHERE YOUR BODY ANTICIPATES THE MOVEMENT.
AND TELL ME WHICH IS THE LAST SACRED BUSH TOAD!
YES, PRECISE AND DELICATE.
THE LAST VIRTUE WAS BROUGHT TO THIS WORLD BY CHUGI REDBACK.
AGH.... IT SPEAKS OF DUTY AND LOYALTY!
AND WHAT DID IT SAY?
THE SAMURAI, PERFORMING AN ACTION OR EXPRESSING SOMETHING, MEANS HE OWNS IT.

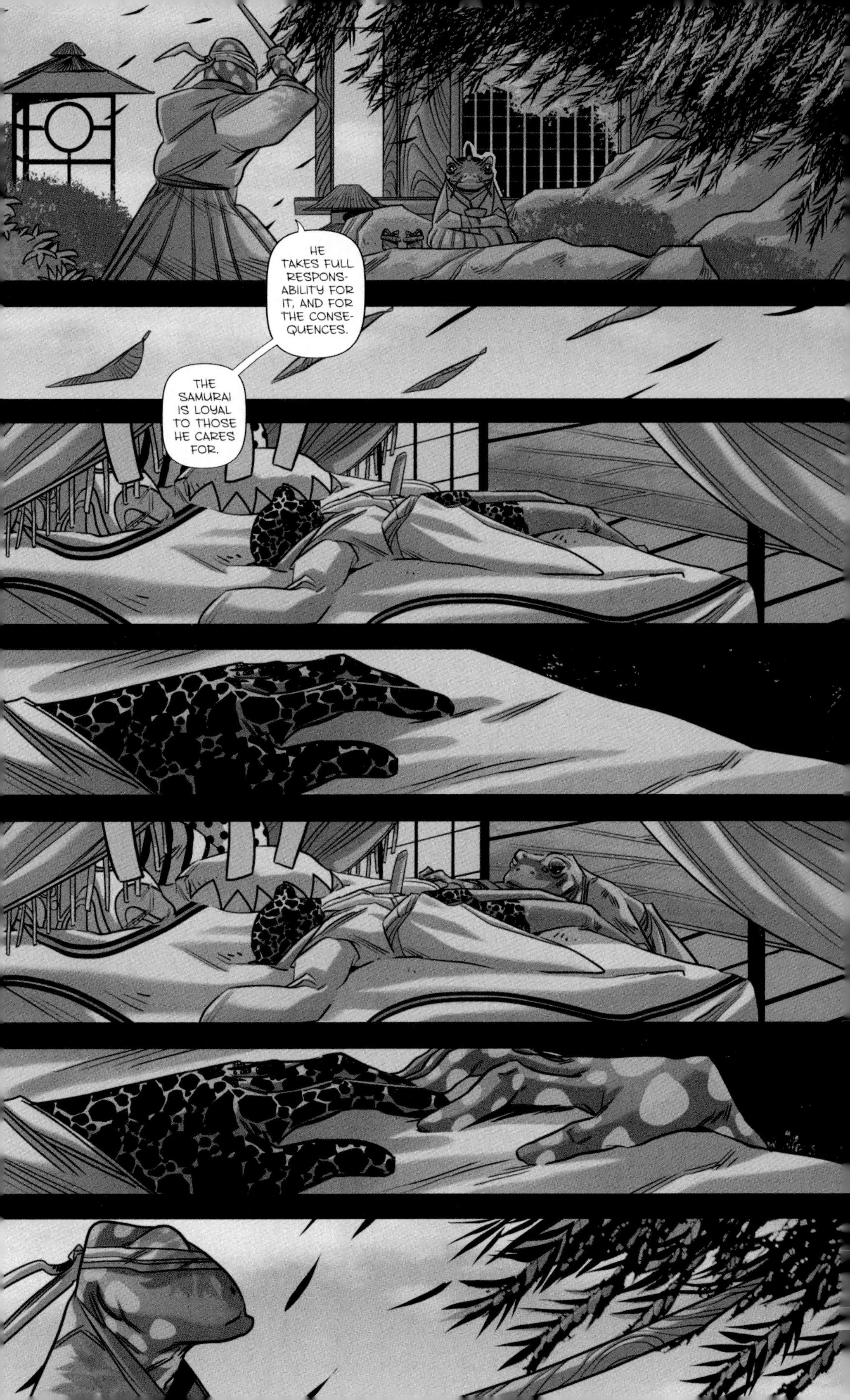
HE TAKES FULL RESPONS-ABILITY FOR IT, AND FOR THE CONSE-QUENCES.
THE SAMURAI IS LOYAL TO THOSE HE CARES FOR.

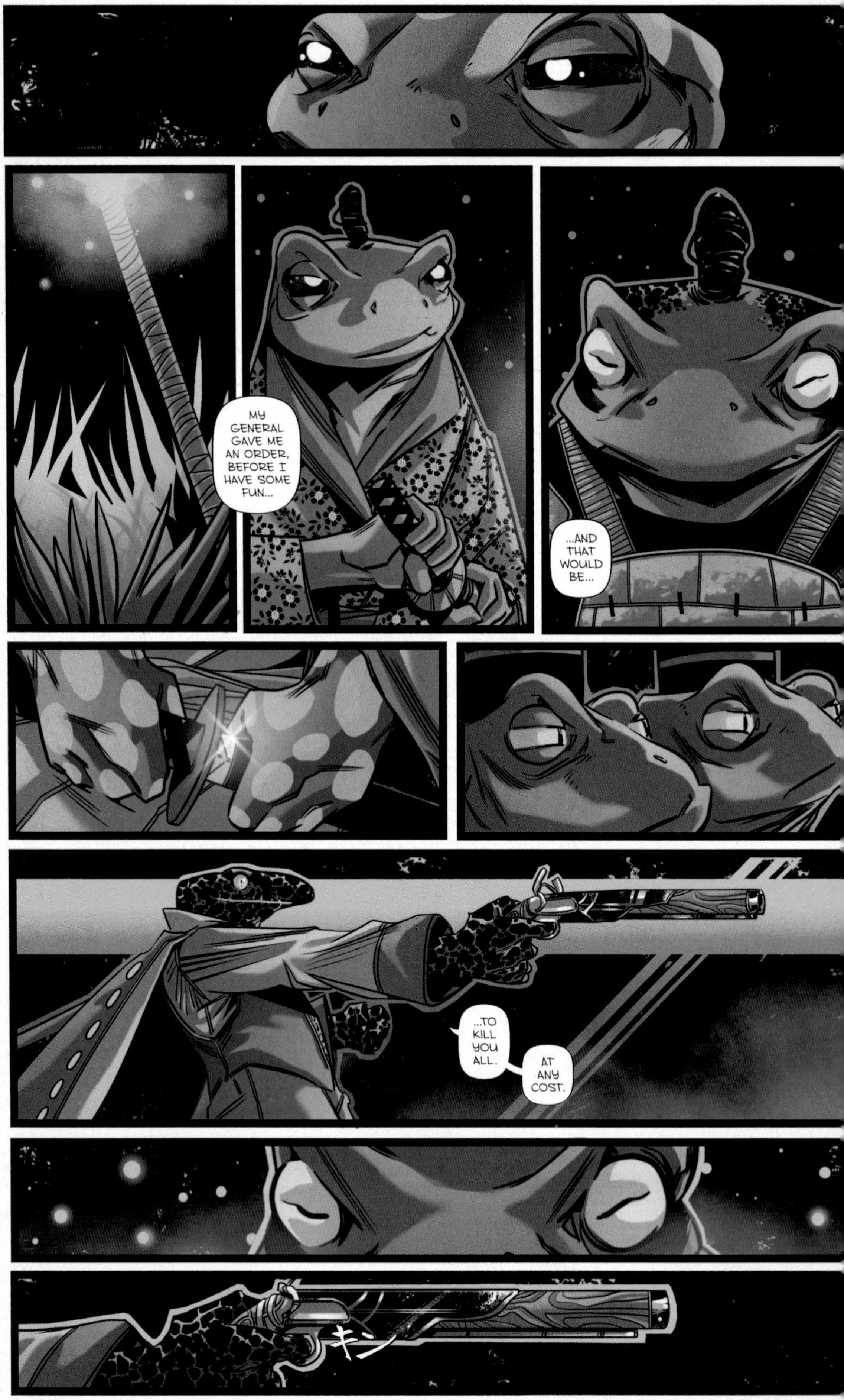
MY GENERAL GAVE ME AN ORDER, BEFORE I HAVE SOME FUN...
...AND THAT WOULD BE...
...TO KILL YOU ALL.
AT ANY COST.
キン

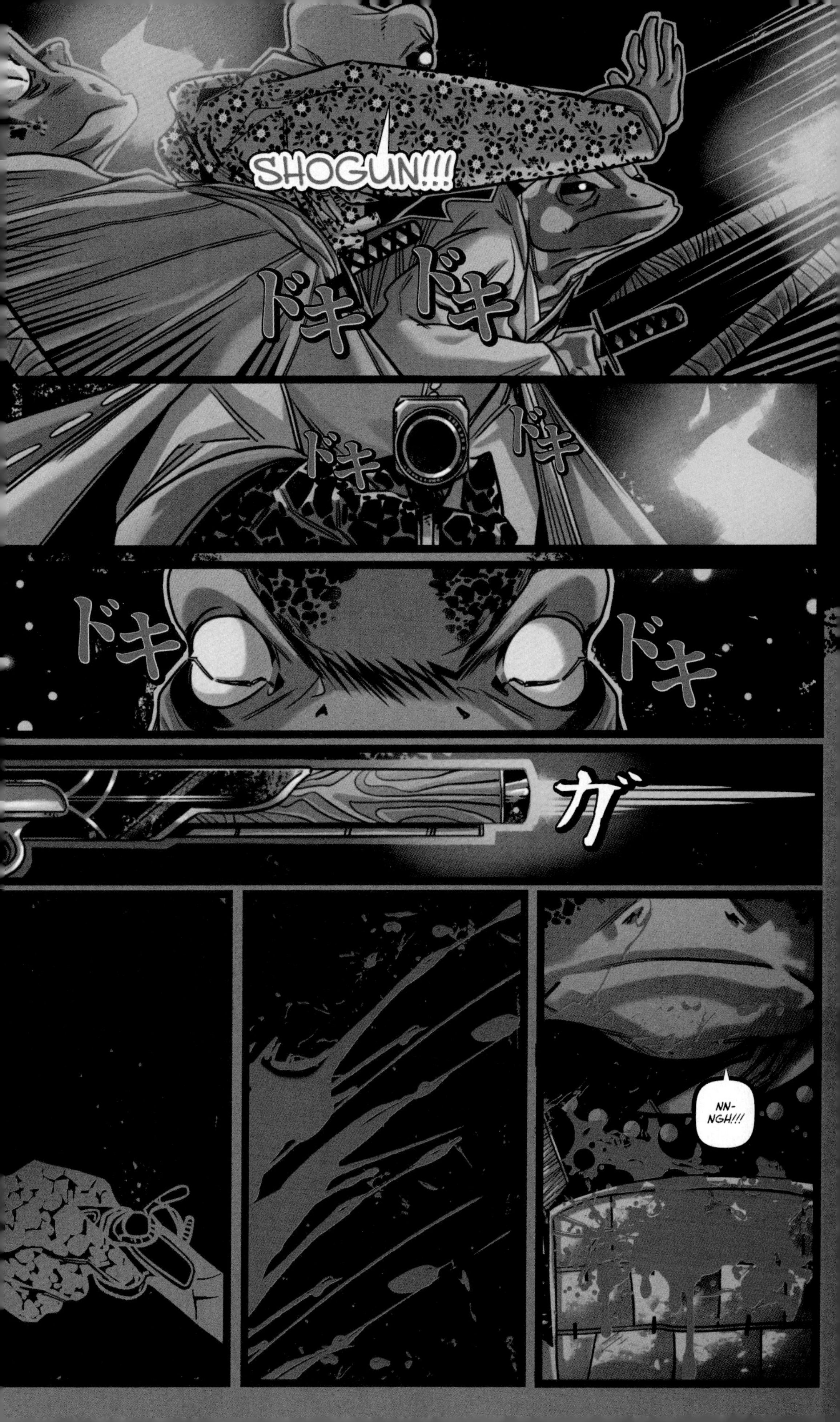
SHOGUN!!!
ドキ ドキ
ドキ ドキ
ドキ ドキ
ガ
NN-NGH!!!

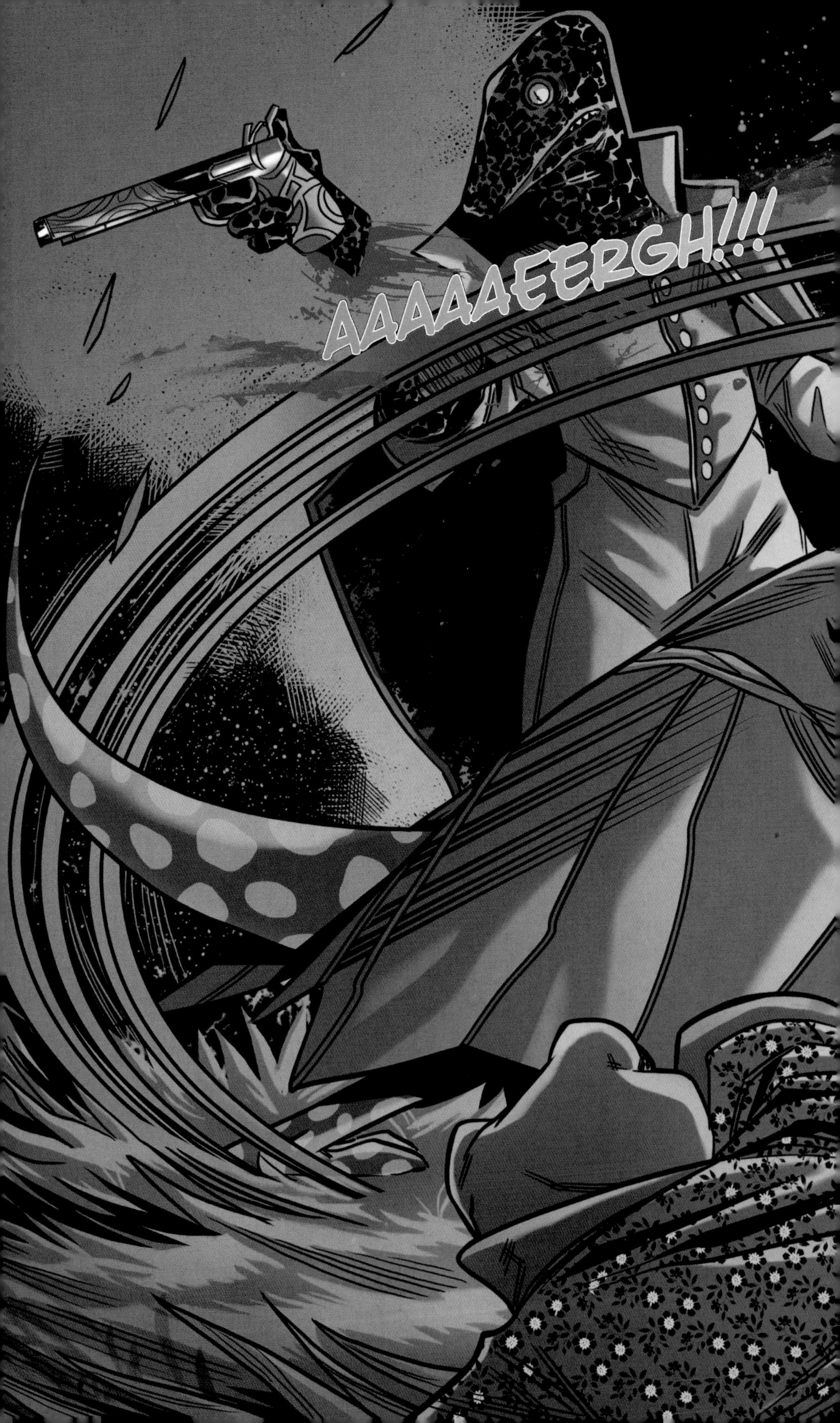
AAAAAEERGH!!!

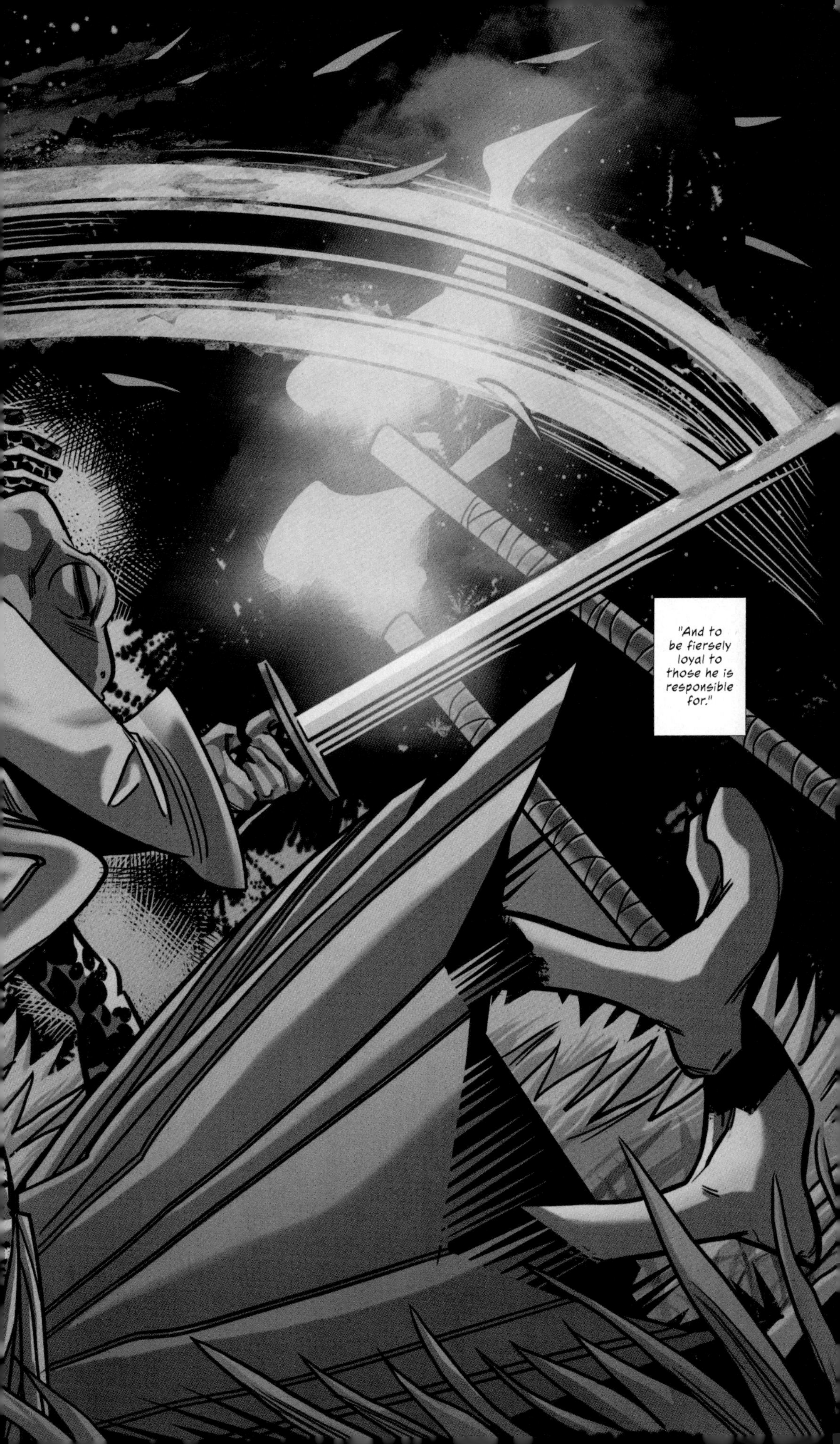
"And to be fiersely loyal to those he is responsible for."

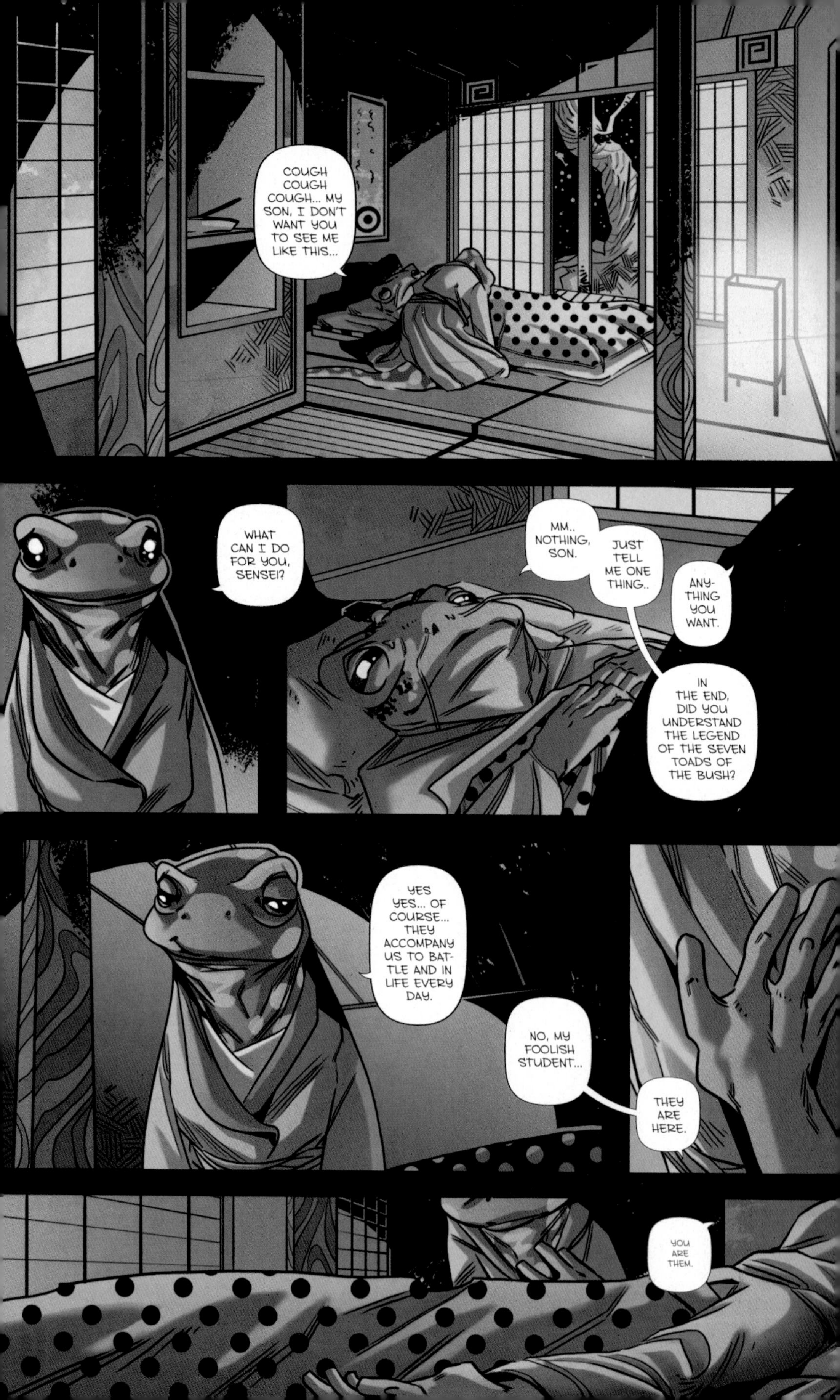
COUGH COUGH COUGH... MY SON, I DON'T WANT YOU TO SEE ME LIKE THIS...
WHAT CAN I DO FOR YOU, SENSEI?
MM.. NOTHING, SON.
JUST TELL ME ONE THING..
ANY-THING YOU WANT.
IN THE END, DID YOU UNDERSTAND THE LEGEND OF THE SEVEN TOADS OF THE BUSH?
YES YES... OF COURSE... THEY ACCOMPANY US TO BAT-TLE AND IN LIFE EVERY DAY.
NO, MY FOOLISH STUDENT...
THEY ARE HERE.
YOU ARE THEM.

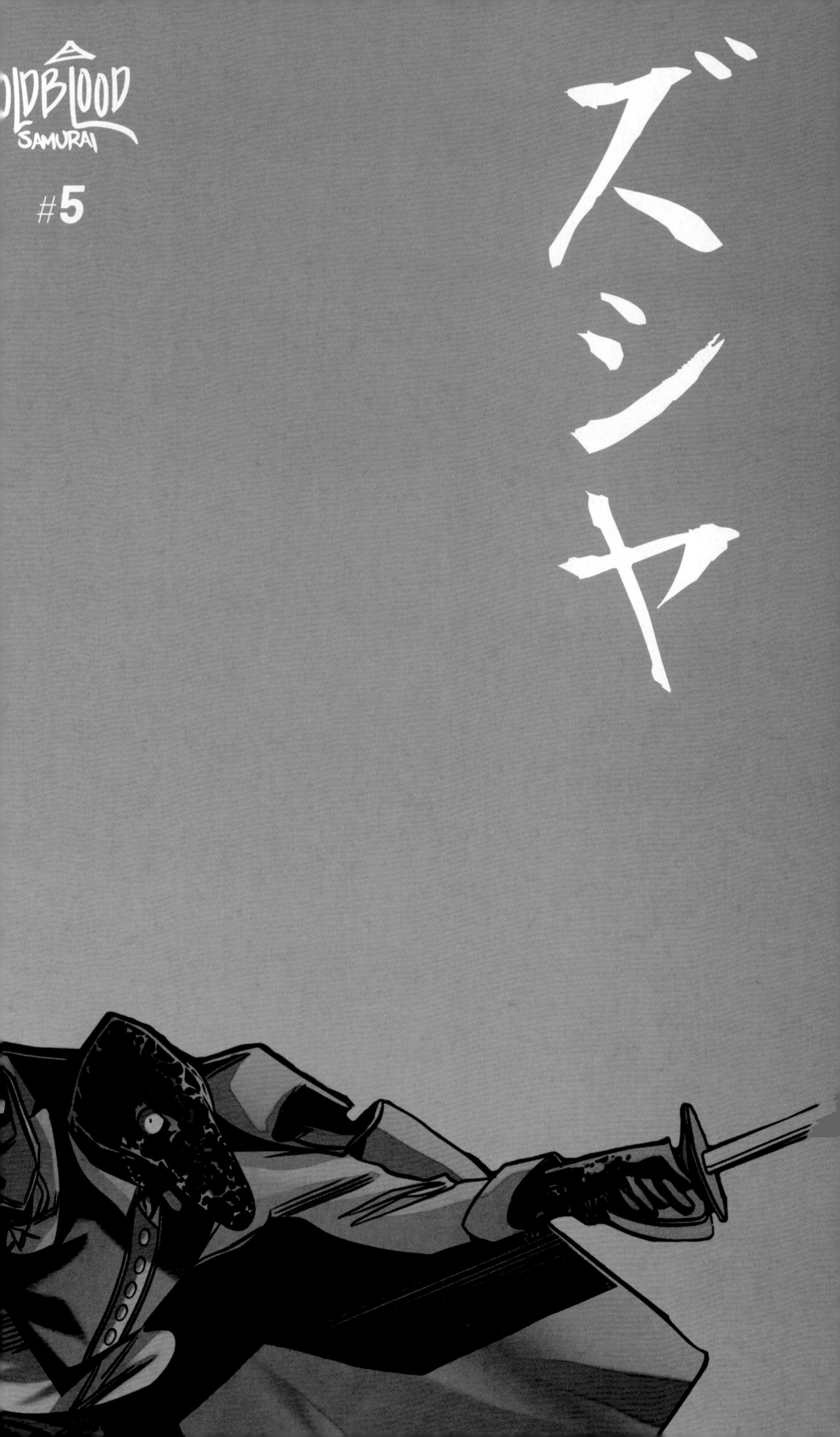
COLDBLOOD SAMURAI
#5
ズシャ

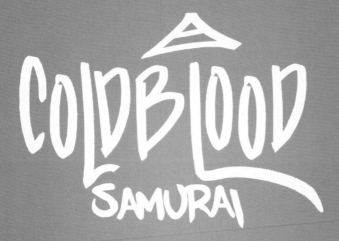

CREDITS

Story
MASSIMO ROSI

Pencils
LUDOVICA CEREGATTI

Colors
RENATO STEVANATO

Lettering
MATTIA GENTILI

Bryan Seaton: Publisher/ CEO
Shawn Gabborin: Editor In Chief
Jason Martin: Publisher-Danger Zone
Nicole D'Andria: Marketing Director/Editor
Jessica Lowrie: Social Media Czar
Danielle Davison: Executive Administrator
Chad Cicconi: King Lizard
Shawn Pryor: President of Creator Relations

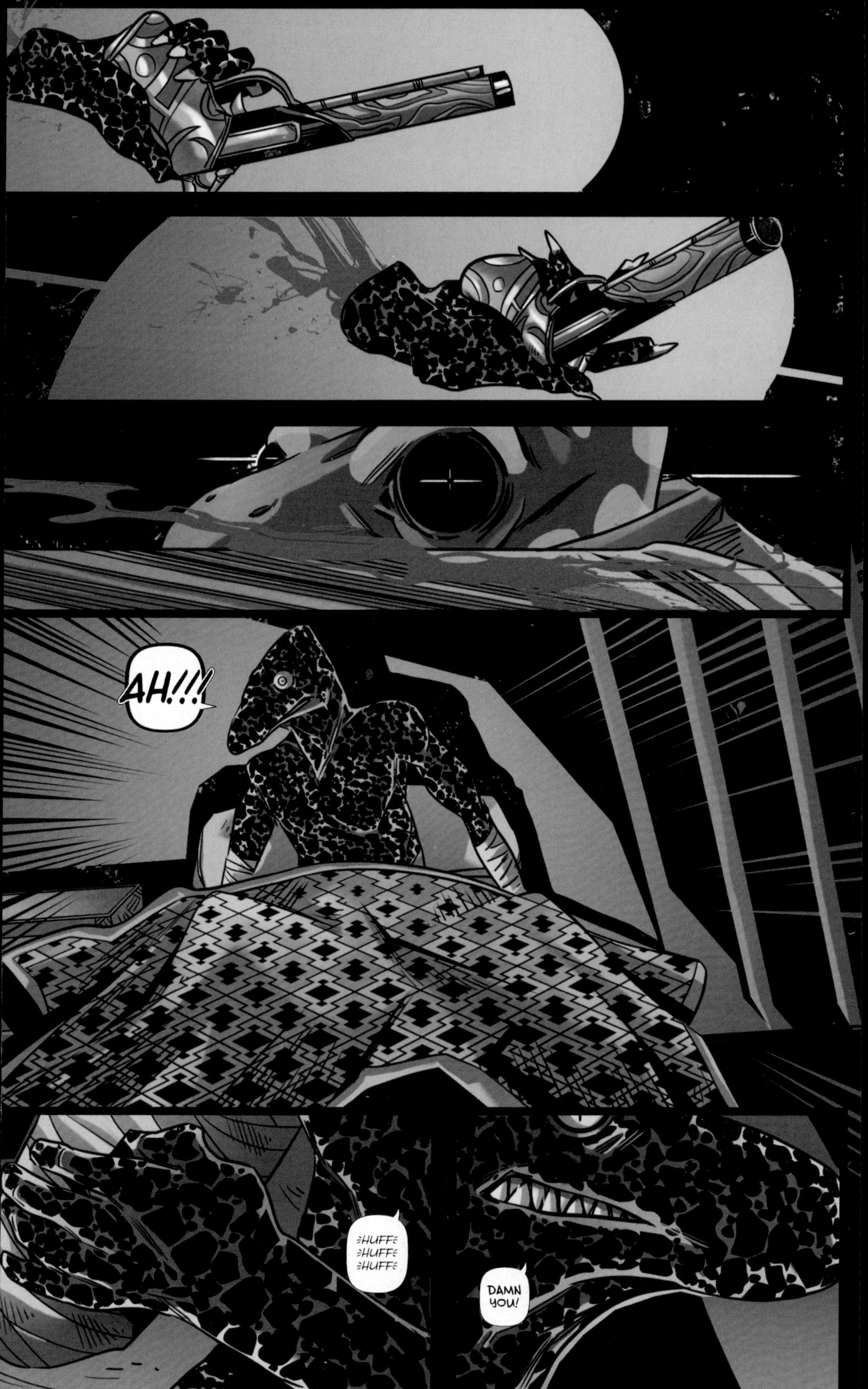
AH!!!
HUFF HUFF HUFF
DAMN YOU!

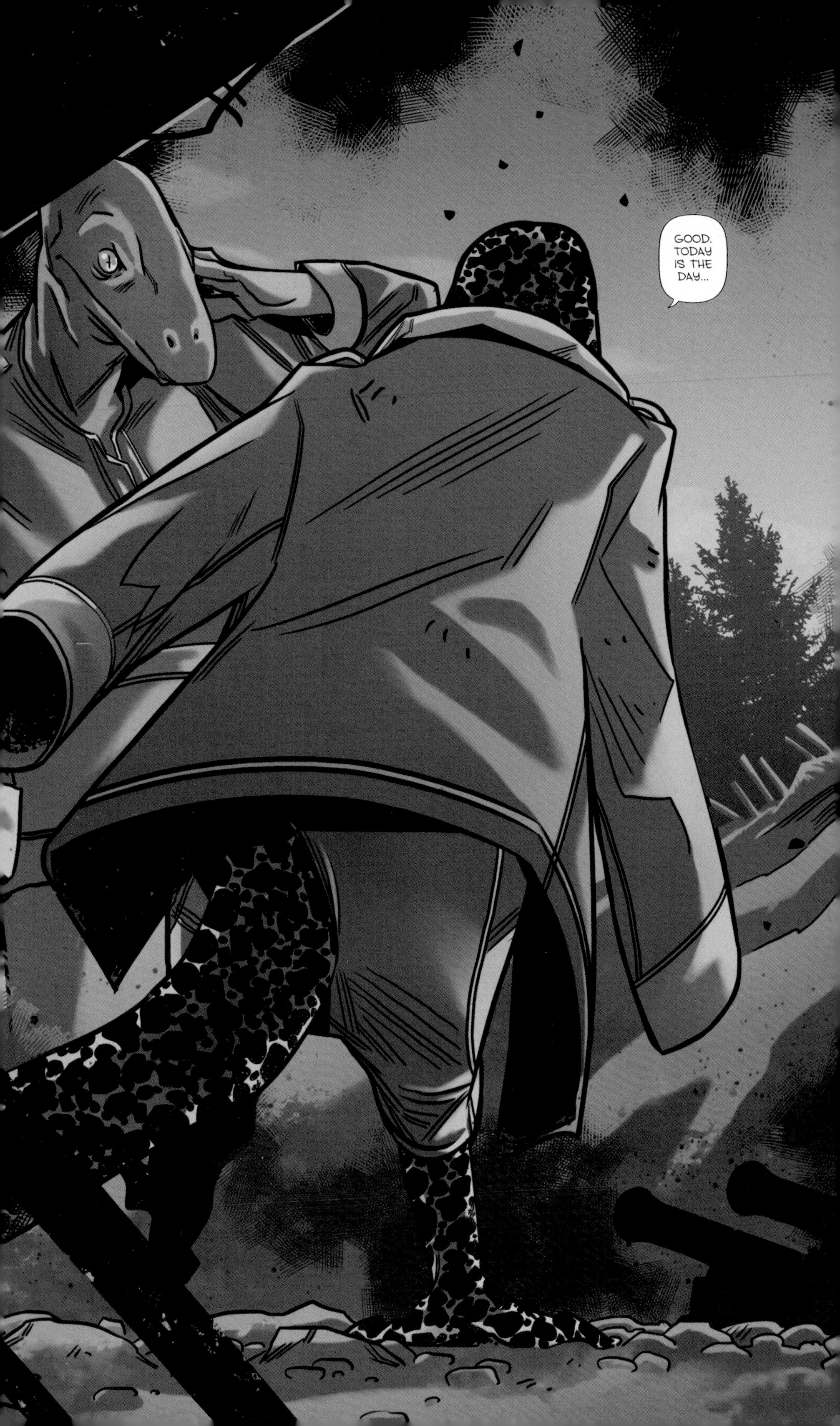
GOOD. TODAY IS THE DAY...

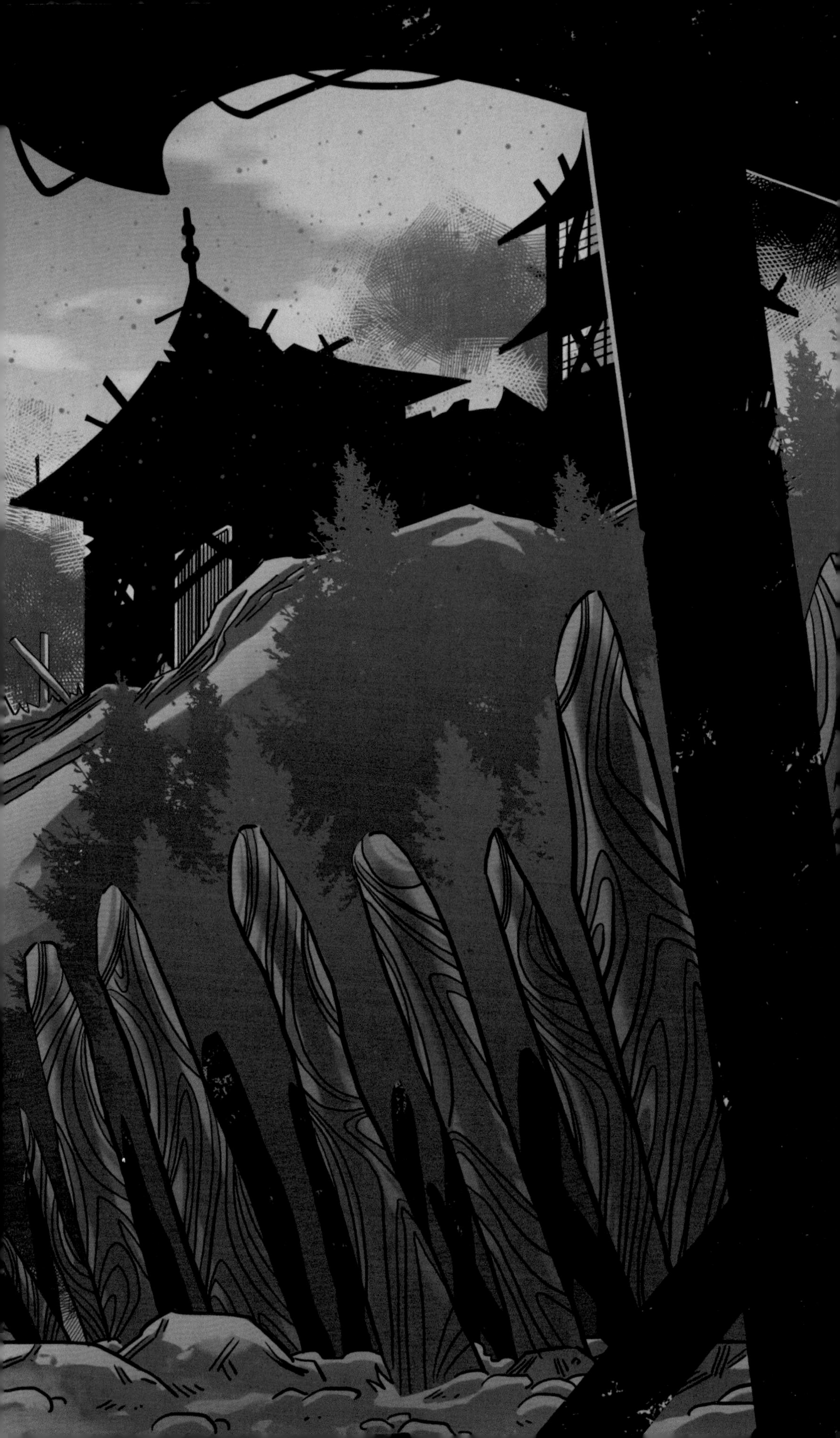

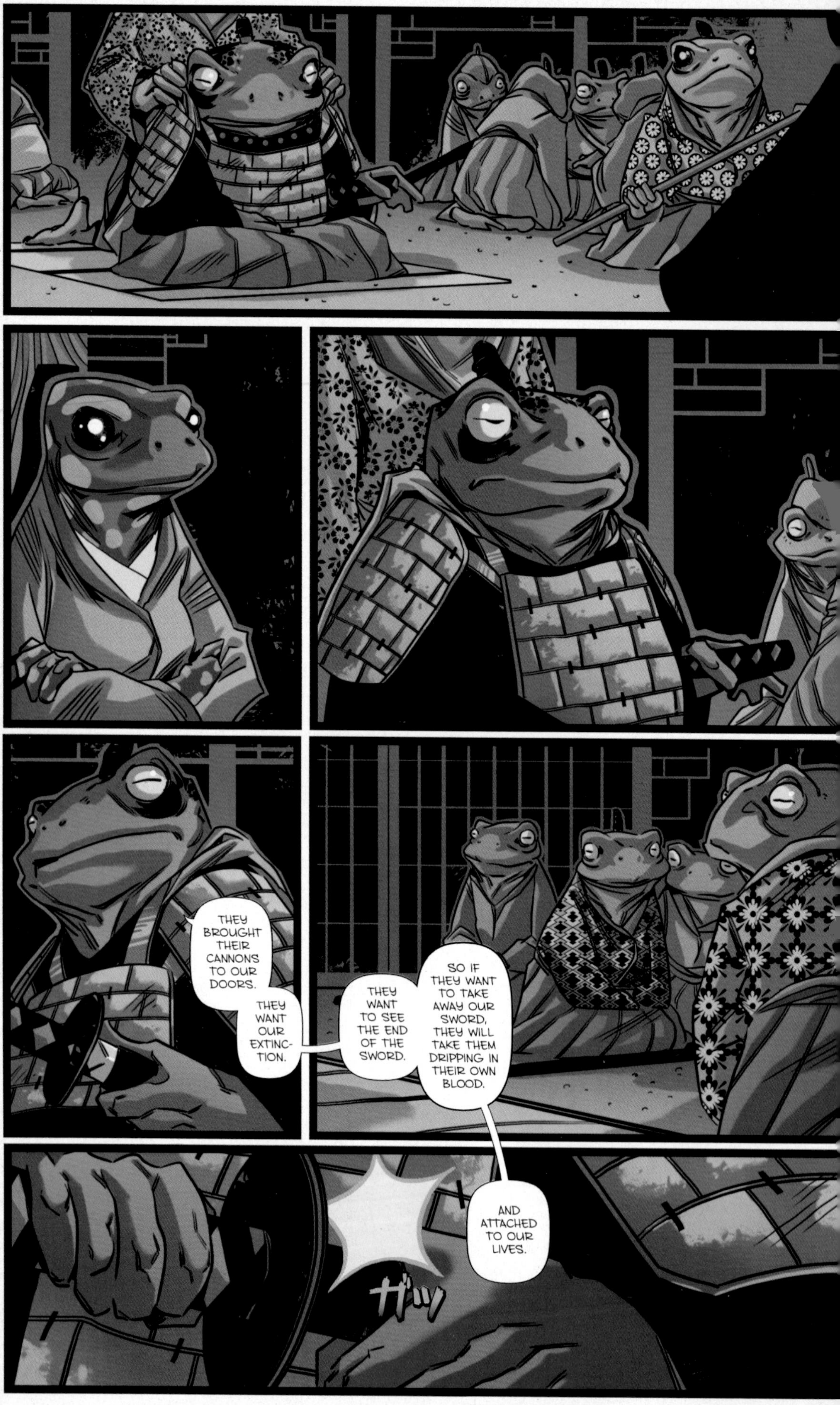

THEY BROUGHT THEIR CANNONS TO OUR DOORS.
THEY WANT OUR EXTINC-TION.
THEY WANT TO SEE THE END OF THE SWORD.
SO IF THEY WANT TO TAKE AWAY OUR SWORD, THEY WILL TAKE THEM DRIPPING IN THEIR OWN BLOOD.
AND ATTACHED TO OUR LIVES.
ガッ

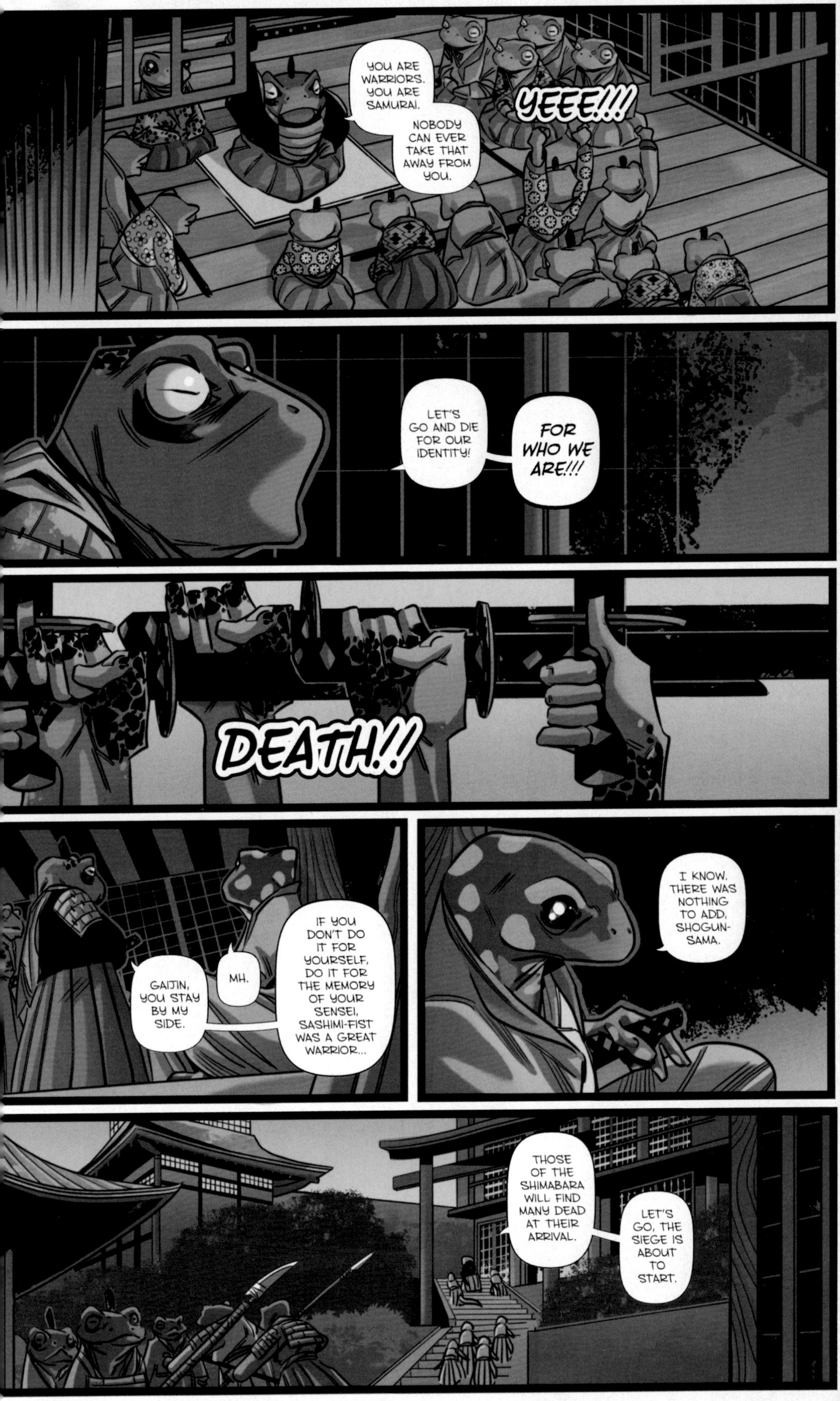
YOU ARE WARRIORS. YOU ARE SAMURAI.
NOBODY CAN EVER TAKE THAT AWAY FROM YOU.
YEEE!!!
LET'S GO AND DIE FOR OUR IDENTITY!
FOR WHO WE ARE!!!
DEATH!!
GAIJIN, YOU STAY BY MY SIDE.
MH.
IF YOU DON'T DO IT FOR YOURSELF, DO IT FOR THE MEMORY OF YOUR SENSEI. SASHIMI-FIST WAS A GREAT WARRIOR...
I KNOW. THERE WAS NOTHING TO ADD, SHOGUN-SAMA.
THOSE OF THE SHIMABARA WILL FIND MANY DEAD AT THEIR ARRIVAL.
LET'S GO, THE SIEGE IS ABOUT TO START.

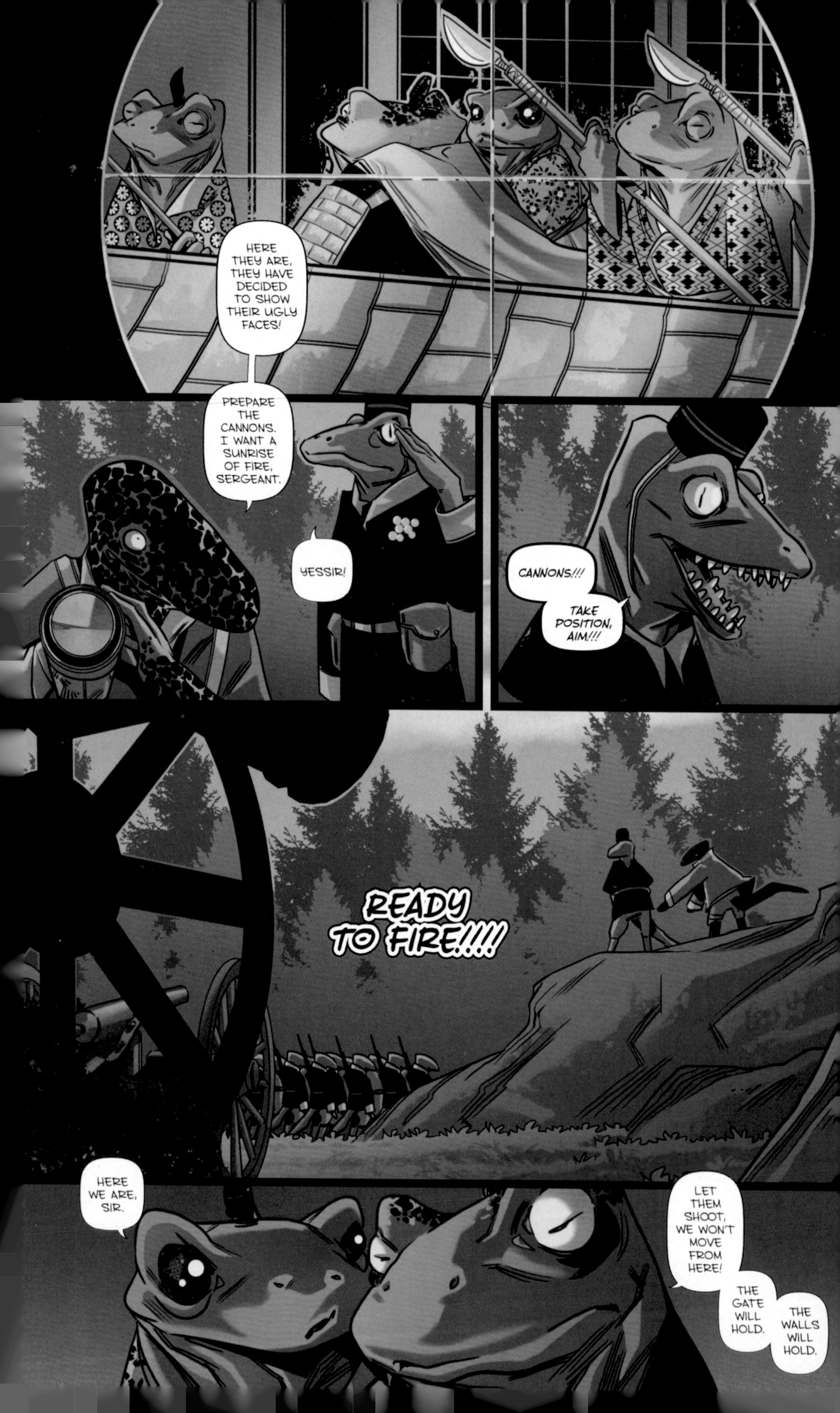
HERE THEY ARE, THEY HAVE DECIDED TO SHOW THEIR UGLY FACES!
PREPARE THE CANNONS. I WANT A SUNRISE OF FIRE, SERGEANT.
YESSIR!
CANNONS!!!
TAKE POSITION, AIM!!!
READY TO FIRE!!!!
HERE WE ARE, SIR.
LET THEM SHOOT, WE WON'T MOVE FROM HERE!
THE GATE WILL HOLD.
THE WALLS WILL HOLD.

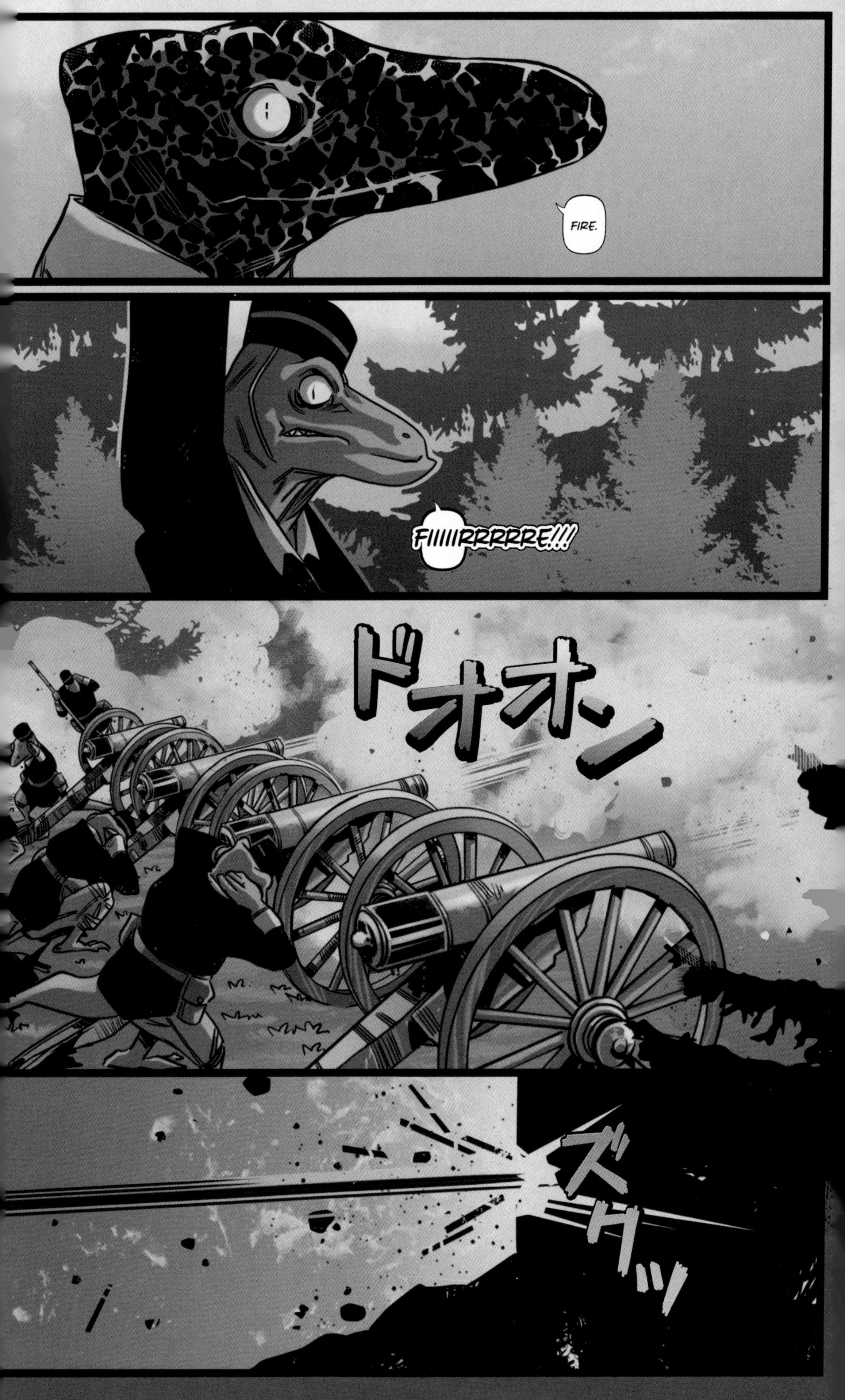
FIRE.
FIIIIIRRRRRRE!!!
ドオオン
ズガッ

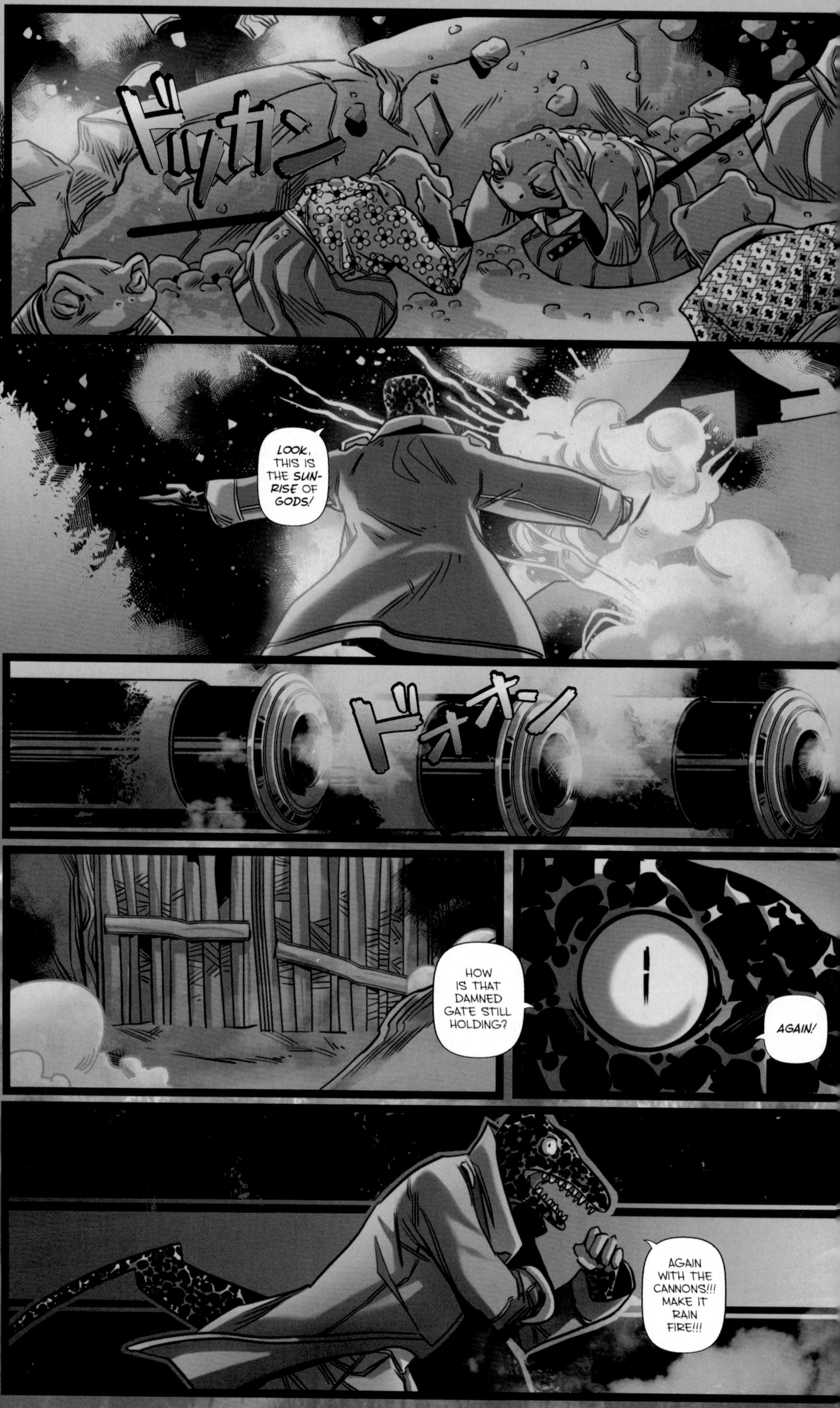
ドッカン
LOOK, THIS IS THE SUNRISE OF GODS!
ドォォーン
HOW IS THAT DAMNED GATE STILL HOLDING?
AGAIN!
AGAIN WITH THE CANNONS!!! MAKE IT RAIN FIRE!!!

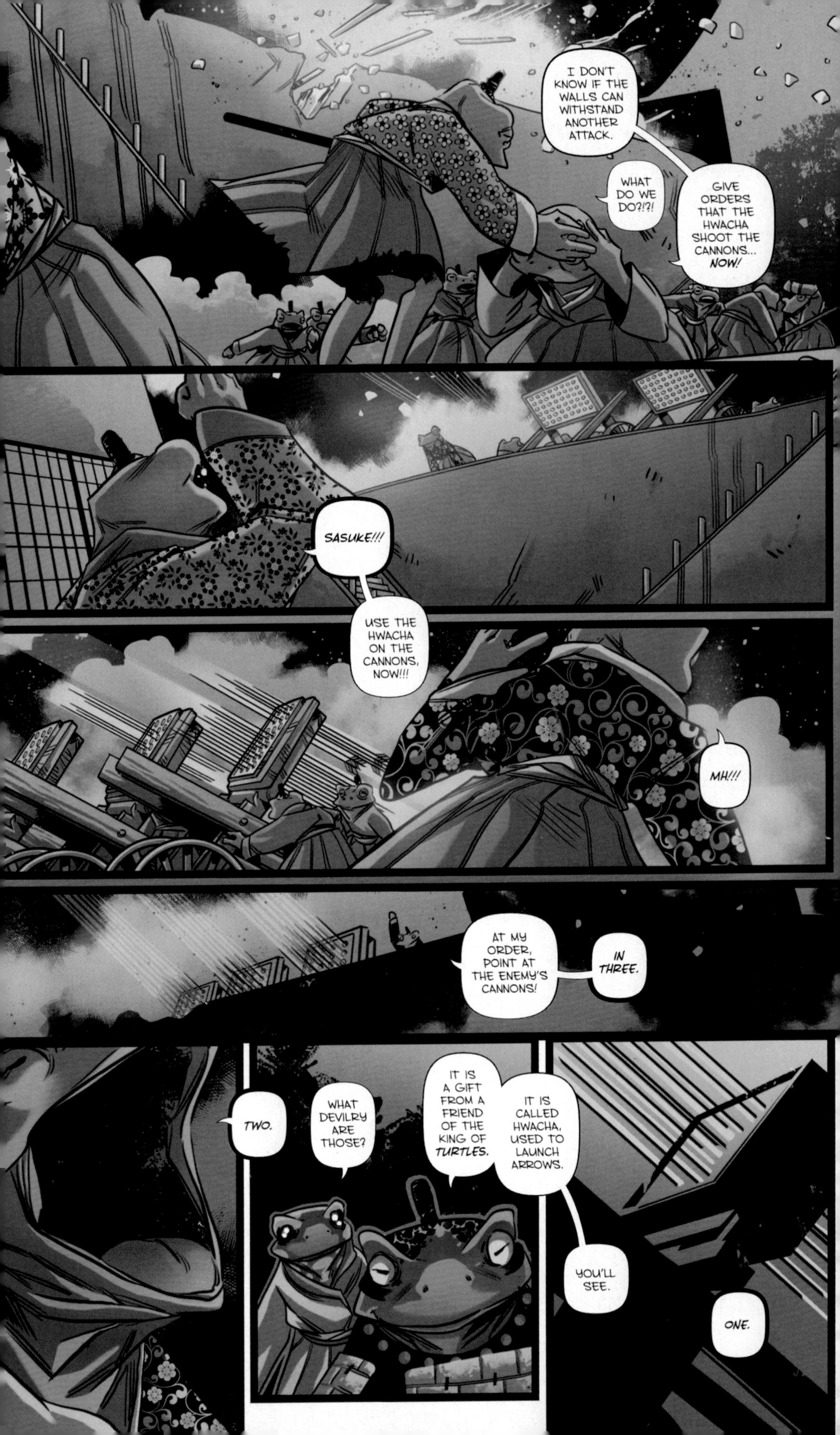
I DON'T KNOW IF THE WALLS CAN WITHSTAND ANOTHER ATTACK.
WHAT DO WE DO?!?!
GIVE ORDERS THAT THE HWACHA SHOOT THE CANNONS... NOW!
SASUKE!!!
USE THE HWACHA ON THE CANNONS, NOW!!!
MH!!!
AT MY ORDER, POINT AT THE ENEMY'S CANNONS!
IN THREE.
TWO.
WHAT DEVILRY ARE THOSE?
IT IS A GIFT FROM A FRIEND OF THE KING OF TURTLES.
IT IS CALLED HWACHA, USED TO LAUNCH ARROWS.
YOU'LL SEE.
ONE.

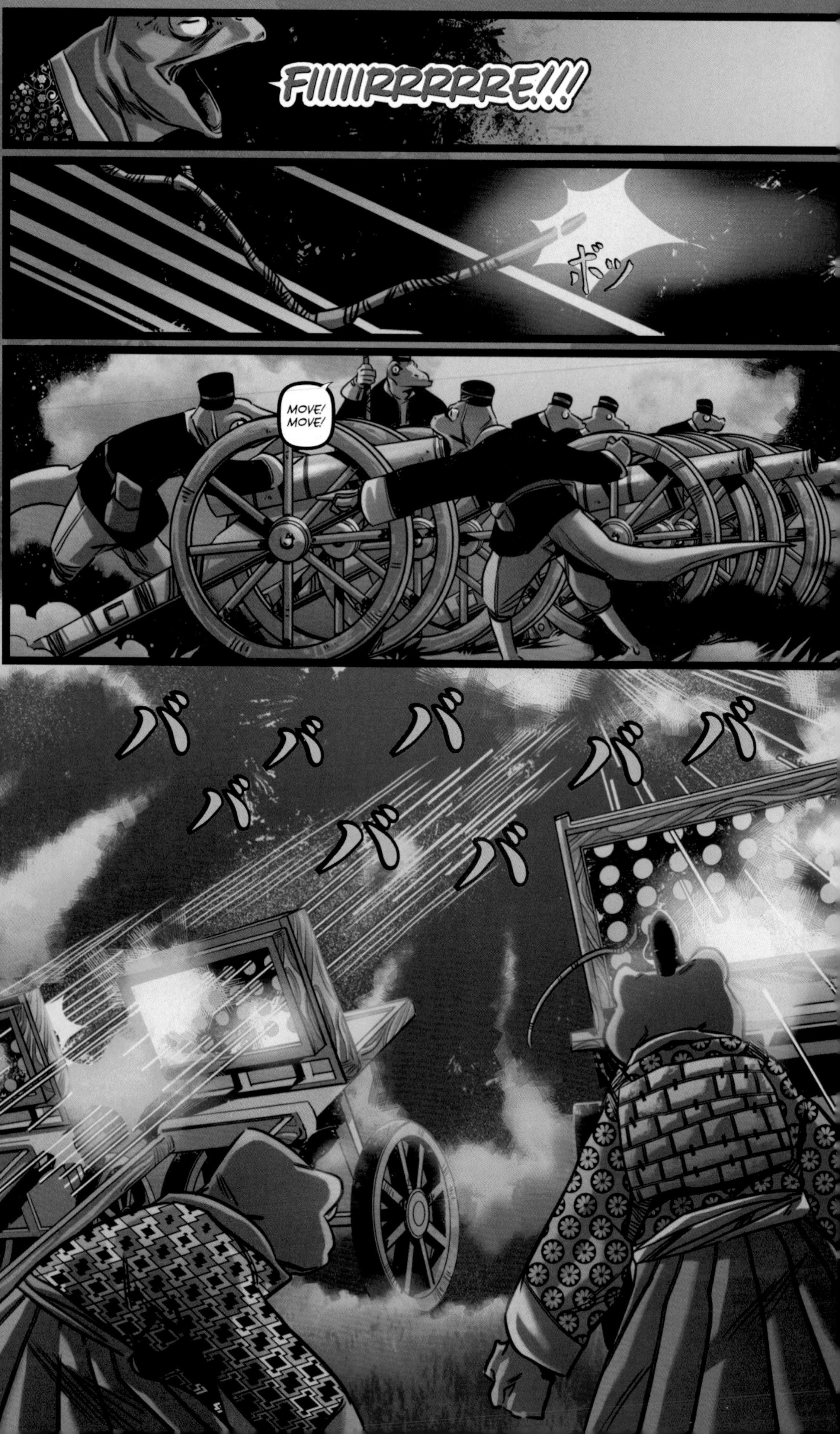
FIIIIIRRRRRRE!!!
ボッ
MOVE! MOVE!
バ バ バ バ バ バ バ バ

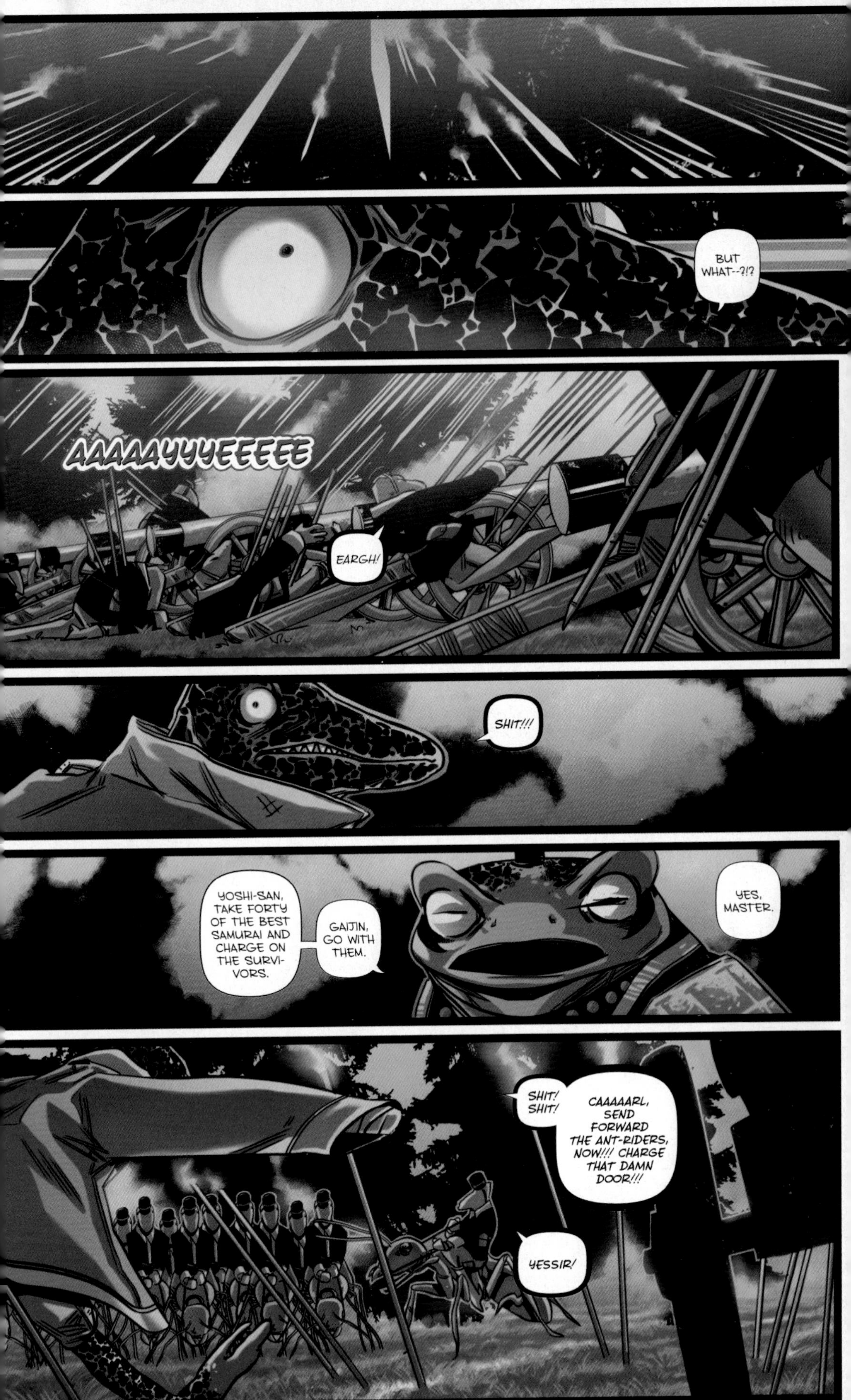
BUT WHAT--?!?
AAAAAYYYEEEEE
EARGH!
SHIT!!!
YOSHI-SAN, TAKE FORTY OF THE BEST SAMURAI AND CHARGE ON THE SURVI-VORS.
GAIJIN, GO WITH THEM.
YES, MASTER.
SHIT! SHIT!
CAAAAARL, SEND FORWARD THE ANT-RIDERS, NOW!!! CHARGE THAT DAMN DOOR!!!
YESSIR!

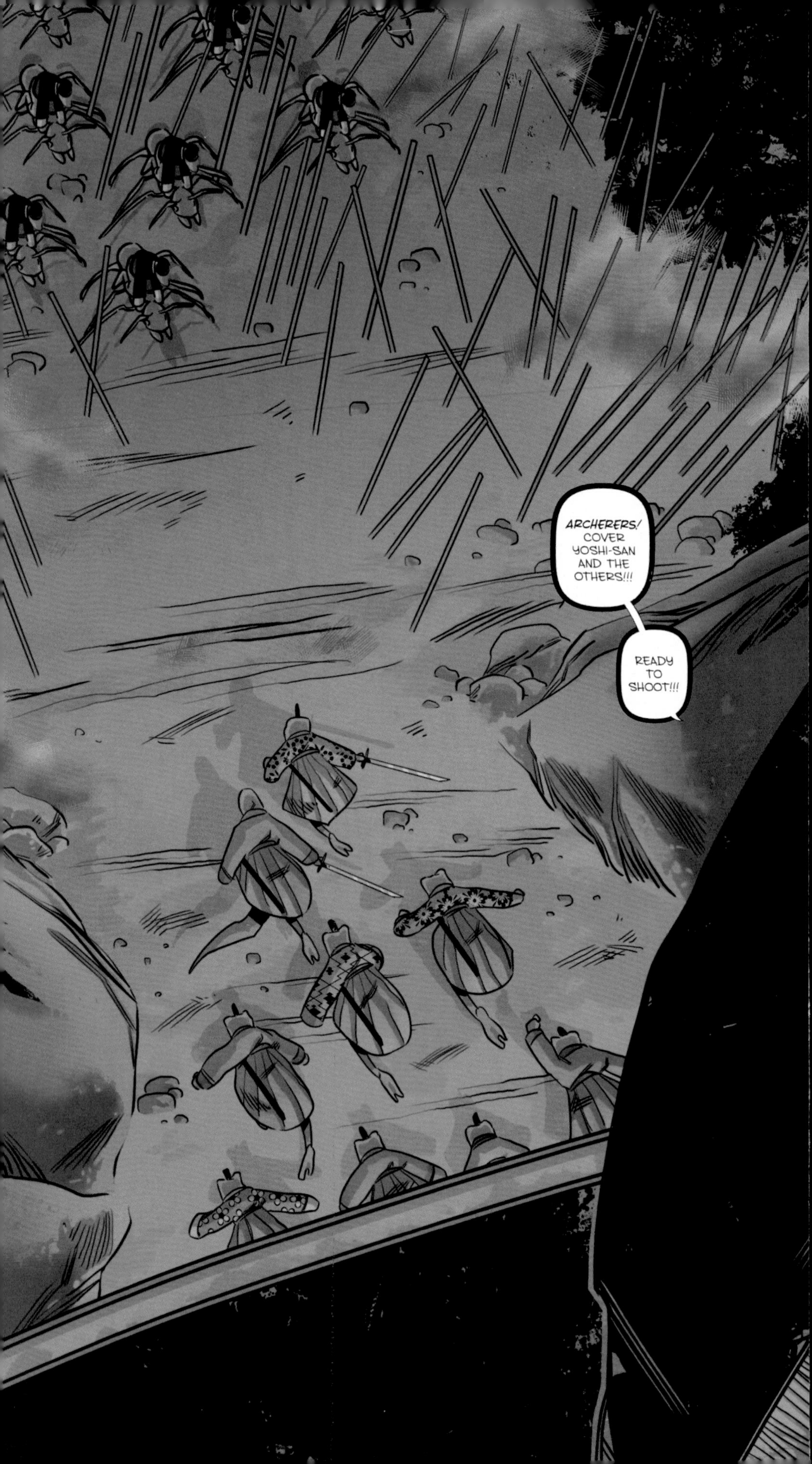
ARCHERERS! COVER YOSHI-SAN AND THE OTHERS!!!
READY TO SHOOT!!!

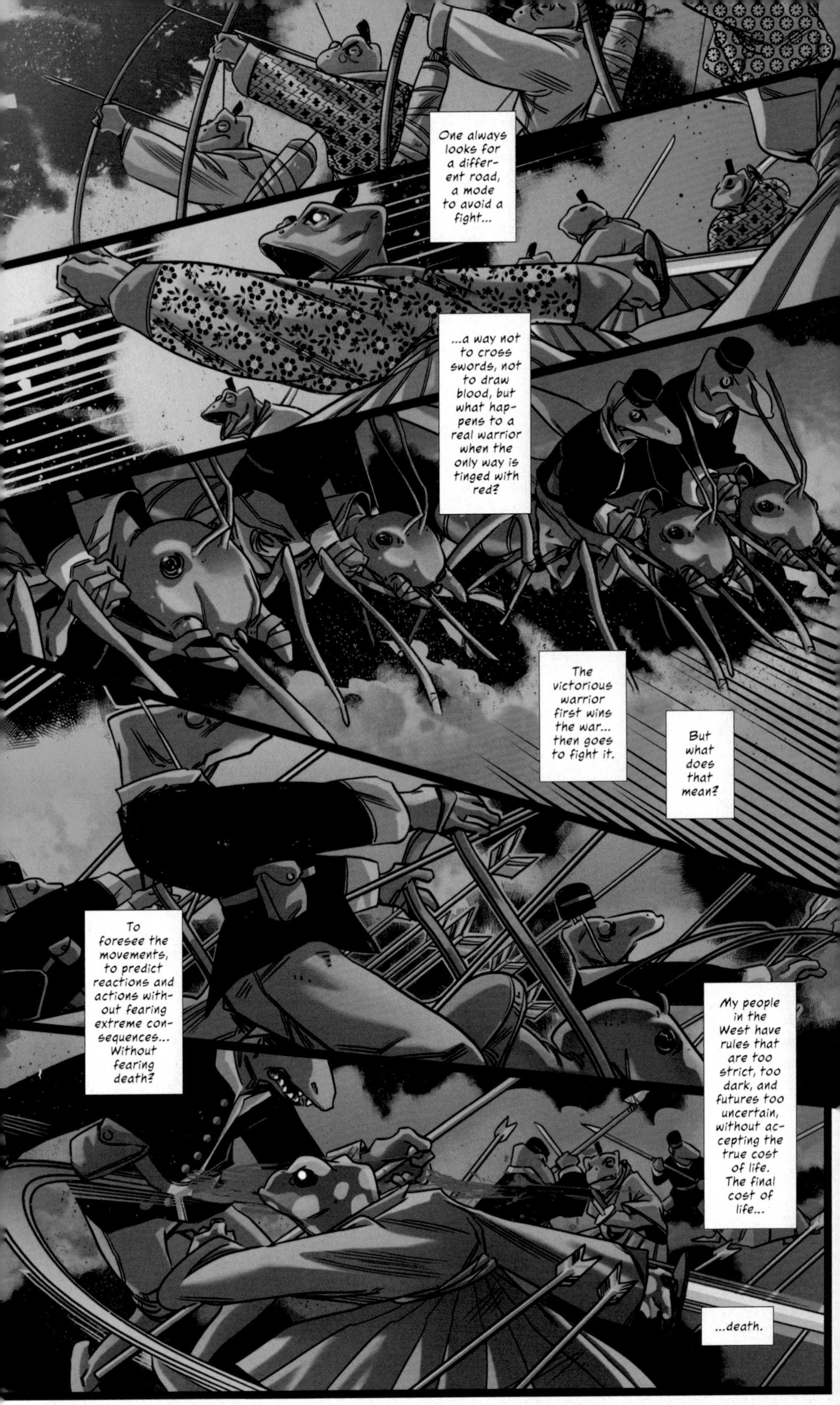
One always looks for a different road, a mode to avoid a fight...
...a way not to cross swords, not to draw blood, but what happens to a real warrior when the only way is tinged with red?
The victorious warrior first wins the war... then goes to fight it.
But what does that mean?
To foresee the movements, to predict reactions and actions without fearing extreme consequences... Without fearing death?
My people in the West have rules that are too strict, too dark, and futures too uncertain, without accepting the true cost of life. The final cost of life...
...death.

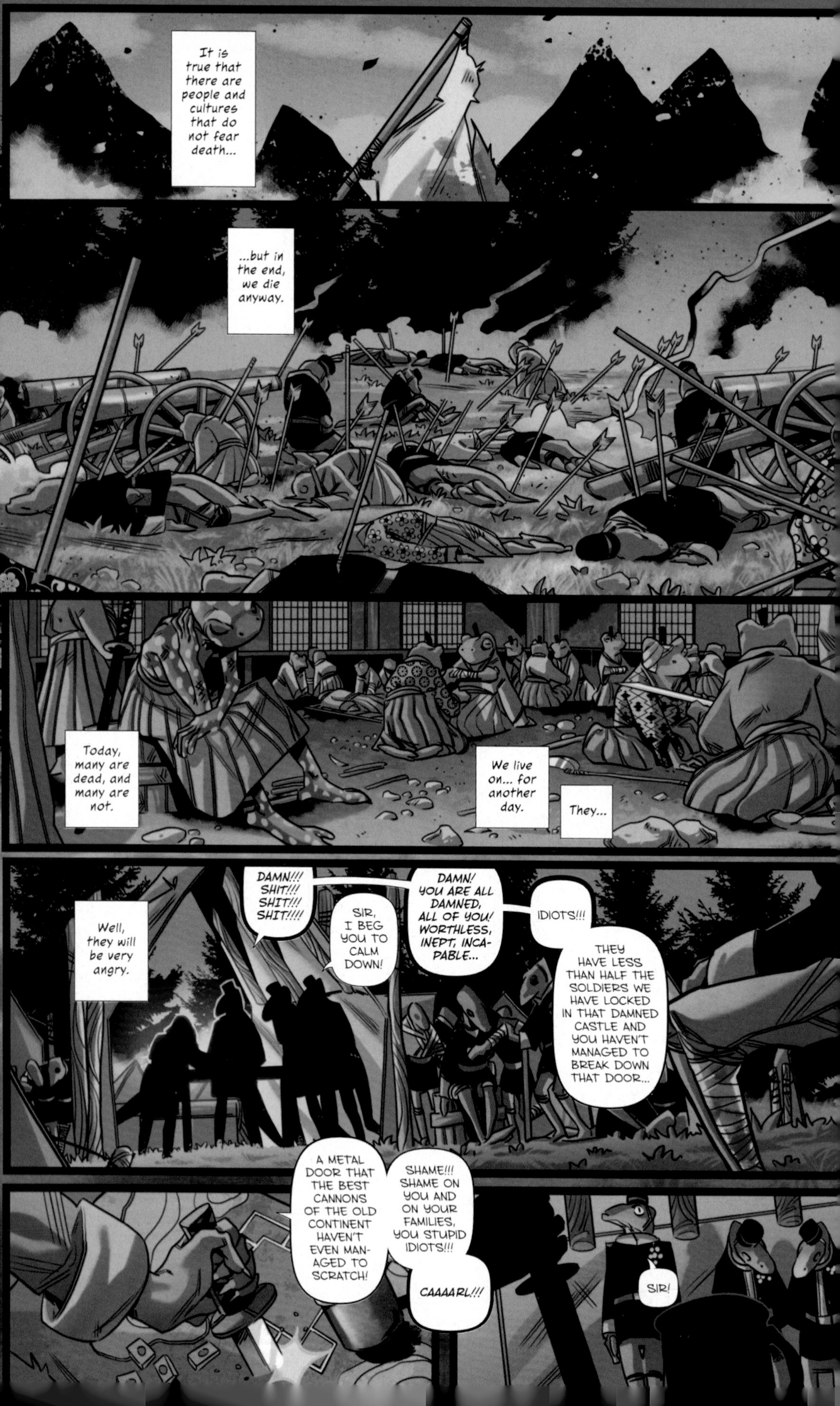
It is true that there are people and cultures that do not fear death...
...but in the end, we die anyway.
Today, many are dead, and many are not.
We live on... for another day.
They...
Well, they will be very angry.
DAMN!!! SHIT!!! SHIT!!! SHIT!!!!
SIR, I BEG YOU TO CALM DOWN!
DAMN! YOU ARE ALL DAMNED, ALL OF YOU! WORTHLESS, INEPT, INCA-PABLE...
IDIOTS!!!
THEY HAVE LESS THAN HALF THE SOLDIERS WE HAVE LOCKED IN THAT DAMNED CASTLE AND YOU HAVEN'T MANAGED TO BREAK DOWN THAT DOOR...
A METAL DOOR THAT THE BEST CANNONS OF THE OLD CONTINENT HAVEN'T EVEN MAN-AGED TO SCRATCH!
SHAME!!! SHAME ON YOU AND ON YOUR FAMILIES, YOU STUPID IDIOTS!!!
CAAAARL!!!
SIR!

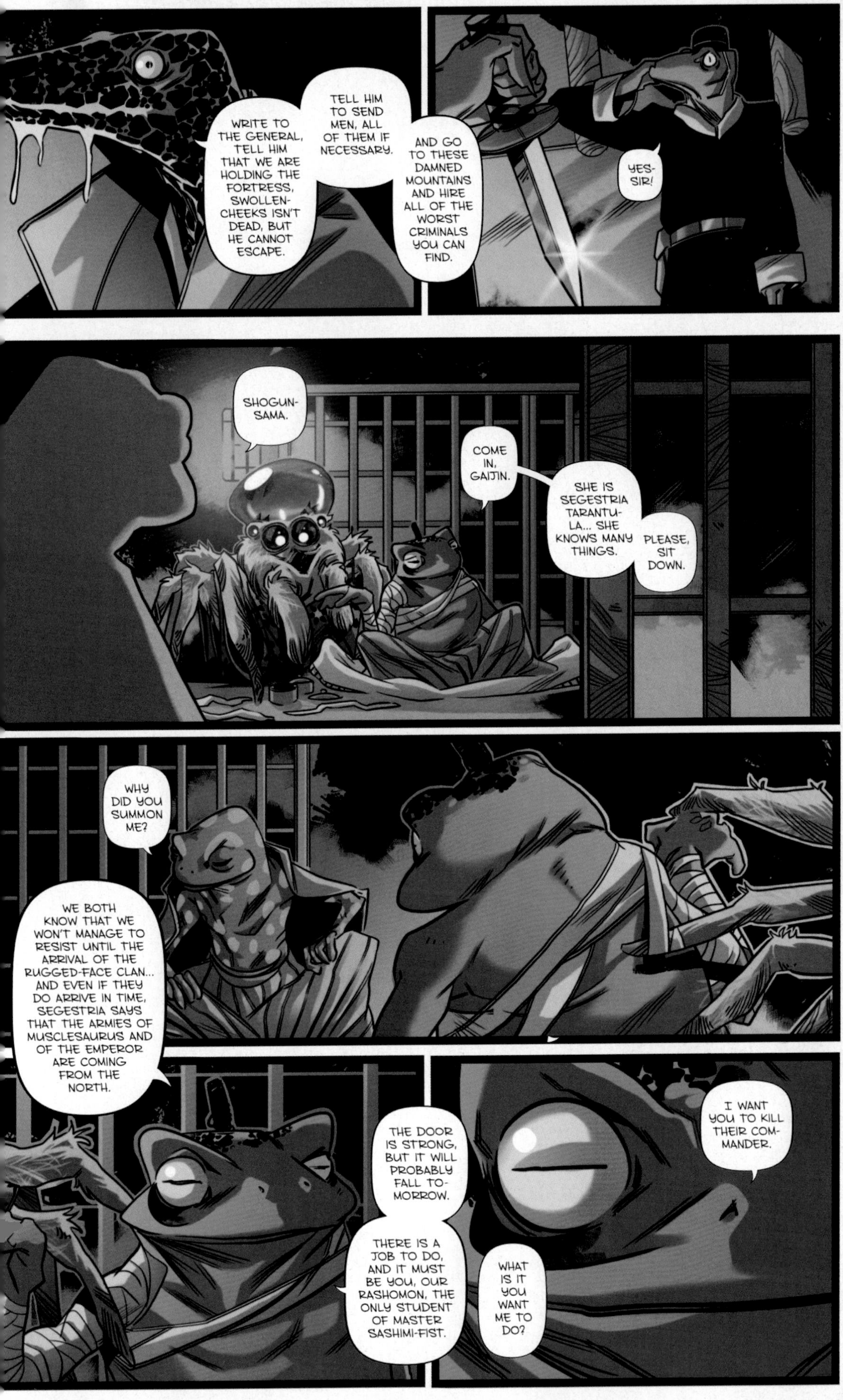
WRITE TO THE GENERAL, TELL HIM THAT WE ARE HOLDING THE FORTRESS, SWOLLEN-CHEEKS ISN'T DEAD, BUT HE CANNOT ESCAPE.
TELL HIM TO SEND MEN, ALL OF THEM IF NECESSARY.
AND GO TO THESE DAMNED MOUNTAINS AND HIRE ALL OF THE WORST CRIMINALS YOU CAN FIND.
YES-SIR!
SHOGUN-SAMA.
COME IN, GAIJIN.
SHE IS SEGESTRIA TARANTU-LA... SHE KNOWS MANY THINGS.
PLEASE, SIT DOWN.
WHY DID YOU SUMMON ME?
WE BOTH KNOW THAT WE WON'T MANAGE TO RESIST UNTIL THE ARRIVAL OF THE RUGGED-FACE CLAN... AND EVEN IF THEY DO ARRIVE IN TIME, SEGESTRIA SAYS THAT THE ARMIES OF MUSCLESAURUS AND OF THE EMPEROR ARE COMING FROM THE NORTH.
THE DOOR IS STRONG, BUT IT WILL PROBABLY FALL TO-MORROW.
THERE IS A JOB TO DO, AND IT MUST BE YOU, OUR RASHOMON, THE ONLY STUDENT OF MASTER SASHIMI-FIST.
WHAT IS IT YOU WANT ME TO DO?
I WANT YOU TO KILL THEIR COM-MANDER.

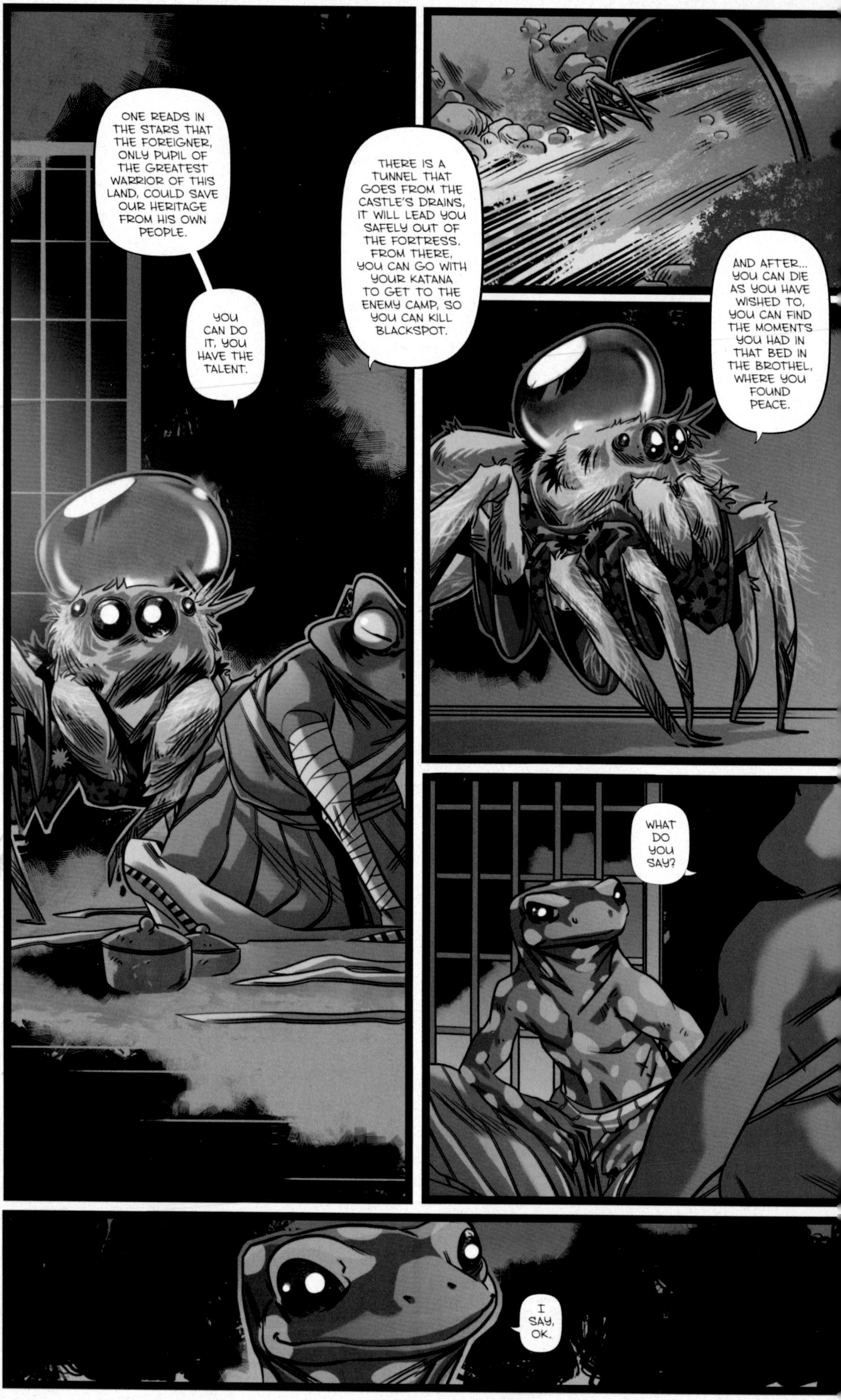
ONE READS IN THE STARS THAT THE FOREIGNER, ONLY PUPIL OF THE GREATEST WARRIOR OF THIS LAND, COULD SAVE OUR HERITAGE FROM HIS OWN PEOPLE.
YOU CAN DO IT, YOU HAVE THE TALENT.
THERE IS A TUNNEL THAT GOES FROM THE CASTLE'S DRAINS, IT WILL LEAD YOU SAFELY OUT OF THE FORTRESS. FROM THERE, YOU CAN GO WITH YOUR KATANA TO GET TO THE ENEMY CAMP, SO YOU CAN KILL BLACKSPOT.
AND AFTER... YOU CAN DIE AS YOU HAVE WISHED TO, YOU CAN FIND THE MOMENTS YOU HAD IN THAT BED IN THE BROTHEL, WHERE YOU FOUND PEACE.
WHAT DO YOU SAY?
I SAY, OK.

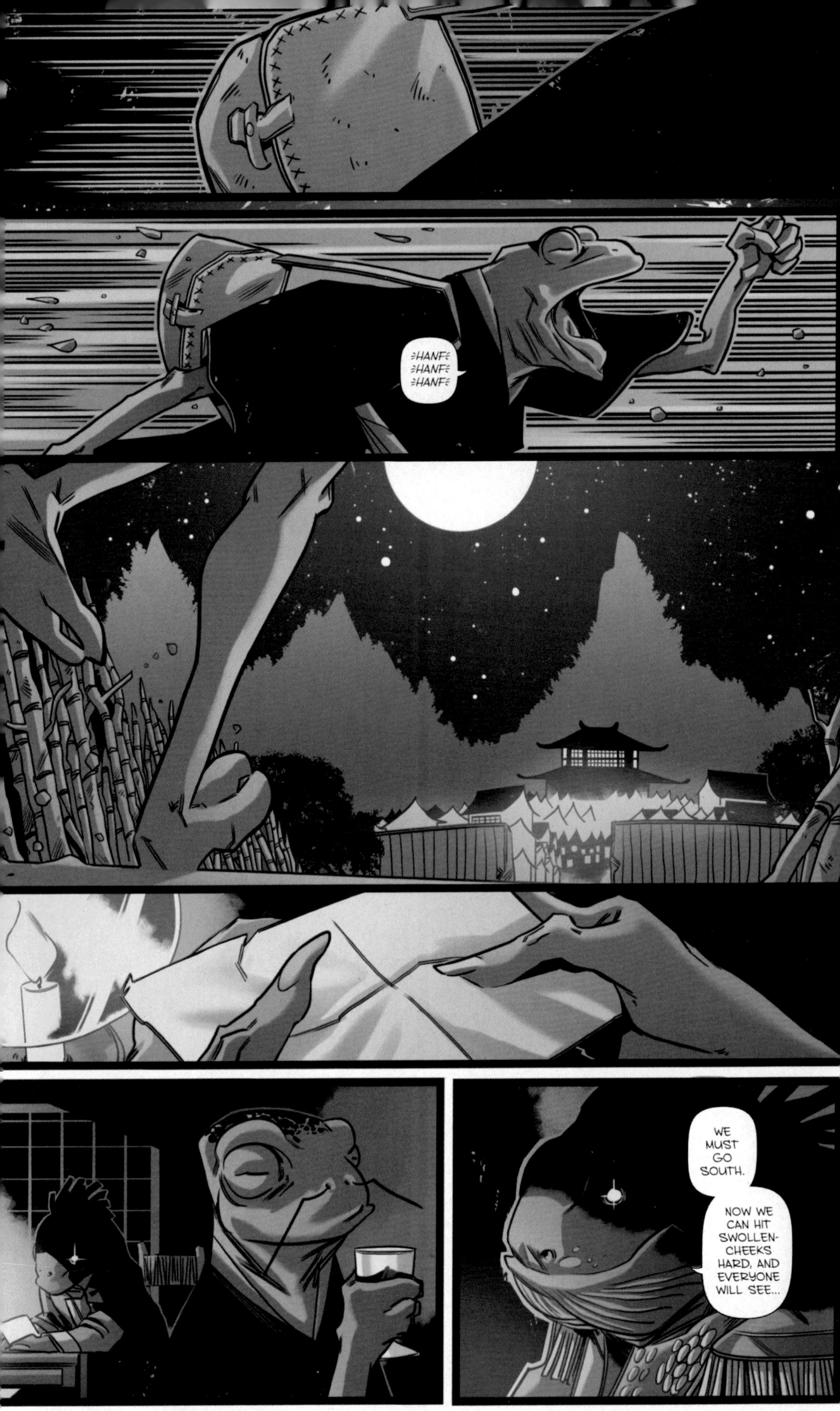
HANF HANF HANF
WE MUST GO SOUTH.
NOW WE CAN HIT SWOLLEN-CHEEKS HARD, AND EVERYONE WILL SEE...

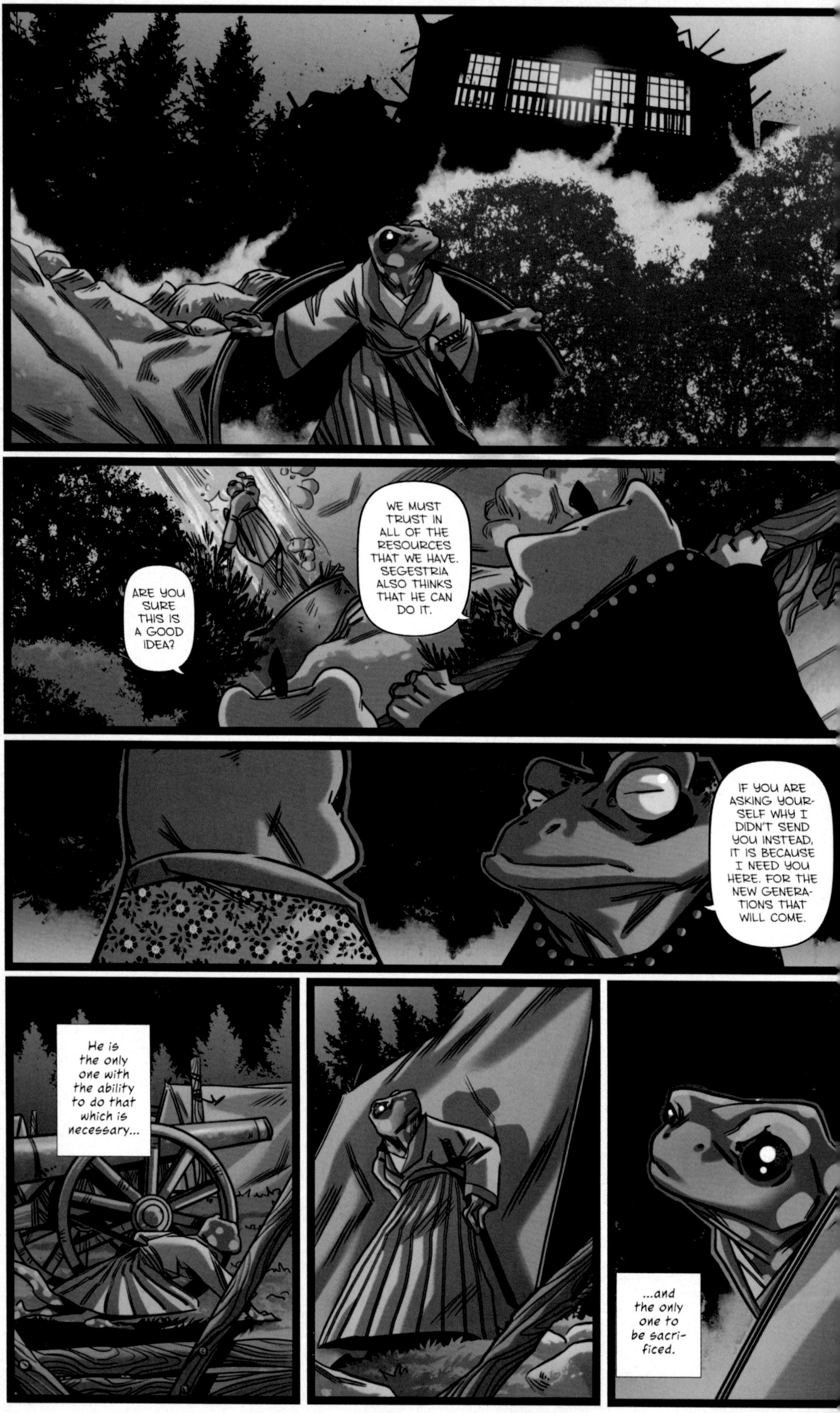

ARE YOU SURE THIS IS A GOOD IDEA?
WE MUST TRUST IN ALL OF THE RESOURCES THAT WE HAVE. SEGESTRIA ALSO THINKS THAT HE CAN DO IT.
IF YOU ARE ASKING YOURSELF WHY I DIDN'T SEND YOU INSTEAD, IT IS BECAUSE I NEED YOU HERE. FOR THE NEW GENERATIONS THAT WILL COME.
He is the only one with the ability to do that which is necessary...
...and the only one to be sacrificed.

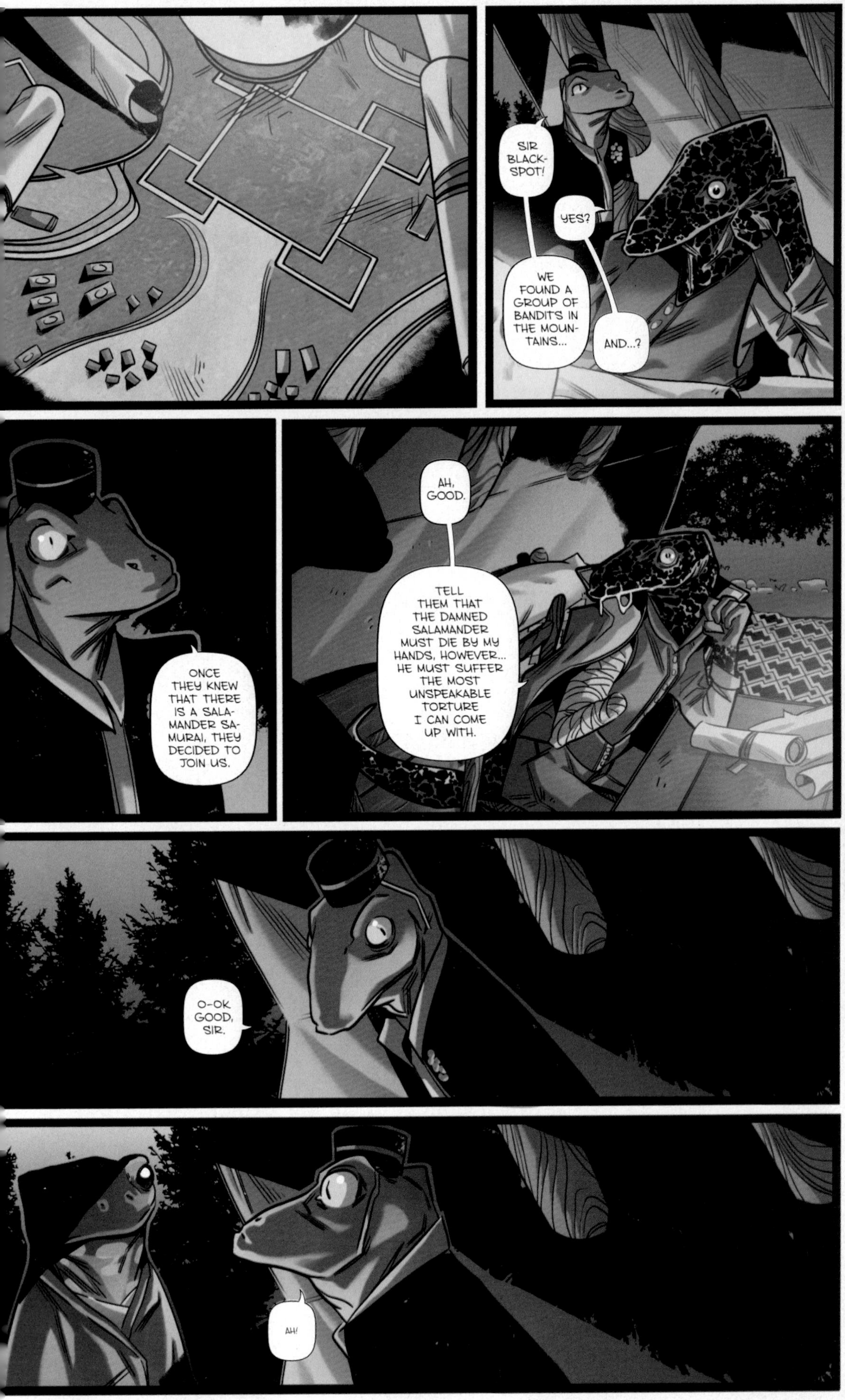
SIR BLACK-SPOT!
YES?
WE FOUND A GROUP OF BANDITS IN THE MOUN-TAINS...
AND...?
ONCE THEY KNEW THAT THERE IS A SALA-MANDER SA-MURAI, THEY DECIDED TO JOIN US.
AH, GOOD.
TELL THEM THAT THE DAMNED SALAMANDER MUST DIE BY MY HANDS, HOWEVER... HE MUST SUFFER THE MOST UNSPEAKABLE TORTURE I CAN COME UP WITH.
O-OK GOOD, SIR.
AH!

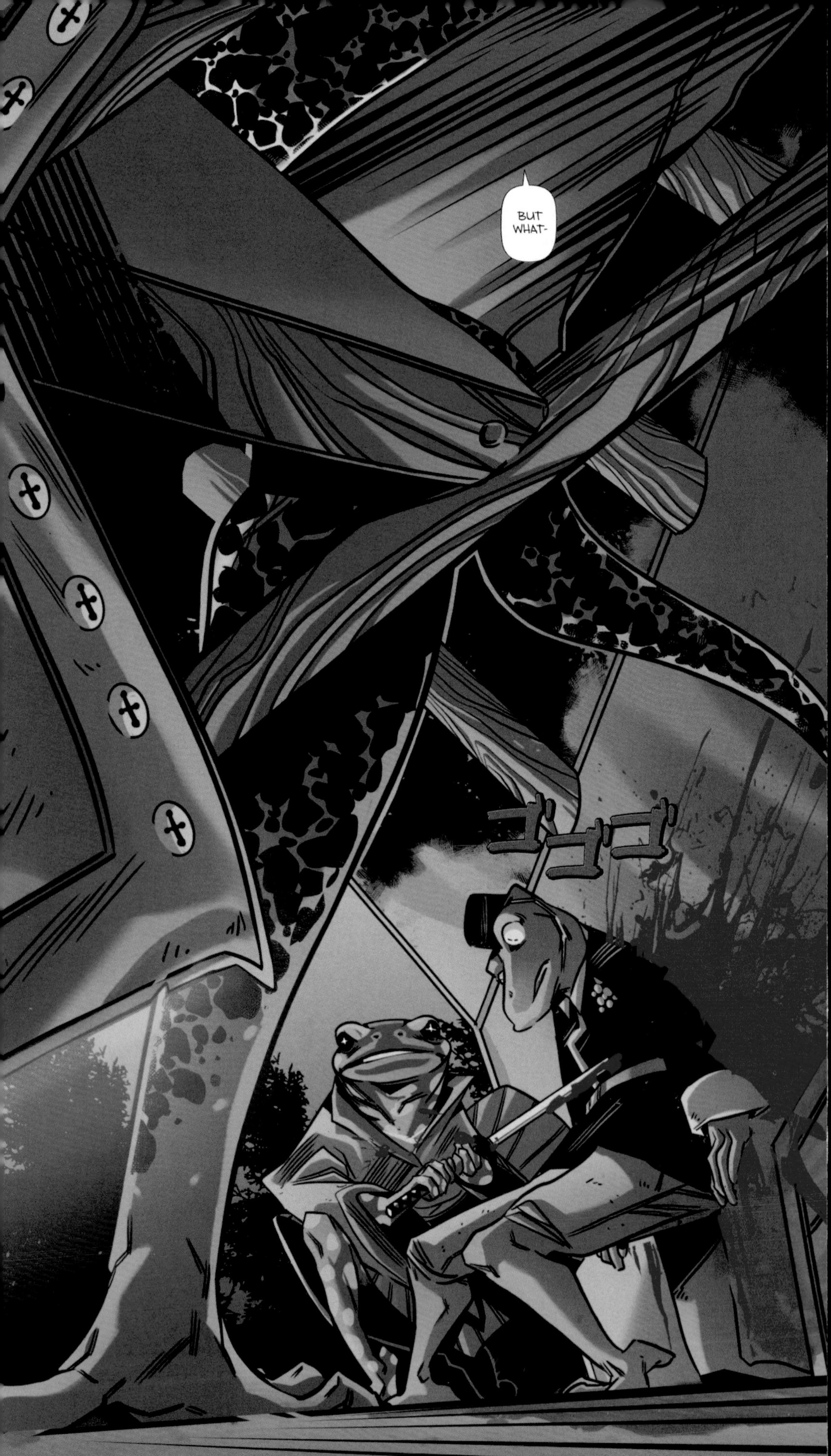
BUT WHAT-
ゴゴゴ

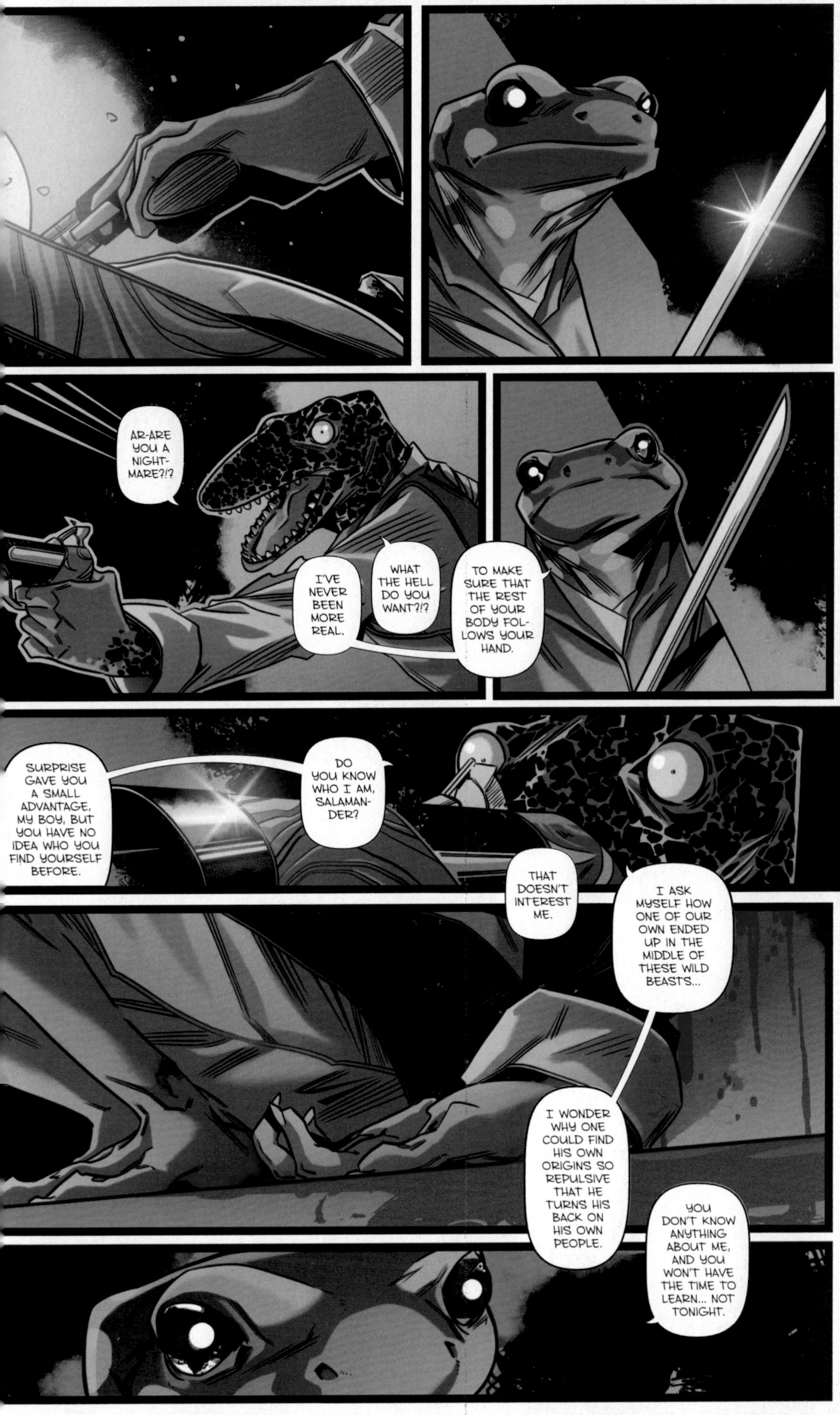
AR-ARE YOU A NIGHT-MARE?!?
I'VE NEVER BEEN MORE REAL.
WHAT THE HELL DO YOU WANT?!?
TO MAKE SURE THAT THE REST OF YOUR BODY FOL-LOWS YOUR HAND.
SURPRISE GAVE YOU A SMALL ADVANTAGE, MY BOY, BUT YOU HAVE NO IDEA WHO YOU FIND YOURSELF BEFORE.
DO YOU KNOW WHO I AM, SALAMAN-DER?
THAT DOESN'T INTEREST ME.
I ASK MYSELF HOW ONE OF OUR OWN ENDED UP IN THE MIDDLE OF THESE WILD BEASTS...
I WONDER WHY ONE COULD FIND HIS OWN ORIGINS SO REPULSIVE THAT HE TURNS HIS BACK ON HIS OWN PEOPLE.
YOU DON'T KNOW ANYTHING ABOUT ME, AND YOU WON'T HAVE THE TIME TO LEARN... NOT TONIGHT.

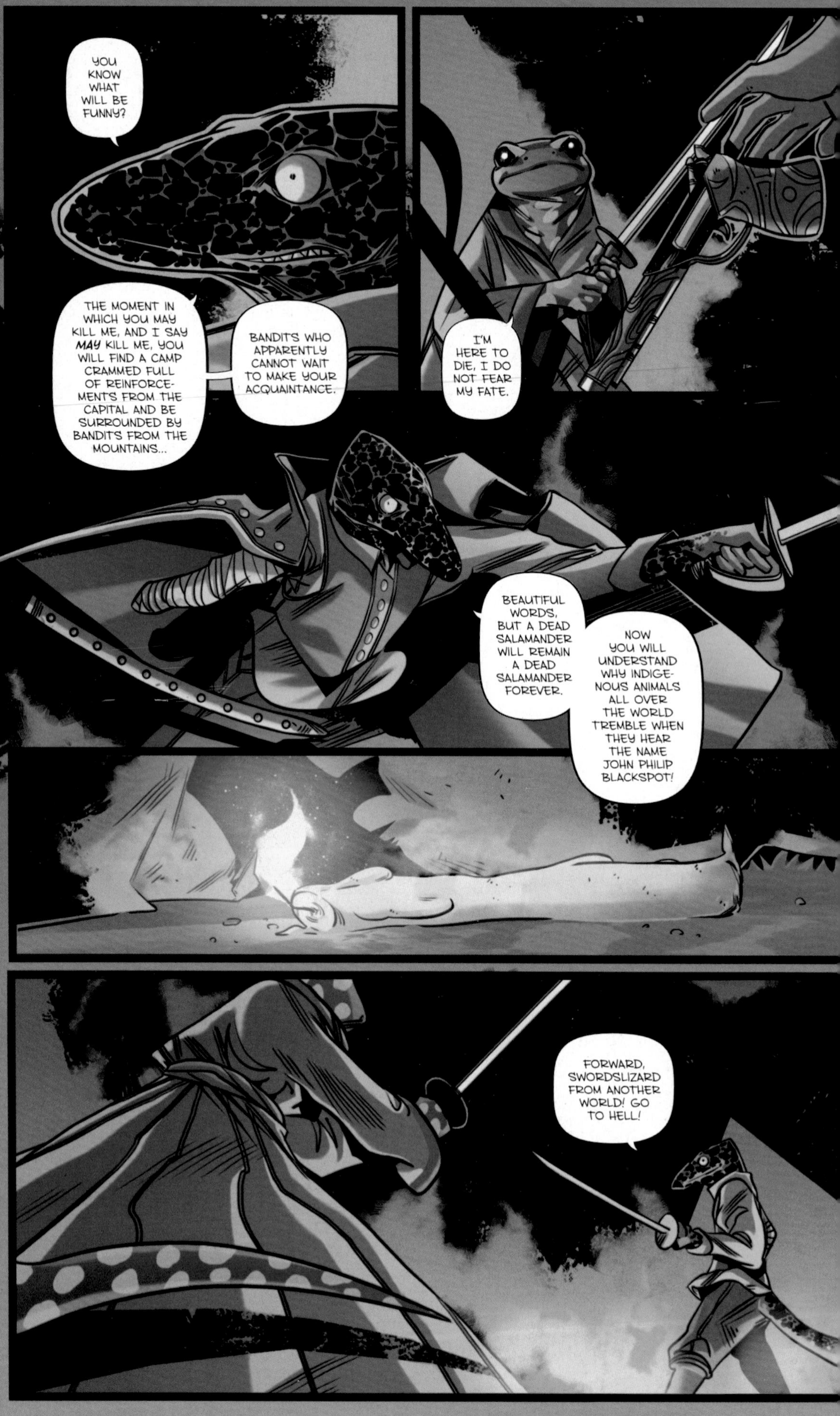
YOU KNOW WHAT WILL BE FUNNY?
THE MOMENT IN WHICH YOU MAY KILL ME, AND I SAY MAY KILL ME, YOU WILL FIND A CAMP CRAMMED FULL OF REINFORCE-MENTS FROM THE CAPITAL AND BE SURROUNDED BY BANDITS FROM THE MOUNTAINS...
BANDITS WHO APPARENTLY CANNOT WAIT TO MAKE YOUR ACQUAINTANCE.
I'M HERE TO DIE, I DO NOT FEAR MY FATE.
BEAUTIFUL WORDS, BUT A DEAD SALAMANDER WILL REMAIN A DEAD SALAMANDER FOREVER.
NOW YOU WILL UNDERSTAND WHY INDIGE-NOUS ANIMALS ALL OVER THE WORLD TREMBLE WHEN THEY HEAR THE NAME JOHN PHILIP BLACKSPOT!
FORWARD, SWORDSLIZARD FROM ANOTHER WORLD! GO TO HELL!

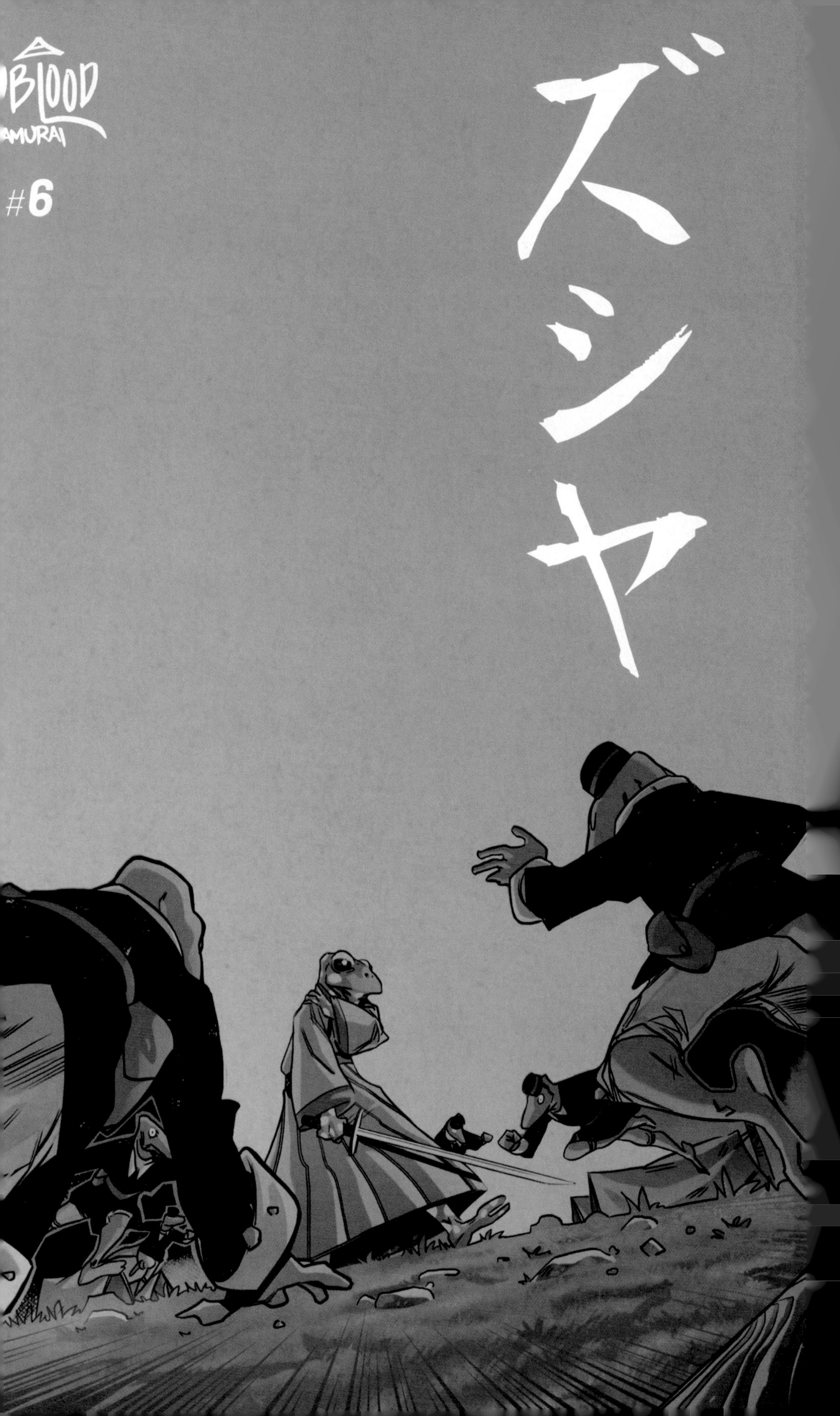
BLOOD
AMURAI
#6
ズシャ

COLDBLOOD SAMURAI

CREDITS

Story
MASSIMO ROSI

Pencils
LUDOVICA CEREGATTI

Colors
RENATO STEVANATO

Lettering
MATTIA GENTILI

Bryan Seaton: Publisher/ CEO
Shawn Gabborin: Editor In Chief
Jason Martin: Publisher-Danger Zone
Nicole D'Andria: Marketing Director/Editor
Jessica Lowrie: Social Media Czar
Danielle Davison: Executive Administrator
Chad Cicconi: King Lizard
Shawn Pryor: President of Creator Relations

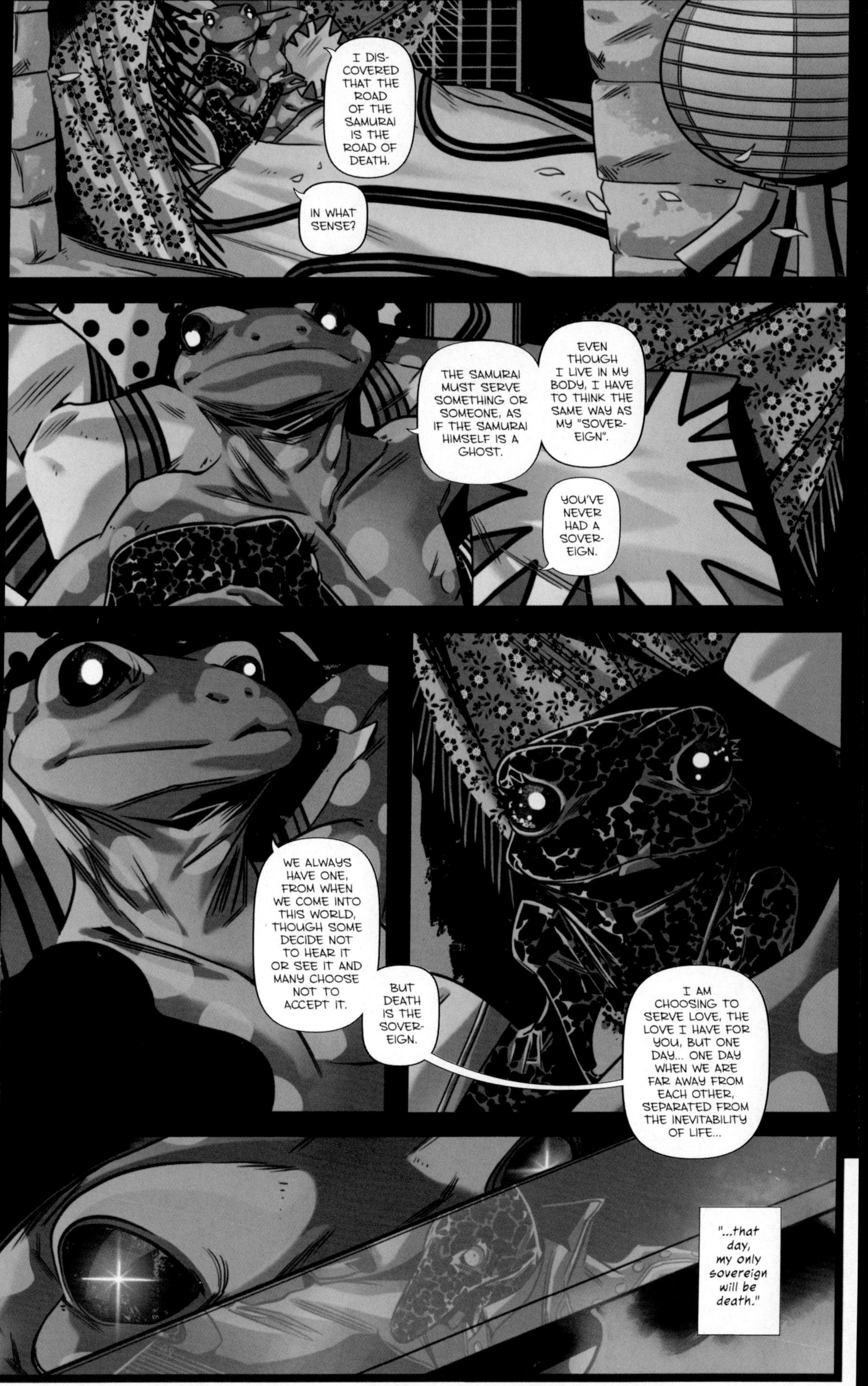
I DIS-COVERED THAT THE ROAD OF THE SAMURAI IS THE ROAD OF DEATH.
IN WHAT SENSE?
THE SAMURAI MUST SERVE SOMETHING OR SOMEONE, AS IF THE SAMURAI HIMSELF IS A GHOST.
EVEN THOUGH I LIVE IN MY BODY, I HAVE TO THINK THE SAME WAY AS MY "SOVER-EIGN".
YOU'VE NEVER HAD A SOVER-EIGN.
WE ALWAYS HAVE ONE, FROM WHEN WE COME INTO THIS WORLD, THOUGH SOME DECIDE NOT TO HEAR IT OR SEE IT AND MANY CHOOSE NOT TO ACCEPT IT.
BUT DEATH IS THE SOVER-EIGN.
I AM CHOOSING TO SERVE LOVE, THE LOVE I HAVE FOR YOU, BUT ONE DAY... ONE DAY WHEN WE ARE FAR AWAY FROM EACH OTHER, SEPARATED FROM THE INEVITABILITY OF LIFE...
"...that day, my only sovereign will be death."

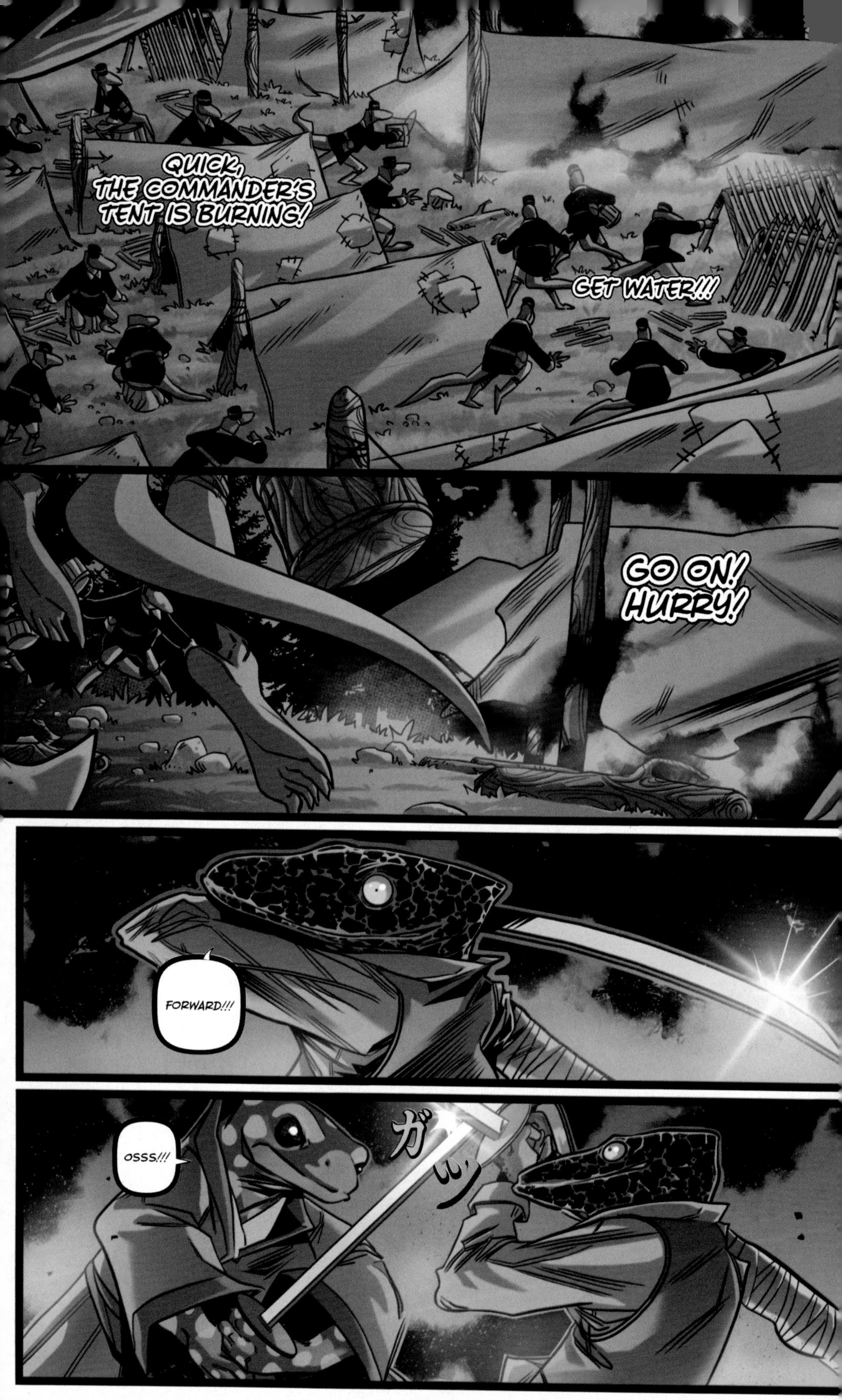
QUICK, THE COMMANDER'S TENT IS BURNING!
GET WATER!!!
GO ON! HURRY!
FORWARD!!!
OSSS!!!
ガッ

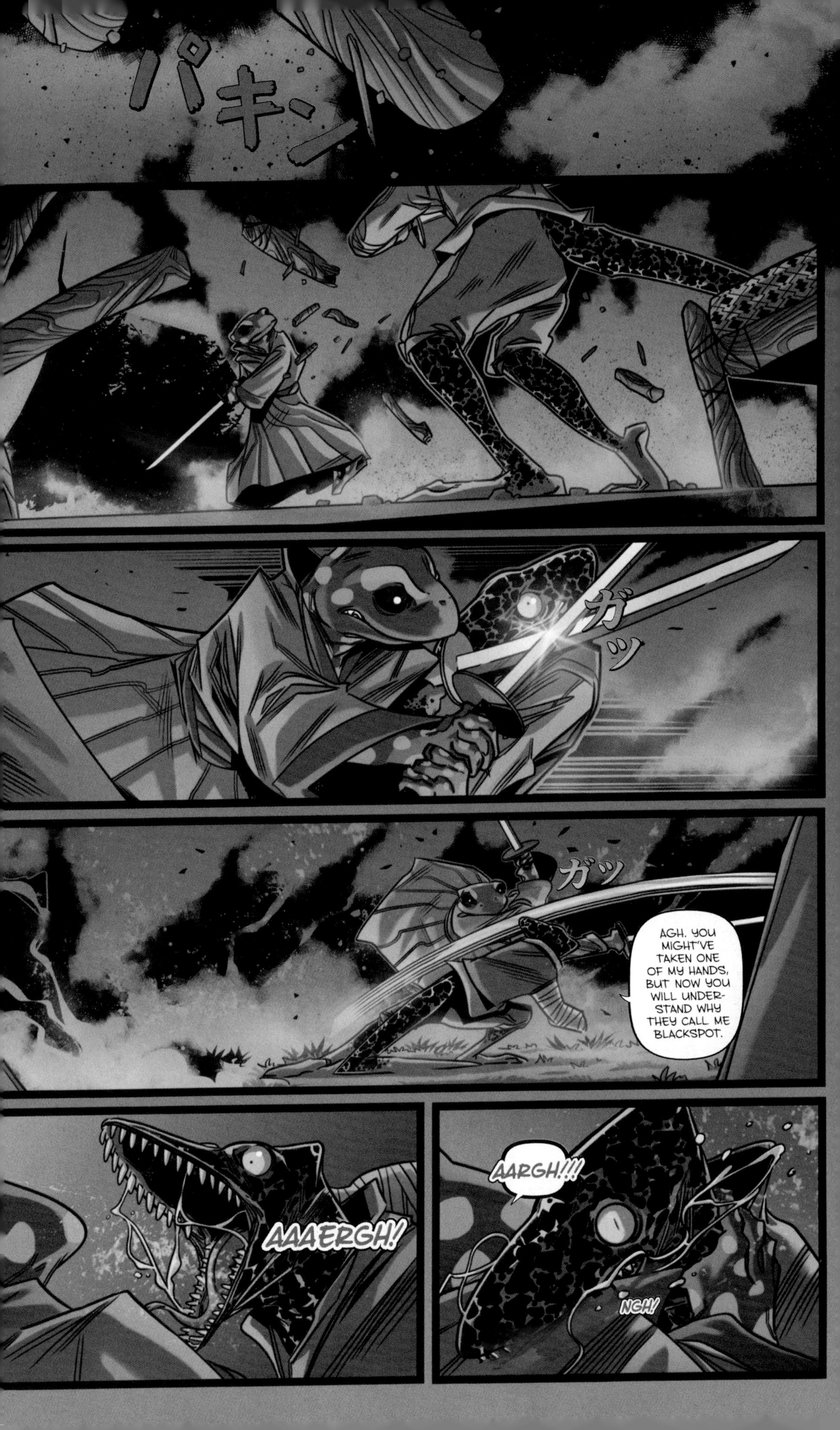
パキン
ガッ
ガッ
AGH. YOU MIGHT'VE TAKEN ONE OF MY HANDS, BUT NOW YOU WILL UNDER-STAND WHY THEY CALL ME BLACKSPOT.
AAAERGH!
AARGH!!!
NGH!

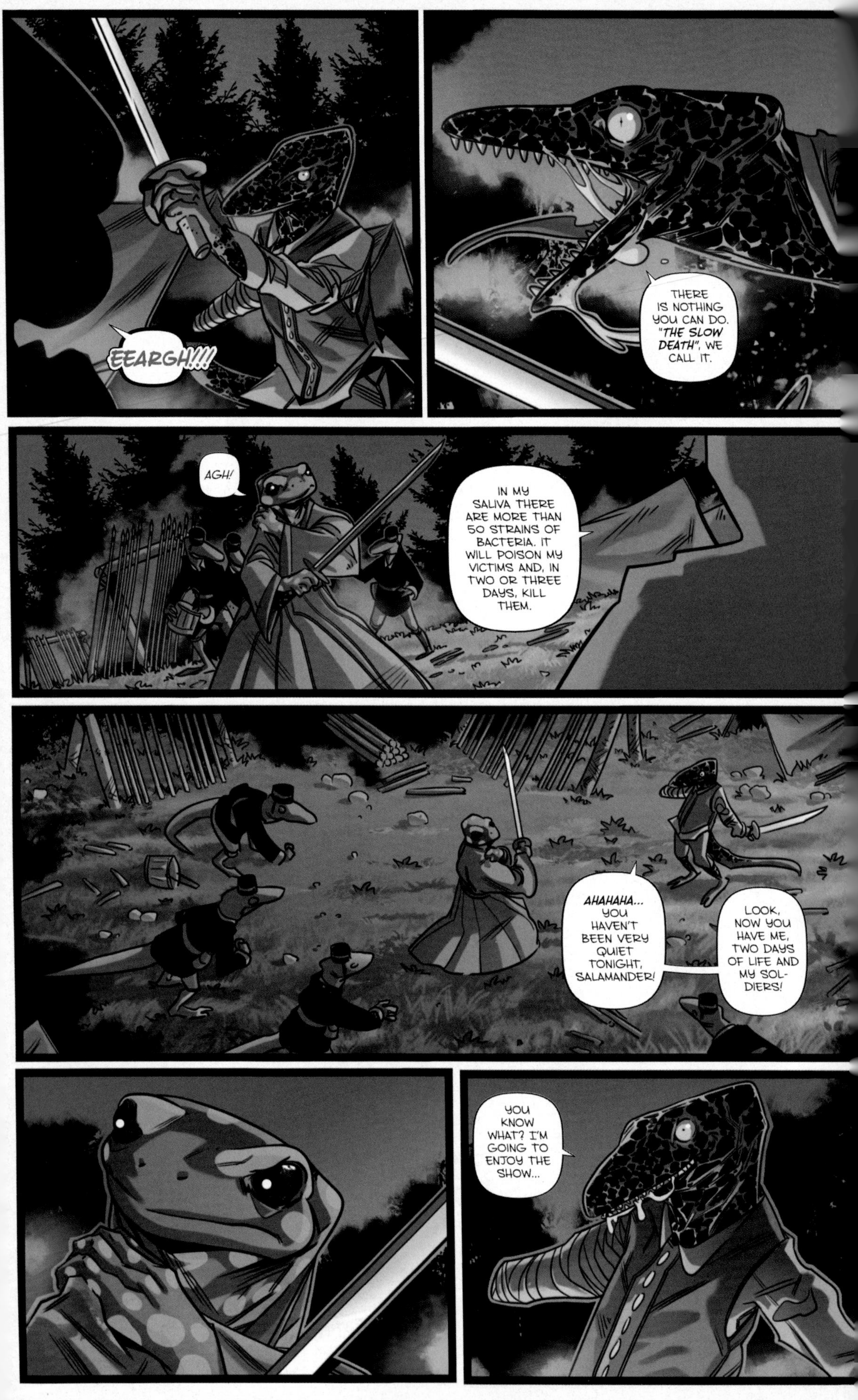
EEARGH!!!
THERE IS NOTHING YOU CAN DO. "THE SLOW DEATH", WE CALL IT.
AGH!
IN MY SALIVA THERE ARE MORE THAN 50 STRAINS OF BACTERIA. IT WILL POISON MY VICTIMS AND, IN TWO OR THREE DAYS, KILL THEM.
AHAHAHA... YOU HAVEN'T BEEN VERY QUIET TONIGHT, SALAMANDER!
LOOK, NOW YOU HAVE ME, TWO DAYS OF LIFE AND MY SOL-DIERS!
YOU KNOW WHAT? I'M GOING TO ENJOY THE SHOW...

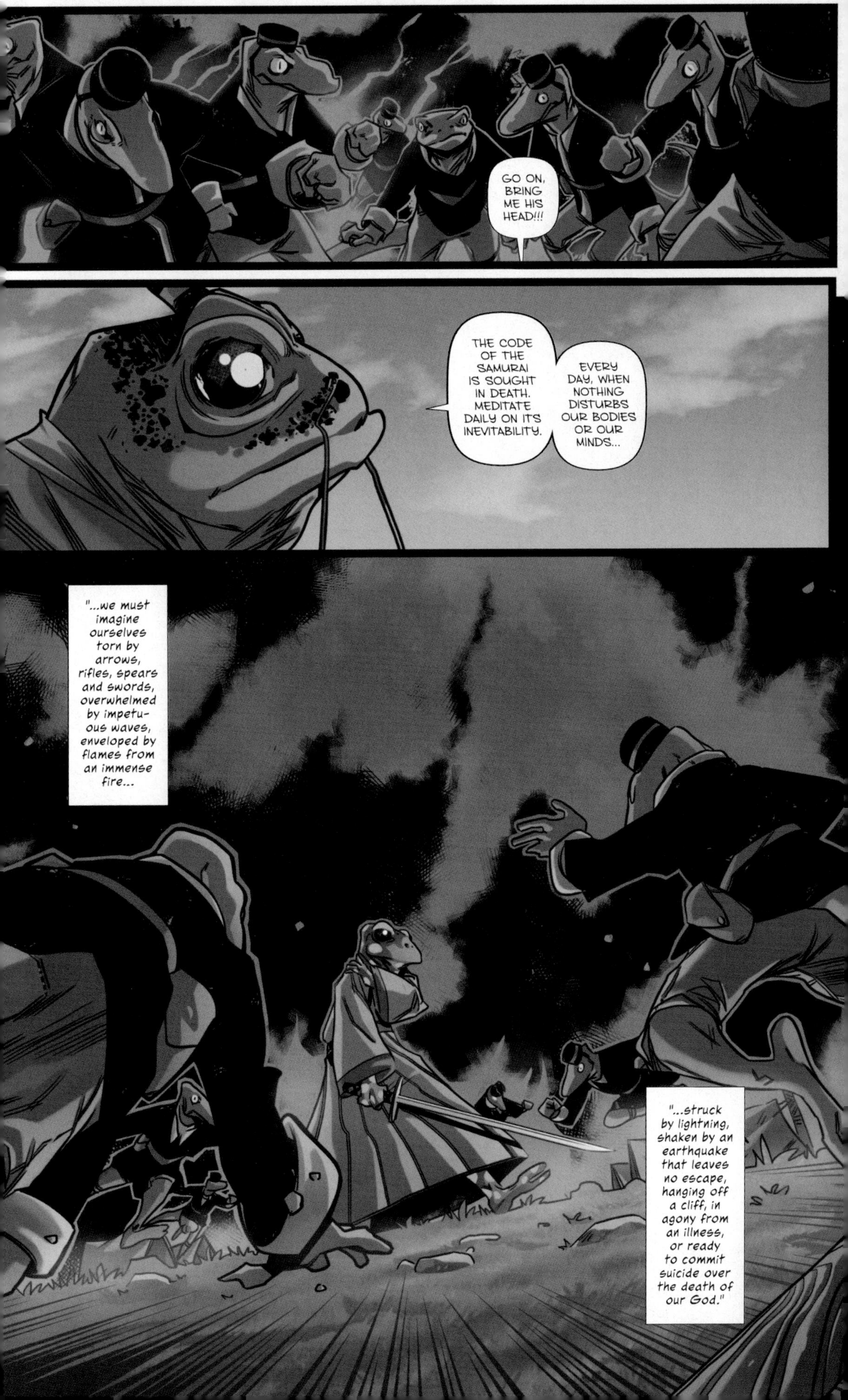

GO ON, BRING ME HIS HEAD!!!
THE CODE OF THE SAMURAI IS SOUGHT IN DEATH. MEDITATE DAILY ON ITS INEVITABILITY.
EVERY DAY, WHEN NOTHING DISTURBS OUR BODIES OR OUR MINDS...
"...we must imagine ourselves torn by arrows, rifles, spears and swords, overwhelmed by impetu-ous waves, enveloped by flames from an immense fire...
"...struck by lightning, shaken by an earthquake that leaves no escape, hanging off a cliff, in agony from an illness, or ready to commit suicide over the death of our God."

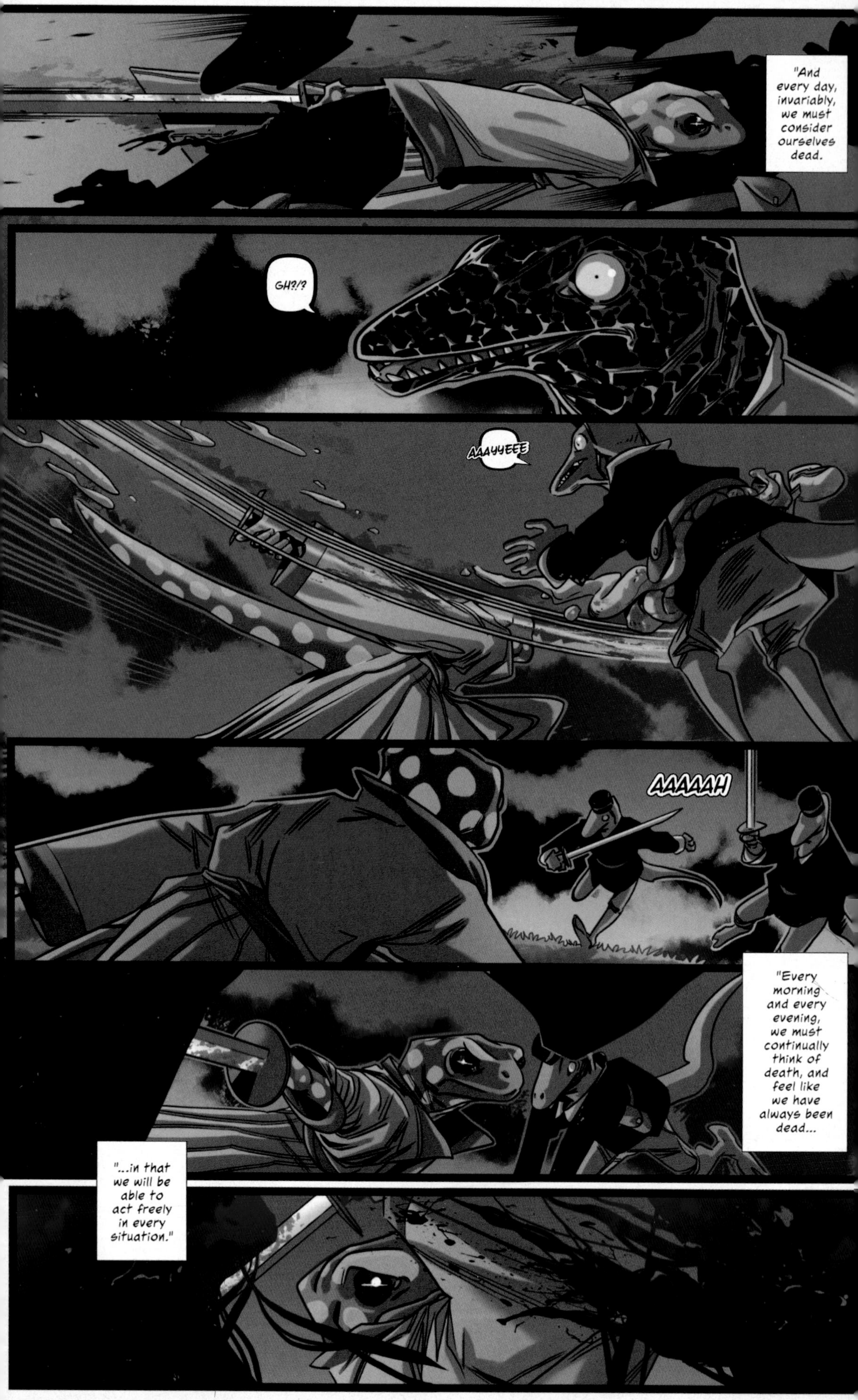
"And every day, invariably, we must consider ourselves dead.
GH?!?
AAAYYEEE
AAAAAH
"Every morning and every evening, we must continually think of death, and feel like we have always been dead...
"...in that we will be able to act freely in every situation."

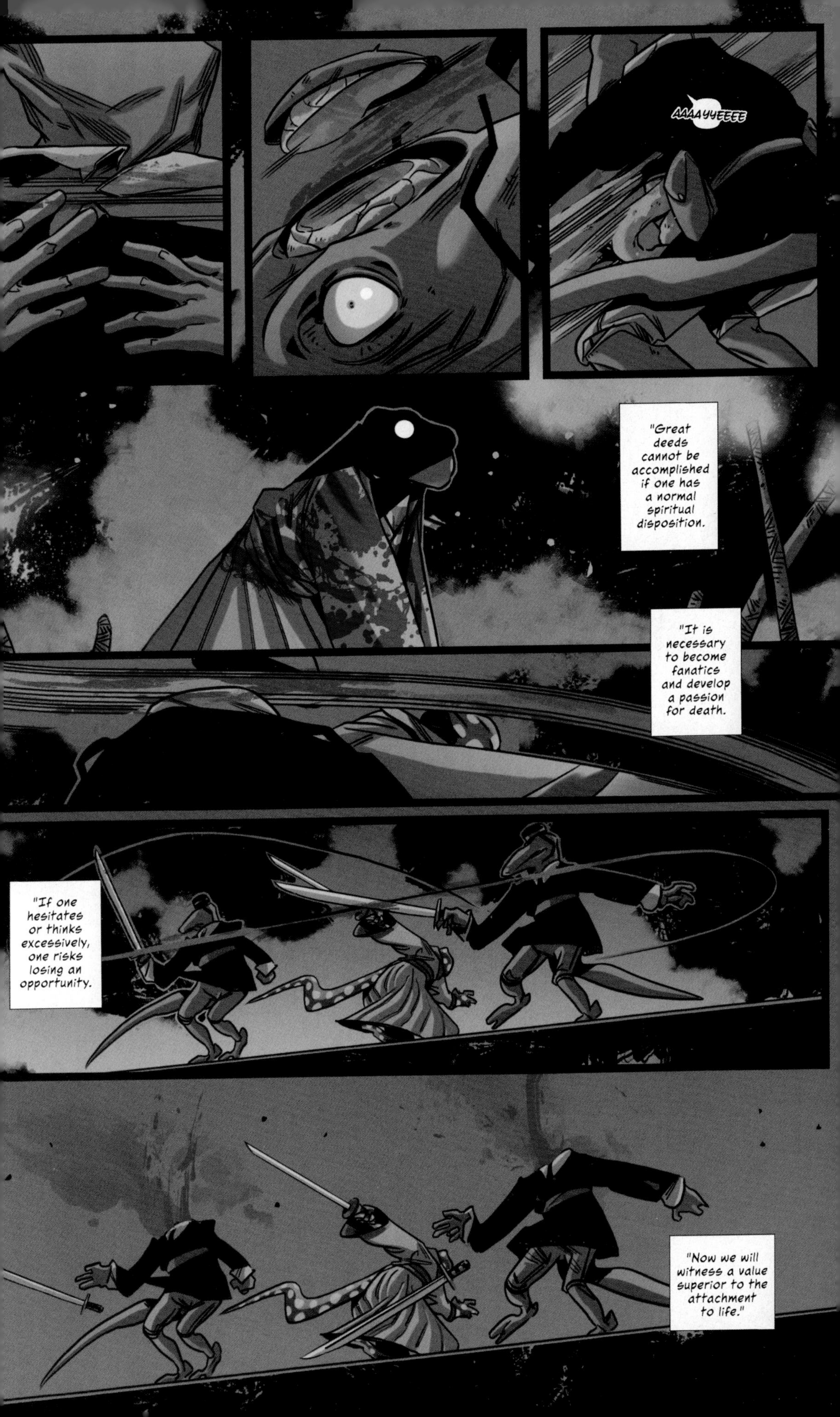
AAAAYYEEEE
"Great deeds cannot be accomplished if one has a normal spiritual disposition.
"It is necessary to become fanatics and develop a passion for death.
"If one hesitates or thinks excessively, one risks losing an opportunity.
"Now we will witness a value superior to the attachment to life."

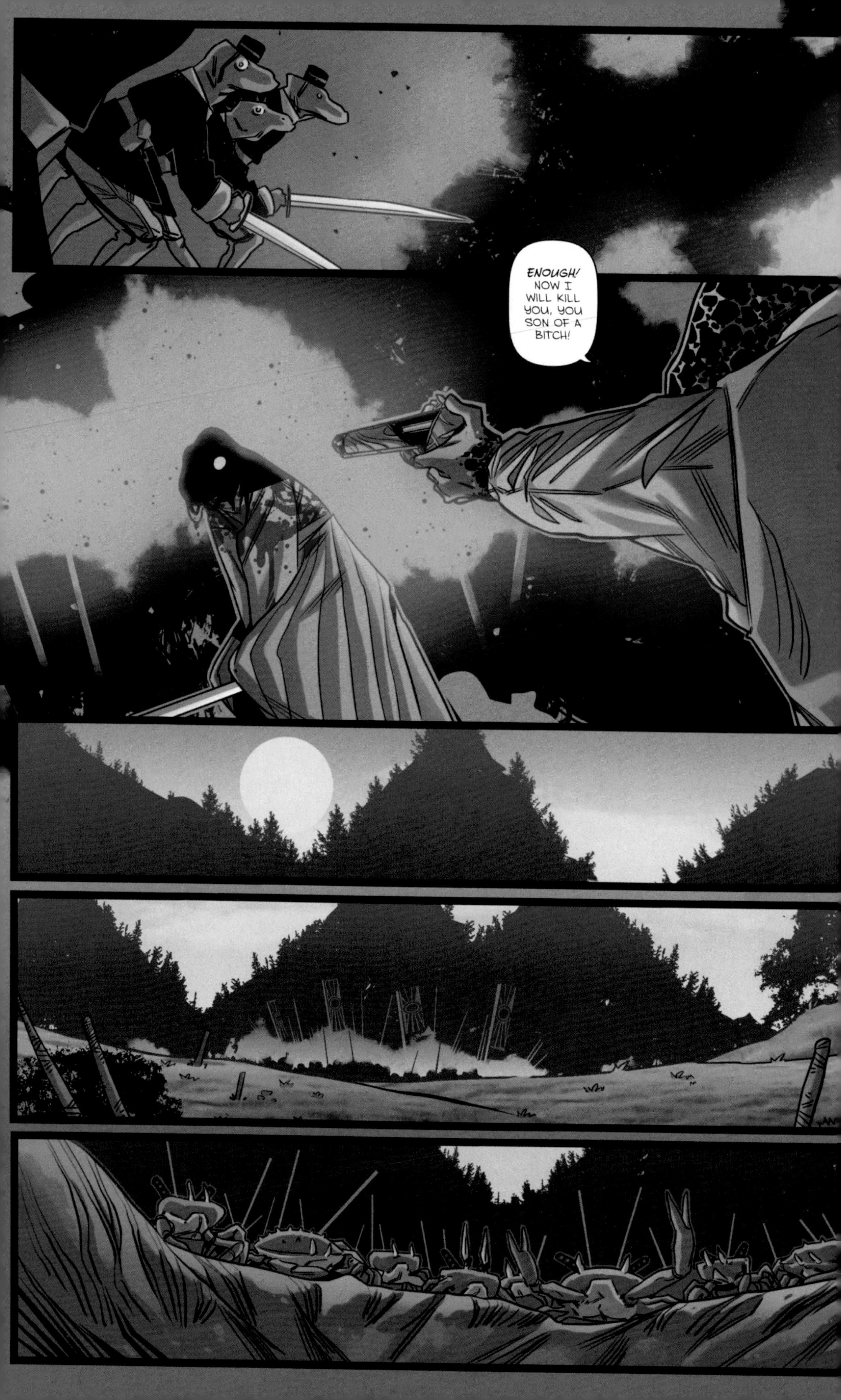
ENOUGH! NOW I WILL KILL YOU, YOU SON OF A BITCH!

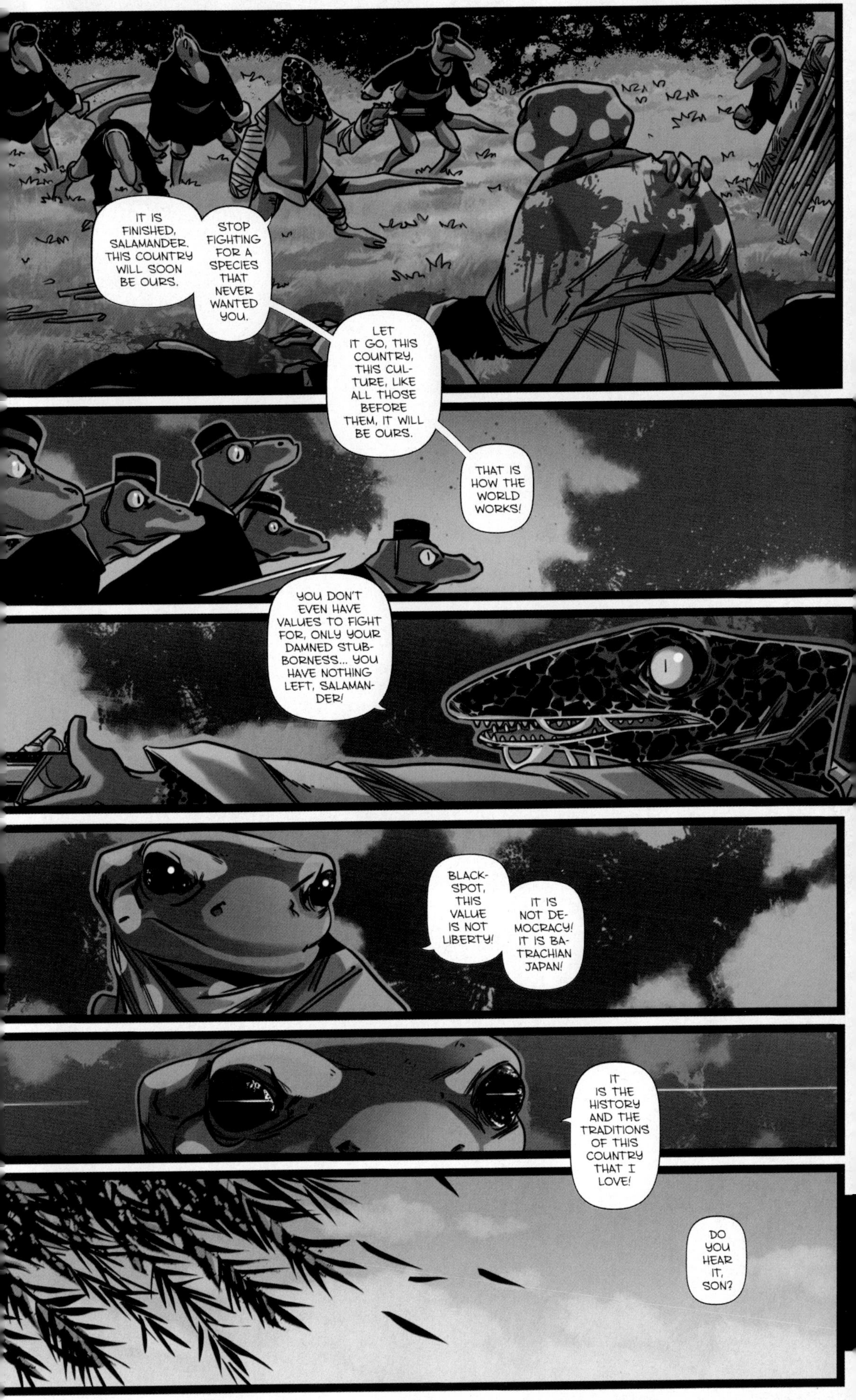
IT IS FINISHED, SALAMANDER. THIS COUNTRY WILL SOON BE OURS.
STOP FIGHTING FOR A SPECIES THAT NEVER WANTED YOU.
LET IT GO, THIS COUNTRY, THIS CULTURE, LIKE ALL THOSE BEFORE THEM, IT WILL BE OURS.
THAT IS HOW THE WORLD WORKS!
YOU DON'T EVEN HAVE VALUES TO FIGHT FOR, ONLY YOUR DAMNED STUBBORNESS... YOU HAVE NOTHING LEFT, SALAMANDER!
BLACKSPOT, THIS VALUE IS NOT LIBERTY!
IT IS NOT DEMOCRACY! IT IS BATRACHIAN JAPAN!
IT IS THE HISTORY AND THE TRADITIONS OF THIS COUNTRY THAT I LOVE!
DO YOU HEAR IT, SON?

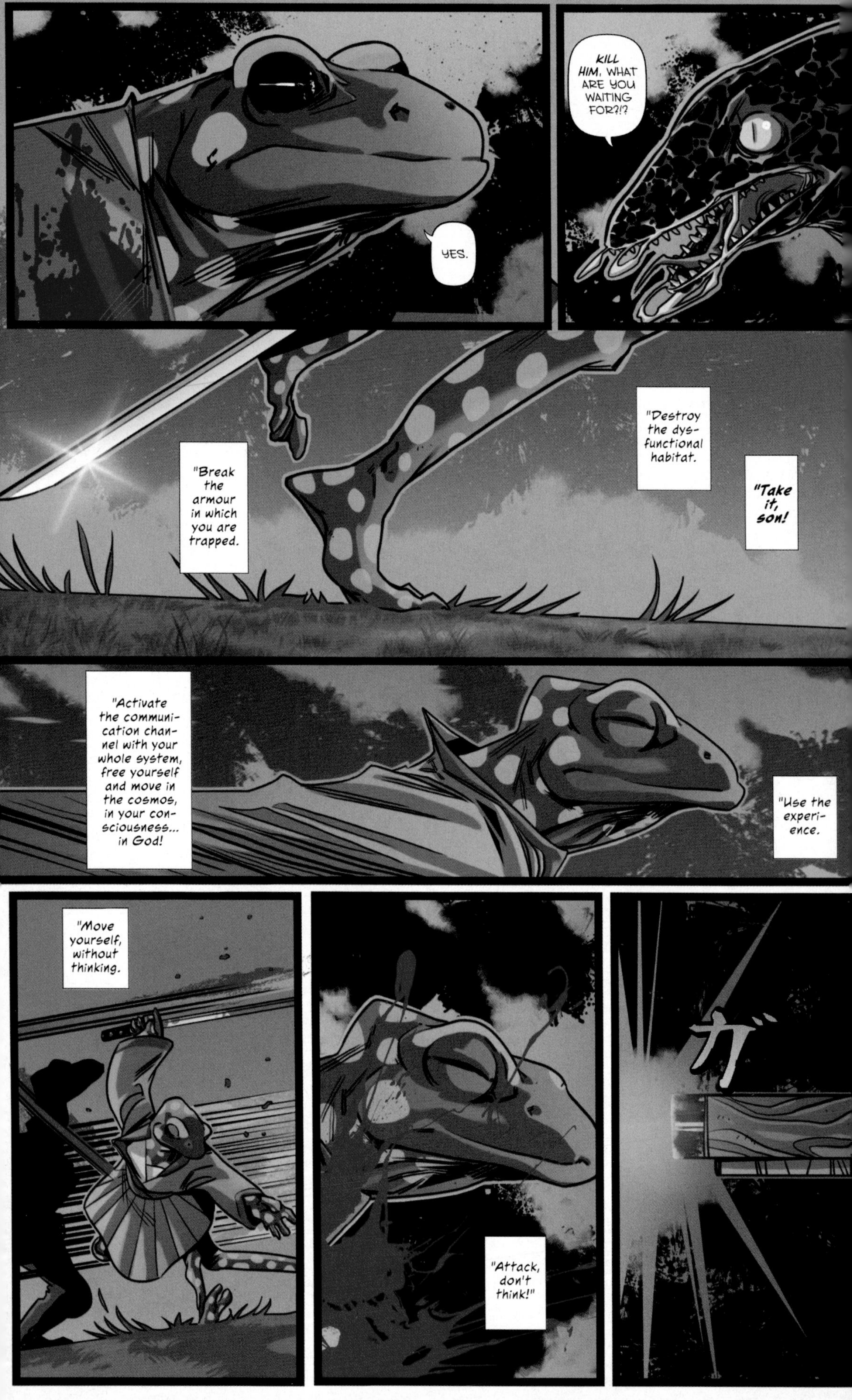

YES.
KILL HIM. WHAT ARE YOU WAITING FOR?!?
"Break the armour in which you are trapped.
"Destroy the dys-functional habitat.
"Take it, son!
"Activate the communi-cation chan-nel with your whole system, free yourself and move in the cosmos, in your con-sciousness... in God!
"Use the experi-ence.
"Move yourself, without thinking.
"Attack, don't think!"
ガ

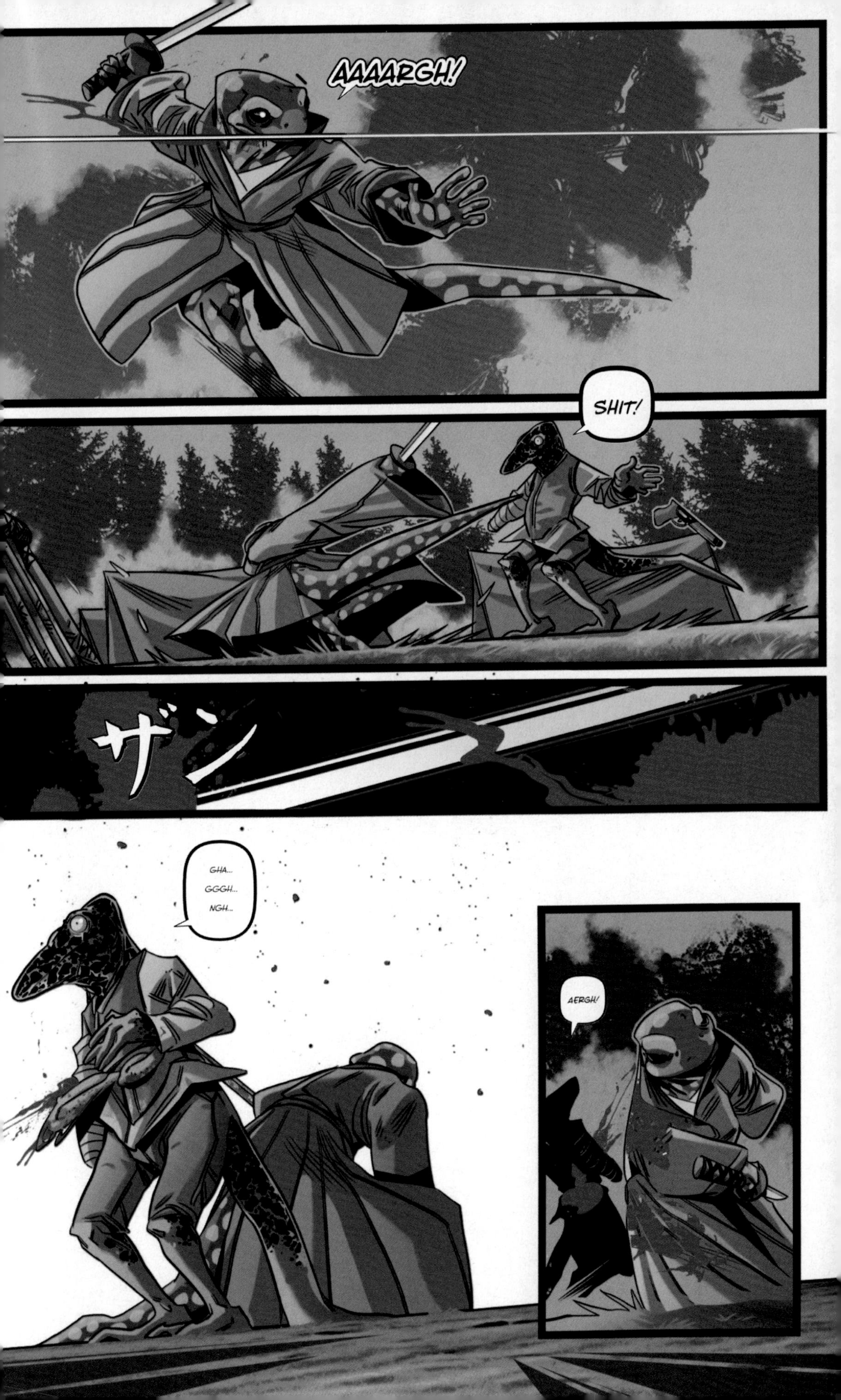
AAAARGH!
SHIT!
ザン
GHA... GGGH... NGH...
AERGH!

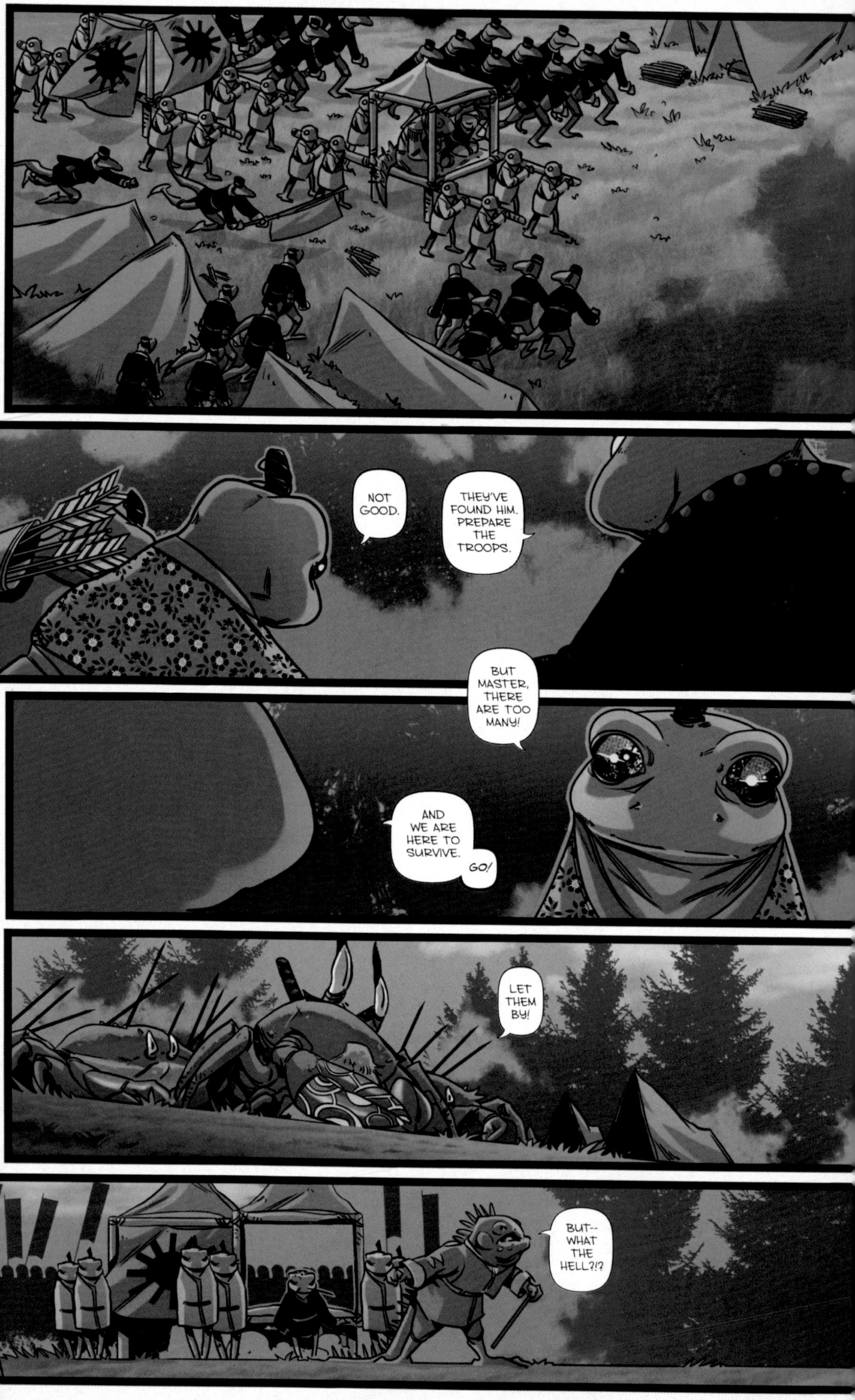
NOT GOOD.
THEY'VE FOUND HIM. PREPARE THE TROOPS.
BUT MASTER, THERE ARE TOO MANY!
AND WE ARE HERE TO SURVIVE.
GO!
LET THEM BY!
BUT-- WHAT THE HELL?!?

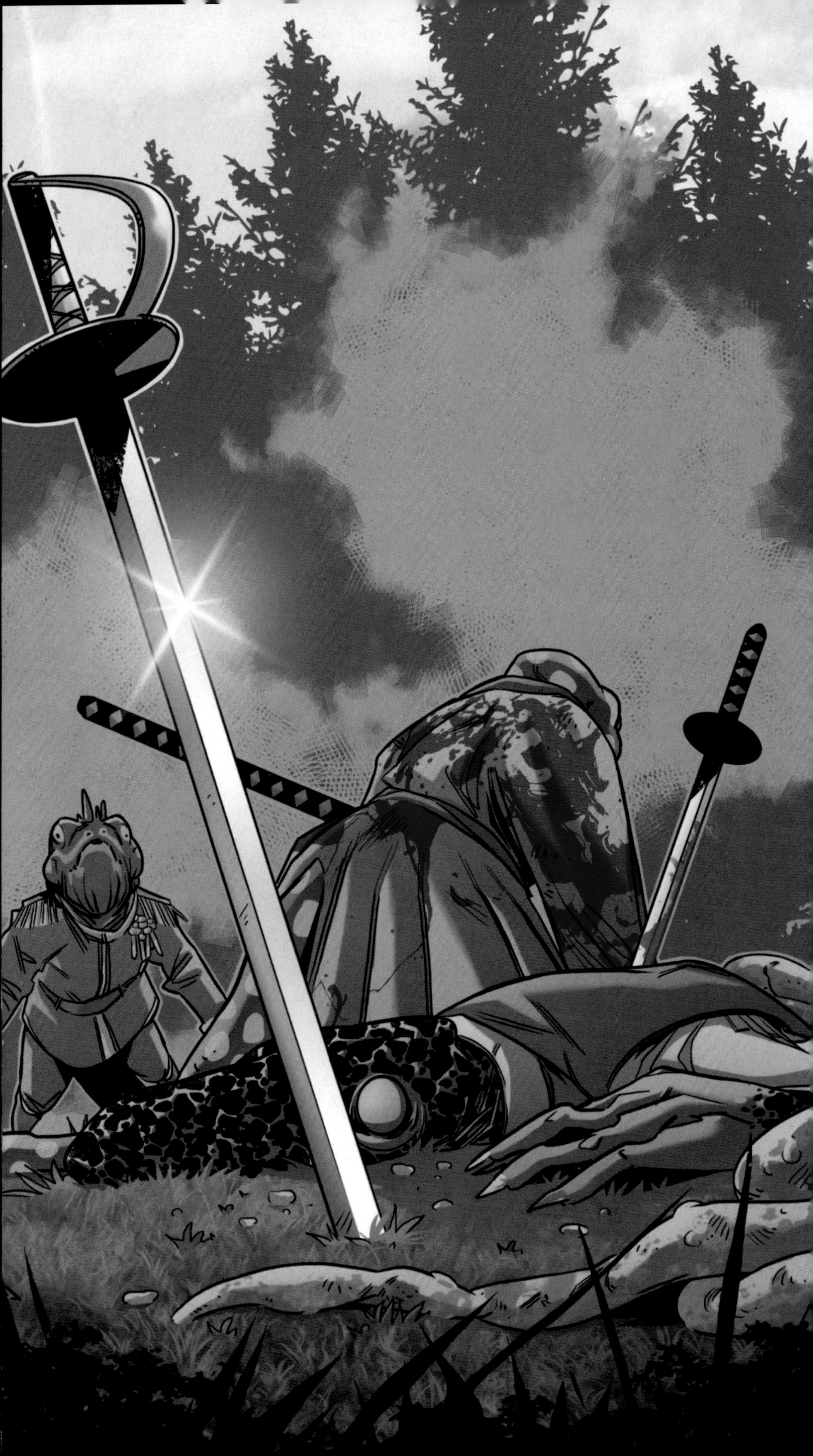

WHAT HAPPENED HERE?!?

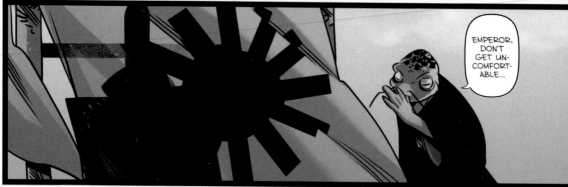

EMPEROR, DON'T GET UN-COMFORT-ABLE...

INCREASE THE GUARD AROUND THE SACRED EMPEROR.

ATTENTION! ON GUARD!!!

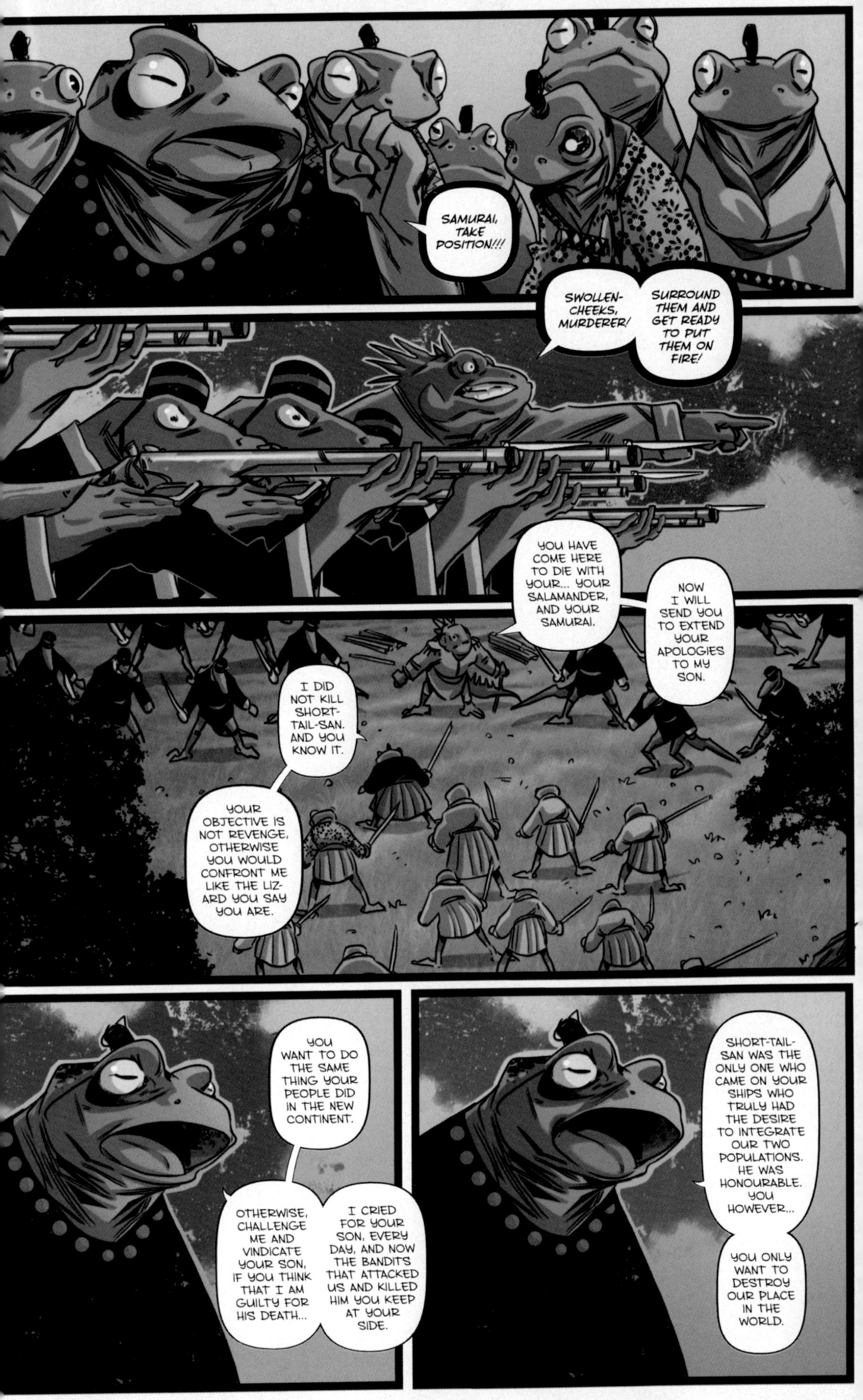
SAMURAI, TAKE POSITION!!!
SWOLLEN-CHEEKS, MURDERER!
SURROUND THEM AND GET READY TO PUT THEM ON FIRE!
YOU HAVE COME HERE TO DIE WITH YOUR... YOUR SALAMANDER, AND YOUR SAMURAI.
NOW I WILL SEND YOU TO EXTEND YOUR APOLOGIES TO MY SON.
I DID NOT KILL SHORT-TAIL-SAN. AND YOU KNOW IT.
YOUR OBJECTIVE IS NOT REVENGE, OTHERWISE YOU WOULD CONFRONT ME LIKE THE LIZ-ARD YOU SAY YOU ARE.
YOU WANT TO DO THE SAME THING YOUR PEOPLE DID IN THE NEW CONTINENT.
OTHERWISE, CHALLENGE ME AND VINDICATE YOUR SON, IF YOU THINK THAT I AM GUILTY FOR HIS DEATH...
I CRIED FOR YOUR SON, EVERY DAY, AND NOW THE BANDITS THAT ATTACKED US AND KILLED HIM YOU KEEP AT YOUR SIDE.
SHORT-TAIL-SAN WAS THE ONLY ONE WHO CAME ON YOUR SHIPS WHO TRULY HAD THE DESIRE TO INTEGRATE OUR TWO POPULATIONS. HE WAS HONOURABLE. YOU HOWEVER...
YOU ONLY WANT TO DESTROY OUR PLACE IN THE WORLD.

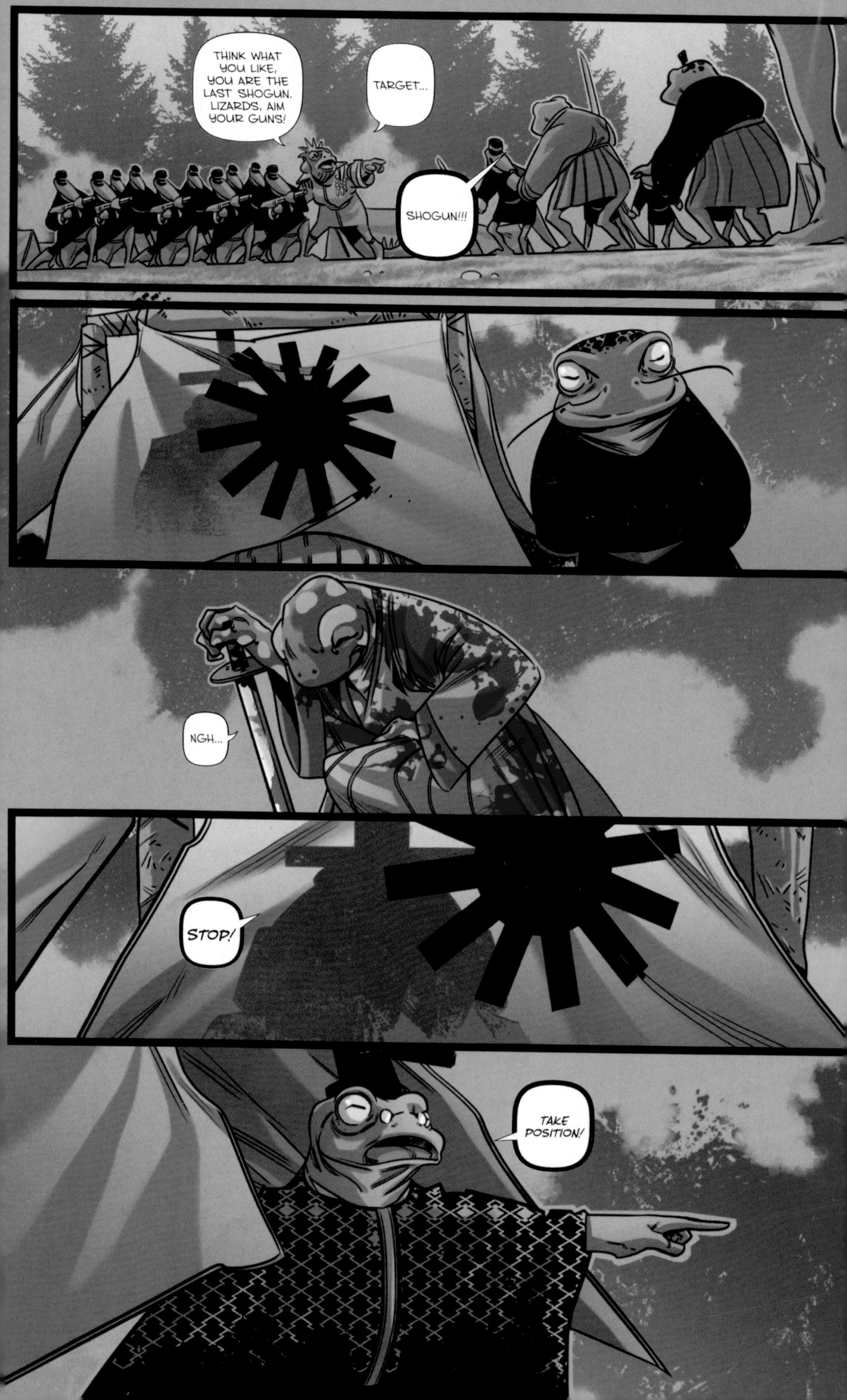
THINK WHAT YOU LIKE, YOU ARE THE LAST SHOGUN. LIZARDS, AIM YOUR GUNS!
TARGET...
SHOGUN!!!
NGH...
STOP!
TAKE POSITION!

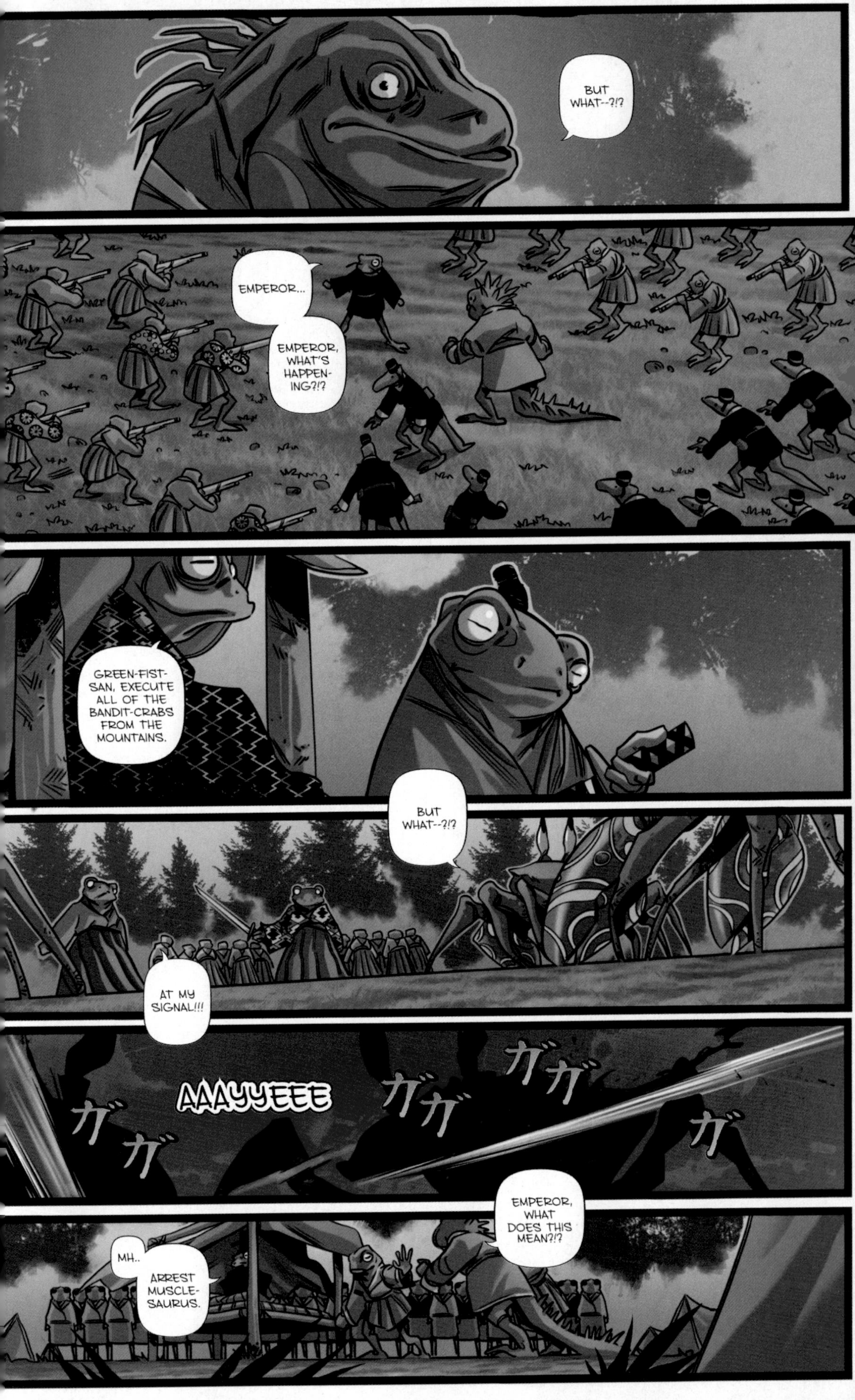

BUT WHAT--?!?
EMPEROR...
EMPEROR, WHAT'S HAPPEN-ING?!?
GREEN-FIST-SAN, EXECUTE ALL OF THE BANDIT-CRABS FROM THE MOUNTAINS.
BUT WHAT--?!?
AT MY SIGNAL!!!
AAAYYEEE
ガ ガ
ガ ガ
ガ ガ
ガ
EMPEROR, WHAT DOES THIS MEAN?!?
MH..
ARREST MUSCLE-SAURUS.

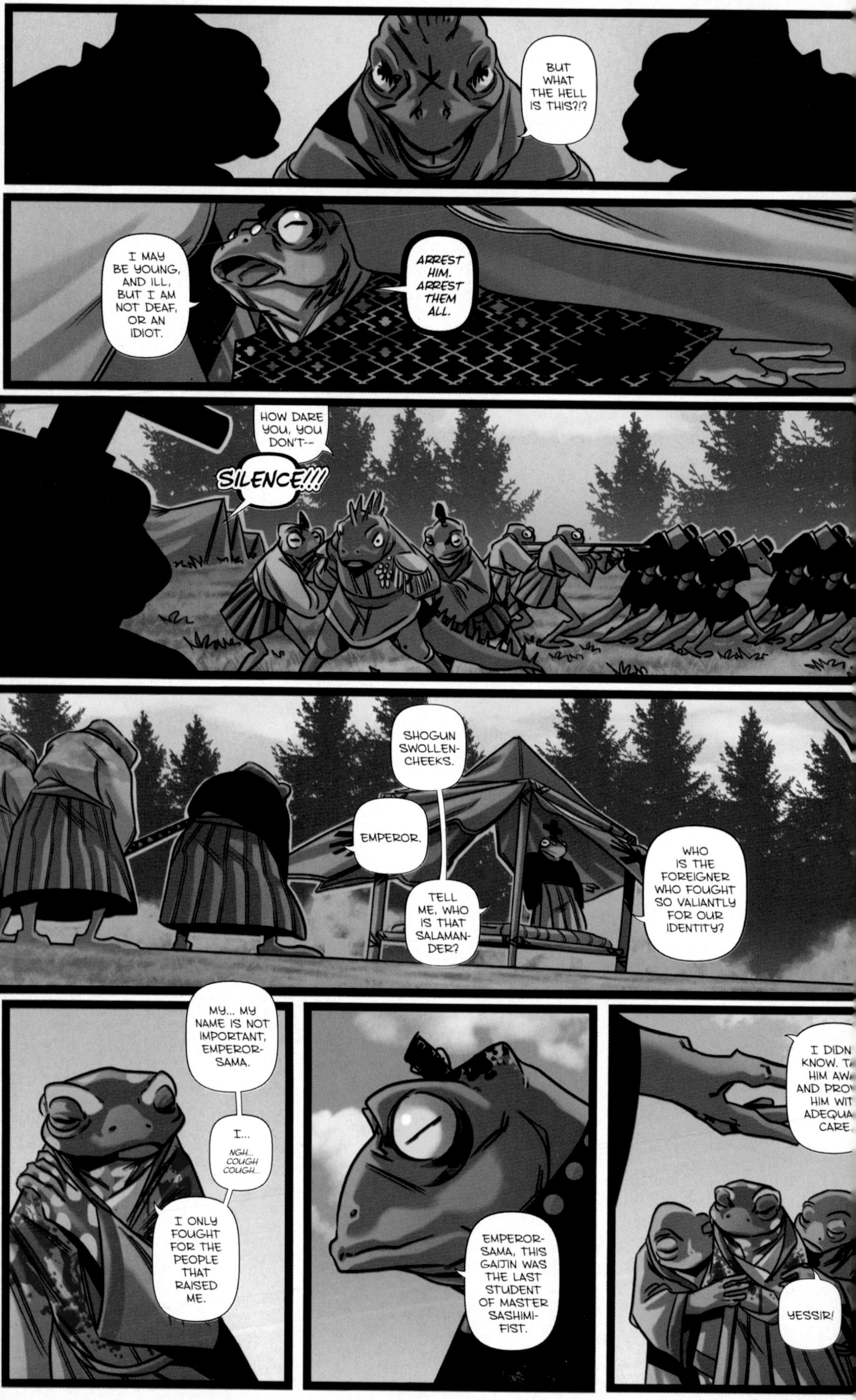

BUT WHAT THE HELL IS THIS?!?
I MAY BE YOUNG, AND ILL, BUT I AM NOT DEAF, OR AN IDIOT.
ARREST HIM. ARREST THEM ALL.
HOW DARE YOU, YOU DON'T--
SILENCE!!!
SHOGUN SWOLLEN-CHEEKS.
EMPEROR.
TELL ME, WHO IS THAT SALAMANDER?
WHO IS THE FOREIGNER WHO FOUGHT SO VALIANTLY FOR OUR IDENTITY?
MY... MY NAME IS NOT IMPORTANT, EMPEROR-SAMA.
I...
NGH... COUGH COUGH...
I ONLY FOUGHT FOR THE PEOPLE THAT RAISED ME.
EMPEROR-SAMA, THIS GAIJIN WAS THE LAST STUDENT OF MASTER SASHIMI-FIST.
I DIDN KNOW. T HIM AW AND PRO HIM WIT ADEQUA CARE.
YESSIR!

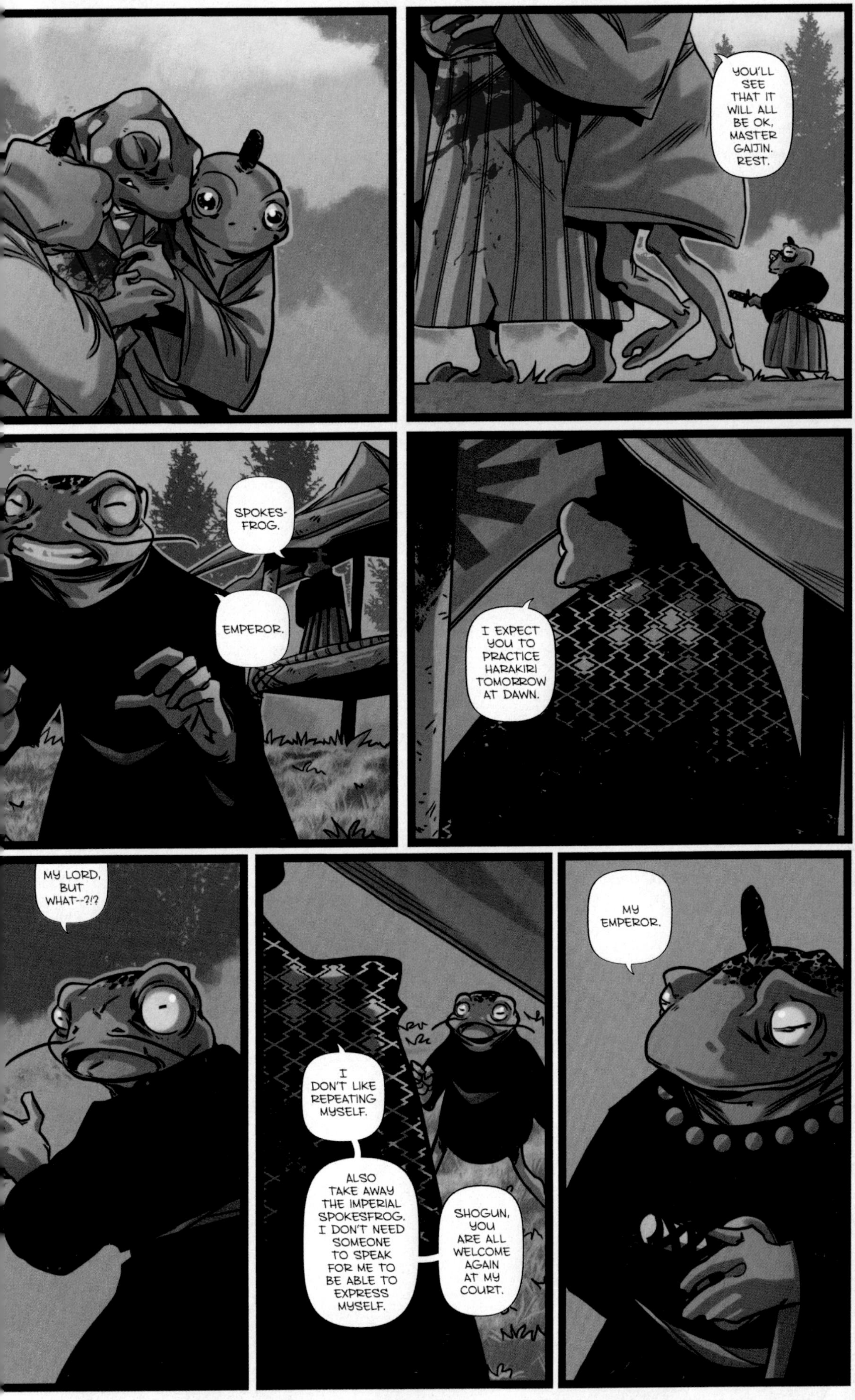
YOU'LL SEE THAT IT WILL ALL BE OK, MASTER GAIJIN. REST.
SPOKES-FROG.
EMPEROR.
I EXPECT YOU TO PRACTICE HARAKIRI TOMORROW AT DAWN.
MY LORD, BUT WHAT--?!?
I DON'T LIKE REPEATING MYSELF.
ALSO TAKE AWAY THE IMPERIAL SPOKESFROG. I DON'T NEED SOMEONE TO SPEAK FOR ME TO BE ABLE TO EXPRESS MYSELF.
SHOGUN, YOU ARE ALL WELCOME AGAIN AT MY COURT.
MY EMPEROR.

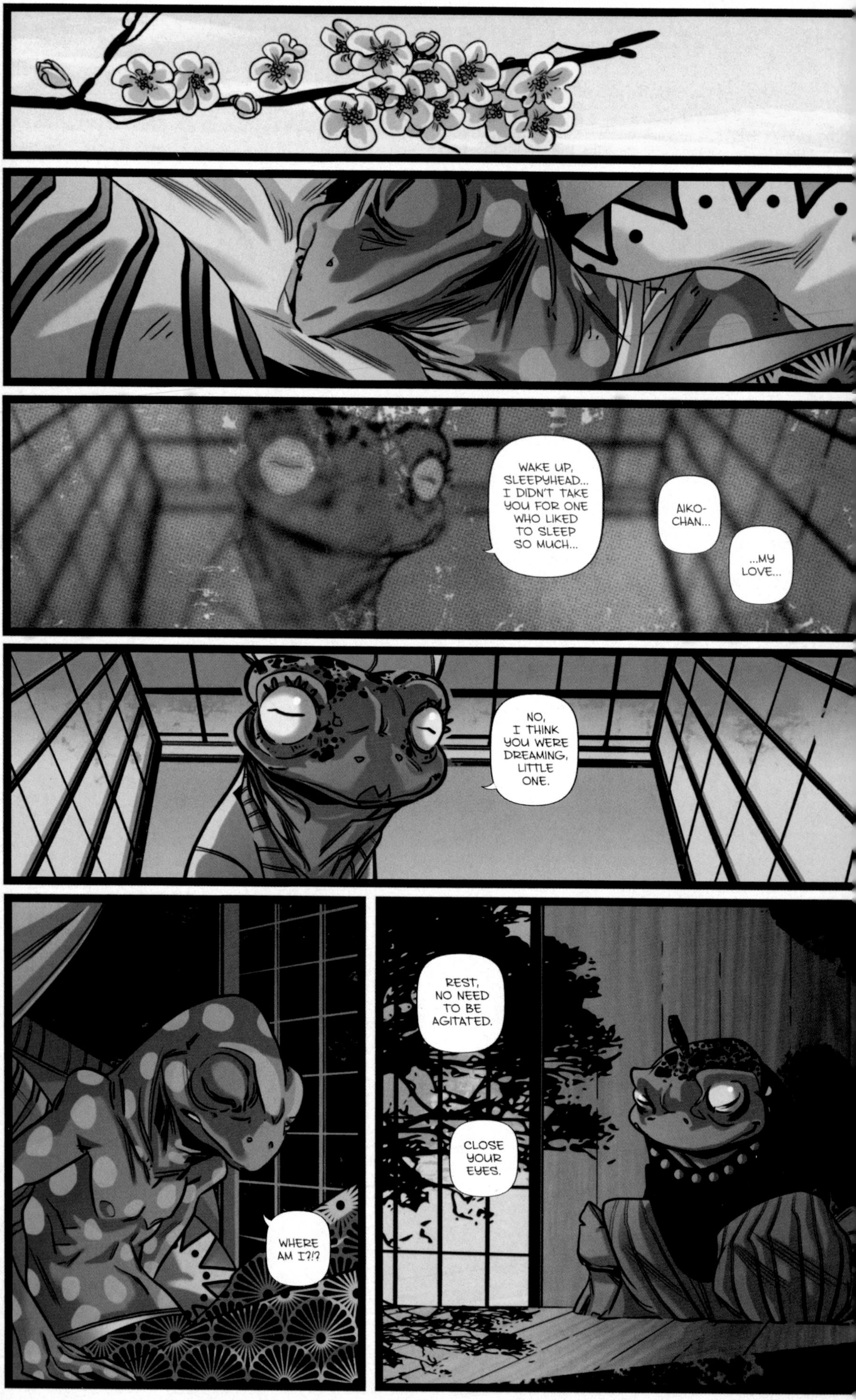
WAKE UP, SLEEPYHEAD... I DIDN'T TAKE YOU FOR ONE WHO LIKED TO SLEEP SO MUCH...
AIKO-CHAN...
...MY LOVE...
NO, I THINK YOU WERE DREAMING, LITTLE ONE.
WHERE AM I?!?
REST, NO NEED TO BE AGITATED.
CLOSE YOUR EYES.

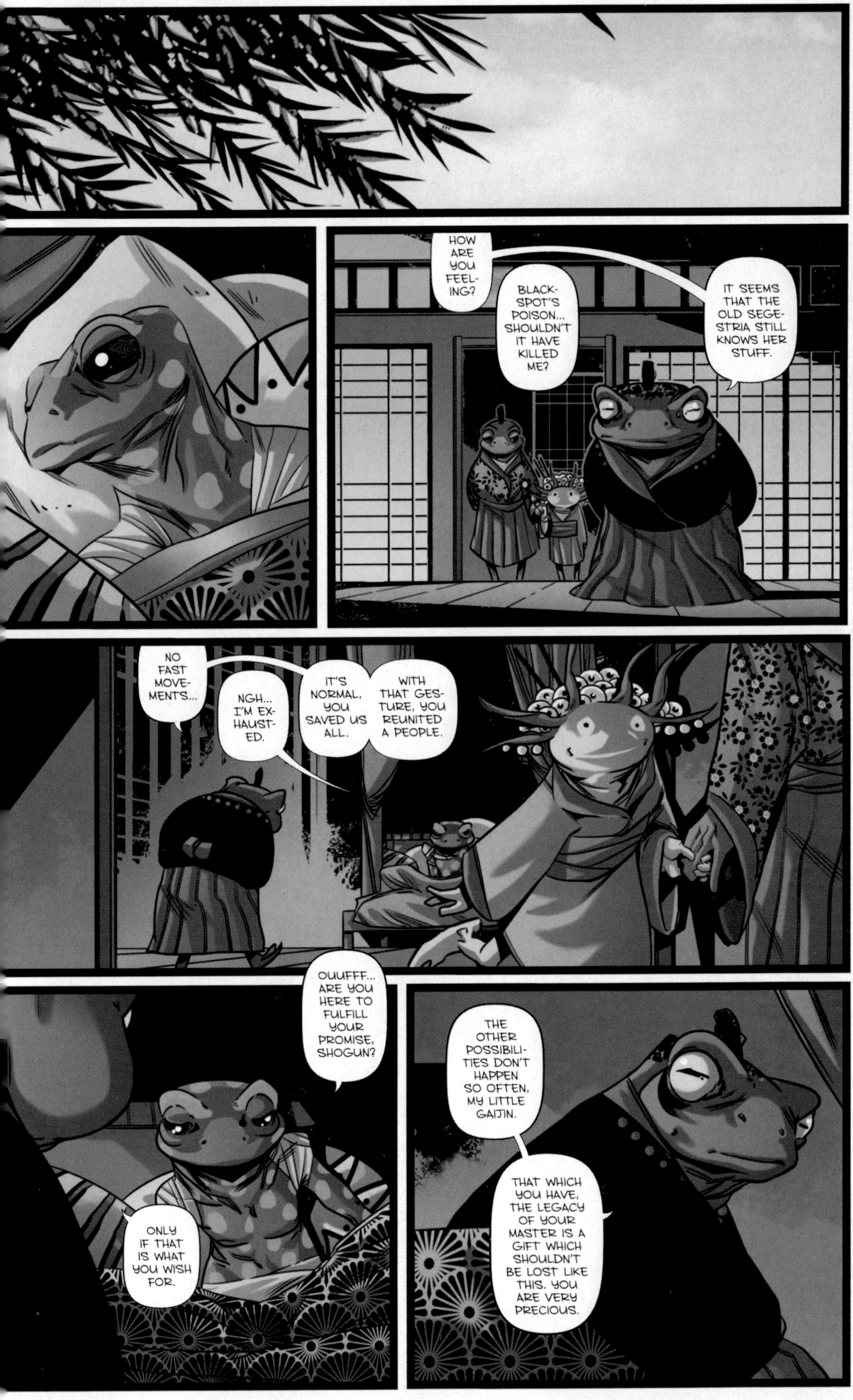
HOW ARE YOU FEEL-ING?
BLACK-SPOT'S POISON... SHOULDN'T IT HAVE KILLED ME?
IT SEEMS THAT THE OLD SEGE-STRIA STILL KNOWS HER STUFF.
NO FAST MOVE-MENTS...
NGH... I'M EX-HAUST-ED.
IT'S NORMAL, YOU SAVED US ALL.
WITH THAT GES-TURE, YOU REUNITED A PEOPLE.
OUUFFF... ARE YOU HERE TO FULFILL YOUR PROMISE, SHOGUN?
ONLY IF THAT IS WHAT YOU WISH FOR.
THE OTHER POSSIBILI-TIES DON'T HAPPEN SO OFTEN, MY LITTLE GAIJIN.
THAT WHICH YOU HAVE, THE LEGACY OF YOUR MASTER IS A GIFT WHICH SHOULDN'T BE LOST LIKE THIS. YOU ARE VERY PRECIOUS.

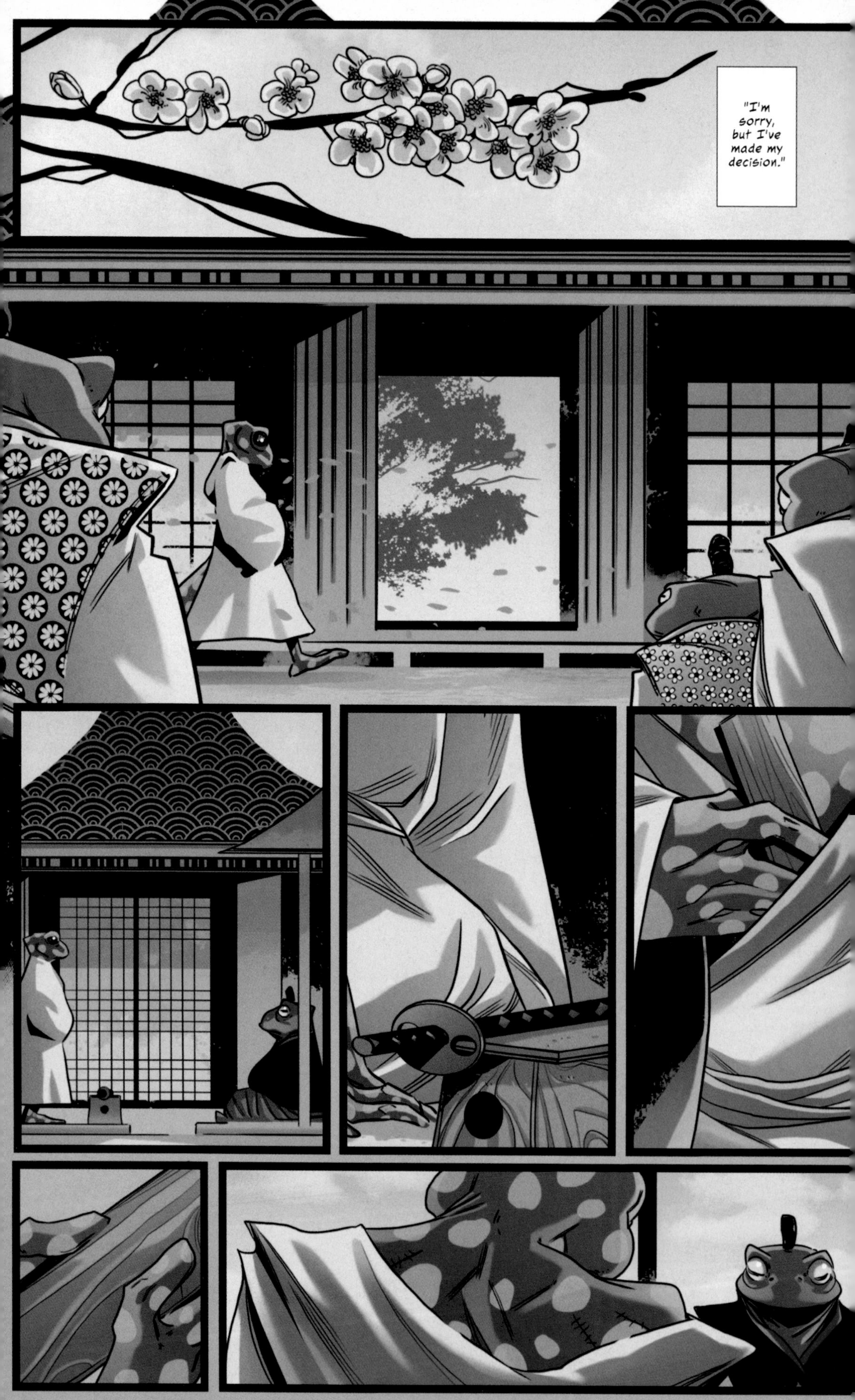
"I'm sorry, but I've made my decision."

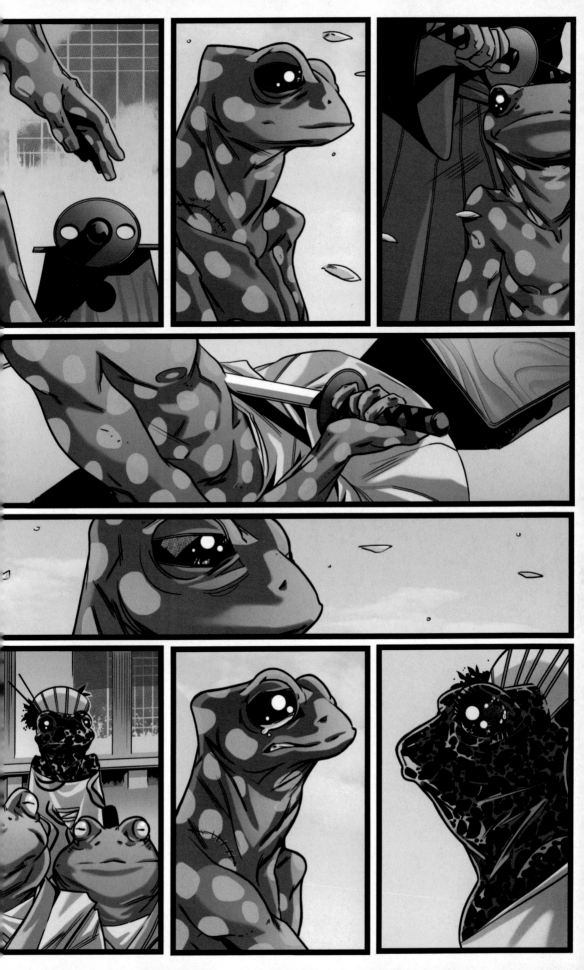

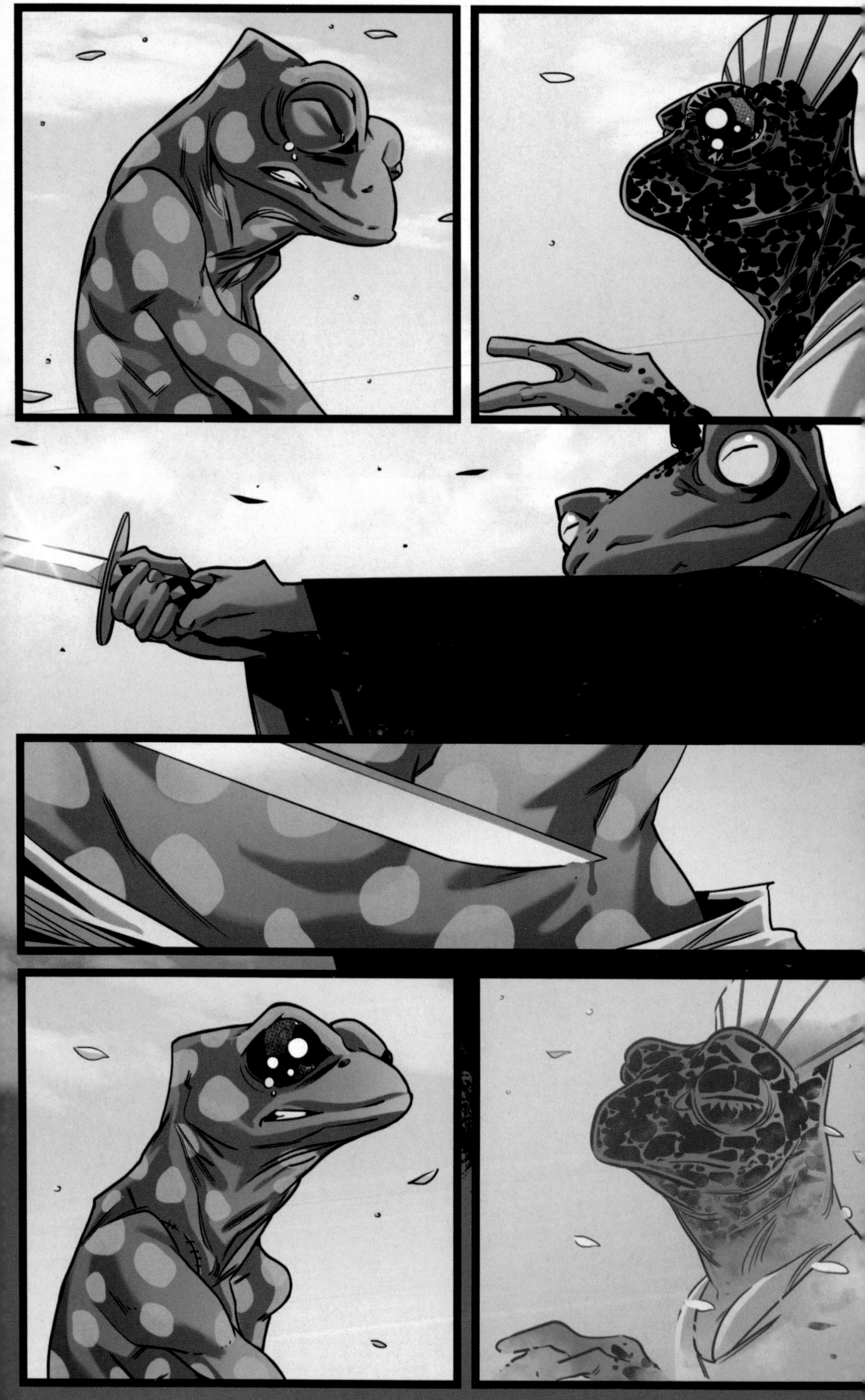

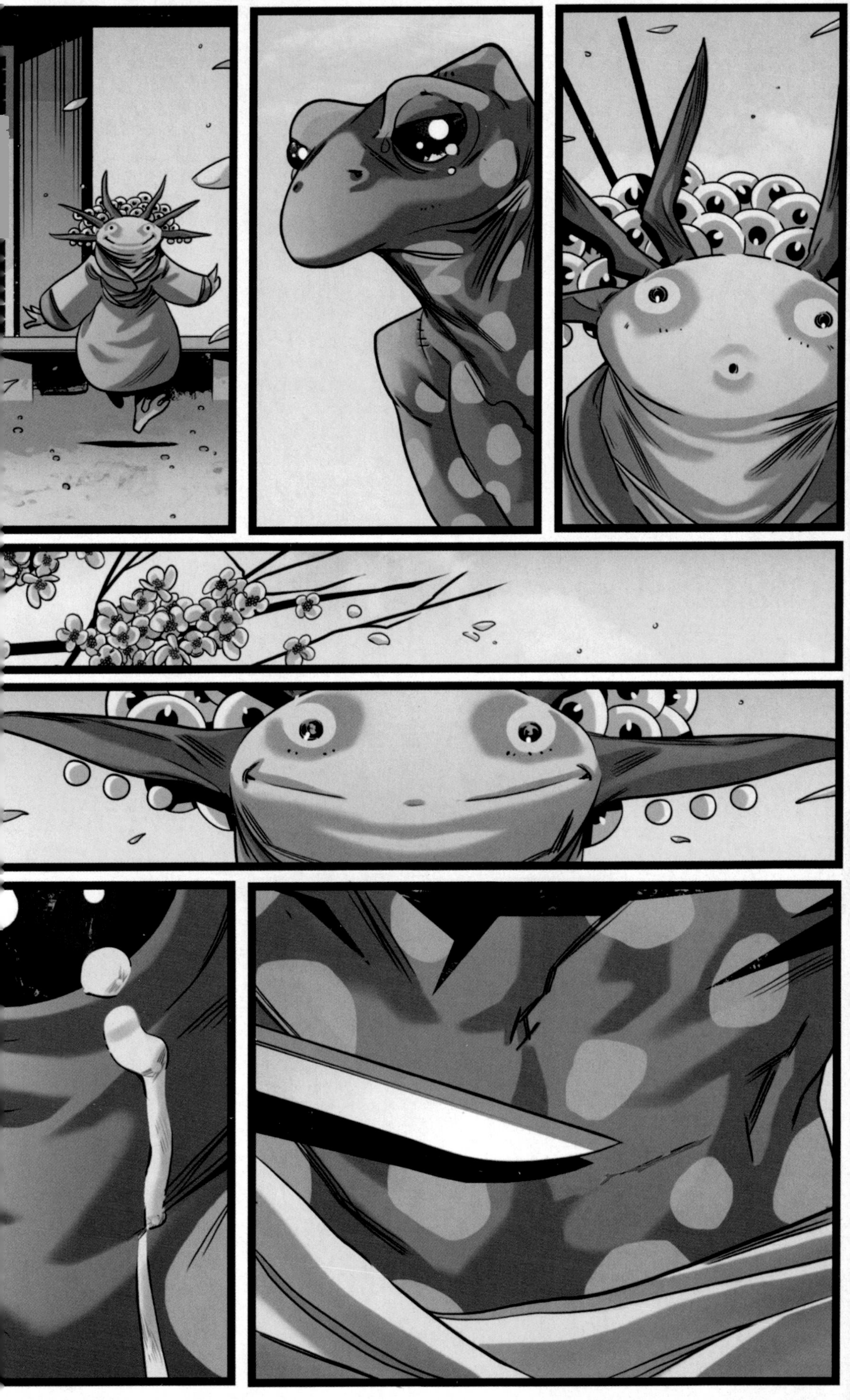

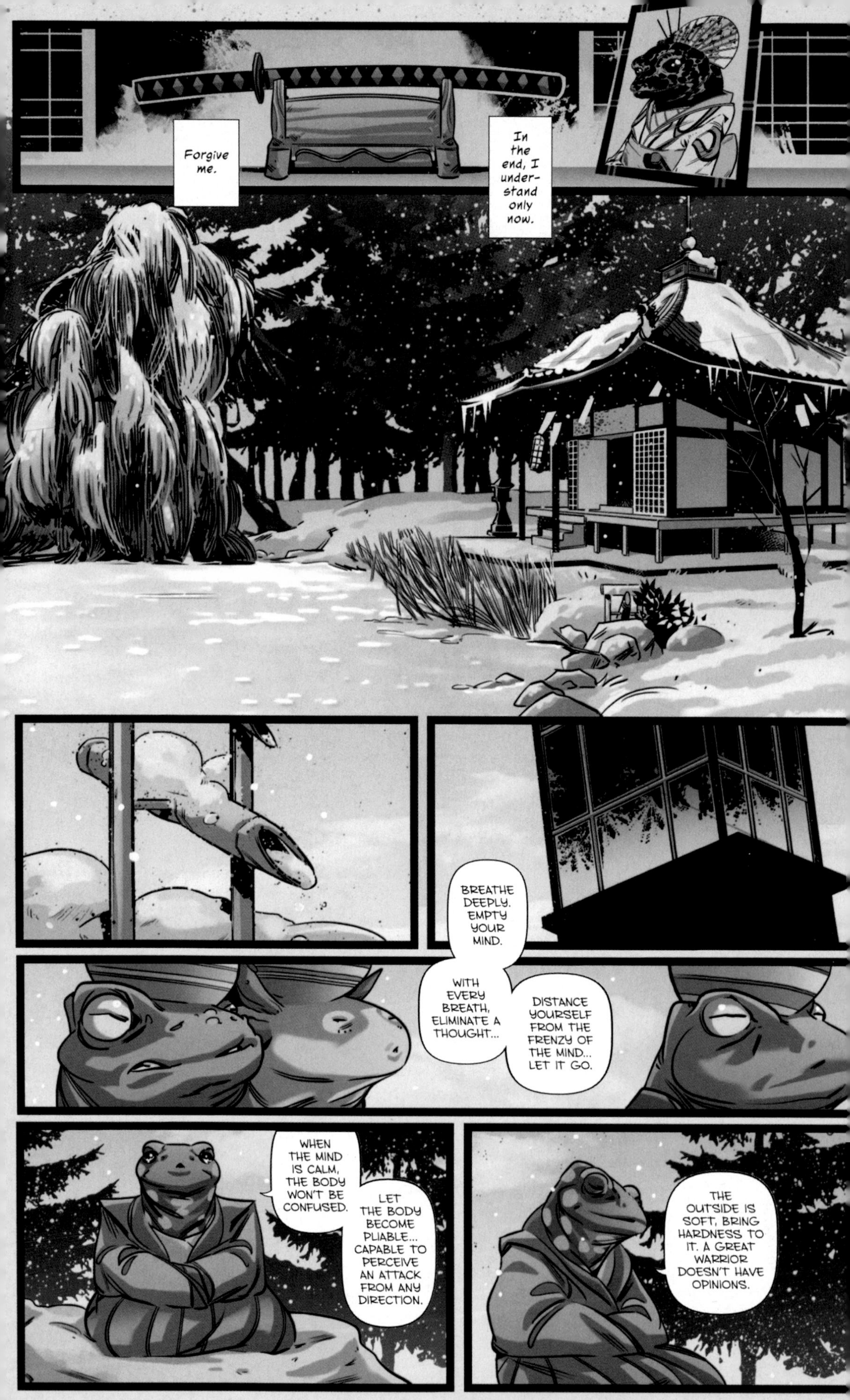
Forgive me.
In the end, I understand only now.
BREATHE DEEPLY. EMPTY YOUR MIND.
WITH EVERY BREATH, ELIMINATE A THOUGHT...
DISTANCE YOURSELF FROM THE FRENZY OF THE MIND... LET IT GO.
WHEN THE MIND IS CALM, THE BODY WON'T BE CONFUSED.
LET THE BODY BECOME PLIABLE... CAPABLE TO PERCEIVE AN ATTACK FROM ANY DIRECTION.
THE OUTSIDE IS SOFT, BRING HARDNESS TO IT. A GREAT WARRIOR DOESN'T HAVE OPINIONS.

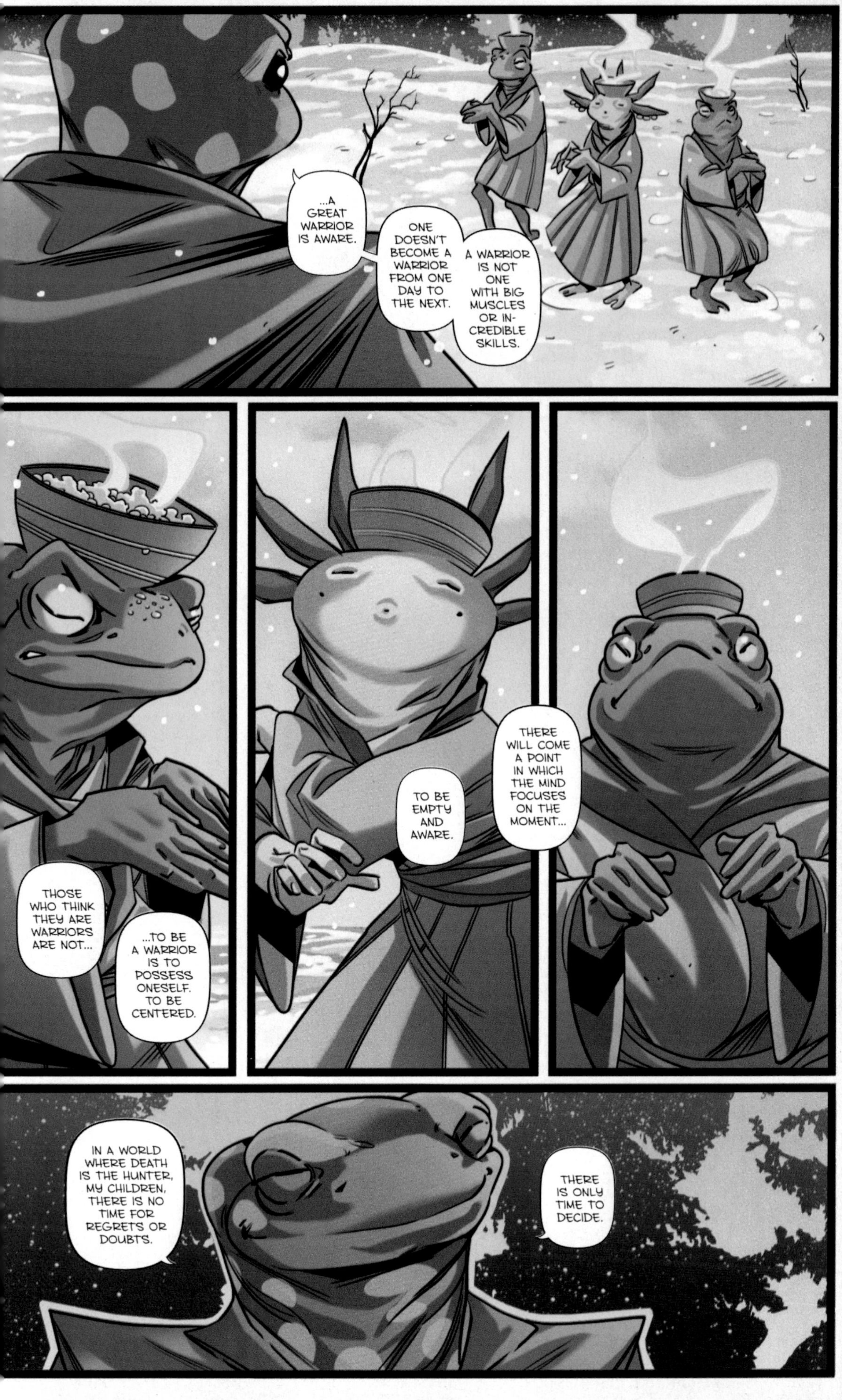
...A GREAT WARRIOR IS AWARE.
ONE DOESN'T BECOME A WARRIOR FROM ONE DAY TO THE NEXT.
A WARRIOR IS NOT ONE WITH BIG MUSCLES OR IN-CREDIBLE SKILLS.
THOSE WHO THINK THEY ARE WARRIORS ARE NOT...
...TO BE A WARRIOR IS TO POSSESS ONESELF. TO BE CENTERED.
TO BE EMPTY AND AWARE.
THERE WILL COME A POINT IN WHICH THE MIND FOCUSES ON THE MOMENT...
IN A WORLD WHERE DEATH IS THE HUNTER, MY CHILDREN, THERE IS NO TIME FOR REGRETS OR DOUBTS.
THERE IS ONLY TIME TO DECIDE.

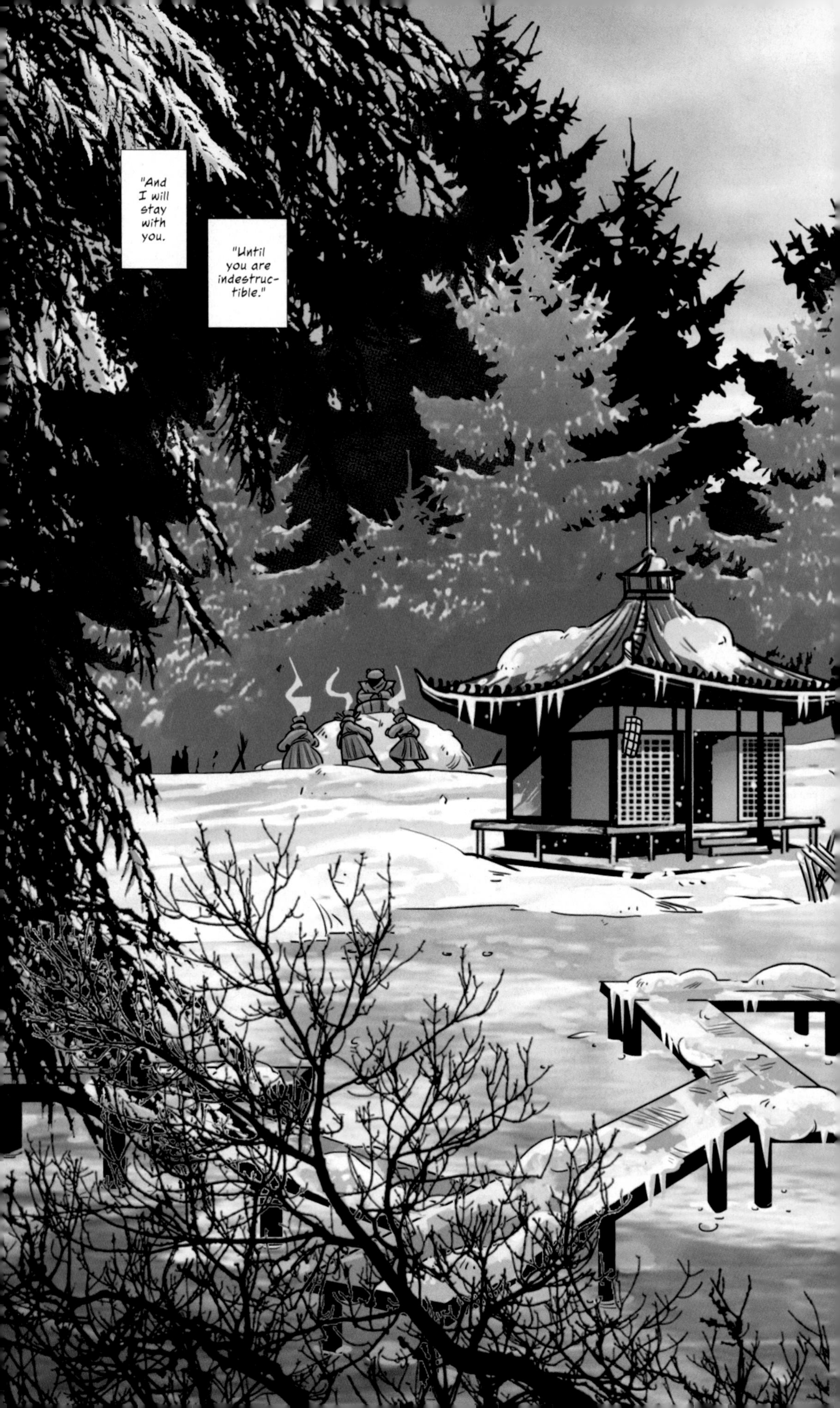
"And I will stay with you.
"Until you are indestructible."

COLDBLOOD SAMURAI

COVER GALLERY

COLDBLOOD
SAMURAI

COLDBLOOD
SAMURAI

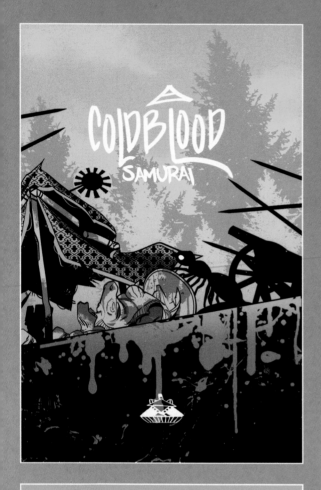

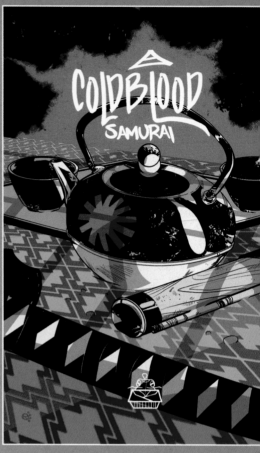

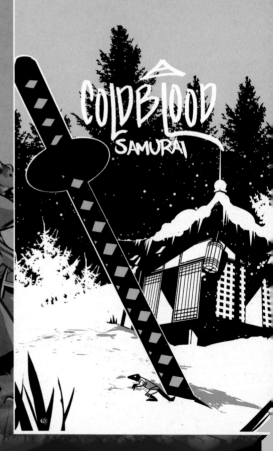